Kim Robinson
Willie Bruce

THE KINGS OF CREDIT

THE KINGS OF CREDIT
A NOVEL

by
Willie Bruce
Kim Robinson

The Kings of Credit

Copyright © 2012 by Kim Robinson and Willie Bruce

Library of Congress Number: 2012912135

First Edition 2012

Printed in the United States

Publisher's Note:

This novel is a work of fiction. Any references to historical events, to real people, living or dead; or real locales are intended only to give the fiction a setting in historic reality. Other names, characters, places, and incidents either are the product of the author's imagination or are used fictitiously, and their resemblance, if any, to real-life counterparts is entirely coincidental.

ISBN: 978-0-9820679-7-0
ISBN: 0 9820679-7-6
June 2012

Cover Concept by: Willie Bruce

Cover Created by: Scott Carpenter

Interior Design and typesetting by: J Bryden Lloyd

Editing by: Eddie

Acknowledgements

Without question, God is the root of all happiness. I thank Him daily, as I realize that any day above ground is a good day, because a lot of people did not awake this morning. Therefore, I'm blessed, because without His presence, I wouldn't have survived the era that I spent in the California prison system, which was collectively over 20 years of my life.

I also want to thank my family members who have had my back for as long as I can remember, especially Ros, she is definitely the glue that holds me together.

Without a doubt, I have to give thanks to my niece, who is actually older than me. Her name is, Kim Robinson. She has been like a big sister to me, and has advised me on so many issues throughout my years of growing up. I haven't told her enough how much that she means to me, but I'm sure that she knows.

Willie Bruce

First and foremost we give thanks to God and our family members who helped us with this project. I want to thank my Uncle Willie Bruce for reaching out to me to help him with this amazing novel and may this be the first of many more to come.

Kim Robinson

Chapter 1

The maximum security prison in the Placerville Desert was designed with one goal in mind, to incarcerate and warehouse the roughest and toughest male convicts the California Criminal Judiciary saw fit to commit to its flawed, overcrowded penal system.

Housed amongst four sequestered yards were killers, cutthroats and knavish prisoners of all ethnicities. Surrounding them were massive brick walls and asphalt walkways insuring that the treacherous convicts had nowhere to go but around and around.

The prison grounds were blazing hot in the middle of July 1999. The shimmering heat-waves emanated from the dirty pavement in the distance giving testament to the temperature. It would melt the soles of the prison-issue boots that were worn by the convicts if they remained exposed to the blacktop too long.

The army of seagulls easily withstood the weather as the birds scrutinized exercise yards with hopes of a caring inmate tossing a half-eaten sandwich or some other morsel their way.

On the A-yard stood the main kitchen, a massive concrete building placed behind the wall where the more privileged convicts prepared bland, processed meals to be delivered via cargo trucks to the satellite kitchens on the other yards.

Behind the kitchen was a concrete loading dock, and beyond that a huge blacktop parking lot filled with mid-sized cargo trucks, scattered piles of wooden pallets, and an array of metal food storage boxes, known as "Hot Carts."

Parked against the dock were 2 refrigerator trucks. One filled with fresh vegetables awaiting its assigned inmate crew to unload its contents. The other contained crates of nonfat milk cartons, manufactured and processed by felons at another prison's dairy farm.

Willie Bruce, a.k.a. "Chill," an adventurous, 35-year-old African-American male, serving a five-year term for 1st degree armed robbery, exited the rear of the truck pushing a dolly laden with milk onto the dock.

He paused momentarily and took in the sight of the seagulls beyond the trucks, "Damn, it's hot as fish grease out in this desert today! And what in the hell are you birds staring at?" he shouted toward the seagulls.

After a moment, he used the back of his long-sleeved chambray shirt to absorb the beads of perspiration that had gathered across his forehead. A correctional officer, Calvin McCoy, a corpulent, 42-year-old African-American male, stepped out of the rear of the kitchen doors holding a small, brown grocery bag. "Are you finished with that milk yet, Chill?" he asked staring upward at the punishing sun.

"This is the last load, McCoy."

McCoy placed the bag on top of a garbage can near the kitchen doors and approached Chill, who continued to glare maliciously at the seagulls. He reached into the rear pants pocket of his blue-denim jeans and pulled out a green apple. "Goddamn birds!" he yelled, and forcefully launched the fruit towards them. "Get the hell out of here!" he blurted, and watched as they immediately took flight from the area.

"Man, Chill, why are you always throwing stuff at them seagulls? Officer McCoy chuckled. "They're not messing with you, they minding their own business. You're just evil! Plain evil, man."

"That's some bullshit, McCoy! I'm not evil at all. I can't stand them damn birds because they're always shitting on me when I'm at the gambling table with my folks, always flying around and messing up our poker games."

3

McCoy laughed. "Yeah, it's probably because you're always messing with them. And believe me, they remember all them apples you've been throwing at them for over three years now."

Chill rolled his eyes at the officer's ludicrous statement. "Yeah, whatever, man." He casually looked up and down the empty dock. "You got my goods with you? You said today, didn't you?"

McCoy nonchalantly glanced up and down the area before replying, "Yeah, I got it, just like I said I would." He tilted his head in the direction of the bag on top of the gray garbage can. "It's over there."

Chill's face broke into a sly grin as he stared at the bag. "You know, Chill, it's a damn shame that prisons don't allow drugs like marijuana on the premises, ain't it dawg?"

"It damn sure is, McCoy." Chill reached inside of his front pants pocket and pulled out six one-hundred dollar bills. "Here you go, man." He handed him the bills, and watched as he slid them into his khaki shirt pocket.

"That's good-looking out, Chill," he whispered. "I'm out of here," he proceeded to walk towards the opposite end of the dock.

"I'll holler at you."

"Okay, Bruce."

Chill wheeled the dolly over to the garbage can and inspected the contents of the bag. "Yeah, three whole ounces of chronic, good old McCoy," he mumbled to himself as he deftly rolled up the bag and hid it underneath his shirt in his pants waistband. Once he was certain it was concealed, he proceeded to push the dolly through the double doors and into the rear of the kitchen.

As he continued along the corridor, he glanced through the window of a walk-in storage freezer and caught sight of Charles "C-Dub" Hicks, his 47-year-old African-American friend, who was engaged in a violent fist fight with two 20-year-old Caucasian convicts.

"C-Dub!" he yelled, and dropped the dolly on the ground rushing into the freezer to render aid. Without hesitation he snatched one of the aggressors by the back of his shirt collar and slammed him to the floor, where he pounded the man's head into the concrete, rendering him unconscious.

He looked up just in time to see a wild-eyed, swastika tattooed kid moving toward him. The assailant emanated a primal howl and charged at Chill, slamming him into the wall of the freezer. As the

4

man began to punch, kick, and bite at his chest, he looked into Chill's light-brown eyes, and whispered in a soft woman's voice, "Willie, honey. Are you all right?"

"What?" Chill yelled in confusion.

"I asked, if you were all right?" his wife Jen repeated. She was his lovely, 32-year-old, Cambodian spouse of 10 years, who was staring at him with concern.

He finally realized that he had been dreaming about being back inside. Copious amounts of perspiration ran down his face and bare chest. Prison related nightmares had plagued his sleep for far too long.

Discombobulated, he sat up in bed and stared out of the apartment window into the chilly December night. He looked at the digital alarm clock on the nightstand where 2:10 a.m., 12-09-04, flashed in bold red lights.

Jen sat up and grabbed a tissue from a box and began to gently wipe away the sweat. "Are you okay, babe?" she implored.

"Yeah, Momma, I'm all right." He continued to stare out the window. "I. I don't know why I keep having those crazy prison dreams. I'm sick of these episodes," he sighed.

"I'm sure you are," she placed the tissue on her nightstand. "You're so tense, sweetheart." She moved forward and began to massage his neck.

"Mm, Momma that feels so good." He reached up and grabbed her hand and kissed it softly. "Whenever we get a chance to move up out of this apartment and get our own house, I'm sure that things will get better for us. It'll be less stressful on us all the way around. I know it will."

"I know it will too, babe." She continued to massage him, "I can hardly wait."

"I know that trying to raise five kids isn't no joke. Now, your mother, she's a great big help around here. She's excellent with the kids. I thank God that she's around, believe that."

He suddenly shook his head.

"What's the matter, babe?"

"Damn, Momma. I've got one hell of a headache!" He turned and rested his head on the pillow.

Jen massaged his temples. "Do you want me to get you some pain tablets?"

"No thanks, Jen."

She laid her head against his chest. "I'm all right. I'm sure that it'll go away."

He began to run his fingers through her long, straight, silky black hair. He lifted her face to gaze into her eyes and kissed her on her forehead. He loved the smell of her strawberry scented hair.

He picked up the remote control on the nightstand and pointed it at the television, which was perched on top of the black lacquer dresser drawer near the bedroom door.

The two of them watched an infomercial that portrayed a blonde, middle-aged Caucasian woman peddling advice on how to become a multi-millionaire, by way of private commercial investments.

"I'd like to look into that type of stuff," he said, as he continued to brush her hair with his fingers.

"It could be profitable, who knows?" She began to gently flirt with him, by skimming the tips of her French-manicured fingernails across his masculine chest. "So tell me, babe, what was the dream about this time? Was it some more the usual prison violence with people getting murdered and stabbed again?"

"Nah baby, not this time." He slid his back up against the headboard and changed the channel to a music video station, depicting Rap superstar, 50-Cent performing his hit song, "*Candy Stick*."

After a moment, Chill shared, "In this dream, I had to save C-Dub's ass again."

Jen rolled her eyes as she repositioned herself. She wanted to be able to press her firm, honey brown breast up against his chest and look into his eyes. "So, tell me what happened with that no-good, son-of-a-blank this time."

"It was crazy, Momma, I mean, it was off the chain! These two crazy-ass Peckerwoods had him hemmed-up in a walk-in freezer. They were whipping on him like he stole something from them."

Jen chuckled, "Knowing C-Dub the way we do, he probably did steal something."

"Yeah baby, but he is my partner. C-Dub's my..."

She interrupted him, "I already know the story, dear... C-Dub's your dawg."

"You've got that right. He and I have been through some real hard times together. I'm talking about some situations that you would never be able to understand. That's my nigga' right there, I'm telling you!"

6

"I thought that I was your nigger." Her beautiful smile broke like the morning sunlight.

He laughed at her strong Cambodian accent, "You are my nigga' baby. Now, if you could just learn how to pronounce the word nigga' the way that we Black folks say it. Because the way you say, "Nigger", that ain't gonna' get you nothing but fucked up."

"Whatever, Willie," she smirked. "Anyway, I still don't understand why you keep having all of these prison dreams. I mean, you paroled from prison almost five years ago. It seems to me that you would have gotten it all out of your system by now."

"Yeah, baby. I would imagine so, huh?" He reached out, pulled her closer and kissed her tenderly on the lips. "I guess in some ways, I have gotten it out of my system. But the memories that I have of that hell-hole will never fade. You dig what I'm saying, baby?"

"Yes my love," she smiled. "Now, let's say that you and I try to focus on making some new memories this morning." She softly began to kiss him around his neck and ear. "Is that okay with you, Mr. Bruce?"

Chill smiled and surrendered to the waves of pleasure that broke over the two of them, "Yes it is, Mrs. Bruce. You know, I can feel my headache fading away already."

She stared into his eyes and leaned in closer to whisper in his ear, "That's good, daddy," she said in a seductive voice.

The two of them engaged in a noisy, passionate kiss. While their tongues intertwined, so did their bodies as she climbed on top of him and moaned pleasurably.

Chapter 2

2 o'clock in the afternoon the next day, Chill was listening to R. Kelly's song, *"Your Body's Calling Me,"* playing from the stereo system inside of the company work truck that he delivered air conditioning parts in. He drove into the long driveway that led to the second level, two-bedroom apartment at the rear of the complex where he lived in a neighborhood populated largely by Hispanics and Cambodians.

He pulled into his parking stall- number F-42 located against the rear brick wall and climbed out of the truck wearing his dark brown khaki uniform and black suede high-top boots and inspected the industrial air-conditioner supplies that he had strapped against the bed of the truck. Once he felt that the cargo was secure, he walked towards the staircase that led to his apartment.

He was greeted by his Cambodian neighbor, Mr. Chung, a cheerful 58-year-old friend of his mother-in-law. Mr. Chung and his wife lived in the apartment/liquor store directly below his family's apartment.

Mr. Chung bowed his head in respect. "Hello, sir. How you today?" he asked in his heavy Cambodian accent.

Chill returned the customary greeting in acknowledgement, "I'm fine, Mr. Chung. And how are you doing this afternoon, Sir?" The two of them shook hands.

"I'm fine, Mr. Willie. I go to market now. Get rice, fish, and oh yeah, lots of beer." He smiled. "Mr. Willie, you off work? Or you lunch break?" He removed his car keys from his denim pants pocket.

Chill chuckled politely. "I am on my lunch break right now. I came home to get my wallet."

"Okay, Mr. Willie." Mr. Chung smiled and nodded his head. "That's good, sir. You go see family now. You have good day. I go now. Me wife get mad, me take too long. She think me have mistress."

"You have a good day also, Mr. Chung," Chill laughed.

The two of them simultaneously bowed their heads to one another and shook hands.

Mr. Chung turned and walked away at a brisk pace towards his white 2003 Chevrolet Tahoe that he parked in his nearby stall.

As Chill entered the front door to his apartment, he was met by Mai, his 62 year old mother-in-law. She was wearing a classy, yet traditional red and yellow sarong, and was sitting with her legs crossed on a blue, oriental-style mat upon the living room floor. Near her, on the mat, were two mixing bowls. One was filled with Cambodian-style deep-fried chicken parts. The other held steamed, white, long-grain rice. She immediately pointed to the bowls. "Willie, you eat rice? You need to eat! No good for strong man like you no eat all day and working hard, too. No good." She shook her head.

"No thank you, Mai," he replied, as he eased the front door shut behind him. "I had some tacos earlier this afternoon while I was on one of my delivery routes." He patted his stomach to reinforce his statement. "I'm still a little full, you know? Besides, I've got to get back to work and pick up my paycheck. Got to get the money, Mai."

Mai smirked. "Yes, you go get paycheck. You no money, no honey." She laughed.

Chill appeared slightly chagrined and laughed briefly, "Mai, you're crazy, you know that?"

9

She laughed uproariously, obviously taking delight in his sudden embarrassment, as she clambered to her feet and pointed at him. He appeared to be visibly flushed. "I know you, Willie." She smiled knowingly. "You come home all the time. You get quickie, then leave, huh? I know you! I'm not stupid!" She chuckled.

Chill laughed uncomfortably, as he looked down and rubbed the back of his neck.

"No Mai. I came back home to pick up my driver's license. I forgot my wallet in the room this morning. That's all."

Mai smirked and shook her head. She knew that he was lying, and he knew that she knew it. He thought about what an *embarrassing mess this was,* as Mai walked pass him towards the kitchen.

"Okay Willie, if you say so." She rolled her eyes and mumbled, "I wasn't born yesterday," as she reached up above her head in the spice cabinet for a bottle of hot chili sauce. "Jen and the kids in room."

"All right, Mai. I've got to get a move on," he told her and then began to move through the hallway to his bedroom door on the left side near the bathroom. Upon entering the room, he was greeted by his five children who were sitting on the carpet near the foot of the bed watching a popular Japanese animation series on the television.

"Hi, Daddy!" they yelled in unison, and jumped to their feet to hug him.

He chuckled heartily as he embraced them. "Okay y'all, daddy loves you too. But I have to hurry up and get back to work," he mentioned, staring at Jen lasciviously while she sat against the wooden headboard.

If his eyes could have spoken, they undoubtedly would have screamed, "*I want you woman, right now!*"

He looked back at the kids. "So, y'all go on into the living room with your grandmother. Your dad needs to talk to your mother about some things for a minute, okay?"

"*And I bet I know what those things are, a quickie.*" Jen thought, before the kids announced, "Okay, Dad," It was not without a touch of disappointment that they all left the room.

Chill shut the door and approached his wife. "Hey, Momma," he whispered, and then planted a passionate kiss on her lips.

After a moment, she wiped her lips with her thumb. "Okay, dear. So tell me, what really brings you home so early?"

Chill sat down on the bed beside her. "I messed around and forgot my wallet in here this morning." He moved in closer to her. "But you know babe, I really came back home for this." He smiled, as he closed in on her and gave her a long intense kiss.

Jen looked upon him with desire in her eyes. "And you wonder why we've got five kids, Willie!" she said, as he began to kiss her, paying particular attention to her neck and ears.

"Thank God that you got your tubes tied," he whispered and immediately regretted his words.

Jen became playfully irritated, as he continued to kiss on her neck. "Yeah nigger, I should've had you get a vasectomy!" she stated in a serious tone.

Suddenly shamed by his thoughtless statement, he attempted to placate her with a sincere apology. "I'm sorry, baby. I know that getting your tubes tied was a hard thing for you to experience. I'll be more thoughtful and careful, I promise. I love you, Momma. I can understand how you feel."

"Willie," she paused. "Continue on with what you were doing! Before I mess around get a headache!"

In an attempt to remove himself from the hot pot of water that he had submerged himself in, he immediately resumed his physical affection. "Mm," she murmured, as he continued to kiss her gently and repeatedly on her neck.

Jen appeared to be lost in pleasure. "Mm, dear... that feels so good," she whispered.

"You like that, baby?"

She began to moan as she closed her eyes, completely lost in the moment.

Soon afterward, the two of them quickly undressed one another and began to make love quietly on the bed.

*****

An hour later, Chill was singing out loud in time with Tupac Shakur's hit rap song, *"Dear Momma,"* which blasted from the company trucks stereo as he pulled it into the parking lot of the air-conditioning warehouse and climbed out of the truck and walked through the rear-delivery garage door, and headed for his supervisor's office which occupied a frontal position within the 50,000-square-foot building.

11

There were rows upon rows of meticulously organized heating and air-conditioning parts, electrical and electronic components, R-22 Freon gas canisters, and thousands of air filters in all shapes and sizes being displayed around the huge complex.

Chill walked past it all and stopped at the threshold of his supervisor's office door. He immediately observed Mr. Jenkins, a 55-year-old balding Caucasian with a decent physique, sitting quietly behind his desk. He was engrossed in whatever was displayed before him on his computer monitor.

Chill knocked softly on the threshold before saying, "Excuse me, Mr. Jenkins."

The man looked up over his silver-frame reading glasses. "Come on in, Willie." He pointed to a chair in front of his desk, "Have a seat."

Chill took the seat closest to him and watched as Mr. Jenkins reached inside one of his desk drawers, and pulled out an envelope containing his bi-weekly paycheck. "Here you are," he said as he reached across the desk and handed Chill the envelope.

"Thank you, Mr. Jenkins. Man," he sighed in relief, "I've got a lot of bills to pay with this particular check. It's pretty-much already issued out, you know?"

Mr. Jenkins developed an expression of doubt. "Yeah, well. I'm sorry to be the one to tell you this, Willie, because you're a very decent and hard-working employee of this corporation. We value you highly, but I seriously doubt that you're going to be happy with this paycheck."

Chill suddenly appeared upset. "Why? What are you talking about, Mr. Jenkins? What's happening with this check?" he questioned in a devastated tone. He seemed to be having a near panic attack, as he ripped the envelope open with his visibly shaking hands.

Mr. Jenkins watched quietly as he quickly transformed from a state of anxiety to anger, and snatched the check out of the envelope and thoroughly examined it.

He finally looked up at Mr. Jenkins with intense fire in his eyes. "What's up with this, man?" he yelled, as he flapped the check high over his head before slamming it down onto Mr. Jenkins desk.

The supervisor flinched and instinctively raised his hands up to ward off any possible blows, but quickly regained his composure and placed his hands on the desk.

"What's happening with the rest of my money, man?" Chill resumed.

"Look, Willie," the rattled man began in a placating tone, "It wasn't my decision to short your paycheck. Please understand that I am following the directives which were forwarded to me earlier this morning. It came directly from our corporate headquarters in Lake Forrest. Please, don't get upset with me. I'm just the messenger here. There is nothing that I could do about this, Willie. I swear to you. This call came in from the very top."

Chill became even more irate and immediately jumped to his feet. "What in the hell do you mean, there is nothing that you could do about it? You can pick up that phone and make a goddamn call, that's what you can do, shit!"

Mr. Jenkins shook his head and sighed. "Look, Willie. I already tried that, but unfortunately, it's absolutely beyond my control. I have no say so in this matter. You see, it turns out that your local child-support agency has given the legally binding order to commence with the garnishment of your wages. That's according to our corporate headquarters. Now by law, I was forced to act upon it immediately. Again Willie, I am extremely sorry for the inconvenience that this mess has caused you."

Chill slammed his right hand against the desk. "Damn!" he yelled, causing Mr. Jenkins to spasm and wipe some fresh perspiration from his forehead.

"Willie, I know that you're pissed off, but why don't you go on and sit yourself down. Try and cool down for a minute, okay? Jesus, man, relax a bit!"

Chill reluctantly sat down in the chair. After a moment, he picked up the check from the floor and stared at it. He began shaking his head and flexing his hand on the check's envelope, crinkling it.

"All right, Willie." Mr. Jenkins rose from his chair and sat on the corner of his desk. "The corporate office has ordered me to forward exactly half of your weekly earnings to the local child-support agency in Encino, California. I'm truly sorry, man. I really am."

"This is fucked up, Jenkins!" Chill growled and glared at the check.

After a moment, he balled it up and then reopened it. He glared at it for a moment, and then squeezed his eyes shut and shook his head in frustration hoping that this was all a bad dream and that he could by sheer force of will, cancel out the unwelcomed reality.

When he opened his eyes, however, nothing had changed.

"I know that it's hard on you, Mr. Bruce. But hey, maybe you can talk to the child-support agency and make some sort of a payment arrangement. Although, in the meantime, you must understand that there is nothing on God's green Earth that I could do about this, you know what I mean? It's totally out of my hands. Otherwise, you would receive what's yours."

Chill wasn't hearing much of what Mr. Jenkins was saying. He folded his paycheck and placed it inside of his shirt pocket. He stared Mr. Jenkins straight in the eyes. His voice laden with resignation when he responded, "Yeah, Mr. Jenkins, I know exactly what you mean, but there ain't no way in hell that I'm going to be busting my ass for this little money! No way, man! Not me." He shook his head in frustration. "I've got too many mouths to feed. This little check ain't going to cut it at all. I'm not working for this, man. No way, Jack! I quit!" he declared.

"Well," Mr. Jenkins sighed and then continued, "I'd really hate to lose you, Willie. But I can't say that I blame you. There is no reason for me to do so because I'm sure that it's tough on you already. I mean, with all of those children that you've got I see your point, I really do." He nodded.

"Yeah, I heard that," Chill muttered, as he stood to his feet. He gave Mr. Jenkins a perfunctory handshake and then walked out of the office. "To hell with this joint!" he told himself, as he exited through the front glass doors and stood in the asphalt parking lot. "This is messed up!"

He walked across the lot and approached his white 2001 Honda Accord. He glared at the brick wall behind it as he began to pace back and forth near the driver's door of his car. He finally unlocked the door and opened it, and stood there scowling silently at the asphalt. "Goddamn Carla, with this punk-ass child-support bullshit!"

He removed the half-garnished paycheck from his shirt pocket and glared at it some more. "Fuck!" he blurted, and then tossed it onto the burgundy leather passenger seat. "All that I get is eight hundred and twenty-two dollars!" He scoffed. "Damn, for two weeks work, that's crazy! What in the hell am I supposed to do with this? Those child-support folks must be out of their rabid-assed minds!" he mumbled slumping down on the driver's seat and staring absentmindedly out of the front windshield.

14

Chill fumed for a moment before he removed his cell phone from his pants pocket and dialed in the telephone number of Carla, his 35-year-old African-American ex-girlfriend and mother of his estranged son, Willie Jr.

Carla answered her cordless phone on the third ring. "Hello?"

"What the hell are you doing, Carla?" he shouted, as he stepped out of the vehicle and resumed his pacing.

"Willie, what the hell are you talking about? And don't be yelling at me! What in the hell's the matter with you? You done messed around and went crazy or something?"

He attempted to calm himself by taking slow, deep breaths. "Girl, you know that the child-support folks done shorted my goddamn paycheck, messing around with you!"

"I don't give a shit about how short your paycheck is!" she declared. "Little Willie and I haven't been getting none of that money anyway. So, I did what I had to do. The fact is, your son is sixteen years old now. That boy is growing out of his clothes as fast as I can buy them. You know that already! But your sorry-ass hasn't done anything to help me out in over two months now! So, don't be coming at me all stupid, because they're making you do what you supposed to be doing anyway!"

Chill continued to pace near the car. "Whatever, Carla!" he shouted. "You did what the hell you had to do!"

"You damn right I did, and I'd do it again, too, you deadbeat dad!"

"Yeah, girl!" he sighed, frustrated. "Whatever!" He continued his pacing.

"Yeah, Chill! Whatever! Whatever the fuck ever!"

"Fuck you, Carla!" he screamed.

"Fuck you, too, punk!"

"Bitch!" he yelled, as he closed his cell phone and tossed it onto the driver's seat. "Man," he blurted, as he resumed his obsessive pacing, which was a reflection of his obsessive thinking. "Damn broad gets on my nerves! Man!" he yelled, and slammed his fist into his palm. "How in the hell am I going to survive, with this child-support bullshit on me this way?" He mused for a long moment while he stared at the ground.

Suddenly, his attention was captured by the song, "*So Rough, So Tough*", by Roger Choplan and Zapp, as it blasted from the sound system in C-Dub's black 2004 SL-500 Mercedes-Benz. He watched it pull slowly onto the premises with the black convertible top lowered.

C-Dub noticed him pacing near his car, as he proceeded to pull into a nearby parking stall.

Chill was still annoyed by his telephone conversation, when he observed C-Dub move the gearshift up to "Park" and lower the stereo volume.

Chill immediately took notice of C-Dub's considerate collection of "bling". He became aware of his platinum Rolex wristwatch, as well as the other various pieces of expensive platinum and diamond jewelry, which C-Dub artfully sported with his light-gray business suit.

Chill walked around the car to the driver's door and admired the German automaker's painstaking craftsmanship, as well as C-Dub's exquisite taste.

C-Dub remained seated behind the steering wheel and extended his right hand. "What's up, my brother?" he asked as the two of them shook hands.

"Not a goddamn thing, Dub!" He immediately noticed that C-Dub seemed to have gone out of his way to flaunt his two-karat platinum and diamond ring on his right "pinky" finger, as he casually brushed it across his graying goatee. He leaned back confidently against the black leather seat, and rested the arm on top of the door. Chill got a good look at his polished Rolex.

"That's a nice watch, Dub."

"Yeah. It's just a little somethin'-somethin', you dig?" he grinned.

"Yeah, I dig. But what's been up with you? What's happening?"

C-Dub beamed conspiratorially. "Ain't nothin' up, Chill. It's just the same old soup, baby boy. It's just re-heated, that's all. You dig what I'm saying, Daddy-O?"

"Yeah man, I hear you." He admired the rich deep wood-grain interior of the vehicle. "Damn, dub! This joint is tight! I see that you still getting your money." Chill was dazzled by Dub's flagrant display of wealth.

"What, you thought I wasn't?" C-Dub nodded in rhythm with the music. "Chill, you know that nothing has changed with me, but the date, the day and the name, and that's it. You know how I get down!" he boasted proudly.

16

Chill nodded his agreement. "Yeah, dub. What this whip hit you for? It's tight!"

"I paid one twenty-eight, with everything. That's it," he bragged.

Chill appeared shocked. "You paid a hundred and twenty-eight thousand? That's it, huh?" he commented sarcastically.

"Yep," he stated as he adjusted his rearview mirror showcasing his diamond ring.

"Damn, homie! It must be nice to be able to spend that much cash on a goddamn car!"

C-Dub smiled, displaying his bright even teeth. "Oh, but of course youngster, it's always good to have nice things. To be able to treat yourself, you know?" He looked judgmentally at Chill's grungy work shirt. "So tell me, young blood, what's up with you? What's your story? I see that you still working your ass off at this nothing-ass job."

"Yeah, well, not anymore because I just quit that job."

"Damn, boy!" he chuckled. "It's about time! Now, what made you finally want to dump that job? Was it those nothing-ass slave checks that you been getting?"

"Nah, Dub, it wasn't that. The paycheck was good enough for me to feed my family. That it was!"

"Well, why'd you quit?" he grinned, as he reached into his ashtray and pushed in the cigarette lighter knob to light one that he produced from a pack of menthols from the inner breast pocket of his suit coat.

"I quit because Carla's ass has got the child-support folks taxing the hell out of me now. I'll be damned if I'm working for nothing. Fuck that! I've got to do something, Dub," he admitted, shaking his head in frustration.

C-Dub appeared overcome with excitement in response to Chill's somber demeanor.

"What? Willie, baby, it sounds to me like you're ready to bring your butt on in out of the rain! You want to start rolling with this counterfeit money I'm dealing with, or what?"

Chill shook his head in a slow, exaggerated motion. "Hell nah! You know that ain't my style. That's your thing, not mine. So you do what you do, buddy. I'm cool on that."

"I am doing what I do." He exhaled a cloud of cigarette smoke and flicked the cigarette over the brick wall in front of his car, "Because getting paid is my thing. I get paid by hook, or by crook, it's all the same, young blood," as he flamboyantly threw out his left arm and glanced at his wristwatch.

"Well, dub, like I said, you do what you do. As for me, I'm cool on that funny-money stuff. That shit is way too risky for me, man. I'm not trying to go back to the joint."

"Well youngster, I suggest that you get your ass to doing something." He gestured with his thumb over his shoulder towards the air-conditioning company behind him. "Because, good old Mr. Charlie up in that joint back there ain't messing with you no more. It also sounds like Carla's pissed off at you, too. Not to mention Jen and the kids. They've got to eat!"

Chill nodded and pondered his current predicament. "That's for real," he whispered, frustrated.

"So Chill, what is it going to be, dawg? Are you in? Or are you out?"

"I'm out, man. I'm cool on that counterfeit money stuff," he admitted after a moment of silence.

C-Dub shook his head in disappointment.

Chapter 3

Later that evening, C-Dub stepped confidently out of the elevator and onto the twenty-seventh floor of the Sky Tower Hotel, in downtown Los Angeles.

He carried a black Crocodile attaché case in his left hand, which contained $50,000 U.S. dollars in $100 bills. As the elevator doors closed behind him, he took a moment to admire himself in the elevator's reflecting doors. "Sweet," he whispered in critique to his freshly shaved, brown-skinned head, his extravagant black wool business suit, and matching crocodile shoes.

"Damn! I'm about one pretty mother-fucker!" he continued, and then glanced at his Rolex and uttered, "6:58," as he strolled along the corridor.

Meanwhile, Armand, C-Dub's flamboyant, 55-year-old Persian friend, was sitting at ease on the couch inside of suite number 2732. Sitting near him was Agonda, a 45-year-old African Nationalist associate who specialized in the manufacturing of counterfeit U.S. currency.

The two men were snorting fine lines of high-grade, Peruvian flake cocaine which Armand had placed on a black lacquer coffee table.

Resting on the carpet near Agonda's reptile cowboy boots was his matching attaché case, which contained $110,000 dollars worth of counterfeit U.S. $100 bills.

Three soft knocks came from the front door of the lavish suite. Armand rose to his feet and proceeded to wipe his nose with a white-cotton handkerchief, which he yanked from his suit coat pocket. He fumbled with the buttons on his dark-blue business suit jacket. "Damn tailor-made suits!" he mumbled, as he finally fastened them.

He checked the time on his gold Rolex wristwatch. "It's seven o'clock on the nose. That's got to be our guy right there, he's right on time."

"That's a good thing, Armand," Agonda commented as Armand walked to the front door and looked through the peephole to see C-Dub before opening the door and greeting him with a welcoming smile.

"Charlie, my friend!" The two of them shook hands and embraced. "Come on in, buddy! How the hell are you, man?"

C-Dub strolled into the suite with his attaché case clutched in his left hand. "I'm wonderful, Armand, my comrade. And how have things been going for you?"

"I'm doing fabulous, Charlie my friend. I want to thank you for coming." He gestured with his right arm towards the hallway leading to the sitting area. "Come, let me introduce you to a new associate of mine. His name is Agonda. He's very cool people from Nigeria."

C-Dub's eyebrows rose in a mild surprise. "Nigeria?"

"Yes, sir, Nigeria."

"That's where the best counterfeit bills are crafted, I'm told."

"That's correct Charlie. I've been told the same thing. Come, let me introduce you to him."

Armand moved towards the sitting area.

"I'd be delighted to meet him."

He immediately noticed the 6'5", slender-built, African man, who was sitting on the white leather couch. He was wearing an expensive, dark-blue tailored silk suit.

C-Dub noticed the attaché case resting on the carpet near Agonda's foot, as well as the parallel lines of powder cocaine on the coffee table.

C-Dub offered Agonda a pleasant smile as he approached, while the tall man clambered to his feet.

"Gentlemen," Armand began, "Allow me the pleasure of making the introductions here." He looked at C-Dub. "My good and longtime friend, Charlie," he turned to Agonda, "I'd like for you to meet my new business associate, Agonda. He hails from Africa."

"Agonda," Armand gestured with his right arm to C-Dub. "This is my very dear friend, Charlie Hicks." Armand placed his right hand on C-Dub's left shoulder. "I love this man," he concluded, while C-Dub and Agonda shook hands.

"Nice meeting you, Charlie."

"It's my pleasure to meet you, Agonda." He sized the man up. "Damn, Agonda, You are tall, man!" C-Dub blurted.

"I know, it is nice meeting you as well," Agonda smiled.

Armand gestured towards the lines of cocaine on the coffee table. "Charlie, would you care for some extremely smooth Peruvian flake this evening? It's some of the best in the world."

C-Dub smiled at the supply. "I thought you'd never ask, I don't mind if I do, sir. But first, answer me this," he mentioned, as he took the vacant seat on the other end of the couch.

"Hold that thought for a moment, Charlie," Armand requested, as he sauntered to the fully stocked wet bar. He grabbed a chilled bottle of fine champagne along with three crystal flutes, and plopped down on the couch between C-Dub and Agonda. "Here you are, gentlemen," he said, while handing them each a glass and filling them with the upscale spirit. After placing the bottle on a coaster on the table, "I appreciate your patience, Charlie. Now, what was your question?"

C-Dub gave him a no-nonsense gaze as he pointed to the cocaine. "Is this Peruvian flake washed with ether or acetone? And please, Armand, don't take offense, but I really don't feel like getting my nostrils burned to hell tonight."

Armand clearly appeared to playfully put on an act of offense before exclaiming, "Why Charlie, I'm appalled! Shocked even! Horrified that you would ask me such an absurd question! And for as long as you've known me, at that! Why, the nerve of you!" He grinned and lifted his glass to his guests as he merrily announced, "Cheers, gentlemen!"

"Cheers!" C-Dub and Agonda responded, as they clicked each other's glasses together before taking a sip of their Champagne.

Each man seemed to be lost in the moment while they savored the spirit, and then place their glasses on the coffee table.

"Now Charlie," Armand resumed in a playful, scolding voice, "to answer your question. You know the business? It's washed in ether, of course!"

C-Dub smirked at Armand's theatrics. "In that case, Armand... rush it!"

Armand politely gestured to the dope on the table, "Be my guest, my friend. Enjoy, but know when to say when, you dig?"

"I dig." C-Dub smiled. "Thanks, man. Besides, I need a wake-me-up, anyway. And oh, by the way my friend... I always know when to say when!" he admitted without hesitation.

C-Dub leaned forward and used the tip of his manicured "pinky" fingernail, to scoop up a small amount of the highly-addictive substance, which he snorted into his right nostril. "Yeah, now that's what I'm talking about!" he exclaimed. He repeated the process in his other nostril and massaged his nose while the other men looked on humorously, obviously entertained.

"Holy shit, Armand! Yeah man, this powder is smooth. And it's been quite a few years since I've had powder this good!"

Armand smiled. "Well my friend, this is a little something from my private stock. It is good, is it not?"

"Oh, yeah! It's as smooth as silk," Agonda cut-in.

"Is there any more of this fire, which you by chance, would care to get rid of?" C-Dub inquired.

Armand smiled broadly. "Perhaps, you and I can discuss that matter later. Now gentleman, "Shall we get down to the business at hand?" he said rubbing the palms of his hands together.

"That sounds good to me, pal," Agonda agreed, while he enjoyed some more of his champagne. "I do not mean to sound impatient, but unfortunately, I have another engagement which I must attend to this evening," he explained, before emptying his glass and placing his flute on a coaster. He grabbed his attaché case and rested it on the end of the coffee table. "Get a look at these, Charlie," he opened it and displayed a breath-taking array of neatly stacked, master-crafted, counterfeit U.S. $100 bills.

C-Dub let out a soft whistle in wordless admiration, while Armand fixed a satisfied gaze upon him.

"Charlie, my friend," Armand began, "These bills are without a doubt, the most incredible, highest quality that I have ever seen in

22

counterfeit one hundred dollar bills. I'm saying that they are the best in the entire continental United States of America. I mean that. Here," he boasted as he handed C-Dub a stack of the bills. "Take a look for yourself."

Armand and Agonda silently watched C-Dub's reaction, as he removed one of the bills from the stack and held it up in front of his face. He analyzed the bill under the fashionable chrome hanging lights that were suspended from the ceiling over the coffee table. After several moments, C-Dub, appeared dazzled and blurted, "Damn, Agonda! These really are some good-looking bills that you've got here! The best that I've encountered, I'll tell you that much, they are fantastic!"

"Thank you, Charlie." Agonda said in a smooth, baritone voice. "They're all right, perhaps. Of course, by far, they're definitely not my best work. I have to admit that fact," he continued, while C-Dub thoroughly examined the counterfeit bill.

"Man, Armand! This is by far some good shit."

Armand nodded in assent. "I'm inclined to agree with you, Charlie. I've already taken the opportunity of checking them out." He looked at Agonda. "Superlative work you've got here, Agonda."

C-Dub returned the stack of bills to Agonda, who promptly placed them in his attaché case. "Thanks, Armand. My brothers and I are very proud of our craftsmanship. You gentlemen should see some of the other sublime bills that we've got back in the Motherland. They're absolutely astonishing, to say the least. They're in great demand, as well. We do a lot of business with these same bills in New York City especially."

"I can imagine." C-Dub mentioned. "Oh, shit!" He stood up and doubled over at the waist, and then began to clutch his abdomen with both hands. "Man y'all!" He nodded to Armand. "I've got to take a mean-ass dump! That's some good powder you've got there. It's got my stomach going already."

"Yes it is, Charlie. But unfortunately, I was forced to cut it with some lactose laxative because of its potency. You know how it is with the good stuff. Am I correct?"

"You can say that again." C-Dub groaned.

He stood upright, but still clutched his stomach. "This is some really potent powder! Do you mind if I use your restroom facility? I swear to you that I won't blow it up too bad. I know all about the down-one, drown-one rule. You know, flushing the toilet. That's some prison rules I learned back in the day."

"Yes, I'm aware of that rule, my friend. It is potent stuff, Charlie. Of course I don't mind. You go right ahead and relieve yourself." Armand pointed towards the hallway leading to the front door. "It's right up the hallway, near the front door on the right."

C-Dub hobbled gingerly towards the restroom.

"Thanks, Armand." He stopped briefly. "Um, look. There's a counterfeit hundred and ten grand right there in that case, isn't it?" he asked as he pointed to Agonda's attaché case.

"Yes, there is. Absolutely," Armand confirmed. "It's a hundred and ten large. As a matter of fact on the nose, I counted it myself. Check it out if you don't believe me."

C-Dub smiled briefly. "That's good enough for me, bud." He pointed to his own attaché case on the floor near the couch. "I've got fifty grand in real U.S. C-notes in my briefcase. So, why don't you go on ahead and count it, Armand? I'll be back in a few minutes. I've got to hurry up and drop this load." He stared intently into Armand's eyes. "I trust you, Armand. You do know that, don't you?"

Armand returned C-Dub's stare and uttered, "That's without a doubt, my friend."

After finishing his necessities, he washed his hands in the beautiful, ornate sink. He stopped cold and locked eyes with his reflection in the mirror, as panic suddenly overcame him. "Damn," he whispered, as he immediately experienced in that very moment, a vivid recollection as to exactly who Agonda was and where he had seen him before.

Unfortunately, as is so often the case with drug-induced epiphanies, this one left him as swiftly as it came. The fast-paced episode created a vague feeling of uneasiness and sudden distrust towards Agonda.

He rushed out of the restroom and was frozen by the scene that lay before him. "What the hell!" he yelled, discovering that Armand was lying face-down on the carpet near the couch, his hands bound behind his back with his own black necktie. His mouth was stuffed with his handkerchief. Armand struggled valiantly while sounds of muffled screams seeped through his plugged mouth.

C-Dub collected himself and quickly rushed to Armand's aid, kneeling down beside him removing the handkerchief while demanding, "What in the hell just happened in here, man?"

He grabbed his switch-blade knife from his pants pocket and used it to cut the necktie away from Armand's wrists.

Armand struggled to his feet, clearly upset and unable to focus for more than a few seconds.

While Armand tried to regain his senses, C-Dub stood close by and howled, "I asked you what in the hell just happened in here, Armand? Talk to me, man! What's going on here?"

Armand seemed visibly shaken. "I... I don't know what in the hell happened, Charlie!" he stuttered. "Fuck, I really don't know! All I know is that... that crazy-ass African bastard shoved this big nickel-plated .357 Magnum in my face. It happened as soon as you left the room. I almost shit my pants, man! I'm telling you, Charlie, I was scared to death!" he said as he shook nervously.

C-Dub noticed that his attaché case was missing from the floor near the couch where he left it. He became even angrier. "Yeah, Armand, it appears as if my fifty large has walked up out of here with that black-ass nigga, too. Didn't it?"

Armand nodded gloomily, "I'm afraid so, Charlie. Look!" He showed his left wrist to C-Dub. "That bastard even took my Presidential Rolex off my arm! Can you believe that?" He shook his head. "Jesus Christ, man! I'm sorry. I really am! Damn!" he shouted in despair.

C-Dub disgustedly tossed the damaged necktie onto the coffee table near what was left of the cocaine.

"Armand, look here, man." He sighed, as he placed a compassionate hand onto Armand's left shoulder. "I've known you forever. I know damn well that you didn't have anything to do with this bullshit. I'm sure of it. Because if I thought for one second that you were in cahoots with this nigga'... man." He sighed, as he opened his coat and displayed a blue-steel, 9mm Beretta in plain view. He had it resting against his shirt inside of an old-style Dockers clutch. "Your ass would be dead right now," he continued, buttoning his coat. "But what I need to know right now is this. How well do you know that monkey-ass, double-crossing motherfucker?"

Armand shook his head and grunted in disgust. "Not well at all. Actually, Charlie, I've encountered only one other business transaction with that imbecile, but it was on a much smaller scale than this one. However, I've got to admit that the bills that he had with him were superb as well. Everything went quite smoothly. Nothing like this transaction! Jesus!" he shouted and slammed his clenched fist into his palm. "Charlie, I messed up big time on this deal, man. I know I did. I whole-heartedly apologize for my carelessness. I should've known that he was shady." He hung his head in shame and stared pathetically at the coffee table for what seemed like forever.

"Don't sweat it, Armand." C-Dub placed his hand back on his shoulder, trying to comfort him. "Don't beat yourself up over this. Shit happens, man. Everything's going to be all right. Besides, it wasn't anything but a lousy-ass fifty gees. It isn't the end of the world."

He removed his hand from Armand's shoulder, allowing him to continue to ponder the situation. After a moment, the two of them sat on the couch and stared absentmindedly at the coffee table.

"Ah. What the hell! I might as well have a blow," C-Dub mentioned, and then he took the liberty of snorting a "pinky" fingernail's worth of the cocaine and smiled. "You know Armand; I think that I should be good for at least a few ounces of this private-stock powder, which you were bragging about earlier, aren't I?"

Armand appeared to be relieved. "Absolutely Charlie, I'll do even better than that." He used the edge of a business card from his coats breast-pocket to line up and snort some of the powder into each of his nostrils. "Mm... good stuff," he said, before his entire face went numb.

C-Dub followed suit by using his "pinky" fingernail again to snort another load.

"Yes it is," he uttered, as he massaged his nose. "Now, buddy, what were you saying?"

"I tell you what, my friend. I know exactly how I could make this right with you. I mean, I really feel bad about this mess." Armand explained, as he nodded and placed his hand on C-Dub's shoulder. "I'm talking about making it up to you big time, buddy!"

C-Dub seemed interested as he raised his eyebrows. "Really big time, you say?" He grinned. "Big enough to get my fifty large back?" He winked and slapped Armand playfully on his back, startling him.

"Charlie, baby!" He smiled, "I'm talking about a hell of a lot more money than that!"

C-Dub continued to smile, engaged and hanging onto Armand's every word. "Well, Daddy-O." He rubbed his palms together conspiratorially, "Let's hear it! Tell me what you got!"

Armand positioned himself so that he could maintain eye contact with him. "Okay my friend, check this out," he began, while he pulled a pack of non-filter cigarettes and a gold-metal lighter from his inside coat pocket, and offered one to C-Dub, who respectively declined.

Armand lit the cigarette and placed the lighter on the coffee table. "Okay, listen," he said, as he exhaled a thick cloud of smoke towards the ceiling lights. "There's an associate of mine. His name is Carlos, Carlos Diaz. The guy's an imbecile! He's definitely an idiot! But, he's filthy rich, and I simply cannot stand him, or his wife's pompous ass. Now look, I've got the whole layout on this cat. I'm talking about his entire daily itinerary." He arched an eyebrow and continued looking directly into C-Dub's dark-brown eyes, with intensity.

He exhaled another cloud of smoke towards the lights. "And, believe me, I'm talking about the complete drawings! So tell me, Charlie, are you interested, or not?"

C-Dub appeared to be lost in ponder. "How rich are we talking about?" he asked, extremely curious.

Armand grinned. "Rich as cream, I tell you. The asshole has got over four million in cold, hard cash stashed away inside of his safety-deposit box in Beverly Hills."

C-Dub whistled approvingly. "He's got four million dollars?"

Armand smiled. "Yes, Charlie. That's correct, four-million smackeroo's, buddy. And that's not counting the other half-million in cash, or the eight-hundred-and-ninety-thousand dollars in diamond-studded jewelry, which is sitting there ripe for the plucking. He has it stuffed inside of his bedroom vault at this very moment!"

C-Dub whistled even louder. "Damn! Now that's a lick!" he mentioned, as he pondered the possibilities.

This could be the job to end all jobs! I would never have to commit another crime, ever again! My loved ones, wherever they are, they would always be provided for. On top of that, imagine all of the cocaine that I could buy! And the bitches I could fuck! Shit!

"Yes, Armand, I'm interested." He smiled. "Now man, tell me more." He ushered him on, nodding. "I want to know everything, every last detail. But first, I want to know everything there is to know about this tall-ass jungle mother-fucker, Agonda, you dig what I'm saying?"

Armand nodded. "Yes, Charlie."

C-Dub clenched his jawbone. "Because Armand, when I catch up with him, I'm going to cut his head off, and then I'm going to shove his dick down his goddamn esophagus! You watch, man!" he blurted without thinking, and then snorted a small amount of the cocaine that he scooped up with his "pinky" fingernail.

Armand informed C-Dub all about his carefully thought out plans for the Diaz robbery. He mentioned that the best time to execute the robbery, and the kidnapping of Carlos Diaz and his wife, would be at 7:00 a.m., on the following Monday.

He assured C-Dub that the entire scheme, should not take any more than two hours to complete, from start to finish. He also mentioned that everyone involved would be rich!

C-Dub added to the plot, by volunteering to have Mrs. Joanna Diaz locked away inside of the storeroom, at his auto detailing shop in Northridge, California. Meanwhile, during the plot, he continued, Mr. Diaz would be forced to proceed as instructed, to the World-Wide Bank & Financing Corporation in Beverly Hills, where he would then retrieve the four million dollars in cash from his safety-deposit box. It was a fool-proof plan," C-Dub assured him.

Armand nodded his approval. "I've been monitoring this knuckle-head mother-fucker and his wife for a long time now. I've wanted to rob them forever, it seems. That's another reason why I wanted to tell you about them, so that you could be in on this plan, Charlie. You're a grimy thinker when you need to be. I know that about you. You're use to this type of shit."

C-Dub smirked. "I don't know if I should take that remark as a compliment or an insult?"

"Trust me, Charlie, it's a compliment, buddy."

"Why, thank you, sir." C-Dub smiled.

Armand returned the gesture. "And you're welcome, my good man."

The two of them agreed that they were going to need some more man-power to properly pull the job off. Their longtime partners, Ken and Mike would be perfect, C-Dub explained. "Yes, Armand, that should do it."

However, Armand mentioned that it was imperative that his identity remain a secret.

C-Dub guaranteed him that his name and position would not be jeopardized in any way, and then he informed him that he knew the right guy to include in on the scheme. They needed a fifth man. His name is Chill.

C-Dub left the hotel suite at 9:02 p.m. He handed a twenty dollar bill to the Hispanic valet employee in the subterranean parking structure. The middle-aged man seemed to appreciate the kind gesture, as he watched C-Dub slide into the driver's seat of his Mercedes-Benz.

He proceeded out of the building and made a cell phone call to Ken and Mike, (47-year-old Caucasian men) who shared a fashionable four bedroom home in the West Hollywood Hills. Thirty minutes later, C-Dub showed up at their residence on Laurel Canyon Boulevard near Mulholland Drive.

After a couple of glasses of fine cognac, C-Dub explained the details of the kidnapping for ransom plot against the Diaz family. "It's the perfect heist."

When Mike asked about the weapons that they needed in the plan, C-Dub informed him that he had all of the artillery and everything else they required to complete the mission. He also explained that the point of entry to the Diaz residence was through the mansion's front door. It would be simple, that Ken and Chill would play a pair of phony police detectives claiming to be in the process of observing a team of highly sophisticated computer hackers that have a clear interest in Mr. Diaz's personal savings account.

C-Dub informed Ken and Mike of how trustworthy his buddy Chill was and that they had had met while locked-up in Placerville Prison back in the days.

Ken asked, "Can this Chill guy be trusted?"

C-Dub responded, "I trust Willie Bruce with my life. He's a down brother! I explained to him the details already. He knows the complete get down. He's fully aware of the risk involved in this kidnapping scheme. He's a father of five little rug rats. Therefore, he's ready and he's hungry! So, don't worry, guys? This is nothing new to him. Chill has executed this type of shit before. Don't trip, fella's." C-Dub lied.

Mike seemed a bit skeptical at first, being that he had never personally met this new guy called, "Chill."

C-Dub eventually convinced them both that Chill was a good candidate for the fifth man's position. A position that was necessary to complete the job, which would also be the last job they would ever need to perform. Riches would definitely be theirs to keep, he informed them.

The three of them agreed to meet up in the parking lot of a Beverly Hills supermarket. The meeting was to take place at 6:30 a.m., the following Monday.

Feeling a bit angry about the robbery in the hotel, but desperately desiring the warmth of a woman's body, C-Dub drove to Hollywood and stopped by a well-known corner on Sunset Boulevard. It was two blocks west of La Brea Avenue.

There, he waited patiently in the car for a few minutes, before he finally spotted the lovely, Ms. Marsha. She was a beautiful, 35-year-old Caucasian prostitute, which he had been paying for sex for a couple of years. He watched her as she exited a brown, late model Cadillac and stood on the curb.

"There goes that bitch," he whispered, and then tapped the horn slightly, which captured her attention.

She waved happily as she crossed the Boulevard and entered his car. "It's about time that you showed up, honey," she exclaimed, and kissed him softly on his cheek.

He seemed happy to see her. "I've been busy, baby," he said, as he proceeded away from the curb.

A moment later, per her instructions, he pulled the car into a nearby shabby little motel over on Yucca Avenue, just north of Hollywood Boulevard.

They checked into room #34, near the rear of the dingy parking lot, and acted as if they were longtime lovers as they entered the room. C-Dub took a seat on the edge of the repugnant, twin-sized bed and smiled at Marsha, as he reached into his coat pocket and pulled out a plastic bag of Peruvian flake cocaine. It was two ounces in the bag, which was half of what Armand had promised him.

Marsha's eyes flew wide open at the first sight of the powder. C-Dub appeased her appetite with a small quantity, which he poured onto a piece of paper on the nightstand near the lamp.

"You're going to like this shit, Marsha," he uttered, as he slid his "pinky" fingernail into the bag and snorted.

30

"Well, let's see, "she said, and then used the tip of the room's door-key to raise the powder to her nostrils.

After an hour-long escapade of sexual gratification, C-Dub handed her two one-hundred dollar bills for her bedroom time, before jumping into his Mercedes-Benz and headed west-bound on Sunset Boulevard. Shortly thereafter, a series of twist and turns had led him into the north-bound onramp to the Interstate 405 freeway.

Chapter Four

Laughter filled the bedroom as Chill and his wife lay in each other's arms in bed. They were clad in wool pajamas watching the eleven-thirty segment of a late night television show.

Suddenly, the cordless phone on the nightstand nearest Jen's side of the bed began to ring. It became quite evident that she was unwilling to part with her warm comfort zone. Nevertheless, she reluctantly answered the phone and, sparing no hint of irritation, wearily croaked, "Hello?"

"Hello, Jen," C-Dub crooned into his cell phone's Bluetooth earpiece.

He was driving along in his Mercedes-Benz with the convertible-top lowered. He was still extremely upset, while he was speeding illegally in the carpool lane on the north-bound Interstate 405 Freeway.

Jen was instantly ill-at-ease upon hearing C-Dub's voice, which seemed to seethe with arrogance.

"Hello, Charlie," she responded dryly, as she rolled her lovely dark-brown eyes, and then looked to Chill to give her a nonverbal clue, as to whether or not he wanted C-Dub to know that he was home.

Chill nodded, as she continued her unwanted conversation. "How are you this evening?" she continued wryly.

C-Dub was barely intelligible over the charging wind and the blaring highway noise.

"I'm okay, Jen. Is that husband of yours around? If so, could you please tell him that I need to holler at him? It's kind of' important, you know."

"Yeah, Charlie," she stated flatly. "He's right here. Hold on, please."

"Okay, Jen. And thank you."

"You're welcome, Charlie." she looked at Chill. "Here, babe," she said softly, handing him the phone.

Chill placed the receiver against his ear as he and Jen continued to stare at the television. "C-Dub!" he blurted. "What's up with it, Daddy-O?"

"Not a goddamn thang', youngster," he replied, as he drove underneath the 101 freeway Interchange. "I lost," he paused. "Allow me to reiterate that statement, Chill. I got straight played up out of fifty grand tonight."

"Fifty gees!" Chill shouted indignantly, as he sat up in bed and rested his back against the headboard, appearing completely absorbed in the conversation.

Jen rolled her eyes and shook her head. For, she knew that C-Dub and his many schemes were all roguish.

"Yeah, youngster," C-Dub resumed, "I got jacked for my attaché case containing fifty-thousand dollars tonight."

"Goddamn?" Chill exclaimed.

"Yeah, man. Well, between you and me. It was actually only five thousand bucks of the real money that I had in the case. Because the rest of that shit was counterfeit," he chuckled.

"You're crazy, Dub!" Chill laughed. "But how'd it happen?" he eagerly inquired.

"I was messing around with that funny green stuff, which I was telling you about earlier this afternoon."

"Oh, okay. I remember." Chill nodded.

"Good," C-Dub said, as he blew some cigar smoke over his head and into the blaring wind. "Anyway, I went to make a buy for a hundred and ten gees of some really good bullshit. But, I messed around and ended up getting my ends jacked by this big-ass African nigga'. He was the same dude who was selling the bullshit."

Chill laughed good-naturedly. "Well, Dub, it sounds to me like you were the one who was trying to get over on the African dude in the first place!"

C-Dub laughed knowingly. "Hell, I was!" he admitted boldly. "However, it didn't work out too cool for a player in the long-run, you dig?" he laughed.

"Yeah, I can see. You're a cold piece of work, C-Dub. Because you were the one who was trying to get over on a counterfeiter, by handing him some counterfeit money!" Chill laughed, while Jen smirked and shook her head. "Damn! You're about one dirty ass dude, Dub! You're scandalous, dawg'!"

"You're just now figuring that out about me, boy?" C-Dub boasted.

"Hell nah! I been knew that about you, nigga'!"

"So, what's the news then?" C-Dub said, as he exhaled some more smoke, while he approached the north-bound 405 off-ramp to Burbank Boulevard.

"Well. It sounds to me like the jacker got jacked tonight, boy!" Chill blurted and rubbed it in with a short laugh.

"Yeah, things went kind of bad for me. Not quite like I expected. It's all gravy though, because I came up on a hundred-thousand-dollar jack move in the process. So it all worked out cool in the end."

"A hundred racks!" Chill exclaimed, and whistled appreciatively.

Jen, who appeared mildly entertained by the television show, stared at him impatiently out of the corner of her eyes with a smirk on her face.

"Yeah, well," C-Dub continued. "It's damn near worth that much, or better, you dig?" He said untruthfully. "And at least half of that money could be going into your pocket. You feel what I'm saying, youngster?"

Chill began to contemplate, although he knew that C-Dub was scandalous.

As he pondered the situation for a long, silent moment, he began to reflect back on his time in prison, when C-Dub was a marked man, whose name was on some prison gangs, "hit-lists." He was marked to be terminated on several occasions because of his foul ways and gambling habits. He was stabbed in his chest on four different occurrences and was lucky to be alive.

"I don't know, dub," Chill finally said, as he stared absentmindedly at the television. However, he failed to notice that his wife was frustrated and shaking her head, as she also continued to stare at the television.

"Man, Chill." C-Dub continued. "At least fifty gees of that money could easily be yours, man. Imagine that, kin folks. This is one sweet-ass lick! So what is there not to know? Your ass is broke! On top of that, I really need you in on this robbery. I mean bad, dawg'! It's a simple robbery. It's a piece of cake! It's you and I, in and out. Real quick like, you know? We can split one-hundred-thousand dollars, just you and me. Straight down the middle. So tell me, what's it going to be? Are you with me, or not? We're talking about a lot of money here, Chill!"

Chill appeared to be lost in contemplation again, as he considered C-Dub's invitation.

Jen looked as if she was disappointed in him.

"Yeah, Dub! Count me in, man." he finally announced. "Fuck it! He blurted, and then observed as Jen rolled her eyes. She sighed deeply, crossed her arms, and glared at the television.

C-Dub was smiling as he continued to drive northbound on the freeway, "Now that's what the hell I'm talking about, Chill baby! Have heart, have some mother-fucking money, boy! Let's get this cheddar, dawg'. You know, like we used to. It's definitely out there. And real hustler knows, that don't nothing come to a sleeper, but a dream! Trust and believe, youngster. I don't want you to know what being poor is all about. So wake up, boy!" C-Dub implored, as he exited the freeway and proceeded east-bound on Burbank Boulevard.

"But what do I have to do?" Chill asked.

"It's a simple jack move, Chill! Now, you know goddamn well that we're not about to have this particular conversation over this telephone like this. We're not suckers, you dig? We done already said too much as it is. Now, I just pulled off of the 405 at Burbank Boulevard right now. So I'll be at your crib in about fifteen minutes. We'll holler about this lick then. Is that cool with you, youngster?"

"Yeah, that's cool, Daddy-O. I'll see you in a minute, then," Chill replied, as their conversation drew to a close.

He reluctantly looked at his visibly upset wife, who continued to stare at the late night show. "That's for sure, young brother. I'm out," C-Dub continued.

"See you in a minute, Dub."

Chill handed the phone receiver back to Jen. "Hang that up for me, Momma, please." he asked, very sweetly.

Jen smirked as she dropped the receiver back onto its cradle.

For a while she stared out of the corner of her eyes at the side of his face. But he tried hard to ignore her by staring at the television.

After a moment, he finally smiled at her. She smirked, as she cocked her head towards him and blurted, "Don't you be cheesing at me, Willie! And don't you call me, 'Momma' either!"

"What, Jen? Why are you mad-dogging me then? You're trippin', baby!"

"No, Willie! You're the one who's tripping. Because you're sitting here grinning with this stinking-thinking stuff that you're doing. You know how scandalous that Charlie is! You just said it yourself! And I know that you're not planning on doing nothing crazy with him! He's bad news, babe. And you know it, too!"

Chill got out of bed and grabbed a box of cheap cigars off of the Chester drawer near the television and exited the room, closing the door behind him.

Jen laid against the headboard shaking her head in frustration.

Moments later, he stood outside of his apartment in his red-wool pajamas and some black-leather house slippers near the driveway.

He was smoking a cigar and mulling over the possibilities of what fifty thousand dollars could do for him and his family.

He could pay on his regular child-support payments for Willie Jr., and continue to feed his family.

He finally observed C-Dub pull into the complex in his Mercedes-Benz with the convertible top lowered.

John Legend's song, "*I Can Change*" blared from the vehicle's sound system, as he pulled up near the curb in front of Chill, and then lowered the music volume.

"What it do, dub?" Chill asked as he reached in the car and gave him some dap.

"You know the business, Chill." He grinned, as Chill opened the passenger door and entered the seat beside him.

Chapter 5

On Monday morning, December 6th, 2004, the early dawn's dew that glistened across the asphalt, reminded C-Dub of the jewels that only he would benefit from after the upcoming heist.

He, along with Armand, Ken and Mike, were all dressed as undercover police detectives in dark business suits, dark sunglasses and black dress shoes.

The three of them stood secretly in the far hidden corner of a Beverly Hills's supermarket parking lot.

A black, late-model cargo van was situated nearby, ready and waiting.

C-Dub flicked his wrist and glanced at his gold wristwatch. "Its six-twenty a.m., gentlemen," he began, "My boy, Chill should be here at any minute now. I instructed him to be here on location, by six-thirty this morning."

"Charlie," Armand said, as he used his gold-plated lighter to ignite a non-filter cigarette. "Exactly how well do you know this kid, Chill?"

C-Dub ran his hand across his freshly shaved head. "I've known Willie Bruce for quite some time now. We met in prison back in the days when I caught that drug-possession beef. Matter of fact, Chill helped to save my black-ass on a couple of occasions."

Armand nodded after exhaling a cloud of smoke. "So, I gather that you trust him then?"

"Yes, I do," C-Dub answered without hesitation. "I trust him very much, with my life in fact. I first ran across him one day on the yard in Placerville Prison. I'd seen him around on the facility for a while, but didn't actually know him. All that I knew about him was that he was a quiet young blood nigga'. He was from the Six-Duce Brims neighborhood."

"Six-Duce Brims?" Armand question curiously.

"Yeah man," C-Dub continued, "it's right off of Slauson Avenue near Normandy. His O.G. homeboy, Big Bruno, and I were real tight. I mean, tight, Armand! He and I had been through a lot of bullshit together. Anyway, how Chill and I officially got cool with each other, and I remember this shit like it was yesterday, It was freezing on the yard. I mean, it was snowing like crazy in Placerville Prison! Chill was standing on the side of a concrete table that we used for playing Poker in front of the 2- building. I was housed in the 3-building. I had just walked out of the rotunda and the cold air hit me like a freight train."

It was December 9th, 1999, at 1:05 p.m. The cold weather was pounding against the A-yard like a 14-pound sledge hammer. The prison grounds were covered in dingy white snow, and the temperature was said to have reached slightly above zero degrees.

C-Dub exited the 3-building's rotunda and proceeded along the walkway, while the black security door slammed shut behind him, "Man, it's colder than a mother-fucker out here!" he blurted, as he zipped up his heavy green prison jacket and glanced around the yard and observed some inmates in the middle of the field playing flag football. "Look at these crazy-ass fools," he muttered, and then observed that the concrete tables in front of each of the five housing units were occupied with inmates playing chess or card games.

Suddenly, he noticed that there were four Black men at the table in front of the 2-building, who had their usual Texas Hold 'em Poker game in progress, and that Chill and two other Black inmates were standing nearby, observing them play.

C-Dub, intent on busting-up the Poker game, began to walk along the walkway that encircled the yard. As he did so, he passed by a few inmates who were jogging in his direction. He nodded to a couple of them as they continued on pass him.

"I'm going to break these nigga's today," he told himself, as he approached the group.

Chill was wearing his thick green camp jacket, and looked as if he was freezing, when suddenly; C-Dub walked up beside him and patted him softly on the back. "What's up, youngster?"

Chill smiled. "Hey C-Dub, what's crackin'?"

"This goddamn weather is, that's what's crackin'!"

"No shit, man. It's cold out here!"

"Cold?" C-Dub scowled, "Man, it's colder than polar bear pussy out here today!"

"Tell me about it, man," Chill replied, and then shivered for a moment as he folded his arms across his chest. He tilted his head towards the table. "Are you getting in this game today?"

"Of course I am, youngster. I'm going to break these busters, just as soon as they let me in, you watch."

Chill laughed. "I think they're waiting on you anyway. You did them kinda' bad yesterday, man. They're pissed off at you."

"I know, huh?" C-Dub grinned. "These cats don't know nothing about no poker. Old fake-ass busters! I cracked them no-playing-ass suckers for two hundred dollars worth of canteen shit." He winked.

"Damn," Chill whistled, as C-Dub stepped to the side of the bench and watched as Devil, a 32 year old Black man dealt the cards across the table.

"What's up, Devil?" C-Dub inquired.

"It damn sure ain't you, Dub! Your ass got lucky on that river queen card yesterday. Course now, today is another day, fool!" He smiled.

C-Dub smirked. "Whatever, boy," he said waving him off jokingly. "Anyway, can a real poker player get in this game, or what? 'Cause these other broke-ass suckers ain't got no money! All they've got is some problems."

Everyone at the table voiced their obscene opinions.

"Fuck y'all, too," C-Dub chuckled.

Moe, a 36-year-old Black man at the far end of the table exclaimed, "Put up, or shut up, Dub!" as he checked his two cards in by sliding them across the table to the dealer.

"I'm trying to put up, Moe. I'm just waiting to get in the game, so that I can break your sorry ass!"

"I heard the hell outta' that! You ain't going to break nobody, blood!"

"We'll see about that. Keep on running your mouth, Moe." C-Dub locked eyes with him. He never liked Moe anyway.

"I'm going to keep on running my mouth until the day I die, blood!" Moe snapped.

C-Dub flashed an evil grin. "Well, that could be a lot sooner than you think nigga'! You never know. Keep on bumpin' your gums!" he announced with venom in his words.

"Whatever, Dub!"

"Yeah motherfucka, whatever, Moe! What's up, man?" C-Dub blurted, challenging him to a fist-fight, as a 40-year-old Black man named, Cassidy, slid his cards to the dealer and then rose to his feet. "Here we go again," he sighed. "I'm out, y'all. You fools are trippin' again."

He yawned, stretched, and then positioned himself near Chill and the other men.

"Yeah, man. You're trippin', Dub." Moe resumed.

"Whatever, nigga'. You don't want to see me about nothing! Because you know that I'll get off in your ass!" he replied, as he looked at the dealer.

"Anyway, Devil, can I get in the goddamn game now, or what?"

"Yeah C-Dub, you can get in the game, goddamn! A seat just opened up, man. Sit on down!"

"Cool!" C-Dub rubbed his palms together as he took a seat on the bench.

Two hours later, Chill was standing behind C-Dub, who was winning at the poker table with a cheap cigar wedged in between his teeth while he studied his cards.

The temperature had risen a bit. However, *it was still cold as hell*, C-Dub thought, as Moe dealt a round of cards to him first, and then to Devil, before he issued two cards to himself. Each of the men discreetly deliberated over their cards.

C-Dub was issued a pair of 3's. His cards were a 3 of hearts, and a 3 of spades.

Moe had a pair of aces in his hands, which were an ace of spades and an ace of clubs. He knew that it was a high likelihood that he had the unbeatable hand. He kept his cool however. "And here we go, y'all," he mentioned, as he laid out the flop, which were the first three cards.

The flop revealed a 3 of clubs, an ace of hearts and a king of diamonds.

C-Dub grinned, realizing that he had a three of a kind with his 3's. "Now that's the business!" he exclaimed.

"Don't get too excited, fool. I've got the aces over here," Moe warned him, as he dropped $40.00 dollars worth of poker chips on the table.

"Yeah, let you tell it! I think that you're bluffing. I'll call that bull-shit that you're talking, though," C-Dub added, while he matched Moe's bet and placed his chips on the table.

"I think he's bluffing, also. Because I've got the aces, too," Devil said, staring into Moe's eyes while he dropped his chips on the table.

"Just deal the cards, man!" C-Dub roared.

"Watch your manners now, boy!" Moe snapped.

"Just deal the goddamn cards!" C-Dub resumed, realizing that he had $165.00 dollars in poker chips on his side of the table.

The poker chips were made out of used playing cards, which were torn into even square pieces.

"Okay, dub," Moe continued, as he placed the forth card on the table, known as the, "Turn Card." It was a jack of spades.

"Jack of spades in the house, ya'll!" Moe exclaimed. "Any bets?" He looked around the table.

"I'll raise you," C-Dub mentioned, and then placed $40.00 dollars in chips on the pile.

"I'm out, y'all. This is hand is way too rich for my blood!" Devil stated, and then stepped back from the table.

"I'll call you on that bullshit, Dub!" Moe said and matched his bet by tossing his chips on the pile.

"Okay Moe, deal the river card, man," C-Dub instructed, peering into his eyes. He knew that he had a lot of money riding on this particular hand.

"And here we go, Dub," Moe declared, as he turned over the last card, which was called, the "River card". They observed as a king of clubs faced upward.

"Damn!" C-Dub sighed, and then tossed $80.00 dollars in chips on the table. "Bet, mother-fucker!" he mentioned, peering into Moe's eyes.

"I'll call, Dub," Moe said, peering back, as he calmly tossed his chips on the table.

"Damn, man!" C-Dub blurted, and then stood to his feet and walked a few steps away from the table with his back towards the men.

He stared upward towards the sky for a moment of ponder, while Chill and the rest of the men watched him closely.

C-Dub had to think of something quick, because there was no way that he was about to let Moe beat him, out of the $360.00 worth of poker chips that was lying on the table.

Therefore, he discreetly reached into his coat pocket and cuffed some extra cards in his right hand. The cards were a king of hearts, and a king of spades. *"Fuck this buster,"* he thought, as he turned around and walked back to the table.

"All right, fool!" he blurted to Moe. "I'll raise that bet another $50.00 bucks then, you soft-ass punk!"

He tossed the chips on top of the pile and plopped himself down at the table.

Moe grinned mischievously. "Bet then, blood!" he yelled, and then tossed his chips on the table. "Matter of fact 'Dub, bet your television! Bet everything else that you've got in your goddamn cell, nigga'!"

"Bet it all then, punk!" C-Dub yelled back, as he slyly used his coat-sleeve to swipe the original cards, the pair of 3's off of the table and into his lap.

Unknowing, Moe smiled. "Yeah, I've got that ass now!" he said, as he boldly dropped his pair of aces on the table for C-Dub to see. "I've got some triple aces, mother-fucker! Now tell me, can you beat that?" he yelled.

C-Dub grinned evilly. "Is that all you got, you little bitch? Well, feast your punk-ass eyes on these, fool!" he said, as he slapped the pair of kings on the table as hard as he could. "How you like me now, nigga'?"

He and the other men at the table observed Moe's near panic reaction, as his mouth opened wide with disappointment.

C-Dub laughed. "That's four of a kind, Moe! That beats your little triple aces. Now, pay up, you little bitch!"

"Mother-fucker!" Moe shouted, and then slammed his palm against the table.

"Yeah-yeah, I know. You weren't expecting this." C-Dub grinned. "Now, pay up, bitch!" he demanded.

"Damn," Moe whispered.

He felt that something wasn't right about C-Dub and his pair of Kings, because he knew that C-Dub was untrustworthy.

"Let me see something right quick, man," he muttered, as he began to sort through the cards on the table.

C-Dub knew at that very moment that he was in deep trouble. "What are you looking for, Moe?"

"I'm just checking something out real quick," he replied, as he continued to search through the cards, where he eventually came across two more Kings. One of the cards was the king of hearts, and the other was the king of spades.

He scowled at C-Dub. "What's up with this shit, Dub?"

"I don't know motherfucker!" C-Dub shouted. "What are you trying to say, Moe? Are you trying to say that I'm cheating or something?" he asked, and then he quickly reached across the table and punched Moe in his nose. He watched as he fell backwards off of the bench and flat onto his back.

C-Dub took advantage of the opportunity and rushed around the table. "Punk-ass nigga'!" he yelled, and then punched him repeatedly in his face, rendering him unconscious.

Big Bundy, one of Moe's friends rushed to his aid. "Get off of my homeboy, blood!" he hollered, and then attempted to stab C-Dub in the side of his neck with a sharpened pork chop bone, which he had wrapped in some black duct-tape.

"Look out, Dub!" Chill shouted, while he hit Bundy in the right side of his face and knocked him out cold.

"Look at you now, Moe!" C-Dub blurted, and then spat his saliva onto Moe's face. "You're paid, punk! Fuck you, and your homeboys!"

The middle-aged Hispanic gunman in the guard tower, noticed the confrontation and immediately pushed his panic button on his utility belt, and then yelled over the loud speaker, "Everybody down! Get down on the ground, right now!" he demanded, as a team of correctional officers ran onto the prison yard and proceeded to secure the premises. All the while, the emergency alarm system continued to ring out.

C-Dub, Chill and the other men in the area proceeded to lie down in the snow near Moe and Bundy, who were still unconscious.

Back in the supermarket parking lot, Ken scowled at C-Dub. "You're one low-down-ass bastard, Charlie!"

C-Dub smiled cheerfully. "I know, Ken. But, I wasn't expecting for Moe to get to looking around through the cards like he did," he admitted sheepishly.

He looked at each of his crime partners. "Anyway y'all, Chill and I have been cool ever since that day. Matter of fact, every now and again, I call him, "Mr. One-Punch." Because that was all that it took. He definitely handled his business that day. I was proud of him."

"Mr. One-Punch, huh? Young Chill's got it like that, Charlie?" Ken wanted to know.

"He's a hard hitting youngster, man. That dude has got some hands on him. I'm telling you! I witnessed it myself. He put Moe out with one punch."

"Anyway Charlie, did you ever pay that guy, Moe?" Armand asked.

"Hell nah! I told the punk that he was paid and to go fuck himself!"

"You're an ass, Charlie!" Mike exclaimed.

"Why, thank you, sir." C-Dub smiled.

"You're welcome, asshole!" he smirked.

"Anyway, Armand," C-Dub continued, "Chill's a good kid, you know? He's nothing like that piece-of-shit, Agonda friend of yours."

Armand appeared embarrassed, as he smirked and looked away, while C-Dub resumed, "Whom I think that I might have a few strong leads on. So, it's only a matter of time before we meet again, and when we do," he chuckled, shaking his head. "Boy, boy, boy, it isn't going to be nice, not at all. Because, I'm going to cut his head off. You can bet that! And I put that on my momma's grave, man!"

"Yes, Charlie," Armand chuckled. "Well, keep me abreast on that situation, will you? I would like to have my way with that asshole, as well."

C-Dub grinned. "I'm sure that you would."

Suddenly, he and his friends observed Chill drive into the parking lot in his Honda Accord. "Speaking of the devil, guys. Here comes my man right now," he stated.

Chill pulled his car into a nearby parking stall. After a moment, he exited the car wearing a black business suit, matching leather shoes, and some dark sunglasses. "Top of the morning, gentlemen," he announced, approaching them.

"Good morning," everyone responded, as Chill and C-Dub embraced each other.

"Top of the morning, fella's," Chill responded.

"What's up, Mr. One-punch?" C-Dub chortled, and then wrapped his arm around Chill's shoulders.

Chill snickered, "Dub, I know that you didn't tell them that story, man!"

"I sure did. I told them all about it. I told them that you're a down, hard hitting ass youngster."

"Yes, Chill. We heard all about you, young man." Armand said with a hint of dry humor.

"Gentlemen," C-Dub mentioned, when suddenly, his attention was captured by an older Hispanic man. He was driving around the parking lot in a motorized grounds sweeper.

It was the previous cocaine-induced paranoid delusion, which actually forced C-Dub to see a uniformed Police officer on the vehicle. He thought that the guy was speaking into a handheld radio microphone, and was staring at him and the rest of his men.

Someone in the group happened to clear his throat, which brought C-Dub back to reality.

"Anyway guys," he continued, "I'd like for you all to meet, Chill. He's a very good friend of mine, and I can truly say that I trust him with my life. And he trusts me as well."

Everyone nodded to Chill.

"Good morning, Chill," Armand spoke up and extended his hand. "I'm Armand," The two of them shook hands.

"Good morning, Armand. I'm pleased to meet you."

"All right, Chill," C-Dub resumed, and then pointed to Ken who was standing near the van with his arms folded across his chest. "This is, Ken. He's also a very close friend of mine."

"How long has it been now, Ken? What, twenty-something years? It's got to be at least twenty years now that I've known you."

Ken smiled. "Charlie, it's been twenty-four years now. You're getting old, pal," he chuckled.

He extended his hand to Chill. "How's it going, dude?" he pumped Chill's fist.

"It's another one like the other one, my brother. I'm trying to get some money today, you know?"

Ken nodded. "I heard that, Chill. You and I both, pal!" He inched open his coat ever so slightly, and revealed a .38 Special, blue-steel revolver. He had it tucked inside of his black leather hip holster. "It's going to be a good day, Chill." he patted the weapon lovingly. "We're all going to get paid today."

"I hope so, man. I sure need the money."

"It's going to happen, Daddy-O," C-Dub cut in. "So don't trip, Chill."

He pointed to Mike, who was standing near Armand. "And last but not least Chill, this is my partner, Mike. I've known him ever since we were in the tenth grade."

Armand laughed. "Shit, Charlie! When the hell was that, in the Stone Age? It's got to be, you old bastard!"

Everybody laughed.

"You go to hell, Armand!" C-Dub blurted playfully.

"Anyway," Mike said as he shook Chill's hand. "It's a pleasure to meet you, man. Any friend of Charlie is a friend of mine."

"Thank you, Mike. It's good to meet you, too"

C-Dub removed his arm from Chill's shoulders. "Very good!" he exclaimed and clapped his hands. "Okay gentlemen." He rubbed his palms together. "Now that all of the pleasantries are behind us, let's get down to business."

He glanced up at the early-morning sunlight. "It's a little chilly today," he said, as he noticed that it was struggling to seep through the overcast sky. He shivered suddenly from the coldness and fastened the buttons on his coat.

"Now you guys, I've got all of the necessary tools for this job." He pointed to the black cargo van. "I've got them secured inside of that van right there. I've got the burners (guns), the handcuffs, detective badges, gloves, duct-tape, etc. You name it and I've got it, guys. This job's gonna' be a piece of cake. Trust me."

"It's going to be as easy as taking candy from a baby, my friends," Armand added, as he flicked his lit cigarette out into the parking lot.

C-Dub made a very brief, yet solemn eye contact with each of the men, and then asked, "Is everybody ready?"

"Yeah," everyone replied in unison.

Armand began, "Yes, Charlie. However, as you and I discussed earlier, it's absolutely necessary that I remain anonymous during this scheme. I ask of this for obvious reasons, of course."

"Don't you worry, Armand. I've got you covered on this job, mainly because of your affiliation with this guy. Your identity will not be compromised. I guarantee you that," C-Dub assured him, and then scanned the area for any hostiles.

He did so only to find that once again, the lonely grounds sweeper was being driven by the same man. Only this time, he didn't appear to be anything other than what he was, a hard-working employee.

"Okay gentlemen. Let's move out," he instructed.

Armand checked the time on his gold wristwatch. "It's six thirty-nine, Charlie. Carlos should be getting ready for the business day."

C-Dub checked his wristwatch as well. "Yes, he should, Armand. At least according to what you informed me regarding his daily itinerary," he said, as Ken and Mike climbed into the van's sliding door.

Chill seemed to be disturbed abruptly, and gently grabbed a hold of C-Dub's arm and whispered, "C-Dub, let me holler at you for a minute, man." He tilted his head towards the parking lot.

"Sure, Chill." The two of them moved a short distance away from the van. "What's up, man?" he asked impatiently, seeming preoccupied.

Chill continued to whisper, "I thought you told me that it was going be you and me robbing a couple of rich folks this morning. You didn't tell me anything about these other dudes!"

"Why, man? What's the goddamn problem?"

Chill glanced toward the open sliding door. "My problem is, I want to know why in the hell do we need all of these cats for only two people? This is way too many people to be involved in this bullshit, man!" He shook his head. It's way too many, dawg'!"

"Don't trip it, Chill! Everything's going to be all right! Trust me on this. I know what the hell I'm doing! Just trust me, man!" C-Dub demanded.

"Trust you? Man, if I didn't trust you, I wouldn't be here! But, Dub, you're on some scandalous shit! That's for real!"

Chill suddenly experienced the vivid recollection of an incident which occurred several years earlier, while he and C-Dub were incarcerated in the Placerville Prison.

It was 2:17 p.m., Saturday, January 2nd, 1993. Chill was trudging laps in the snow-burdened track on the "A-Yard." His friend and fellow inmate, Charles "C-Dub" Hicks, was shoveling some snow on the opposite side of the track. This was bestowed upon him as a punishment, for being caught in his cell, engaging in a fist-fight with

Andre "Chip" Donaldson, his 31-year-old African-American cellmate.

C-Dub was given thirty days by the prison's administration to perform 40-hours of "extra-duty." Otherwise, he would have to endure more intense consequences.

The cell-fight with Chip was a result of him attaining some information from his African-American wife, Lydia. She stated that C-Dub had boldly sent her an unsolicited and unwanted, sexually explicit love letter. The parcel was addressed to her home in Sylmar, California. During that precise moment, she immediately informed her husband.

Chill waved to his friend from across the yard and C-Dub waved back. The weather was bitterly cold and both men were dressed in very heavy thermal clothing.

Chill had to keep moving and C-Dub had to continue working to prevent them from freezing. The majority of the inmates weren't brave enough to go out onto the yard when the weather hit below-freezing temperatures.

Chill and C-Dub's only "companions" on the yard numbered less than twenty inmates, including three seasoned correctional officers who were walking on the track in the opposite direction of everyone else.

Chill happened to see something suspicious; he noticed that C-Dub saw it, too. The compelling sight was a group of Asian gangsters who were congregating near the Southern fence.

C-Dub happened to be the closest however, and was able to get a clearer view of them when the turn of events began. One of the men passed something to another man, who seemed to have panicked and dropped what appeared to be a small bundle wrapped in plastic.

As each of the men scattered, none of them seemed to notice that the officers had suddenly taken much interest in the grouping itself. The group was immediately gathered up, and ordered to stand-up against the fence. They were thoroughly patted down and handcuffed. As soon as another officer arrived on the scene, they were all escorted to the "lock-up" cages located inside of the yard's Program office.

C-Dub quickly made a bee-line for the area where he saw that the bundle was dropped. He found it half-buried in the snow, and realized that it was a tightly wrapped package of powder cocaine.

He greedily stashed the bundle in the ground in another location and returned to his cell.

Chill couldn't believe what he had witnessed with his very own eyes.

"*Was C-Dub on a death-wish trip? Or was he just plain stupid?*" he mused.

He genuinely worried about the fate of his friend, but Chill wasn't the only one to witness C-Dub's foolish opportunism.

C-Dub was later approached by the leader of the Asian gang, and was given twenty-four hours to return their dope, or die.

Unfortunately for C-Dub, he had used a small amount of the drug. He was in his new cell and suddenly became apprehensive. During his panic attack, he flushed the rest of the dope down the stainless steel toilet.

Chill spoke with C-Dub about the incident, but he stubbornly refused to admit his actions, even to his friend.

Out of love for his disgraceful partner, Chill paid the Asian gang leader, a heavy-set, 32-year-old Cambodian named, Tony Kin. Tony happened to be one of the cousins of Chill's wife, Jen.

Chill paid him and his gang members for the value of the cocaine, plus 10% for their troubles. Family or not, it was business on Tony's part.

In any case, Chill had saved C-Dub's life, but he never once told him of it.

C-Dub was completely ignorant as to just how close he had come to being stabbed to death in the yard.

It was with this in mind, which Chill snapped out of his reverie and back into the present.

"You're wicked, Dub! So you can miss me with all that, "Trust me shit! I may not be a rocket scientist, but I didn't get to be as old as I am by being stupid, neither!" he whispered. "Something's not right about this lick, man. And I think that you've got some explaining to do, homeboy! Or, you can count me out of this robbery, right here, and right now!

C-Dub looked around furtively and shook his head. "Man, Chill. You really get on my nerves sometimes!" He sighed and leaned in close and placed a comforting hand on Chill's shoulder, then whispered, "This is some top-secret-type, high-power shit that I'm about to lay on you, you dig? And you can't say a word of it in front of those other cats."

Chill nodded as he stared downward at the black-top while C-Dub resumed, "Now look, Chill. I said that this lick was worth $100 large, which is supposed to be split right down the middle between you and me. But no way, no how is that enough kibbles to feed all of these Cats." He tilted his head towards the van. "But you're right, boy. And all that I can tell you right now is that these other cats have already been fed, you know? And what's ours, is ours. It ain't going to be shared by anyone else, but you and I. Trust me, Chill," he continued, while he tapped his right hand gently against the backside of his left wrist. "It's all about this blackness right here, my nigga. Fuck them crackers in that van! I don't care how long that I've known them fools.

"When this shit is over and done with, they ain't getting a goddamn dime! Now, we don't have the time for this philosophy bullshit. We're behind schedule as it is. So I'm asking you one more time, homie." he said, as he impatiently craned his head towards the van's open door, where he noticed that Armand was impatiently tapping his wristwatch and motioning for them to hurry up. "Are you in, or you out?"

"Yeah, whatever, man. Let's go!"

C-Dub laughed and clapped Chill on the back. "That's right, boy. Let's get!" The two men jogged towards the van and jumped inside along with the other men.

Dub drove the van incognito towards the Diaz residence, and then moments later, he pulled it slowly over to the curb which was covered with brown leaves. The leaves seemed to spill over into the street and danced in the breeze.

He positioned the van in front of the semi-circular driveway, which led to Carlos & Joanna Diaz's Beverly Hills mansion.

"That's a sweet ride he's got there," C-Dub mentioned, as he pointed to the red 2004 Bentley Azure that was parked in the driveway. Near it was a black 2004 Mercedes-Benz, E-Class Wagon. Both cars were parked in front of the double-door entrance of the home.

"Yes, it is a sweet ride, Charlie. That clown, Carlos, paid over two hundred thousand dollars for that disposable machine. It is not an ordinary ride," Armand explained. "It happens to be one of the finest, precision-crafted motorcars that Great Britain ever designed, and introduced to the United States. I guess that you can call it an exquisite present to you tacky Yankees," he added snobbishly,

50

before mentioning, "it's well deserving of its present location as well."

The men stared at the illustrious estate.

"That's a beautiful house he has, too," Ken chimed in, as he opened the van's sliding side door. He instantly impersonated an official police officer's voice, as he asked Chill with authority, "Are you ready to do this, Detective Randle?"

"Yes, without a doubt, Lieutenant Monroe. Let's roll," he replied confidently.

"Come on, then. Let's move out and handle this situation."

The two of them stepped out of the van and walked to the front doors, where they stood quietly on the porch.

Ken, being the seasoned veteran, observed that Chill appeared to be a bit anxious. "Are you okay, Detective?"

"Yes, Lieutenant," he responded nervously.

It was quite some time since Chill had actually been involved in any type of criminal activity since his release from prison, but he genuinely tried his best to recapture his composure. "I'm all right, lieutenant," he uneasily assured him.

"That's good, officer. All right, then, let's rock and roll, dude!" he whispered.

He reached out and pressed the doorbell button on the right-side of the stained-glass door. The doorbell chimed, as Carlos Diaz and his wife, Joanna Diaz, who were both in their late 50's, were in the bathroom wearing matching silk pajamas, and brushing their teeth in the sink in front of the gold-trimmed, Victorian-style mirror.

Mr. Diaz looked at the digital alarm clock on the towel cabinet and saw that the time was 7:10 a.m. He scowled as he placed his toothbrush in its holder near the mirror. "That's rather peculiar, honey. I wonder who in the hell could that be?"

"I don't know, Carlos," she replied, appearing a bit irritated as well as she dried off her face.

"Didn't Maria tell you that she was showing up to work at nine o'clock this morning? She's kind of early, don't you think?"

"Yes, dear," she said, as she began to brush her luxuriously long, brunette hair. "That woman is so unpredictable. I think that we should start looking for her replacement as soon as possible. I'm sick of her!" she told him as the doorbell rang once more.

"I have to agree with you, honey. Now, let me get that goddamn door!"

"Okay, dear."

Carlos left the bathroom and walked down the steps into the foyer. He hastily looked through the windows in the front doors.

"Who in the hell are these guys?" he wondered, as Ken pressed the doorbell once again.

"All right, all right, shit! Get off my goddamn doorbell!" he yelled, before he opened the front door and saw that there were two strange men in dark suits and sunglasses, standing on his porch. "Who in the hell are you guys?"

"I'm Lieutenant Monroe, Mr. Diaz," Ken answered and then pointed to Chill. "This is Detective Randle, sir. We're with the fraud division downtown. Good morning."

"The hell if it is a good morning, Lieutenant! It's far too early for this visit. That is, unless someone that I actually care about has died. I'm really in a rush and you're making me late! So let's cut out all of the chit-chat shit and get down to the point of this completely unannounced visit! Shall we?"

Ken glanced at Chill and shared a menacing, knowing look. *Why, the nerve of this arrogant bastard! If he only knew what was about to happen to him, he'd shut the hell up!*

He looked at Mr. Diaz. "Well sir, based on our preliminary investigation, we are convinced that a syndicate of highly motivated computer hackers have taken a sudden interest in your personal savings account."

"Which account are you talking about?" Mr. Diaz demanded.

"Your savings account at the World-Wide Bank & Financing Corporation. The branch right here in Beverly Hills, sir."

Mr. Diaz panicked. "Oh my God!"

"Sir, you need to know that these same criminals have already compromised your checking account," Ken fabricated, and then relished at the fear that his words had instilled in the man.

"Dear Lord!" Mr. Diaz shouted, but his fear quickly gave way to anger. "Well!" he blurted. His words seemed to reclaim their pompous stench. "What in the hell are you two assholes doing about it?"

Chill forced himself to remain calm during the blatant disrespectful questioning. "Sir," he interjected, "may we discuss this matter further inside?"

Mr. Diaz suddenly appeared apprehensive. "Hackers, you say?"

"Yes, Mr. Diaz. It appears to be some of the best that I've ever encountered in my twenty-six years on the force. The good news is that your bank is federally insured, so all is not lost," Ken explained carefully.

Mr. Diaz began to scrutinize the two imposters. "May I see some badges? You never can tell who is who these days, you know?"

"Absolutely, sir," the imposters said in unison, and then reached inside of their coat pockets and displayed their phony badges.

He carefully examined them before he reluctantly backed away from the front door and into the foyer. "Come on in, detectives."

"Thank you, sir. This won't take more than a few minutes," Ken assured him.

Ken and Chill placed their badges away as they successfully entered the house.

Mr. Diaz closed the door behind him. "Right this way." He led them into his contemporarily furnished living room. "Have a seat, detectives." he gestured with an arm towards the white lambskin couch near the familiar tinted, lacquered coffee table.

"No thank you, sir. I'd rather stand. I hope you don't mind. It's the hemorrhoids, you know," Chill said, gazing around the room.

"Suit yourself, detective." Mr. Diaz replied, appalled. He took a seat next to Ken on the couch.

Ken quickly noticed his odd behavior. He seemed very uneasy as he watched Chill's every move.

Chill was unaware of Mr. Diaz's behavior, as he stood nearby, but was busy admiring his lavish surroundings.

"This is a really nice home you've got here, Mr. Diaz." Chill admiringly stated, attempting to soothe the victim's restlessness.

"It's okay, I suppose. It's just a house. Nothing special," Mr. Diaz replied, waving the compliment dismissively.

"Okay, Mr. Diaz. I've got a few necessary questions to ask you," Ken mentioned, while he focused on the cherry-wood flooring.

"Go ahead, detective. Make it quick."

"Okay, sir. Is Mrs. Diaz present here in the house?"

The gray, straight hairs on the back of Mr. Diaz's neck instantly stood up, as he became more suspicious. "Yes, detective," he responded hesitantly. He seemed to be lost in his own thoughts, as he stared absentmindedly at the small crystal unicorn sculpture on the coffee table.

He glanced at Chill standing nearby, but swiftly focused his attention back to Ken.

"My wife Joanna, she's in our bedroom. Other than that, we're alone in the house. However, our servant, Maria is supposed to be here around nine o'clock this morning. I actually assumed that it was her when you cops rang my door bell."

"She doesn't have her own key, Mr. Diaz?" Ken asked off-handedly, making eye contact with Chill, whom he noticed seemed quite apprehensive.

"Hell no!" he snapped, shaking his head. "We don't trust that, bitch!" He scowled.

"You don't?" Ken asked, appearing surprised.

"Of course not, Lieutenant!"

"Then why would you employ someone to work in your home, if you identify the person as being deceitful?"

Ken saw that Chill was becoming more impatient.

"Because, the damn peasant has six kids, and she accepts the crumbs that we toss her for her services! That's why, Detective!" he blurted.

"All right, sir." Ken stood up and moved into Chill's vicinity. "Where exactly in this house, would your bedroom be?"

Mr. Diaz felt the *butterflies* develop in his stomach. He also felt the bile rising from his esophagus, as he failed to make any sense of Ken's line of questions.

"It's upstairs, Lieutenant. It's straight ahead at the very end of the hallway." His growing apprehension compelled him to ask, "Why must you ask, Mr. Monroe? What exactly does my wife and the location of our bedroom have to do with your investigation of some computer hackers at the bank? And frankly, I'm finding this whole line of questioning of yours to be odd and irrelevant, to say the least. Please, leave my home. Now!" he shouted. "And I must warn you; you'd better be prepared, because I will make sure that your superiors learn of your incompetence!" he bellowed, pointing towards the front doors.

Ken nodded his head to Chill. *This was when they needed to begin.* Chill seemed content, as he had been longing for this very moment.

"You want us to leave your home, Mr. Diaz?" Ken asked, making sure that he sounded calm.

"Yes, immediately!"

54

"Well, we'll be out of here as soon as we're done with your arrogant ass!" Ken blurted, and then brandished his .38 Special revolver from its holster underneath his suit coat. "You asshole!" he continued, as he pointed it directly at Mr. Diaz's forehead.

Mr. Diaz appeared petrified and began mumbling and babbling incoherently.

Chill followed suit and pointed his 9 mm Beretta towards the center of Mr. Diaz's chest.

"What...? What the hell?" he stuttered. "What are you two imbeciles doing?" he managed to ask. "What the hell is the meaning of this? This is absurd!" he yelled, pointing an accusing finger at Ken.

"I know it is, Mr. Diaz." Ken grinned. It's completely absurd."

He noticed that Carlos Diaz couldn't fully grasp the enormity and gravity of his predicament. "But right now, you will shut the hell up, stand up, turn around, and place your hands behind your back. You will carefully follow these instructions, right now. Otherwise, I will kill you, right here!"

Mr. Diaz nearly lost control of his bowels and quickly complied with Ken's demands.

"What in the Sam hell is going on here? What kind of cops are you guys anyway?"

"We're not cops, stupid!" Ken announced, and harshly grabbed onto Mr. Diaz's hands. "So, like I told you, shut the hell up, before I put a hole in your head."

He removed a pair of handcuffs from his waistband and secured them tightly onto Mr. Diaz's wrist.

"Hey, asshole," Chill whispered into his ear, "Have you ever tried to think with a big ass hole in your head? It's hard buddy. Believe me, it's hard."

"Of course it is, Mr. Diaz," Ken chuckled. "It does sound pretty hard to me. So, my advice to you is to chill out."

Mr. Diaz's face twisted into an expression of rage as he screamed, "You won't get away with this bull-"

Ken immediately cut his tirade short by pistol-whipping him across the back of his head. He watched as Mr. Diaz crumpled to the floor and began to snore.

"Holy shit, dude! I think you knocked him the fuck out!" Chill chuckled, appearing excited by the unexpected violence.

"I put his ass straight to sleep, didn't I? Listen to him snore, man. I told him to shut the fuck up, didn't I?"

"Yep," Chill answered quickly.

"He's lucky that I can't kill his ass right now!"

Mr. Diaz moaned in agony as he slowly began to move around on the floor. Ken noticed that he appeared to resemble a turtle that was stuck on its back.

"We've got to get this asshole awake so that we can finish this mission and get the hell out of here."

Chill nodded his head and immediately located the kitchen. He then began to rifle through the expensive, ornate cabinets and cupboards until he found a large glass pitcher.

He walked to the sink and filled it with cold water, and then rushed back to Ken, who was standing over Mr. Diaz. He noticed that Mr. Diaz was still sprawled out on the floor.

"Here, sir." He handed him the pitcher.

"Thank you, Detective."

"You're welcome," Chill giggled.

"Wake up, mother-fucker!" Ken exclaimed, and then he upended the pitcher and splashed the water into Mr. Diaz's face.

He jolted upright, panting and wheezing, and then he peered about like a wounded animal.

"Get your ass up! Right now, motherfucker!" Ken demanded.

"You heard the man!" Chill whispered.

"Yes, whatever you say, sir!" Mr. Diaz begged. "I'll do whatever you want. But please don't kill me!" he said, while he clasped his hands together as if he was about to die at that very moment. He quickly began to sob.

"Like we said already, do as you're told. If you scream, try to use your phone, signal for help, and attempt to escape, or, try anything else stupid with any of us... I will shoot your ass until I am completely out of bullets. Do you understand, Mr. Diaz?" Ken asked.

"Yes, I do. I understand." He shook uncontrollably.

"Now, sir," Ken resumed, "let's go on upstairs and get your wife in on this little party. After that, I need for you to take us to your vault in your master bedroom."

"What vault?" Mr. Diaz asked in an obviously deceptive tone.

Ken raised his pistol high over his head and made it look as if he was going to bring it crashing down on top of Mr. Diaz's face.

"Oh God, no! Please!" He howled and fearfully threw up his hands in surrender. "Okay, okay. I'll take you to the vault. I'm sorry! Please don't hurt me or my wife!"

"How many times do I have to repeat myself? You and Mrs. Diaz will be fine, as long as you two do what the hell you're told, and don't try anything stupid. Because if you continue to play stupid, Mr. Diaz," Ken mentioned, as he used his pistol to simulate shooting the man multiple times, "it'll all be over for you. One more false move from you and you're dead." He drew his hand across his neck, adding emphasis.

Mr. Diaz clutched the back of his head and winced, as Ken jammed the muzzle of his pistol against his ribcage and grabbed his right arm.

"Now, Mr. Diaz, let's go!" he demanded, as he began to lead him up the marble staircase.

Ken's crazy, Chill mused, as he began to follow closely behind them.

Moments later, inside of the Diaz's master-bedroom, a frightened Mrs. Diaz was forced to sit on the foot of the bed with her hands cuffed behind her back.

Her eyes were completely bloodshot from her unrelenting tears, as she was forced to wear some blacked-out snow goggles to cover her eyes.

Clad in only her pajamas and some black leather slippers, she shook and sobbed uncontrollably.

"That's way more than a hundred grand," Chill whispered to himself, while he stood a few feet away from Mrs. Diaz, and was staring at a plastic garbage bag on the bed. The bag contained well over a half of a million dollars in cash. He seemed to be placing all of his attention on the amount of the currency within it. "What the hell are these idiots doing?" he muttered, obviously troubled by the unexpected and unannounced turn of events.

He simply couldn't believe what he was witnessing. He shook his head, as he looked at Mike, whom was placing what appeared to be an explosives vest over Mr. Diaz's shoulders.

"*These crazy-ass fool's are turning this man into a suicide bomber!*" he thought, while C-Dub and Ken stood near the vanity mirror supervising the procedure.

"Man, I could end up getting the death penalty for this shit!" he whispered.

He finally whisper-whistled to C-Dub and captured his attention. "Come here, man," he muttered.

"What's up, man?" C-Dub replied, as he approached him.

Chill briefly inclined his head towards Mike and Ken standing near Mr. Diaz.

"What's up with all this crazy-ass shit, that y'all have got going on up in this joint, man?"

C-Dub instantly became upset. "Don't worry about it, man! Just chill out, dawg'! Just be cool and keep an eye on this bitch!"

Chill scowled. "You're telling me to chill out, while your boy what's his name over there... he damn near bashed the man's brains in downstairs!" He nodded towards Mike, who was busy attaching the explosive device over Mr. Diaz's chest. "And what's that vest thing that he's putting on the man's body? What's up with that old weird-ass shit, man?" he whispered, as Mike began to help Mr. Diaz to slip a black wool sweater over his shoulders, apparently, to conceal the bomb vest.

He observed the look of terror etched across Mr. Diaz's face, while he helplessly stood there in his sweater, some black wool slacks and black socks.

"That's all a part of the plan." C-Dub grinned.

"What plan, man?"

"Plan-B., fool!" C-Dub snapped.

"What in the hell is, 'Plan-B.'?" He sighed. "Man, you mother-fuckers are putting too much drama in the game with this here bullshit!"

C-Dub became completely disturbed at Chill's insubordination. He clenched his teeth and gently bit his bottom lip. "Damn!" he whispered, shaking his head in frustration. He managed to finally calm himself down with a soft smile.

"Plan-B., that's bigger figures, man," he whispered, "which is a hell-of-a-lot more cash than this chump change right here." He pointed to the bag of money on the bed. "That ain't shit. Not compared to the $1.2 million in cash that this Carlos Diaz fool has got stashed away inside of his safety-deposit box." C-Dub lied.

He glanced at Mr. Diaz as he slipped his feet into some black-leather shoes. "And with or without you, youngster... we're going to get it, you dig?" he mentioned, staring deeply into Chill's eyes.

Chill was infuriated at not only the fatal turn that the so-called, "simple robbery" had taken, but also at the fact that he was kept completely out of their other plan, on purpose it seemed.

His trust for C-Dub was pretty much gone, and if he decided to continue on, it would only be to help provide for his wife and children.

He glared at the black leather duffle bag sitting on the shag carpet, which contained roughly over a million dollars worth of diamond-studded jewelry.

He finally locked eyes with C-Dub and continued to whisper. "Yeah nigga', and apparently you forgot to mention the other night that it was going be all of this drama, because I damn sure wouldn't have signed up for this shit!" He pointed to the bag of money on the bed near the wailing Mrs. Diaz. "Now, we've got the money that we came for right there. Which is way more money than the figure that you described to me." He then pointed to the duffle bag on the carpet. "Not to mention the fact that we've got all of this goddamn jewelry right here, too! Man! Come on, dawg'! Let's leave these people alone and get the hell up out of here. We've already gone too far with this shit! This robbery is straight up bullshit, playa'! I'm telling you, homeboy!"

Chill noticed that C-Dub's harsh demeanor had softened.

"Come on Chill. Lighten up, man," he said smiling, and placed his arm around Chill's shoulders.

The two of them watched as Mike lifted up Mr. Diaz's sweater. He seemed to be inspecting some electrical wires, which were attached to what looked like some explosive plastics in the pockets of a green hunter's vest.

"We're already committed on this job, man," C-Dub continued. "So, kick back and enjoy the ride, Chill! By the end of the day, your pockets will be straight, man. I promise you that. You'll be papered up out the game, son! Trust me, boy!"

Chill had no more trust for C-Dub. Matter-of-fact, he trusted him about as far as he could throw him, which wasn't very far at all. He realized that he had come much too far in their madness to turn back at this point. He had to remain willing and able to ride this out, otherwise, he'd have absolutely no compensation for his efforts.

"Man!" he sighed and He shook his head. "Damn, I have never been a part of no bullshit like this before! This shit is way out, Dub!"

C-Dub smiled and whispered, "I know it is Daddy-O. I know. Just finish rolling with me on this, man. I promise you that things are going to be all right."

Chill sighed deeply, and contemplated his answer. He finally nodded. "Yeah, nigga'! Whatever, man," he sighed.

C-Dub seemed to force a bright and friendly smile, and said, "Cool Daddy-O. Now, that's what I'm talking about!"

He removed his arm from Chill's shoulders.

Mike noticed as C-Dub smirked and rolled his eyes, as he and Chill watched him lower Mr. Diaz's sweater back over the bomb.

He took a few steps backward and then stared intently at the sweater. "Okay, Mr. Diaz. I need for you to turn around very slowly, okay?" he asked politely.

"You mean, like this?" he replied, appearing petrified, as he held his arms out and rotated slowly in place.

"Yes, sir, like that," Mike agreed. "But not so fast, though," he chuckled. "Hell, we wouldn't want to inadvertently trigger the bomb and blow us all to smithereens, you know what I mean?" He grinned at Ken and C-Dub, who found his comment humorous.

Mrs. Diaz began to weep as C-Dub moved in closer to Mike and examined the sweater.

"Is he ready yet?" C-Dub asked.

"Yes, Captain," Mike replied. "Everything looks good to me. The bomb appears to be well hidden, sir."

"Indeed, it does." C-Dub smiled. "I can't see it at all underneath that thick sweater of his."

"That's some very good work you've done, dude," Ken mentioned.

"It's perfect. It's excellent work, man," C-Dub continued. "Now, let's hurry up and get him inside of the Bentley, and then we need to hurry up and get the hell up out of here."

A short while later, Chill was driving the Diaz's Bentley Azure. He was heading southbound on Cohen Place in Beverly Hills. He made certain to conceal his fingerprints by wearing some black leather gloves.

C-Dub was smiling, as he was nestled in between Mr. & Mrs. Diaz in the rear seat, who were both handcuffed and blinded by the blacked-out goggles, which covered their eyes.

"All right, Mr. Diaz," C-Dub began, as he removed the blinders from his eyes.

He watched him squint painfully for a brief moment, as the sudden influx of the bright daylight temporarily blinded him.

Before he fully adjusted, C-Dub shoved a small box-like electronic device in his face. "This remote control device is my little friend, sir," he told him, as Chill drove the vehicle over Santa Monica Boulevard. "Why, you might ask? Well Mr. Diaz, with this little beauty right here... I can blow your rich-ass up at anytime that I choose. I can do this from as far as a mile away even. So, if I were you, I wouldn't try anything stupid, you hear?"

Mr. Diaz nodded vigorously. "Yes sir. I hear you!"

"Good." C-Dub smiled. Now, Mr. Diaz, while you're inside of the bank retrieving the cash out of your safety-deposit box like we discussed, and I do mean all of it! We'll be situated close by in a different vehicle with this little transmitter. So, remember what I said. You've got exactly twenty-two minutes to load that money into a duffle bag that I'm going to supply you with. At which point, you'll exit the bank and walk south toward Trolley Lane. Otherwise, my associate, whom you haven't any knowledge of, will press this button right here. Well," he grinned, and then shouted, "BOOM!"

Mr. Diaz and his wife were quickly startled and screamed.

C-Dub laughed uproariously. "Okay now, sir. Need I explain to you what would happen next?"

"No sir, you don't have to. I completely understand,"

"That's very good, sir. I'm glad otherwise, your death, and the innocent bystanders in the bank with you... well, that would completely be your fault! And oh, I almost forgot about your lovely wife here, Joanna. Well, let's just say this, one false move on your part, and her body will be found somewhere near the bank. Now," he smiled. "This pretty little head of hers," he brushed his hand across her hair, "it'll be found decapitated somewhere else. So, her well-being depends on your actions from this point on. Is that understood, sir?" he said, as he observed the anger being displayed upon Chill's face in the rear-view mirror, behind his sunglasses.

"Yes, sir!" Mr. Diaz cried out.

"Jesus, Carlos! Please honey, just do what they say! I beg of you!" Mrs. Diaz pleaded.

"Don't you worry, honey. I won't let these awful people hurt you! I swear to you. I'll do exactly as they say, mi amor."

"That's very good, Mr. Diaz. You're not as dumb as you look," C-Dub continued. "Okay, my friend, you'll have exactly twenty-two minutes from the time that we drop you off at the bank. That's it. No more time. Do you understand?"

"Yes sir, I understand," he blurted, as rivulets of perspiration dripped from his head and onto his sweater. He closed his eyes and began to pray.

C-Dub looked into the rear-view mirror and smiled at Chill, who was fuming in the driver's seat, shaking his head.

"That's excellent, Mr. Diaz," C-Dub resumed, nodding. "Excellent. You do as you're instructed and nobody, yourself included, gets hurt. It couldn't get any simpler than that," he added, as Chill drove the vehicle into the supermarket parking lot of the original meeting place.

C-Dub re-blindfolded Mr. Diaz with the blackout goggles, while Chill pulled the car adjacent to his Honda Accord.

Armand discretely parked the cargo van in the stall on the opposite side of Chill's car, away from the Bentley Azure.

"Okay, Detective Randle," C-Dub said to Chill, "Stay in the car and keep an eye on this bitch. Meanwhile, I'm going to take this Carlos Diaz motherfucker to the van."

Chill seemed to ignore him.

C-Dub scoffed, and continued to Mr. Diaz, "Okay, man. Let's go."

He discreetly escorted him to the cargo van's sliding side door and placed him in the rear seat.

Armand, Ken and Mike, stepped quietly out of the van and stood near the rear end.

Shortly thereafter, C-Dub was ranting as he approached them. "Damn, Mike!" he muttered. "I'm going to kill this son-of-a-bitch, man!"

He glanced around the parking lot and observed that it was gradually filling with vehicles and shoppers.

Armand inquired, "Who are you talking about whacking, Charlie?"

C-Dub tilted his head toward the Bentley. "This fool, Chill!"

"Why, Charlie?" Armand probed. "What the hell did he do?"

"He did some punk-ass shit, man! Damn bastard! He done messed around and pissed me off now!"

"Yeah, Charlie," Mike cut in. "I was wondering what in the hell was going on between the two of you back in that bedroom. It sure looked like trouble to me."

"You're telling me! This coward-ass nigga' started tripping out on me right in the middle of the goddamn mission! I thought his scary ass was about to walk out the house on us!"

"For real, that's what it looked like to me," Mike resumed. "You two were really going at it for a minute there. Hell, I thought you guys were about to come to blows or something!" he chuckled.

"Damn, Charlie! What the hell happened back there?" Armand asked anxiously, as Chill stepped out of the Bentley and joined in on the meeting, leaving Mrs. Diaz in the rear seat of the vehicle.

"What's up, y'all?" he mumbled, visibly upset.

"Not a goddamn thing, Chill!" C-Dub answered sarcastically. "We were just talking about you."

"Talking about me?" Chill asked, as he felt some ice develop in his stomach. He locked eyes with C-Dub. "What about me, man?"

C-Dub grinned devilishly. "Nothing man. Don't trip. Anyway, I want you to meet up with us at my carwash around 11 o'clock this morning. We should be done with this mission by then." He paused a moment. "On the other hand, you can roll with us to the bank if you want to. It really makes me no difference at all. So, Chill, what's it going to be?"

Chill shook his head. "Man, I'm cool on that kidnapping bullshit! Because you didn't tell me that it was going be all-"

"Yeah, yeah, man! Whatever!" C-Dub blurted, cutting him off. "So, what's up? Are you going to meet us at the carwash? If so, I need you to be there around 11 o'clock." he continued in a no-nonsense tone of voice.

"Yeah, man. I'll meet y'all at the carwash. Because this kidnapping shit is way too deep for me! I didn't sign up for this part of the game!"

Ken and Mike glanced at one another. They seemed to have had the same thought about C-Dub, A *liar.*

C-Dub nodded. *I thought you'd say that. You old coward-ass nigga'!* "Yeah, youngster, I understand. It's all good, though. I'll talk to you later on, then. I'll see you at the carwash at 11 o'clock. And oh yeah, Chill; make sure that you come by yourself, All right, boy?"

Chill felt another wave of dread in his gut, but concealed it from C-Dub and his friends. "Yeah, Dub, whatever, man. I'm out this joint!"

He discreetly handed C-Dub his handgun, handcuffs, and the fake detective badge. "Peace, y'all," he mentioned, and entered his Honda.

Under everyone's hostile gaze, he pulled out of the stall and drove quickly out of the parking lot.

C-Dub flipped him off with his middle finger, as he continued to his friends, "I'm telling y'all. That's a coward-ass mother-fucker! I'm going to smoke that fool! I hope that he bring his scary-ass to my carwash. He's history! Through! Dead! He just doesn't know it yet!" he resumed, as he watched Chill's car until it disappeared from view.

Armand grilled him for some more information. "Man, Charlie, whatever Chill did in that house, it must've been bad. Jesus!"

"It doesn't matter, Armand. Because he's dying today! Fuck his wife! Fuck his rug rats! Fuck everything, man!" He took several deep breaths and then continued, "Anyway-"

"Say, Charlie," Mike interrupted. "I've known you for a long time now. But I got to know, man."

"Know what, Mike?" C-Dub snapped.

He analyzed C-Dub's eyes for a long moment, before saying, "Did you tell Chill about everything that what was included in this mission today? Because it sounds to me like he was under the impression that this job was just a simple robbery. Did he know that there was going to be a kidnapping involved? If he didn't, well, I understand." He gazed levelly at C-Dub. "But it sure does change things."

C-Dub studied his friend for a moment. "Changes things like what, Mike?"

"I don't know. I'm not sure."

C-Dub waved him off dismissively. "Anyway Mike, I told that scary-ass fool everything that we were going to do this morning. He knew the whole get-down! That punk knew the business!"

Mike maintained his gaze and nodded, as he pondered deeply about what C-Dub had mentioned. "Are you sure, Charlie?" he asked in a grave tone. He knew that if C-Dub would lie to Chill, he would lie to him as well.

C-Dub avoided Mike's gaze and blurted, "Yeah, yeah, man! I'm sure! And I'm sick of talking about that punk motherfucker!"

Mike shrugged his shoulders and looked away.

"Anyway, man," C-Dub continued to Armand. "I want you and Mike to take the wife and the Bentley to the carwash. Make sure that you lock her whining ass up inside of my storage room. Watch her ass real close, too, until Ken and I get there with the loot from the bank. You got it?" he glanced at his wristwatch.

"No problem. I've got it, boss," Armand assured him.

"Understood, Charlie," Mike said, looking over his right shoulder toward the rear end of the Bentley.

"All right, guys." C-Dub glanced at his wristwatch again. "Look, it's a quarter to 9, and the bank's about to open. So we better get a move on. You guys be careful and drive at the posted speed limits. Make sure that you come to a complete stop at all stop signs and traffic signals." He pointed at the Bentley, "Especially with all that cash and jewelry in the trunk."

"We got you, Charlie." Armand replied.

The meeting ended and everyone shook hands before heading to their respective mission vehicles.

Chapter 6

The time was 9:08 a.m., and the posh, Polanski Drive's World-Wide Bank & Financing Corporation in Beverly Hills, wasn't busy due to the chilling weather. The dozen or so customers present were dressed in their winter attire and seemed pleasant enough, as they were being attended by equally pleasant tellers. The peaceful ambiance was suddenly shattered when Carlos Diaz barged into the bank, sweaty, anxious, and overall, uneasy.

Diaz tried unsuccessfully to regain his composure. The ongoing trauma of having what he believed to be an explosive vest strapped to his chest blotted out any other considerations from his mind.

He carefully wiped the perspiration from his forehead with the left sleeve of his sweater, while he held a folded duffle bag underneath his right underarm.

"You can do this," he whispered to himself, and approached the desk of the manager, Mrs. Clark, a 55-year-old Caucasian, who was staring at her computer monitor.

A snobby patron scoffed and turned up her nose at Mr. Diaz, as she quickly got out of his way.

"Good morning, Mr. Diaz," Mrs. Clark greeted, as she looked over the rim of her gold-plated reading glasses. A fraction of a second later, Mr. Diaz's appearance had fully registered in her mind.

She inhaled sharply and exclaimed, "Oh, my God! Is something upsetting you, sir?"

She took in his demeanor and his apparent mood of excessive anxiety, as he stood quietly near her desk, sobbing.

"Mrs. Clark, I've been forced to wear an explosive vest and come down here to retrieve a large amount of money. Otherwise, these terrible men will blow me up and kill my wife, who has been kidnapped! Please help me!"

"Dear God in heaven, Mr. Diaz!" she yelled. "I hope that she's all right!"

"So far, I think she is. But I have a more pressing problem to deal with. You see, I'm scared to death of this," he said, exhaling heavily and placing a shaking palm against his chest. "They have a remote control detonator. My God, it could explode at any moment and kill us all!"

The woman uttered an unintelligible string of obscenities and leapt up out of her chair. She staggered back from her desk appearing to be scared out of her wits.

"Yes, Mrs. Clark. Now you know how I've felt for the past hour and a half!"

"What should I do?" she screamed, attracting the undivided attention of everyone in the bank.

"Call the authorities, please!" he advised, as he eased himself into the chair behind him, while everybody looked on with their mouths wide open, obviously in shock.

Moments later, C-Dub was gripping the wood-grain steering wheel in his Benz, while Ken sat beside him in the passenger seat.

The two of them were staking out the front entrance to the World-Wide Bank & Finance Corporation, which was a half-block up the street from where they were parked against the curb.

C-Dub looked in the rear-view mirror at his neatly kept teeth, and said, "Yeah, man. I started to shoot that sucker right there on the spot, Chill had me hot as fish grease!" "I can understand, Charlie. But tell me, how long have you actually known this character? I ask you this, because I've never met him. I mean, you never brought him home into the fold."

"Like I mentioned earlier, I've known Chill's punk-ass for quite a few years now. We met when we were in Placerville Prison. We've done a couple of small-time licks together, but nothing to this magnitude. I'm glad that I didn't bring him home to meet you

67

guys. Just look at how he got down today! That punk-ass fool! But forget about his sorry-ass, because his time has come." He looked at his wristwatch. "Man, Ken, Carlos Diaz has been in the bank for twelve minutes now."

"No shit," he sighed, as he and C-Dub continued to stare through the front windshield of the vehicle at the bank's main entrance. Their adrenalin was racing while they eagerly awaited any sign of Carlos Diaz and the handsome ransom money.

The scene became eerily quiet, as C-Dub released a deep sigh. "So far, so good," he uttered. Ken chuckled to himself. "What's up Ken? What's so funny, man?"

"I was just thinking about something." He laughed.

"Thinking about what, man? Enlighten me. What's up?"

"I was thinking about that bogus bomb vest that Carlos Diaz is wearing. I hope that he doesn't figure out that it's nothing more than some harmless clay, that's wrapped in cellophane."

C-Dub chuckled, "Yeah, those dead-end wires that we've got stuffed inside of it was genius! He's a stupid motherfucker, anyway. He'll never figure it out."

They both laughed as Ken resumed, "But honestly, Charlie, I believe that Carlos is way too ignorant and distracted to figure it out, like you said. Besides, he knows that we've still got his wife hostage. And we know that Mike did a really good job on that vest to fool even me. Also, if I were Carlos Diaz, I wouldn't be taking any chances."

C-Dub smiled and continued to watch the entrance to the bank. "Why thank you, sir," he mentioned snobbishly. "I'll take that as a compliment. Because I designed that vest myself. But, I'll agree with you, though. Because if some crazy-ass dudes were to strap something like that onto me, man," he shook his head. "I'd probably shit on my goddamn self!"

Ken laughed. "Shit, Charlie. No pun intended. But you and I both, pal."

"Man, Ken," C-Dub chortled, "You ain't right, man, you nasty fucker!" He howled between spasms of laughter.

The chit-chat in the car was suddenly cut short by the ominous wailing of a complete line of emergency vehicles.

The police department's bomb squad and other emergency and medical vehicles whooshed past them at rapid speeds and converged onto the bank's premises.

"What the hell!" C-Dub blurted in confusion, as he witnessed an armored S.W.A.T. carrier shoot past them. "Oh, goddamn, Ken! This punk done snitched on us! We've got some problems now, man!"

"Fuck!" Ken shouted, as they watched the vehicles empty out and established a line of scrimmage near the street. The S.W.A.T. teams confidently took up their covered firing positions. "It's all bad, Charlie!" he shouted, and pounded his balled fist against the dashboard. "I can't believe that stupid-ass, inconsiderate mother-fucker! Just like that, to hell with his wife! He don't give a shit about her life!"

"I know," C-Dub sighed.

"Damn, man," Ken exhaled. "We had to do this hostage shit with an asshole whose only love is his money!" he growled, as they continued to watch the activity proceed down the street.

Their faces were struck with disbelief, as they observed a large group of cops with K-9 police dogs rushing into the bank.

"That little shit!" C-Dub yelled, and banged his palm against the steering wheel. "Come on Ken; let's get the hell up out of here!" He started the engine.

"Yeah, man, but let's drive super normal, you know? We sure as hell don't need to get pulled over right now."

"Don't trip, Ken. I've got this here," he mentioned, and pulled away from the curb.

He made a slow but legal u-turn and eased away from the area at the posted speed limit.

In the Northridge, California parking lot of C-Dub's auto detailing shop, Armand and Mike were leaning up against Mr. Diaz's Bentley. The two of them were smoking on non-filter cigarettes and looking out at the vehicle traffic on the boulevard. Armand exhaled some smoke and admitted, "Man, Mike, I'll sure be happy when this shit is over and done with."

"I heard that!" He yawned and rubbed his tired eyes. "What time you got, Armand?"

Armand yawned, as he glanced at his wristwatch. "It's ten-forty."

He flicked his cigarette out into the empty parking lot. "We should be getting close to acquiring a shit-load of cash, my friend."

"I hope so," Mike replied, giving him some dap.

Meanwhile, nearby, inside of the secured storage room, Joanna Diaz was shivering nervously. Her eyes were blinded by the goggles, and she was completely unsure of what her assailants would do to her, as she sat handcuffed to a lounge chair that Mike had provided for her. A dingy, gray wool blanket was draped around her narrow, frigid shoulders.

In spite of the circumstances, she didn't seem as stressed-out as she was previously.

Apparently, her kidnappers had been so kind as to place a boom-box radio in the room with her.

"This is for your listening pleasure, Mrs. Diaz," Mike told her, giving her at least one thing to do.

Luther Vandross's mega-hit song, *"Here and Now"*, played at a soothing volume and seemed to put her a bit at ease.

Soon afterwards, the stern voice of Rex Gordon, a 48-year-old Caucasian news station anchorman, interrupted the radio communication to broadcast the morning news.

"… A high-speed chase which started in the City of Bell, California, ended in the deaths of three suspects. According to the local authorities, three male Hispanics, all minors, entered a convenience store on Burris and Central, demanding cash at gun point from the Hispanic male clerk."

"Sheriff's deputies arrived on the scene as the suspects were making their getaway in a stolen 2003 Range Rover. The deputies pursued the erratic, reckless vehicle for more that twenty-two minutes. Their speeds reached up to 95 miles per hour, in 25 mile per hour residential areas."

"The suspects finally lost control of the S.U.V. when they hit a speed bump traveling at 80 miles per hour, causing the white Range Rover to fishtail and roll-over several times. It exploded against a Ford cargo van near Cypress Park, on Meade Avenue."

"The total amount of cash that was taken from the store was less than $100 dollars. The incident is still undergoing investigation, according to the police."

"And now," he continued, "we'll proceed with some local news in Beverly Hills. Earlier this morning, a badly shaken, Mr. Carlos Diaz, a prominent Investment Banker, walked into a local branch of the World-Wide Bank & Financing Corporation where he informed the female manager that he was being robbed, and that the robbers had forced him to wear an explosive vest underneath his clothing. He stated that the bandits had threatened to blow him up, and

70

murder his kidnapped wife, Mrs. Joanna Diaz, if he failed to retrieve an undisclosed amount of cash from his safety deposit box."

"Mr. Diaz was led to believe that the vest he wore was loaded with Military-grade C-4, a highly combustible plastic explosive."

Mrs. Diaz gasped and sat up in the chair. "Jesus," she whispered, as she listened closely to the anchorman.

Rex Gordon cleared his throat and continued, "The local police department's bomb squad extensively and thoroughly examined the vest, where they determined that it was actually filled with harmless clay."

Mrs. Diaz shook her head and began sobbing.

"The victim himself, Mr. Carlos Diaz, was relieved at the news to say the least. Police refused to further comment on what was called an active and ongoing investigation. That's the news, and I'm Rex Gordon, reporting for, K-SARK, 108.9 F.M., your easy-listening station."

Smooth Jazz began to play, while Mrs. Diaz shook her head in frustration. "Oh my God, Carlos! What have you done? You're an idiot!" she wailed, and slumped back into the chair.

Outside in the parking lot, Armand chuckled suddenly and said, "I'm telling you, man. I really felt helpless for the first time in my life. I mean, the way that African bastard had me lying on the floor, bound and gagged like that. I felt like I was participating in some kind of a West Hollywood surprise party. I couldn't do a damn thing about it, but lie there on the carpet, and hope like hell that he didn't rape me!"

Mike chuckled, "I can imagine."

Suddenly, their attention shifted to C-Dub's Mercedes-Benz, which flew onto the lot at a high rate of speed.

"What the fuck?" Armand blurted, as C-Dub slammed on the brakes and brought the car to a screeching halt. Both doors flew open simultaneously, and C-Dub and Ken stormed out of the car and walked briskly towards them.

"Check this shit out, y'all!" C-Dub yelled, and then pointed at the Bentley. "We've got to hurry up and get the goods up out of that trunk! Then, we've got to get rid of that damn car! After that, we've got to kill that bitch!"

"Why, Charlie?" Armand asked.

"Because, that stupid-ass husband of hers done called the cops on us!"

"What a selfish son-of-a-bitch!" Armand shouted through clenched teeth.

"You can say that again," C-Dub muttered.

He opened the Bentley's trunk and removed the bags of cash and jewelry and sat them on the black-top behind the vehicle.

"That rat-ass bastard! He obviously doesn't give a damn about his wife, Joanna," Armand mentioned.

"I guess not," C-Dub said, shrugging his shoulders. "That's why she's dying, too."

"What do you mean, too?" Armand asked. "Damn, Charlie, you were serious about killing that kid, Chill. Weren't you?"

"Yeah man, as serious as a motherfucking heart attack!" he declared, and then glanced at his wristwatch. "Speaking of which, it shouldn't be much longer now. It's almost 11 o'clock."

He looked at Ken. "But first, man," he pointed to the Bentley, "You've got to ditch this car somewhere. This thing sticks out like a sore thumb. I'm sure it's got one of those vehicle-locating devices hidden up in it somewhere."

"That's a damn good idea, Charlie. I'm on it. I'll be back," Ken replied, as he approached the driver's side of the Bentley.

"Ken?" C-Dub called out.

"What's up, Boss?" he asked, as he grabbed a hold of the door handle.

"Make sure that you wipe the car down real good. You know, just in case we left any of our fingerprints on it, you dig?"

"I dig, Boss." He opened the car door.

All of a sudden, the men were surprised by a heavily-armed contingent of law-enforcement personnel that swarmed onto the lot. An all Caucasian male team began aiming their pistols, shotguns, and assault rifles at the dumbfounded and slack-jawed criminals.

Police Sergeant Cole, the 54-year-old officer in charge, assumed control and began shouting orders toward C-Dub and his men.

They were advised to immediately get down on their knees, cross one leg over the other, interlace their fingers above their heads, and hold still.

At the same moment, Chill was singing along with, Notorious B.I.G.'s hit song, *"Juicy,"* which was blasting from his car's stereo system. He was definitely in a pleasant state of mind and looking forward to his riches, as he drove south-bound on Reseda Boulevard.

He activated his left-turn signal indicator as he approached the driveway entrance to C-Dub's auto-detailing shop on the opposite side of the street.

"Oh, shit!" he blurted in a state of panic, after he instantly caught full view of the heavy police presence on the premises. "Fuck!" he whispered, as he spotted C-Dub and his crew members kneeling down on the pavement and facing the street with their hands behind their heads.

"Goddamn, Dub," Chill continued, shaking his head.

He quickly flicked off his turn-signal, and tried hard not draw any unwanted attention to himself. His mind was spinning rapidly, while he covertly stared at C-Dub who was being roughly hand-cuffed by Sergeant Cole. C-Dub happened to take notice of Chill's car on the street, and the fact that he seemed to be observing the entire event, while Sergeant Cole was reading him his Miranda Rights.

As C-Dub continued to grin mischievously, he peered intensely into Chill's eyes, and muttered, "Yeah, Willie-boy, you got lucky, punk." He nodded. "You got real lucky, man!" he said, as Chill secretly proceeded to drive away from the scene.

Moments later, C-Dub and his accomplices were ordered to sit on asphalt against the wall near the office of the detail shop.

Mrs. Diaz was still physically shaken as she stood near the Bentley.

She had a police blanket wrapped around her shoulders, while Sergeant Cole thoroughly interviewed her.

"That's correct, Sergeant," she stated firmly, "I am absolutely positive that I heard Armand's voice coming in through that open window right there."

She pointed to the open, barred window on the door to the storage room. Sergeant Cole concentrated on the window and then pointed at C-Dub. "Okay, Mrs. Diaz. You're sure that Mr. Hicks was the guy who was in charge of this little operation?"

"I have no doubt about that, Sergeant Cole!"

"Yes Ma'am. I understand. And Mr. Hicks was the man who ordered for you to be murdered, is that correct?"

"Yes sir. I heard him tell the man myself. He also mentioned something about killing the younger guy who was supposed to show up here at 11 o'clock. I heard Armand say that the man's name was, Chill."

73

She pointed to Mike on the ground. "And that fellow right there was the man who helped to place that fake bomb thing on my selfish, good-for-nothing husband, I witnessed it myself."

She paused, appearing clearly angered by her husband's careless actions. "I mean my ex-husband!" she blurted. "After all, with his actions regarding this mess, I'm divorcing his selfish ass! Hell, I'm the one who has the money anyway! He was broke when I met him. I taught him everything he knows, and I let him tag along because I felt sorry for him. But now that I look at this situation, and how he handled things, to hell with Carlos! That no-good, son-of-a-bitch! I can't wait to tell my sons about this shit!"

"Yeah," Sergeant Cole chuckled, "If you don't mind me asking, do you and Mr. Diaz have kids together? You mentioned, "My sons.""

"No sir. My first husband, Mitchell, we had three boys, who are now grown men. Mitchell passed away due to colon cancer.

"I'm sorry to hear that, ma'am."

"It's okay. I really miss him sometimes."

Sergeant Cole nodded. "Yes ma'am. But anyway, you're absolutely, positively, one-hundred-percent sure, that the name of the younger assailant, the fifth suspect, is Chill? As in, C-H-I-L-L?"

"Sergeant Cole, sir, I am certain! Beyond a shadow of a doubt!" she drew the sign of the Holy Cross onto her chest.

Sergeant Cole seemed lost in thought. "Chill, huh?"

He pulled out a small notepad and a pen from his shirt pocket underneath his bulletproof vest, and wrote Chill's name on a piece of paper.

"That's correct, Sergeant. I distinctly heard the name, Chill."

He placed his pen and notepad back inside of his pocket. "Chill," he mentioned, as he watched a flatbed tow-truck pull into the parking lot and positioned itself in front of the Bentley. "Well, Mrs. Diaz," he sighed and raised his eyebrows, while shaking his head, "you are a very fortunate woman, indeed! Because, had it not been for your vehicle locater..." his voice trailed off as he glanced at the handcuffed men sitting on the ground.

C-Dub grinned arrogantly and turned his head and spat on the ground.

Mrs. Diaz was unmoved by C-Dub's vulgar and futile gesture, as she closed her eyes and blew a kiss towards the heavens, and smiled at the officer.

74

"Oh, yes, Sergeant Cole. Believe me. I've already given thanks to the Man upstairs! I've been thanking Him for a lot of things, lately. Believe that!" she scowled.

"I know you have," he uttered, as his fellow officers loaded C-Dub and his gang into separate patrol vehicles, while the Bentley was gingerly loaded onto the flatbed tow-truck.

Damn, I hope this bullshit don't fall back on me." Chill thought nervously. He felt as if his heart was about to jump out of his chest. His mind was speeding at a thousand miles an hour, while he sat on the foot of his bed at 5:28 that evening.

His hands shook uncontrollably, as he picked up his cell phone and dialed a number, and then pressed the phone against his ear.

"Beverly Hills Police Department, Officer Moore speaking," answered the 34-year-old Caucasian female, who was the front desk officer. "How may I help you this evening?" she asked, seeming polite, yet forcefully professional.

"Good evening, ma'am," Chill responded nervously.

"Good evening to you, sir. What can I do for you?"

Jen entered the room and sat quietly on the bed beside him.

"Yes, ma'am," he uttered, and uneasily cleared his throat, "Could you please tell me if you have a Charles Hicks in custody there?"

"Charles Hicks, sir?"

"Yes ma'am, that's Hicks. It's spelled, H-I-C-K-S."

"Hold on a moment, please. I'll have to check our computer."

"Sure ma'am. No problem."

His ear was suddenly filled with some pleasant jazz music while he was placed on hold.

Jen was smirking at the television on the dresser. "Is he in there, babe?"

"I don't know yet. The lady's checking for me right now. She's got me on hold," he explained, as the officer returned to the phone.

"Hello, sir?"

"Yes ma'am. I'm here," he mentioned anxiously, and unable to keep his emotions out of his voice.

He glanced at his wife, who immediately acknowledged his nervousness.

"Okay sir, according to our computer records, currently, we do have a Charles Hicks in custody here at our station."

"Damn," he whispered inadvertently. "I apologize for my language, ma'am."

Knowing her husband the way she did, Jen shook her head in frustration.

"That's quite all right, sir. It's understandable. I get that all the time."

"Ma'am," he sighed deeply, "could you please tell me what he's being charged with and, what is his bail amount?"

He stared blankly at the television, not really seeing the sports segment on the news.

"No problem, sir. Well, first off, all of Mr. Hicks's charges are Class-A felonies. His charges consist of one count of conspiracy to commit murder. Along with two counts of 209 (A) - kidnapping for the purpose of ransom," she informed Willie who now appeared despondent. "Mr. Hicks is also being charged with two counts of robbery in the first degree. Now sir, his bail amount is presently set at four million, one hundred and fifty thousand dollars."

Chill's eyebrows flew up in surprise, as he repeated, "Four million, one hundred and fifty thousand dollars!" as if he could not believe what he was hearing.

Jen sighed and shook her head, as she continued to quietly stare at the T.V.

Officer Moore resumed, "Yes sir. That's what our computers are indicating." She paused a moment. "Now sir, may I have your name?"

Chill was highly agitated by the news. He quickly closed his cell phone and dropped it on the bed. "Man," he sighed deeply and stared at the television in silence.

"Four million, one hundred and fifty thousand dollars," He seemed to be having trouble comprehending what he had heard. "Damn! That'll hold him!" He sighed and pondered the possibilities of himself being caught-up in C-Dub's predicament.

Could it happen? Would it happen? He mused. He wasn't certain. All that he knew was that C-Dub could not be trusted.

Jen finally broke the silence. "Willie, we're lucky that you're not sitting in jail with him right now facing a life sentence!" she said sternly, avoiding his eye contact. "I told you that he was bad news, didn't I? He's not as solid as you think he is, babe. I already told you that. But a hard head makes a soft ass, as my mom used to say."

Chill offered no reply because he didn't hear her speak. His mind was spinning much too fast to pay her words any attention.

Chapter 7

Six months later, Chill was lying on the living-room couch in his red-silk pajama pants and a white cotton tank-top. He was laughing at a particularly funny scene on an afternoon talk show. The highly respected African-American female host was interviewing a legendary comedian.

"Let's see what's on the cable channel," he said to no one in particular, and grabbed the remote control from the mirrored coffee table and pointed it at the television, which lay within the matching entertainment center against the wall. "This looks like a pretty good movie." He sat the remote back on the coffee table and began watching a 1980's blockbuster. "Excellent flick," he said.

Jen entered the room and her sweet perfume filled the air. She handed him the cordless phone. "It's Jo-Jo," she informed him and headed back to their bedroom.

Chill sat up and placed the phone against his ear. He suddenly heard Jay-Z's multi-platinum song, "*99 Problems*" blaring through the line.

"Jo-Jo!" he shouted appearing excited to hear from him. "Turn that damn music down, boy! I can't hear you, dawg!"

Joseph "Jo-Jo" Milton was his 41-year-old, flamboyant, African-American brother-in-law.

As they spoke on the phone, Jo-Jo slowly pulled into the driveway of Chill's apartment complex with his blue-tooth wireless ear set attached to his right ear, and thought that he heard Chill say that he *couldn't hear him.* He lowered the volume on his car stereo.

"Can you hear me now, nigga?" he asked in his best impersonation of a world-famous commercial, while he carefully backed his customized 2005 light gray S-600 Mercedes-Benz into the empty parking stall next to Chill's Honda Accord.

"Yeah, Jo-Jo, I can now, where you at, boy?"

"I'm sitting right here in your parking lot next to this car of yours. So bring your triflin' ass on out here. I got to holler at you about something."

Jo-Jo saw a bunch of Hispanic and Cambodian kids tossing water balloons at each other in the driveway, fully enjoying themselves underneath the scorching sun.

"Yeah, man," Chill replied, and slipped his bare feet into some black leather slippers. "Hold tight, fool. I'll be out there in a minute."

He cut the phone off and stretched and yawned. "Let me see what this fool wants?" He sat the phone on the coffee table and headed out of the front door.

"Give The People What They Want" by the Legendary "O-Jays," played softly in Jo-Jo's car, while he was in the middle of a business call with Rick, his credit client; a 42 year old, Hispanic male. "Yeah, pretty Ricky. That'll work, man. You said you've got twelve gees, right?" as he bobbed his head to the music.

"That's correct, Jo-Jo, as you requested of course. I've got twelve thousand dollars in cash in my office, along with all of the credit reports."

Jo-Jo observed Chill approaching his car wearing his slumber attire. He thought about what a pathetic wretch that Chill had become and shook his head in frustration.

He finally glanced at his platinum Rolex wristwatch, and asked, "Exactly how many reports are we talking about here?"

"It's nine credit reports in all. There are nineteen derogatory statements between all nine of them."

Jo-Jo nodded to Chill as he got into the front passenger seat and shut the door. "Nineteen derogative statements, huh?" he asked, giving Chill some dap, as Chill began to nod his head to the music as well.

"Yeah, Jo-Jo. So tell me, how soon can you come to my office?"

"Well, I'm over at my brother-in-law's crib right now handling some business. So give me a couple of hours and I'll swing by, all right?"

"Yeah, Jo-Jo, That'll work. I'll see you at around 5 o'clock then.

"All right, Ricky baby. Later, man."

"Later."

Jo-Jo closed his cell phone on the center console, "So Chill, what's your story?"

"Ain't nothing going on, Jo-Jo," he admitted, as an ice cream truck pulled into the driveway.

The truck was instantly swarmed with hooting and cheering kids, as well as their unenthused parents. "It's just hot as hell in this Valley today, man." Chill continued.

"You ain't lying about that."Jo-Jo pointed to Chill's pajama pants with his right thumb. "I see that you still got your broke ass in your damn pajamas."

"So?" Chill smirked.

"So?" Jo-Jo scowled as he checked his Rolex again. "Boy, its three-twenty in the afternoon, man!"

"And?" He said sarcastically and shrugged his shoulders. "Your point is? I'm lounging, nigga'. Why, what's up?"

"What's up is… you've been lounging way too long,. And from what I've been hearing through the grapevine lately, it damn sure ain't you, that's what's up. That's for sure boy, I might add."

Chill became upset and smacked his lips. "Yeah man, I see that old Jen's been running her goddamn mouth to Lena again, huh?"

"What you thought she wouldn't? Man, you know that sisters are going to gossip! Besides, you've been jobless for seven months now. Matter-of-fact, ever since that dumb-ass robbery that y'all did. It spooked the hell out of you, huh?" he chuckled. "That was a stupid-ass move altogether," he continued, shaking his head.

He could definitely see that his scolding was angering Chill whose tone and body language gave way to how he really felt. "Since you got to know, it's been six months since that move with C-Dub went down." He sighed. "Exactly who in the hell do you think you are anyway? My goddamn score keeper?" he asked, as he observed his wife step out onto the wrought-iron balcony.

She was wearing a black and gold sarong, and her hair was draped down her back.

She appeared to be smiling at the kids around the ice-cream truck, while she held the hands of Jolina and Jovont`e, their two-year-old fraternal twins.

Jo-Jo saw them too, and lowered his side window and then stuck his head and arm out. "What's up Jen?" He smiled and waved, as Chill tried to play along as if nothing was wrong.

He noticed the striking garment that she wore with her bare feet, and that the beautiful brother and sister twins were clad only in their form-fitted diapers.

"Hi, Jo-Jo!" Jen exclaimed, as she playfully forced the twins to wave their tiny hands to him.

"Say 'hi' to Uncle Jo-Jo!"

"Hi, Uncle Jo-Jo!" they said, barely audible, and smiled shyly as they tried their best to shout.

"Hi, Jolina and Jovonte!" Jo-Jo yelled back. He was happy to see how they were growing up.

It was way too hot outside, and the cool air-conditioning in the car was seeping out of the window. He raised it back up and turned to Chill.

"Now, where the hell was I at? Oh yeah, nigga', I ain't your damn score keeper. That job belongs to your wife right there." He pointed to Jen on the balcony. "She's your official scorekeeper, not me. I happened to be called in because I love you. I have the obligation to help your lazy ass, and to get your poverty-stricken ass up off of that goddamn couch." He looked Chill up and down conceitedly, "And up out of them damn pajamas, for Christ sake. It's three-something in the afternoon, man and you're still lounging, like you rich or something! Well, consider this your intervention, Homie. But make no mistake, Chill. If it weren't for the fact that our wives are sisters, well, how could I put this politely?" He paused. "I wouldn't give a mangy dog's shit what you did with your time. But you've got all these babies, man! All of those little Afri-bodians that you've got to provide for."

Chill laughed. "Afri-bodians?"

"Yeah, man. You know, Half African and half Cambodian! Anyway, that's for real. The truth is that this ain't about us. Not at all! It's all about the kids, Chill. The kids, man!" he whispered aggressively, and then pointed at Chill's family on the balcony, with Jen seeming mildly shocked at the mass of people around the ice-cream truck. "The babies, you know?" he continued.

Chill appeared to be lost in ponder as he nodded.

"That's where it's at, man," Jo-Jo resumed. He lit up the tip of his cigar. "Your boy Jo-Jo is here to the rescue," he exhaled a smoke ring towards Chill, who waved it away.

"And how are you going to do all that, with that credit-cleaning bullshit that you're always doing?" he asked sarcastically.

Jo-Jo became irritated at his brother-in-law's disrespect. "Chill, let me explain a little something to you about this "credit-cleaning bullshit", that you so disrespectfully described. This is some serious stuff, man. This game will have you living like a millionaire, if you roll with me. And you know this, man!"

He paused to open his sun roof a little, and then leaned in close to Chill and whispered, "Can you smell that exquisite suede-leather upholstery up in this ride?" He leaned back against his black-suede seat and smiled with his eyes closed. "Get a whiff of that scent, man," he said, as he seemed to take pleasure in the feeling as he grasped the leather subtly, yet firmly. "This is what the hell I'm talking about." he blurted, and invited Chill to admire the black-suede headliner and the matching dashboard.

Jo-Jo pressed a button on the steering wheel and, "*For the Love of Money*" by the "O-Jays," filled the car.

The music played through some of the most premium stereo components known to man. "You smell it Chill. Don't you, boy?" he smiled.

Chill nodded to the music and smiled. "Yeah, man. I can't lie. I smell it, Jo-Jo. It smells nice, too," he finally admitted.

Jo-Jo smiled and leaned in close to him again. "You damn right it smells nice."

Chill took in the aroma of the interior and closed his eyes. "I like it!" He rested his back against the comfortable ergonomic seat. "It feels good, too," he mentioned, as he opened his eyes and took pleasure in observing his wife, as she escorted the twins down the steps towards the ice-cream truck.

"Listen to me, Chill, you know that if you applied yourself like I know you could, you could be rolling in one of these cars, too. This ain't nothing but a car note, man. I know that you would be able to handle that once you've got your shit together."

Chill shook his head, and appeared to be contemplating Jo-Jo's offer, as he enjoyed the view of his family near the screaming children by the ice-cream truck.

He finally looked at him and said, "Man, I've thought about it. But I can't see it, Jo-Jo. I mean, this is a nice car. But, there ain't any way in hell that I'm ready for no car payment this high. This joint is way up out of my league!"

"No it's not, Chill," Jo-Jo replied, as the two of them observed Jen and the twins standing near the ice-cream truck.

"This car note ain't nothing but eighteen a month. That's it. That ain't shit!"

Chill's face seemed to register a state of shock. "Eighteen what?" he exclaimed.

"18 hundred dollars, boy, that's all!"

"18 hundred dollars?" Chill scowled. "That's crazy!" he exclaimed, as he immediately caught sight of Jen herding the twins back home. He noticed that they had a soft-serve ice-cream cone clutched in their little hands. He couldn't help but to smile at his adorable creations.

Jo-Jo grinned. "That's reality, Chill," he told him, as he observed the delightful sight as well. "And 18 hundred dollars ain't nothing! That's chump change! If you've got one ounce of game in your brain, which I know you do, you'd be rolling with me. You'd be making that kind of money in a couple of hours, man, that ain't shit."

He smiled and waved at Jen, as she patiently ushered the slow moving toddlers back toward the stairs to their apartment. *The half-devoured ice-cream cones that they held in their tiny hands* was *cute.*

"Look at those little-bitty sandals they're wearing, Chill." he chuckled, and pointed towards their shoes.

"Yeah, man," Chill laughed. "I bought those shoes for them last week," he said, and enjoyed the sight of the twin's messy little faces. "But I'm going to be real with you, Jo-Jo. I don't know anything about this credit cleaning stuff. Although, I do know that I don't have any credit. Not any good credit, anyway."

"Look here, Chill. It could take you..." Jo-Jo began, as he suddenly turned his attention to his ringing cell phone on the center console. He quickly picked it up and looked at the caller I.D. "That's Michael Glutzinberg calling." He sat the phone back on the wood-grain console near the gear-shift. "He works at Collins and Beasley Investments firm, in Century City. He's another credit client of mine. I'll let it go to voicemail," he said as the phone stopped ringing. "I'll bet you 10 gees, that he's trying to give me at least that much to clean up some credit reports for his clients. You want to take that bet, boy?"

Chill laughed and shook his head. "Hell nah, fool!"

"Anyway man, as I was about to tell you. It could take you twenty years to establish what they call, "A-1" credit. But it could take you exactly thirty-two days to completely destroy it,"

"Thirty-two days? How is that?"

"By not paying your bills within a timely fashion, that's how. You know, like you agreed upon when you signed your name on the dotted line on the contract. It's usually a thirty-one day period. Whether you know it or not, credit is what makes the world go around. Without it, you don't mean anything to anyone. Not anyone who counts anyway. I'm talking about the creditors, the lenders, so to speak. If you listen to me, I'm going to put you up on some game that's going to blow your mind, man. Your boy Jo-Jo's going to show you how to ball, Chill. I mean, really ball! Look at me. I'm ballin' like a motherfucker."

Chill smiled and nodded. Jo-Jo's remark held little humor but the way it sounded made it seem a little funny.

"Yeah, I see." Chill grinned.

"And you want to know why I'm ballin'?"

"Why, man?"

"Because, I'm one of the kings!" Jo-Jo blurted, arrogantly.

"The kings of what?"

"The kings of credit, boy! I'm one of the kings in this business!" he boasted, while tugging lightly on the collar of his white dress shirt. "And don't you forget it, either!"

"The kings of credit, huh?" Chill smiled. "Yeah Jo-Jo, that sounds pretty catchy. I like that phrase, Daddy-O."

"Mr. Willie Bruce, you're going to like a whole lot of things, if you play your cards right. That's the truth, brother-in-law." He straightened his blue silk tie and then reached inside of his shirt pocket, and pulled out a white business card. "Here, boy." He handed it to Chill and watched him examine it.

"Now, as you already know, I've got some credit clients to meet and collect some money from. So, make sure that you drop by my new office. The address is on the card. I'll be there around twelve o'clock tomorrow. So try and be there." He pointed his finger directly in Chill's face. "So don't forget!"

83

Chill smiled. "I won't. I'll be there for sure."

"Now, that's what I'm talking about, Chill! Get money, boy!

Chill smiled as Jo-Jo gave him some dap. "Yeah man, you're crazy, that's sounds good to me!"

"You've got that right, Chill, I'm crazy about this money! So let's get it. You feel me?"

"Yeah dawg, I feel you."

Jo-Jo took on the accent of a California surfer. "Cool, dude! Kowabunga, bro'!"

Chill doubled over, and burst out in laughter.

Chapter 9

Chill felt as though his life had finally found some purpose, as he drove his Honda into the Subterranean parking structure of a high-rise office building, in Westwood, California.

He merrily sang along to *"Fifty-Fifty Love"*, by Teddy Pendergrass, as he lowered the music volume and approached the valet station, where he was immediately approached and greeted by Andre, the 55-year-old Panamanian valet.

"Good afternoon, sir," he welcomed Chill with a warm smile, after opening the driver's side door. "My name is Andre," he mentioned, and handed Chill his parking validation ticket. "You have a nice day, sir."

"You too, Andre. Take care, man," he uttered, and stepped out of his car in his professional outfit for the day, which was a denim-suede combination. He even wore his favorite blue suede boots, while he moved with purpose through the stylish and well-polished corridor, and then approached the information station in the lobby's center.

He looked over his shoulder through the tinted windows at the heavy mid-day Wilshire Boulevard traffic, and then turned his attention to the heavyset, 56-year-old Caucasian security guard.

"Hello, sir. How can I assist you this fine afternoon?" the older man asked.

Chill glanced at the nameplate on his tan, short sleeved khaki shirt. It read, "Bob", in gold-accented print.

"Hi, Bob. I'm here to meet with Mr. Milton, in suite number 1506. My name is Willie Bruce. He's expecting me."

"Well, in that case, Mr. Bruce, allow me to guide you," he mentioned, while he glanced at the tenant registry. "Walk that way, sir," he continued, pointing to a row of elevators in the corridor. "You can take any one of those elevators over there up to the fifteenth floor. At which point, you proceed to your right, sir."

"Thank you very much, Bob."

"You're very welcome, Mr. Bruce. You have a nice day, sir."

"You too, Bob," he headed towards the elevator doors.

Sabrina, the 30-year-old Caucasian receptionist was sitting comfortably at her desk perusing some files, while Chill sat quietly on the leather, dark-brown couch reading a current issue of a business magazine which catered to the serious entrepreneur.

Jo-Jo entered the lobby from beyond the inner-lobby door. He wore an elegant, expensive, light-gray business suit. He smiled at his receptionist and uttered, "Thank you, Sabrina."

"You're welcome Mr. Milton," she smiled back.

He greeted Chill on the couch as he approached the coffee table.

Chill placed the magazine on the table and stood up. "What's up, Jo-Jo?" The two of them briefly embraced.

Jo-Jo smirked. "It's good to see that you're not in your goddamn pajamas, nigga."

Chill laughed and whispered, "Shut up, fool."

"Yeah boy, whatever. But, I'm glad that you could make it today."

"Man, I had to make it. I've got to do something, Jo-Jo. Hell, Jen's starting to look at me all crazy."

Jo-Jo laughed. "Don't feel like the Lone Ranger, man. I get those exact same cross-eyed looks from Lena's slanted eyed-ass, too. Don't trip it, though. That's a problem that money will solve. The minor problems can always be resolved that way. And I'm going to show you how to get it. Now, come on, man. Let's go to 'our' new office."

"Lead the way, Daddy-O."

He followed Jo-Jo through the inner-lobby door and down the hallway to the fifth office door on the right side. The two of them were laughing as they entered the lavishly decorated office. The room contained two mahogany executive desks, two up-to-date computer systems, and a fully functional telephone system.

"*Olivia*", by The Whispers played softly from the brand new IPOD system on top of the matching filing cabinet, which was placed near the wall behind Jo-Jo's desk.

"I'm telling you, Chill... your kids are off the chain, man." Jo-Jo chuckled, while he sat in his black, leather executive chair behind his desk. He pointed to the smaller, but nonetheless luxurious chairs in front of the desk. "Sit down, man."

"Yeah, my kids are a trip, huh?" Chill agreed, and sat down. "Especially that little bad-ass, Jolina. She thinks that she's running shit. That heifer's only two years old, can you imagine that?"

"Of course, I can," Jo-Jo replied, as he attempted to tidy the space around him. "That's because she is running shit, you wait and see. I'm telling you, boy. She's going to have you wrapped around her little finger."

"I know, huh?" Chill chuckled.

"You're goddamn right! And that twin brother of hers, he ain't no joke, neither."

Chill sighed. "Tell me about it, man!"

"Damn, Chill. You and Jen have got five kids, man! Don't you and your wife have a T.V. or something? Y'all don't have anything else to do, but fuck?" They both laughed.

"Yeah, man," he mentioned, seeming embarrassed.

Jo-Jo laughed. "But seriously, man. I've got to agree with you. That's one hell of a squad you've got there," he said, while he lowered the music volume with the remote.

"Yeah, that's my squad. That's my team right there, boy. I wouldn't trade them for anything," he declared, and pounded his fist proudly against his chest.

"I heard that. You've definitely got a beautiful family, though. You're a lucky man, Chill."

"That I am, Jo-Jo, and thanks. Speaking about kids, when the hell are you and Lena going to give Grandma some more grandchildren? What the hell are you guys waiting on?"

"Shit, don't get it fucked up! I love rug rats and all. Just as long as I am not the one who has to take care of them. Besides, you and Jen have got enough kids for Mai and a few other grandmothers; you old tender-dick ass, nigga'!" He blurted.

Chill laughed. "Shut the hell up, Jo-Jo! You ain't right, man!"

"I know," Jo-Jo chuckled, as Chill looked around the office and appreciated the fine decorating. "Man, this sure is a nice joint you've got here."

Jo-Jo began to rifle through his desk drawers in search of some paperwork. "Yeah, as much as I'm paying for this office space it had better be nice. A-ha! Here it is," he said, after he found the document he was looking for and placed it on the desktop in front of Chill, who glanced at it.

"Chill, you need to study each and every one of those items on that page until you've got them memorized. I can't tell you enough how important this is." Chill picked up the sheet and perused it.

Jo-Jo pointed to the paper. "That's what my associates and I call, our 'price list'. It displays the per-line item fee that we charge our credit clients. It's for the items that they either want removed, or 'cleaned,' as we prefer to call it."

Chill placed the list back on the desk, hunched over it, and furrowed his brows while he concentrated. "I got a quick question, Jo-Jo. I mean, I really hate to sound stupid, you dig?"

"How could I mind? And there are never any stupid questions. Remember this you are learning something that's brand-new to you. So, go easy on yourself. You'll get it. Trust me. Oh, one more thing I almost forgot. There is only one stupid question. It's the one you never ask." Jo-Jo winked and smiled. "So what's your question?"

"Okay," Chill said, leaning back in his chair. "Explain to me what you mean by removing, or, 'cleaning' something?"

"Well, that means to get rid of it." He gently thumped his manicured fingernails against his desk top in sync with the soft beat of the music. "It means to wipe out that particular item. for example, one of the items on an outstanding credit-card balance. One that has not been paid within the contractual period is what we call, 'charged off'."

He paused for a moment to sip from a bottle of water. "Now, Chill," he continued, placing the bottle back on a coaster on his desk, "a 'charge-off', can be, and usually is a fatal blow to your credit score. It reveals to the creditors that you are irresponsible, incompetent, and that you do not pay your bills. It tells the world that you can't be trusted. It's plain and simple. Now, what I'm able to do is erase the derogatory information from the targeted credit company's computers, and presto!" He waved his hands dismissively in the air. "You've got a clean slate, a fresh start. Just like that. That's only the beginning, though. I can clean anything, Chill! I'm the man, baby!"

Chill seemed confused. His mind began to wonder. "What?" he exclaimed. "How in the hell can you actually do something like that? I mean, that's other people's personal information."

"No shit, Sherlock." Jo-Jo smirked as he stood up. He removed his coat and hung it over his chair and sat back down. "That's a very good question there, boy," he grinned and pointed to Chill. I want you to remember this, it's not what you know, but who you know. Now, I need for you to keep this information up under your hat. But me, I'm engaged with some very serious affiliates. Some affiliates who has inside contacts who work inside of the credit companies. The insiders are the ones who actually press the buttons on their computers. Naturally, everyone is paid handsomely for their services."

Chill became dumb-struck by what he was hearing. "Damn, Jo-Jo! You mean to tell me, that you've got it like that?"

"Yep," he nodded. "I got it like that. Hell, you do, too. We've got it like that, my man. We could be a hell of a team, Chill, you and me."

He noticed Chill's pondering state and took it as a clue that he was thinking about the profitable possibilities. "Loved one we can add some made-up, exceptionally good credit items onto a credit report as well. I'm talking about some extravagant, paid-off homes, yachts, even some top-of-the-line credit cards. We're what you might call, a one-stop shop. There isn't anything that we can't do to a credit report. I guess that you would call us the royal family of this business, man."

"And you're one of the kings, huh?" Chill grinned.

"You're goddamn right I am, kinfolks."

"Damn!" Chill whispered, while the wheels were definitely spinning inside of his mind. "Can we clean up child-support from a credit report, too?" he asked enthusiastically.

"Yep, we damn sure could. We can fix anything on a credit report. However, there's a list of items that we simply won't touch, child-support, I'm sorry to say this, buddy, but, it's at the very top of that list."

Chill appeared slightly disappointed. "Why is that, though?" he asked, intently staring at a gold framed photograph of Jo-Jo in a trendy West Hollywood nightclub.

He was standing with Lena, his beautiful, 36-year-old Cambodian wife of six years. The two of them were smiling while holding champagne filled glasses.

Jo-Jo looked him straight in the eyes. "Well, all that I can say is that we choose not to get involved with that type of stuff. It's bad for business, you know? I'll just leave it at that."

Chill sighed. "Man, Jo-Jo. You're not bullshitting, are you?"

"I don't have any time to be bullshitting, dawg. Life's way too short for that. Besides, bullshitters are all about the decrease. Me, I'm about the increase, you dig? Momma needs a new pair of shoes. So, we've got to get this money while we can." He stared deeply into Chill's eyes again. "Preferably, without pulling guns on people, you know? I'm sure you understand what it is that I'm getting at?"

Chill nodded and began to re-examine the price list on the desk. He knew what Jo-Jo was referring to. "Yeah, man, I hear you." He pointed to a particular item on the list. "Tell me about this, 'Public Records, $1500. What's that mean?"

Jo-Jo flipped the page around towards himself. "That's our fee to clean a credit item that's in the public records category. The cost is fifteen-hundred dollars. If it's a public record, it means that anybody can view it. Some examples of public record credit items are your bankruptcies, civil judgments, repossessions, evictions, student loans, Federal and State tax liens, as well as your foreclosures. That's just naming a few."

He pointed to another item on the price list. "Now Chill, as far as the non-public record items are concerned, they're not publically accessible, usually. They include your late payments, collections, charge-offs, failure to pay as agreed, account negotiations, Rolling 30, 60 and 90 day late charges, and so on. We provide impeccable service to our clients because we can and with precision wipe out any bad credit completely. If in some cases the item can't be totally erased, for whatever reasons, we can leave the negative entry on the credit report. But, we can clean it up so that it would show as being in good standing. Anyway, getting back on the topic, we charge a thousand dollars per line for non-public record items."

"Understand this, Chill. Our prices are totally non-negotiable. Our clients can pay the listed price, or, they can go elsewhere. There are no specials. No two-for-one deals, no season passes. None of that type of shit. It's not much of a worry, though, because our clients pay us in advance. Without question, I might add. You see, the average American is not worried about their credit score, until it comes time for them to use it. Usually in the case of buying a house, a boat, a car, a bike, or a flat-screen television set. The fact is we get results, fast. Man, Chill, this game is better than selling dope." He paused and leaned in close to Chill and whispered, "Or kidnapping folks, you dig?"

Chill received the message completely, while he continued to ponder and concentrate on Jo-Jo's words.

"Yeah, Jo-Jo," he smiled and crossed his legs. "Man, this credit stuff ain't a joke, huh?"

"Hell nah it ain't a joke! Like I told you yesterday, credit makes the world go around. Without it, your life doesn't mean anything, and that's for real." He reached into a desk drawer and pulled out a sheet of paper, a silver writing pen, and a white box containing one thousand customized business cards. Check this out," he said, as he placed them on the desk.

"What's all that for?"

"It's for your new life. This is for your alternate personality, so to speak." He smiled.

Chill appeared overwhelmed as he sat back and folded his arms across his chest.

"What do you mean my new life? My alternate personality?

"Just roll with me, Chill!" Jo-Jo exclaimed. "Now, I need for you to write down your complete name, date of birth and your Social Security number on that piece of paper."

Chill silently complied with the rushed demand.

Jo-Jo took the paper and smiled. "Give me about 48-hours with this information right here. I guarantee you that your credit score will be on A-1 status."

"What is a credit score, anyway?" Chill frowned at his own ignorance. It was a shame that he didn't know the business' basics. He would frown upon that later.

"A credit score is your credit rating. It thoroughly describes how risky it would be to give you a loan. American commercial organizations, as well as Government institutions, predicate your personal credit and your trustworthiness, on this particular number. The higher the number is, the lower the risk. Also, the greater your trustworthiness is, the more money that you can borrow. My associates and I control that number, you dig? You know what that means don't you?"

"Yeah, I get it. You're the king!"

Jo-Jo smiled again. "Well, I'm one of them, anyway." He high-fived Chill across the desk. "Now you're learning, son!"

"I like this shit!" Chill blurted, as he and Jo-Jo reveled in the hype of the moment.

The future held such promise for Chill. For the first time in his life, he saw a way to provide lavishly for his family, without the risks that accompanied robberies and burglaries, home invasions and kidnapping for ransom.

Jo-Jo tapped his fingernails on his desk to the beat of "*Just Gets Better with Time*", by The Whispers.

"Chill, give me about two days and I'll get you all the way in the game, as far as your credit score is concerned. I'll take you shopping for a Mercedes Benz at Stuart's car lot. He's one of my credit clients. Afterwards, you and I will roll to the Beverly Shopping Center. I'll buy you some new garments."

Chill was delighted with his newly developed itinerary. Jo-Jo observed this and continued, "Chill, man, the car and some designer suits are the tools that you'll need to establish yourself in this line of business,"

He enjoyed the smile on Chill's face, as he began to stare at the business-card box on the desk.

"That sounds cool to me, Jo-Jo." He pointed to the box. "Now, what's in the box?"

"Open it up and see for yourself. Check them out."

Chill grabbed the box, placed it in his lap and opened it. He retrieved one of the eloquently designed and printed cards. The cards design depicted a clear summer night. A beautiful, well-lit back yard showcased an inviting, superlatively crafted, aqua blue swimming pool, which amplified the artificial radiance of the lighting to an unparalleled degree of form and artistry. Contrasting perfectly was a white, illustrious Bel-Air mansion, which seemed to project beyond and embrace the card itself, with the essence of quality. Chill was beside himself with appreciation, as he admirably read the light blue and white lettering. "These are some tight-ass business cards, man!"

"Those are your business cards, Chill. I grabbed them from my printer on my way over here today. I picked them out myself. They're okay cards, I suppose," Jo-Jo stated humbly.

"Okay?" Chill scowled. "Man, these cards are nice!" His gratitude was obvious, as he continued to admire the card. "Hey man, whose mansion is this on the card?"

"The hell if I know," he replied, shrugging his shoulders. "I picked it out of about two hundred different cards on the wall at the print shop."

"Damn," Chill chuckled. "You sure work fast, man. I mean, you got at me about all this stuff yesterday afternoon."

Jo-Jo cracked a smile. "That's because I know you, boy. I move quickly. We don't have any time to be dragging our feet. Besides, I already anticipated you joining up with me, before I ever brought it to your attention."

"Man," Chill sighed, as he glanced out of the window and marveled at the other buildings in the area. He especially enjoyed the Westwood College campus in the distance. "Am I that predictable?"

Jo-Jo nodded and smiled. "Yeah, man. Pretty much, and that's without a doubt. I know you, man."

"Yeah," Chill chuckled, as he took on a regal posture. He cleared his throat and read the business card with a tone of false arrogance. "W.B. Financial Services. Specializing in personal, business loans and mortgages. C. E. O. Willie Bruce," he declared and looked at Jo-Jo. "Damn, man. This card is bad, and your office is out of this world! Well, it is to me, anyway. But I'm very grateful to you. Although, I got to tell you man, I don't know nothing about all of this financial stuff that you're involved in."

"Don't trip on that, my brother. Because you are now, my representative, and by the end of the day, you'll know everything that you need to know about this weird and wonderful world of mines. So pay attention, because school is now in session, Grasshopper."

"You're crazy," Chill chuckled, as they began to laugh heartily.

Chapter 10

The time on his gold-plated, Chromatic Mariner wristwatch read Friday, 9:51 a.m., as Chill stood back from his bathroom mirror and praised his gray denim outfit, black tennis shoes, and baseball cap. He thoroughly enjoyed the particular feeling of promise and excitement that the day held for him.

Jen stepped up behind him and admired his appearance as well. "Yes, babe," she said, as she began to brush some lint off of his shoulders and back. "You are very attractive, as always."

"Why thank you, my love. And so are you," he mentioned, and turned his head and gave her a soft kiss on the lips. He seemed to enjoy the sight of her blushing in the mirror. "You are beautiful, baby!"

Jen smacked her lips and smirked. "You're just saying that, whatever, Willie. I feel like I'm gaining some weight. I'm getting heavy, aren't I?" she frowned.

"Baby, you're crazy! You are not gaining weight! You're just as beautiful as you were the day that I met you in that gas station. You're still my lovely Cambodian Queen."

As a vivid recollection filled his mind of being at a family reunion the summer before, he immediately noticed his faux pas. It was scorching hot at a vacation spot in Lake Havasu City, Arizona. Some of his family members were enjoying the weather and splashing about in the warm, fresh water. Others were hiding from temperatures beneath an array of tents and canopies. Chill had noticed his wife standing near the water's edge, staring admiringly into its clarity. He rose from his lounge chair with a tall can of beer in his hand and approached her. He was somewhat intoxicated when he wrapped his arms around her. She sported a black one-piece swimsuit. "You know baby," he slurred. "You're getting a little fat around the edges."

Jen's eyebrows rose instantly. "Oh yeah, nigger?" Jen blurted, and threw his arms from around her. Chill instantly regretted his blunder. However, it was much too late, and there was no way he could take his unforgiving statement back.

As a punishment, after they returned home to their Van Nuys apartment, he was forced to spend the next two nights on the living-room couch.

Sasha, their two-year-old Siamese cat, was his only companion.

Jen was grinning as she pointed in the bathroom mirror, "You must've remembered that day when you told me that I was fat, huh? And you don't want to sleep your butt on the couch again, huh?"

"Hell nah! Fuck that couch shit! I'm serious, baby! You're still a sexy ass woman to me," he insisted earnestly, sensing that he was walking on very thin ice.

She smacked her lips again, "Yeah Willie, let you tell it."

"I'm telling you the truth, momma," as he began to scrutinize his mustache in the mirror he responded to the soft smile on her face. "You know that you're beautiful, baby!" He felt as if he was on safe ground with her again. "Jo-Jo should be here any minute now." He quickly changed the subject and glanced at his wristwatch. "It's almost ten o'clock now. It looks like it's going to be a pretty long day for us. I can't be sure what time I'll be home this evening. I hope it's not too late."

"Whatever time that you get home, you know that your wife and kids will be here when you make it back," She held him from behind in a prolonged embrace, while he turned his head and kissed her gently on the lips, before turning back to the mirror.

"You know that's the best part of my day, don't you baby?" he mentioned, as he began tweezing hairs from his nose.

"What is, dear?" she asked, hugging his waist.

"Me coming home to my family, I always enjoy that."

Jen felt absolutely loved at that moment.

95

"Well, you already know that we love you, too, don't you?"

Chill smiled as he placed the tweezers on the counter and returned to primping himself in the mirror. "Of course I know that, babe!"

While he seemed to have fallen in love with his own reflection, she began to fuss with the fabric around his collar.

"But I do know one thing, Momma," he continued.

"And what might that be, dear?"

"I can't wait until tomorrow."

"Tomorrow?" she asked curiously. Tomorrow's Saturday. What's going on tomorrow, babe?"

He noticed that she seemed to be wracking her brain with curiosity, as he turned to face her. "Oh, baby! Please tell me you're joking! You must be joking!" he declared as he encircled her waist with his arms and saw that she was consumed by confusion.

"It's not your birthday," she finally said.

"Nope," he grinned.

"I know it's not our anniversary."

"No, it's not." He toyed with her, loving the fact that she was completely bewildered. "Guess again, babe."

"It's not my birthday, that's March the third. I give up, Willie!" she sighed. "I don't have a clue as to what is going on tomorrow. Just tell me what's happening tomorrow!"

Chill tugged gently on his shirt collar and boasted, "Damn, momma'! I get's better-looking everyday! I thought you knew that!" he chuckled.

Jen broke out in laughter and playfully punched him in his abdomen.

He laughed at her as he grabbed her gently, spun her around and then embraced her tightly.

"Baby, you so crazy!" she blurted, and kissed him softly on his lips.

"I'm crazy about you, that I am!"

"Ditto, but you're right, Willie. Because every day that passes by leaves you looking better than you did the day before."

"Thank you. And so do you, my love. And I mean that, sweetheart," he admitted, before they fell into a passionate kiss.

An hour later, Chill was standing in the exterior lot of Exotic Motoring Auto Sales in Sherman Oaks, California. He was there admiring a sparkling black, customized 2004, S-500 Mercedes-Benz.

"This ride is clean!" he told himself, as he promptly slid behind the glossy wood-grain steering wheel and into the rich, black leather seat.

He seemed delighted, as if he had just won the lottery. "Really nice," he said, while he nodded to 50-Cent's song, "*In Da Club*," which pounded throughout the sound system.

Jo-Jo seemed to be enjoying the vehicle and the music as well, while he and Stuart Magnum, his 58-year-old, suave Caucasian business associate, who was the sole owner of the car lot, stood nearby relishing the moment.

Appearing pleased with his vehicle choice, Chill turned off the music and exited the car. "Well, Willie, what did you think?" Stuart asked.

"This is a nice ride, Stuart,"

"A nice ride!" Stuart blurted, sounding offended, as he jabbed his finger toward the Mercedes. "She's an absolute S-Class dream is what she is! She has a premium, triple-diamond black paint job and a new transmission added. She's had a recent two-hundred point inspection, which included a tune-up, micro-detailing, new carpeting, and some new, soft-black leather interior included. She's barely a year old, man! Hell, her mileage is so low, she should be barely a month old, no doubt!" He softened up a bit. "She's a beautiful piece of work. A gorgeous S-500, isn't she?"

"You're damn right she is!" Chill exclaimed. "She's a mighty fine S-500. I could definitely see myself rolling in that car. She's got a smooth, comfortable feel to her. I like her, Stuart."

He looked at Jo-Jo. "She's nice, huh?"

"It is a beautiful car, Chill," Jo-Jo replied, as his cell phone began to ring. He reached into the pocket of his dark-blue velour sweat suit and retrieved his phone, and checked the caller's name. "It's Ilene Bartley," he mentioned, cancelling the call and replacing the phone back inside of his pocket. "It's a nice car, Chill. You'd look good rollin' in it."

"No doubt I would!" Chill exclaimed.

"But of course, it's definitely not as nice as mine," Jo-Jo gloated, and then pointed to his S-600 Mercedes-Benz parked nearby. "However, it will do for our purposes." He continued, and turned to Stuart, "So you've already verified Chill's outstanding application and his sky-high credit score? So, what do you think? Because if you ask me, I think that he deserves to roll up out of here in this beauty, right now, with no money down." Stuart scowled.

"No money down?"

"Yeah Stuart, just like you did for me when I bought my ride."

"Come on, Joseph!" he protested.

"Look, Stuart. Willie's an excellent risk, man. He's got the job, the income and the credit score. So, what do you say, my friend?" Jo-Jo smiled.

Stuart grimaced. "Jo-Jo, you're killing me, man! Jesus! Can't he at least pay for the goddamn taxes and licensing fees? Come on, Joseph, Damn! You want me to totally eat this sale? I wouldn't do you like that. I've got to make something off this deal." Stuart was irate and offended, as Jo-Jo confidently smiled and winked at Chill.

"I'll tell you what, Stuart," Jo-Jo resumed, "I believe that I have an outstanding proposal which will satisfy you and me both," he said, and glanced around at the large number of foreign luxury cars on the lot. "I can take care of the taxes and that other fee by taking care of your little sister's blemished credit report. How's that sound to you?"

Stuart was all smiles now. "It sounds great, my friend!"

Jo-Jo and chill smiled at one another. "So, we have a deal then?"

Stuart grinned. "Absolutely, hell yeah we've got a deal! So, when can you get started on it? Because Lizzy needs it done immediately, I mean like yesterday, man."

Jo-Jo flashed a soft smile. "I can get started on it immediately. If not sooner! I'll need her full work-up. You know the usual, full name, social security number and date of birth, which are necessary to achieve our goal."

"No problem, Jo-Jo. I'll get you that information sometime today."

"Cool. It'll take me about a week. That way, I won't have to rush. Does that sound good to you?"

"Yes sir, no doubt!" he happily pumped Jo-Jo's fist.

Jo-Jo saw that Chill appeared to be suppressing a great deal of excitement on his face.

"Chill brotha', are you ready to sign on this deal and roll your new whip up out of here?"

The excitement finally won over Chill's self control and he exclaimed, "Hell yeah, Jo-Jo!"

Jo-Jo turned to Stuart. "Are you ready to do this, Stuart?"

"I'm as ready as I'll ever be, you guys follow me to my office," he instructed and leading them into the showroom.

"Poppa' Was a Rollin' Stone", by The Temptations filled the luxurious interior of Chill's Mercedes-Benz S-500.

He felt really cool, wealthy even, as he followed closely behind Jo-Jo's Mercedes into the fancy valet station, which was on the ground floor of the Beverly shopping center.

After a two hour shopping spree, exorbitant sums were spent. During which time, Jo-Jo was constantly conducting credit business on his cell phone's blue-tooth earpiece.

He checked the time on his Rolex, and noticed that it was 3:11 p.m., as he and Chill stood confidently in front of the counter of an exclusive men's shoe store on the main floor.

"I got this again, Chill," Jo-Jo whispered, as he handed his Platinum credit card to Alfred, the middle-aged, homosexual Hispanic salesman,

After a moment the man returned to the counter. "Here you are, Mr. Milton," he said, and handed Jo-Jo back his card and receipt.

"Hold on a moment, Eileen," Jo-Jo said into his blue-tooth.

He winked at the man and placed his hand over the ear-piece. "Thank you, Alfred. You're a jewel, you know that?" he mentioned in a very soft voice.

Alfred appeared to blush. "Thank you, sir." He smiled, "And as always, you're very welcome, Mr. Milton."

Jo-Jo dropped the receipt in his sweatpants pocket and placed his palm over the earpiece again smiling at Chill, "I told you this credit shit was saucy!" he growled through clenched teeth. "I'm one of the kings of this game, boy!" he whispered.

Chill was also overcome by triumph, and suddenly felt the emotion of victory. He smiled broadly as Alfred handed him their purchases.

"Hell, yeah, Jo-Jo! You ain't lying about that!" he whispered. *Man, six pairs of crocodile shoes, just like that!* He mused, obviously dazed by the cost.

"Thank you once again," Jo-Jo told the salesman, who smiled and bowed his head.

"You are very welcome, Mr. Milton."

"Chow," he replied with a wink.

"Chow, Mr. Milton," Alfred mentioned softly with a wink in return, as Jo-Jo helped Chill to gather up their shopping bags. The two of them swaggered out of the store and into the lively main floor of the mall. After visiting the nearby food court, the two of them moved towards the elevators.

"Okay, Ilene," Jo-Jo resumed into his earpiece. "I do apologize for that delay. But, I'm in the Beverly shopping center right now with my brother-in-law. At any rate, you can bring the money to the restaurant tonight. Give me a call when you pull up to the valet. I'll send Lena out to get it." He checked the time on his Rolex. "Yep, that's correct. It's La Shawn's, in Century City. And you did say that you were bringing me nine grand, right?" He enjoyed the look of shock on Chill's face. "Cool, Ilene, I'll talk to you later then." He glanced at his ringing cell phone. "Ilene, sweetheart, I've got to take this call. So I'll hear from you later, love," he paused- "You, too, darling."

He pressed a button on his phone and blurted, "Michael Glutzenberg! How's life treating you at Collins and Bensley, buddy?"

Upon leaving the mall, Jo-Jo continued his cell phone conversation with Michael Glutzenberg, while Chill stood nearby on the red carpeted valet station.

"That'll definitely work, Michael. I'll be at your office in about twenty minutes or so to pick that up. We're leaving the mall right now. So, I'll see you when I get there." He winked at Chill. "That's perfect, buddy. Be there soon, I promise." He closed his cell phone and checked the time on his wristwatch again.

"That's ten more, Chill," he boasted, and then dropped his phone back into his sweat pants pocket.

"10 thousand dollars?" Chill exclaimed, in disbelief. "You ain't no joke, Jo-Jo! You ain't about the business, you are the business!"

Jo-Jo laughed and clapped Chill on his shoulder. "I'll take that as a compliment, dawg'. But anyway, the pen is way mightier than the sword, my brother. And game is meant to be sold, not told. Of course now, here I am, serving it to you on a silver platter for free, just because we're kinfolks. Hell, if that ain't love, well, I don't know what is, Chill."

"I sure appreciate it, man."

"I know you do. But don't you worry my brother. Because next weekend, the fun and shopping is going to be on you. You'll be receiving your credit cards in the mail, as well as a complete enhanced layout of your credit report."

Suddenly, a 34-year-old Hispanic male valet brought Jo-Jo's Mercedes up to the stop sign. He exited the vehicle and "*In Case You Need Love*", by Smokey Robinson floated out from the car's stereo system. The music seemed to ease even the darkest spirits.

"Oh, yeah!" Jo-Jo blurted, and reached into his Mercedes and cranked up the music volume. "That's my jam right there!" he mentioned, as a Caucasian valet guy parked Chill's Mercedes directly behind his car. "I'm feeling this joint!" he continued, as the mall patrons in the area began to observe him while he executed a flawless "*Cha-cha*" solo dance near his car.

Everyone seemed to enjoy the recreational respite from the otherwise mundane day. The crowd smiled and offered words of praise and encouragement for Jo-Jo's performance.

He pointed at Chill, and, without missing a beat, challenged him to a dance-off. "Boy, you don't know anything about this Cha-cha shit!

"You must be out of your mind, man! Check this out!" Chill exclaimed, and then quickly established an impressive rhythmic step, giving Jo-Jo a complete run for his money.

Jo-Jo brought his performance up a notch, as his playful competition brought about entertainment for all.

After a moment, Chill stopped dancing and conceded defeat to Jo-Jo's superior skills.

Jo-Jo however, continued to dance to the music until Chill finally interrupted him.

"Hey, Jo-Jo, man. Knock it off for a minute. I need to ask you something. And turn that damn music down!"

"All right, nigga'," he muttered, and reached inside of his car and turned off the stereo, while their audience of shoppers, and even the valet employees broke out into cheers and applauded their dance show.

Jo-Jo smiled at everyone, and then bent over at the waist and nodded towards them. "Thank you, ladies and gentlemen! Thank you very much!" He told them, as he bowed his head again, and then turned towards Chill, "Now dawg', what's up?"

"Well, I've been meaning to ask you something," Chill said, as he picked up his shopping bags from the bench nearby.

"Ask me what?"

Chill placed his bags in the rear seat of his car and then returned. "I was wondering why you instructed me to write down on that car application, that I made eight thousand dollars a month. 'Cause that's a lot of money! Especially for a nigga' who ain't got no goddamn job!"

"Chill!" Jo-Jo chuckled. "You trippin', man. You know who you sounding like now, don't you? You're sounding like your wife, boy! Now, check this out, eight grand a month ain't nothing! It's chicken-shit pay! Chump change, man! It's only an insignificant ass $96,000 a year. That's crumbs! Just watch and you'll see. 'Cause everybody loves me and don't be saying that you ain't got a job, neither. Because you do have a job now, you sell credit, boy!"

"That ain't no goddamn job!" he smirked, "That's a hustle, Jo-Jo!" he whispered, as he watched Jo-Jo place his spoils of the shopping spree into the rear seat of his Mercedes. "And it doesn't matter how you look at it, man, fifty dollars an hour is far from being chump change. In fact, it's a whole lot of money!"

Jo-Jo clapped Chill's shoulder. "Yeah, for some folks it is. I guess." He smirked.

Chill nodded. "It is, Jo-Jo. It really is man."

Jo-Jo smirked. "I guess it is. If you say so, anyway, I'm tired of talking about this nonsense."

"Whatever, man." Chill smirked.

"Anyway, Chill. You and your wife are going to meet us at La Shawn's tonight, right?"

"Of course we are! You said to be there at seven-thirty, right?"

"Yeah, brother." Jo-Jo pulled his ringing cell phone out of his pocket and checked the caller I.D. "It's One-Eye. He's one of my record producer partners," he mentioned, and answered the phone. "Hey, One-Eye," he said into his earpiece. "I presume that you are satisfied with our services, am I right?" He smiled and gave Chill some dap. "That's splendid, One-Eye. Just splendid buddy," he chuckled, as he sat down behind the steering wheel of his Mercedes.

Chapter 11

Chill and Jen were dressed for a classy night out on the town, while the two of them stood by the front door in their living-room. He appeared to be somewhat impatient, as he checked the time on his wristwatch.

"Come on babe, its five fifty-two. We've got to get a move on," he announced, and then addressed their children, "Okay y'all, you better behave yourselves while your mother and I are gone. And make sure that you listen to everything that your grandmother tells you, you hear me?"

"Yes dad," they all responded simultaneously, as Mai looked on regally sporting one of her usual sunny colored sarongs.

"Dad," said Buetrie, their eight-year-old and oldest daughter.

"Yes, Buetrie?"

"Can you bring us back a surprise? Please, oh please?" she begged.

"Sure sweetie." Chill smiled and looked at all the kids. "Does some Chocolate cake sound good to y'all?"

"Yay!" The children cheered in unison.

"Okay, you guys, listen up!" Jen cut-in. "I don't want to hear nothing bad when we get back home! Otherwise, your little butts will be grass. And guess who the lawn mower will be?" She grinned, looking into the obedient eyes of each child.

Monica, their six-year-old was the first to respond through her missing front teeth, "You mommy," she said shyly.

"You got that right, Monica. So don't you forget it! And that goes for you too, Kyle," she pointed to their four-year-old son, before addressing them all, "Mommy's not playing either. So you all behave yourselves!"

"Okay, Mommy!" They all said in unison.

Chill clapped his hands together. "All right, you guys. Give Mommy and Daddy a kiss."

The two of them kissed each of their children before leaving the apartment, even the twins who were fast asleep on the couch.

Shortly thereafter, Chill and his wife were cruising northbound in his Mercedes-Benz, over the Sepulveda Pass on the 405 freeway. Alicia Keyes's hit song, "*A Woman's Worth*," was playing soothingly from the superior Rockford-Fosgate sound system.

The traffic was as always a pain due to its frequent congestion. As Chill passed over Mulholland Drive, he seemed a bit agitated and opened the moon roof. The sound of the whooshing air filled the car while he lowered the volume and addressed his wife, "Jen, why are you so goddamn pessimistic about things? Damn!" he shouted.

"You need to calm down, Willie!" she blurted back. "I am not a pessimist! I am however, and always have been, a realist! You should know that by now!"

"That's a lie, babe! If you weren't a pessimist, which you are, then you would see exactly how much money that we're going to be making in this new business. I mean, you've seen it for yourself already. You know how bad my credit report looked before Jo-Jo changed it. And now look at it! It's A-1 status."

Jen remained unconvinced as she leered at the bumper-to-bumper traffic. "Yes, Willie. Your credit score is almost perfect now. I already know, it's just that-"

His agitation increased, as he cut her off, "It's just that, what, Jen? You are a damn worry-wart! That's what you are! Just for once, could you go along with the flow of things and trust me on this! I mean, damn!"

She pointed at him and mentioned assertively, "Love, you listen up! I trust you with my heart, my soul, my life, and everything else for that matter! And you know that! You also know that we've got five children to care for. And I'm sorry, babe, but I'm a mother.

Which means that I'm going to worry, because that's what mothers do? It's our job. It's in our genes."

"I already know that."

She smirked. "And if you did, you would know that it's our duty to make sure that there's food in their bellies, clothes on their backs, and a roof over their heads! But with you doing all of this shady stuff with Jo-Jo..."she paused and shook her head. "Just look at what happened to your friend, C-Dub. That's a sign right there that you need to be paid close attention to. Have you thoroughly thought about this new project of yours? I'm sorry, babe, but it does nothing at all to ease my troubled mind. Not the least bit. Oh, and there is another thing."

Chill rolled his eyes. "What, Jen? What now!" he bellowed, as he glared at the tailgate of the red Ford Explorer in front of them.

"I just thought that since we were on this subject, I would ask you, do you really need this expensive car? After what happened with C-Dub, you promised me that you were going to straighten up and fly straight. You promised me that you were going to keep things on the up and up from now on, and look at you now!"

"Jen, do you see me pulling guns on people? No! Not anymore. I'm done with that kind of shit."

"It's true. You have stopped your little robbing thing. Thank God for that! However, you're still robbing the system, even without a gun. Because that credit stuff that you'll be doing with Jo-Jo isn't legal at all. In fact, it's a Federal offense. And if you got caught robbing someone with a gun, you'd probably do a hell of a lot less time in prison, than you would if you got caught doing this. What would that do to me? What would it do to the kids? My God, Willie, what would it do to you, babe?" She began to cry silently, as she discretely released her frustration while looking out of her side window.

"Whatever, Jen," he sighed.

She shook her head and whispered to herself, "Man, here we go again."

"And what the hell is that supposed to mean?" he snapped.

"Nothing, Willie, nothing at all!" She turned up the music volume. "Man," she continued, as she pressed the repeat button on the remote to the C.D. player.

After a moment, she began to dramatically sing along with, "*A Woman's Worth*", as it resumed playing.

Century City's La Shawn's restaurant was filled to maximum capacity. The sounds of conversation, laughter and the clinking of utensils filled the air, as families, lovers, friends and business associates of all cultures enjoyed their meals.

The best booth in the prominent establishment was occupied by Jen, Chill, Jo-Jo, and his flamboyant, 36-year-old Cambodian wife, Mrs. Lena Milton.

Jo-Jo seemed pleased, as he was cautiously counting a large stack of $100 bills. "That's four, five, six, seven, eight, nine, and one more, makes nine thousand dollars exactly," he said, more or less for Chill's benefit, who couldn't stop grinning and shaking his head.

As Jo-Jo proceeded to slip the cash inside of his brown suit coat pocket, he turned to Lena. "Yeah, baby. Its nine gees, right on the nose. You know that Ilene is always about the business."

"She's my girl, and she's always been about her money. She also told me that she needs our services to clean up her mother's credit report as well," she mentioned, sipping on her glass of Chardonnay.

Chill blurted out of excitement, "Damn, Jo-Jo, you're the man! You are one money getting mother-fucker!"

Jo-Jo smiled and glanced at Lena. "They love me, baby! They all do!"

He looked back at Chill. "I already told you, son! I'm one of the kings of this shit, boy! What?" He scowled. "You thought I was bullshitting? I ain't lying," he winked at him. "You better recognize, nigga'!"

"Man, they got to have some mad love and trust for you. I mean, damn, for them to be cutting you into their mother like that!" he said, while he savored a bite from his gargantuan, Porterhouse steak.

"They can't get enough of me! They all love me, Chill!" he mentioned, and then he smiled at Lena.

"Ain't that right, Lena?" he boasted.

"No doubt, sweetie," she said, and then glanced at Jen and rolled her eyes. "Everybody in California," she paused. "No, sweetie, everybody in the whole United States of America, loves you, baby!" She slyly smirked at Jen.

Jo-Jo chuckled and kissed Lena on the lips as she was trying to stuff some salad into her mouth.

"Don't get it fucked up, Lena," he snickered. "Everybody in this goddamn universe loves my black ass, so get it right!" he was obviously beginning to feel his cognac on the rocks.

He grinned evilly at Chill. "Now, Chill. Ah, hell," he blurted, as he picked up his vibrating cell phone from the table and looked at the caller. "It's my boy, Victor Goldberg, Chill."

"Now this cat puts the 'M' in 'money'! But I need to chop it up with you tonight. I'll call his rich ass back," he said, as he placed the phone back on the table.

"Anyway, Mr. Bruce, come Monday, you need to wake the hell up in the morning, and, not at no goddamn ten-thirty, neither. I need for you to be out of the house by 7:30 a.m. I want you dressed in a suit, a white-shirt, and a tie. And make sure that you gas up the Benz, and go that-a-way," he declared, and pointed to the western section of the restaurant.

Everybody at the table followed his out-stretched hand with their heads, and saw nothing but a fully stocked liquor bar at the back of the stylish establishment.

"What the hell is that-a-way?" Chill inquired, appearing thoroughly confused.

"It's credit clients, boy! Thousands of them are waiting for you right now!"

Everyone at the table laughed heartily at the unusual gesture. "So, go on and get them, soldier! Tighten your game up and charge! Charge, I tell you! Charge!" he exclaimed, as he continued to point toward the bar while the laughter resumed.

Chill chuckled, "Jo-Jo, man, you're burnt the hell out, dawg'!"

Jen chimed in. "Jo-Jo, you're incredibly insane, and that's for real!" She took another drink from her iced rum and coke.

"I'll tell you what, Jen, I am a clown. This I know. But I try to stay light about things and keep the humor in life, you know? Life's way too short."

"Yeah, Jo-Jo," she replied, and sat her glass down on the table.

"But on the real, Chill," Jo-Jo said, and pointed westward again with an expression of utter seriousness. "I need for you to roll that-a-way." He then pointed in the opposite direction towards the restaurant's entrance doors. "Because I've already got this side of town all sewed up, and it doesn't make any sense for us to be all bunched up together in one spot. You understand where I'm coming from?" His eyes narrowed nearly imperceptibly, as he awaited Chill's response.

"No doubt. I understand, man," he answered, as Jen shoved some prime rib into her mouth.

"Cool, because I need for you to be as sharp as a tack. Focused, you know?"

Jo-Jo relaxed his back against the booth, and then he gobbled up a large chunk of Porterhouse steak and washed it down with a sip of cognac.

"You've got to approach every realty office, income-tax service, title and escrow company, stock-brokerage firm, jewelry shop, loan office, as well as every foreign and domestic auto dealership that you can find. I'm talking about from here, to West Timbuktu!" he uttered, pausing for another sip.

"Listen, Chill. You've got to approach these businesses with caution, though." He winked.

Jen sighed and rolled her eyes at his advice.

"You need to feel them out and make sure that they're not associated with the cops. Once you've established that, and you're feeling good about these folks, you can hand over one of your business cards. The card always speaks for itself. And don't forget to let these potential clients know all about your ability to add some solid trade lines onto their personal credit report and how you can clean up their derogatory entries. That always gets them interested." He reached across that table and gave Chill some dap. "You dig?"

Jo-Jo saw that Chill was dutifully processing his detailed instructions.

"No doubt, man, I dig," he agreed. "It sounds like a piece of cake to me," he said, and then scowled at Jen.

"Whatever!" She scoffed in return.

"You can do this, man. I know you can. Because you're a sharp, quick-thinking young brotha', I recognized that about you a few years ago. And I know you're going to be a professional at this game in no time. I believe in you, brotha'," he admitted sheepishly, while savoring a bite of his Alaskan lobster.

"I believe in him too, Daddy!" Lena crooned, obviously intoxicated. "It's about time that my brother-in-law graduated up to the big time."

"You mean this big time world of high finance, don't you, Momma?" Jo-Jo grinned, and sipped from his drink once more.

"Of course I do, Daddy," Lena answered, and noticed the look of skepticism on Jen's face.

She smiled at her sister. "Don't trip on it, Jen. Everything's going to work out fine. You'll see," she slurred, and swooned in her seat.

"Lena, you already know how I am. I'm just concerned about the kids, that's my main worry. I can't be living a footloose and fancy free lifestyle like you and Jo-Jo. I've got way too much to worry about. It's different for a woman when there's kids involved. It really changes how you feel about stuff," she advised, and avoided eye contact with her sister.

"Damn," Chill blurted, and intentionally clanged his fork rather loudly against his plate. "This woman's always trippin', man. Goddamn!" He sighed and began to breathe heavily while he stared at his meal.

Jo-Jo cut in, as he suddenly sensed a marital meltdown in progress.

"Jen, now you just stop it with all of that nonsense. Trust me, you guys are going to be all right. I'm going to see to that, personally." He took another sip from his cognac glass.

"I really hope so," Jen commented dubiously, as Chill began to crack his knuckles.

Jo-Jo cast a worried glance upon him, as Chill fumed at his lobster.

"Listen here, you two," Jo-Jo resumed. "Everything's going to be all good for y'all. It will be beyond your wildest dreams after a while. Because as soon as Chill's credit cards hit your mailbox, you all are going shopping. And then about a couple weeks after that, you guys will be moving up out of that apartment and into your new crib. Lena and I found a nice four bedroom house right down the street from us." He looked at his wife.

"Isn't that right, Baby?"

"Yep," Lena verified, and then belched rudely, "Oh, God!" She blurted, covering her mouth. "I'm so embarrassed! Excuse me, you guys." She smiled and pointed to Jen. "Boy! But anyway sis, check this out, my Baby's got the whole deal in the works right now with Henry Floyd. He's very good at what he does."

She looked at Jo-Jo. "Tell them, Daddy," she continued, as she attempted to give him a sloppy kiss.

Jo-Jo smoothly deflected her. "Mind your manners now, sugar-foot," he whispered, and turned his attention to Jen and Chill.

"But yeah, you guys. Mr. Floyd is a longtime partner of mine." He glanced at his Rolex. "He's the one who put Lena and me in our house. The man knows the realty game as if it were the back of his hand. He has his own real estate firm over on Ventura Boulevard.

It's right off of White Oak Avenue. He's solid people, you know? One of the best in the business, I might add," he informed, while he eagerly cut into his steak.

"Well," Chill uttered, as he sipped on his cognac-straight up. "I'm ready to get on the road and get busy with this credit cleaning shit on Monday morning, I'll tell you that!"

"I believe you, Chill. Just make sure that you're dressed for success. I need for you to hit the boulevards in one of your white shirts and a nice tie. And poof! You'll never be denied. That's for real!" he said, chomping on his steak.

"Yeah, I hear you, man." Chill nodded. "And with all of those expensive suits that you bought me, I'm ready, like Freddy baby!"

Chill seemed confident that he would be able to take on the task. But Jen thought different, as she smirked and shook her head. She was still unconvinced as to what exactly was occurring.

"Don't worry about a thang', chicken wang!" Jo-Jo added, primarily for Jen's sake. "You watch, Jen. You guys won't have enough space for all of the things that you're going to be able to buy. Especially when your husband gets to handling his business, like I know he can," he mentioned, and then pointed to Chill's inexpensive wristwatch.

"By the way, Chill, what time does Mickey have?"

Everyone at the table laughed. Everyone except for Chill, of course, who seemed quite offended when he heard the thoughtless remark. "Mickey?"

He scowled. "Mickey?"

"Yeah boy, I said, Mickey!"

"Why you've got to be clownin' my watch, nigga'? It works, shit!" he blurted, seeming embarrassed but totally defiant.

Jo-Jo chuckled. "I should've said, piece of shit! Because that's what I'm looking at! That watch looks like you've got a brown turd wrapped around your wrist. I can even smell it. It's all stinking and shit! It's real trifling, Chill. But anyway, what time does it have?"

Chill self-consciously examined his so called, 'turd'. "It's eight thirty-eight, man," he answered, not sure whether or not he should feel offended. "And this ain't no turd, neither! It's a 17-Jewel, Chromatic Mariner," he continued, as the maniacal laughter erupted again.

Chill grabbed a napkin from the table and vigorously cleaned its cheap crystal face.

Jo-Jo wiped his mouth with a cloth napkin, and chuckled, "Chill, it's a turd, man. It's a piece of shit! And that's for real, brother. So throw that piece of shit away, right now!"

He pulled a black velvet wristwatch box from the pocket of his suit coat draped over the booth and handed it to Chill.

"What's this?" Chill asked, surprised.

"Open it up and see." Jo-Jo smiled.

Chill opened the box. "Oh, damn!" He exclaimed, and nearly choked on his own saliva, as he gasped in delight.

The box contained a beautiful, stainless steel, Rolex, Daytona wristwatch. Chill was speechless, while Jen and Lena seemed shocked.

Jo-Jo smiled. "Now, that's a wristwatch!" he declared, nodding.

"Thanks Jo-Jo, man! It's a Rolex, damn!" he blurted, as he removed his cheap Chromatic Mariner and tossed it on the table. "I can't believe this," he whispered, and then with reverential deliberation, he happily fastened the superlative Rolex onto his wrist.

Jo-Jo continued to smile. "Chill brother that is your new Rolex. I mean, we sure as hell can't have you gallivanting around town and representing us, with a smelly ass turd like your 17-Jewel Chromatic Mariner dripping from your wrist. Now can we, brother?"

"Thanks a lot, Jo-Jo. Damn!" he stammered.

"Look, baby!" he continued, as he flashed the wristwatch in front of Jen's face, presumably hoping for her praise.

She smirked. "It's a watch, dear," she mentioned, totally unimpressed. "Does it tell any better time than your other watch did?"

He scowled at her and blurted, "Oh my God! Why you always hating on a player? You're a natural born, pre-approved, H-A-T-E-R! Ugh!" he exploded, and felt as though he had enough of her views for one night.

Jen was unmoved by his temper tantrum. "Shut the hell up, nigger!" she whispered calmly, and then swallowed the remainder of her beverage.

Chapter 12

It was Monday, 9:42 a.m. The traffic on Ventura Boulevard in the upscale district of Encino, California, was heavy. Chill was feeling like he had a million bucks, as he soaked in the glorious cloudless sky through the sunroof of his freshly detailed Mercedes-Benz. Considering the fact that he and his car stood still at a red stop light, he took the time to admire his extravagant vehicle, which held some 22" premium chrome rims and rich, black leather interior. Even the stereo system was expensive. He smiled as his rims caught the glare of the sunlight, and caused a reflection from the store-front windows along the strip. He took in a deep nasal breath and thoroughly enjoyed the new car's scent. "*Treat her like a Lady*", by The Mighty Temptations played at a modest volume.

"Bring on the money," he said toward his reflection in the rear-view mirror, when suddenly, he caught sight of a Caucasian businessman through the front windshield. He noticed that the man seemed to be a crafty-looking, 47-year-old, and well fit-looking guy.

Chill observed that the man was standing in front of a prominent business known as, The Montoya Realty Group wearing a navy-blue business suit, black-silk tie, and a light-blue cotton shirt.

Nice tie, Chill thought, as the guy concentrated on the Boulevard and adsorbed the spectacle of morning commuters while enjoying a cigarette.

Chill muted the stereo and drove slowly through the green light, while he thoroughly examined the man. The guy seemed oblivious to the attention that he was receiving. Chill spoke aloud to himself, "Now, he looks pretty promising," while he fully passed the man by and continued to check him out in his rear-view mirror.

The man appeared to be a laid back kind of person.

He's definitely not a Cop, Chill contemplated, as he pulled his car over to the curb and parked.

His point of view may have been right, but to take an extra precaution, he remained inside of the vehicle. He casually positioned himself and enabled him the opportunity to continue his clandestine surveillance through the rear window.

Chill seemed to take every possible step in order not to draw attention to himself. He finally looked at the building behind the guy and read the name of the billboard, "Montoya Realty Group," he said, as he processed it all. "Hmm, it looks good enough to risk it," he uttered, and then turned back around in his seat and turned off the engine.

He took a moment to ponder his approach as to not place himself in a position where he would end-up in handcuffs... This was his first time dealing with a stranger in his brand-new business venture. He gave himself a quick pep-talk. "Let's do this, Chill. Go get 'em, Champ!" he whispered, and then grabbed his black suit coat from the hook over the rear door and exited the vehicle.

He hung his suit coat elegantly over his shoulders in an attempt to look like any other businessman, as he patiently fed some loose change into the parking meter, until his allotted time was set to the maximum amount.

"Keep it pimpin', Chill," he said, as he straightened his gold necktie against his white shirt, and casually walked towards the gentleman, who continued his cigarette break.

"Hello, sir. How are you this morning?" Chill asked, while he closed the distance between them.

The guy looked at Chill and smiled. "I'm okay, man. I appreciate your concern," he said, and instantly preoccupied himself as he looked up at the sky. "I believe that today is going to be another beautiful day for us. Well, hopefully it will be."

Chill followed his glance and concurred, "Yes, sir. I predict the very same thing. Allow me to introduce myself. My name is Willie

Bruce," he informed, as he carefully examined the guys demeanor while he shook his hand.

Chill assumed that the gentleman was a business professional, and he tried his hardest to appear professional, too.

"I'm Nick Crane, Mr. Bruce. I'm honored to make your acquaintance."

"Thank you, sir. The honor is all mine," Chill replied, and then pointed at the facade of the real estate building and asked, "Is this your place of business?"

Nick chuckled lightly and extinguished his cigarette underneath the sole of one of his black leather shoes. "Is this my place of business? No sir!" He chortled. "I would love for it to be, though. Unfortunately, Mr. Bruce, I'm only an agent here. I'm under the employment of the owner, Stanley Montoya - he's the one who earns the big bucks, not me. We call him, Mr. Moneybags," he explained, as he smiled and waved at a strikingly beautiful, red-headed Caucasian woman jogging towards them.

"Wow!" he whispered, as he nonchalantly eyed her form-fitting, hot pink running suit.

The woman noticed the attention and smiled and winked lasciviously, as she continued on.

"Mary, sweet Mother of Jesus!" Nick whispered to himself as he gawked at her buttocks.

He glanced at Chill. "Man, Mr. Bruce! Would you look at that!" he chuckled, as his eyes returned to her derrière while she continued along the sidewalk.

Chill grinned. "Yeah, Mr. Crane, I see it. So, anyway, you mentioned that you're an agent, huh?"

"That's correct, sir," he admitted, while he was completely sidetracked by the receding jogger's majestic butt.

In an attempt to suppress his noticeable lust, he bit gently into his knuckles and murmured, "Mm."

Chill laughed. "Well, that's fantastic, sir. And in that case, I actually believe that you are the man that I need to speak to, then."

"Is that a fact? I'm that guy, huh?" He said sarcastically, as he finally turned his attention back to Chill.

"Yes, sir. You're definitely the man. I guarantee it."

"Well, Mr. Bruce, in that case, you have my undivided attention, sir. So, how might I assist you this morning?"

"Sir, I'm willing to bet you that I could be of great value to you."

Nick observed Chill's confidence, his demeanor, and his apparent wealth. He finally arched an eyebrow and asked, "How so?

"I was just about to inform you," Chill mentioned, and then glanced at his Rolex.

Nick pointed to the watch. "That's a nice Rolex you've got there." "Thank you, sir. The wife bought it for my last birthday."

"Nice present."

"Yeah I think so too, she's sweet like that. So, Mr. Crane, just think of me as a closer. I will help you to close any deal that comes across your desk. Now, I understand that my claim is grand, but it is also guaranteed."

Nick's skepticism faded away. He smiled. "Okay, Mr. Bruce, you have definitely piqued my curiosity. Proceed, if you will. I'm listening."

"Fantastic." Chill casually surveyed the area, and spotted nothing more ominous than a city bus passing them by in the west-bound lane. "Allow me to give you one of my business cards," he said, as he retrieved one of his professional cards from his coat pocket and handed it to Nick. "That's my line of work, sir."

He studied the man while he read the card out loud to himself.

"W.B. Financial Services, specializing in personal & business loans and mortgages. C.E.O., Willie Bruce." Nick looked at Chill and smiled. "Mr. Bruce, I think I understand you, now. By the way, this is an excellent business card."

"Why thank you, sir. It reflects my work, and myself, and believe me when I say, what I have printed on that card right there accounts for only a small fraction of the magic that I can actually perform." Chill cracked a smile, "Mr. Crane, I guarantee that you're going to absolutely, positively love the rest of what I have to offer."

Nick smiled, obviously interested. "I can imagine. Hell, I love it already!" He held up the business card. "May I keep this?"

Chill bowed his head slightly. "But of course, the card is yours."

"Thank you, my man," Nick said, as he slipped the card inside of his shirt pocket.

"You're quite welcome, of course. Could I bother you with one more question before I continue?"

"Absolutely. I see no reason not to. Inquire away," he said, as Chill moved in closer to where they were now eye-to-eye.

"Okay, sir. Are you presently, or have you ever been associated with any sort of Municipal, State, or Federal Law Enforcement agency?"

Nick suddenly appeared apprehensive. "Sir, I don't believe that I've ever been asked such a question before."

"Mr. Crane, please. You may call me, Willie. All of my friends do. Now, first of all, understand that I come to you in peace, and in the name of business," he said, as he flashed a peace symbol with his fingers to Nick, who smiled once more, much to Chill's relief.

"All right, Willie," Nick mentioned, without apprehension. "And please, call me, Nick."

Chill smiled and nodded. "Once again, it's my pleasure, Nick." He shook his hand.

"Likewise, my friend", Nick continued. "Now to answer your question, of course not, do I look like an officer of the law to you?" he asked, as he opened his coat, and displayed the absence of gun or badge. "I have never been involved with any form of law enforcement, never planned to either." He fastened his buttons.

"That's great news, Nick. Because I haven't either! Now, I will ask you this: How many clients have you had, who turned out to be a total waste of your valuable time?"

Nick sighed. "Christ, man! I lost count some years ago."

"I can imagine." Chill glanced at his Mercedes-Benz up the street near the curb. "Picture this, my man. You get a call one day from a Mr. & Mrs. Ellen and Clifford Smith. They're a cute little middle-aged Caucasian couple who live in an apartment unit somewhere right here in the San Fernando Valley. The couple decides that they want to purchase their dream-home in the range of five-hundred thousand dollars. Therefore, as the professional that you are, you do all of the necessary footwork involved."

"Yeah," Nick chuckled. "Tell me about it."

"I can imagine." Chill laughed. "But anyway, you escort the clients on a grand tour of the many prospective properties that you cover on your books. After a short while, a final decision is reached and the three of you settle into your office, where you, among other things, check their supposedly, 'wonderful' credit score."

"I know the story well, Willie."

"I am sure you do, because I hear it all of the time, but only from new clients like you. I never hear this type of a story from my clients whom I have a history of doing business with. Well anyhow, it unfortunately turns out that their credit score is so poor, that they would not be capable of financing a tricycle. Let alone, a beautiful, half a million dollar piece of property! Does this sound familiar, Nick?"

Nick was laughing and shaking his head, as he lit up another cigarette and offered Chill one. "No thank you, Nick."

"Sure. Anyway, you hit the proverbial nail right on the head, Willie. The scary thing about the scenario that you just described has, in today's troubled economy, become the rule instead of the exception. Even the co-signers nowadays are rejects. Hell, I'm barely keeping my head above water as it is, and I'm not sure as to how much longer I'm going to be able to survive in this business. In any case, there must have been thousands of these cases," he explained.

"I hear you, buddy," Chill continued. "But the good news about it is that with my assistance, this will never happen again. That's guaranteed."

Nick arched his eyebrow again and prompted Chill to continue.

Chill easily glanced at his Rolex again, and checked his local surroundings. He noticed a small group of middle-aged Korean businessmen off in the distance, who seemed normal as they walked into the law offices across the Boulevard.

"Nick, your solution is as simple, as it is effective. Continue to take in these potential clients. If one of them has a less than stellar credit score, you refer them to me. I'll use my resources to clean up their credit in no time, and send them right back to you. You close the deal. You make your commission. I make my fees directly from your client. Everyone is happy. It's an outstanding concept, isn't it?" He smiled.

Nick appeared to perform the necessary mental math. "Damn. I make my six percent in commission in the process."

"That's right Nick, my man. You make your six percent and you keep all of it, plus, whatever referral fees that you choose to tack onto my fees, which your clients will cover. However, a token of gratitude from you for my unique services, would not be at all inappropriate. Meanwhile, your client is now magically able to finance and acquire his, her, or their dream home! Everyone's happy. It sounds like a vision of paradise, doesn't it?"

Nick just laughed. "It most certainly does! And it sounds like a dream come true to me, my friend. Indeed it does."

"Well, sir. I must now ask you the most important question thus far."

"And what is that?"

"Are you interested?"

Nick smiled broadly and answered without hesitation. "Only a fool would turn down such a handsome proposal, even if only half of what you're saying is true."

"Willie, believe it or not, I have 14 clients right now who could use your immediate attention. Just tell me how to proceed. I'm very much interested."

"In that case, we can clean their files all at once, or one by one. It really makes my associates and me no difference at all. You see, Nick, our guiding principle is trust. This trust is for the process, the consumer, and in your case, the realtor. It's an uncompromising field that without which we have nothing."

Nick became overwhelmed with gratitude for his newfound friend and potential business partner. He shook Chill's hand and said, "Why don't we go inside and discuss the finer points of your proposition, in greater detail. We have coffee, donuts, and a rather diverse wet bar." He grinned.

Chill smiled as he tilted his head towards the front doors to the building. "Lead the way my friend," he said, as he followed Nick into the regal, two-story, mirrored-glass building.

*****

It was Tuesday, June 14th, the following afternoon. Chill was standing next to the trailer office of the Universal Sales Automotive Company, in Tarzana, California.

The weather was sizzling hot while he negotiated his business with the owner and his new client, Mr. Al Hakeeshi, a 56-year-old Iranian man whom Nick Crane had referred to Chill, and mentioned that Al was an unusual character, who was rumored to be devious, deceitful, and greedy.

Chill was dressed in a dark brown business suit, and held a manila envelope containing a five-page credit report, which Al had just handed him.

Al leaned up against his black 2005 Range Rover and uttered, "I can't wait to see the results, Willie."

Chill smiled, "I know you can't. Therefore, I'll be sending these reports to our home base to be processed later on this evening.

Before long, Al, this report will have an A-1 credit rating for sure. I promise you this."

Al shook his hand, "If this little transaction goes well, I've got forty more vehicle applicants who could use your expertise."

Chill smiled, knowingly. "Al, buddy, I can personally guarantee you that this is going to happen for you. It's not a question of if, but when. And I'm looking forward to serving every one of those forty applicants of yours. I also look forward to meeting other individuals in need of my services, which some of your friends might know." Chill winked conspiratorially.

"I'm looking forward to that myself." Al shook his hand again. "You're what I need, Willie. And I have to know, man. Where have you been all of my life?"

"Right here, Al. I've been right here all along, man," Chill said smiling, while he pondered the possibilities of his new business venture. "You take it easy, my friend."

"You take it easy, also," Al replied, as he watched Chill swagger across the parking lot which was filled with shiny, imported European vehicles.

Chill climbed into his Mercedes-Benz and shut the door. He then began to admire his confident reflection in the rear-view mirror.

"Yeah man, handle your business then," he whispered to himself, as he became grateful for his experiences in the military program in junior high school during which time his summer-break trainings were executed at the Marlboro Hill Military Academy, in Oxnard, California. He learned, among other things vital to his childhood, how to write and speak in the proper manner, as well as the ability to be a leader and to take charge of a situation.

Young Chill had excelled in academics and had toyed with the farfetched idea of becoming an author. That was, until the neighborhood gangs and drugs seized Willie Bruce in their relentless grip.

He never fully appreciated the knowledge that he so easily absorbed, until he found himself, today, reflecting on how he was interacting with these successful businessmen. He was able to communicate with them on their own, more sophisticated level, in their own comfort zones.

He may have been able to speak like a businessman, but he could never throw away the skill of speaking street ebonics, the neighborhood levels of his childhood homeboys.

He knew that if things continued on as they had, the future would truly be his to enjoy. "Get this money, boy," he said as he started the engine and pulled away.

On Wednesday morning, at 10:22 a.m., Chill was conducting his business inside of the executive offices of the Landmark-Trade Investment Group, located in Woodland Hills, California.

He appeared quite confident as he sat before the desk of the owner, Mr. Michael Leon. He was a 47-year-old, slender-built Italian man. He carefully handed Chill a stack of papers, and said, "Okay Willie, let's start with these five credit reports." He leaned back in his white leather executive chair and observed Chill, while he perused the first set of papers.

"This report is pretty beefy, Mr. Leon," Chill said, while he weighed the documents in the palm of his hand.

"Yeah, well, that report is 32 pages long, if I remember correctly. And that particular gentleman has a bunch of negative accounts. Therefore, Mr. Bruce, you've got your work cut out for you."

"Yeah, it's not a problem, though. After all, I receive these sorts of files all the time."

"I'm sure that you do," Michael replied as Chill leaned back in his chair and crossed one leg over the other. He wanted to make sure that he seemed relaxed, while he examined the first report. After a moment, he looked up at Michael. "I'm going to need a couple of minutes to tally up the charges. You know, crunch the numbers, Mr. Leon. Please excuse me for a moment, if you will."

"Absolutely, sir! Take as much time as you need, and please, call me Michael."

"Okay, Michael," he mentioned, while he pulled out a slim silver calculator from his gray, suit coat pocket. "And please, call me, Willie."

"Okay, Willie."

Chill began to re-examine the documents while he calculated the figures.

He easily worked his way through the five credit reports. When he finished, he removed a silver pen from his suit coat pocket, and scribbled a figure on the top page of the first report.

"Here you are, sir." He slid the papers across Michael's desk. Michael read the figure and smiled, while he silently nodded his approval, "That's a fair price you've got here, Willie. My partner, Nick Crane, he told me about your connections within the credit companies. I'm telling you, man. I am impressed! You couldn't have come in my office at a more opportune time, I tell you that! Hell, I've been waiting for someone like you to come along with your superb capabilities. You're just what I've been seeking. Hell, you're a dream come true!"

Chill smiled and nodded.

In an instant, he reflected upon the days in the early 1990's, when he was peddling rock cocaine on the street corners in his old neighborhood.

He understood then, the concept that rock cocaine sold itself, and those who possessed what was needed by the users, had the power. Those without the products were powerless and completely dependent upon him. It became the same scenario in this case, he mused, while he smiled and replied, "I know, Michael. I know, buddy. God bless America, eh?"

"Yes, sir! God bless America!" Michael chuckled, and then shared, "I had an inside man, once who worked inside of the credit bureau. He was really good too. I mean damn good! I guess that it was about three years ago, now. He was heaven sent, I tell you." Michael shook his head while he stared at his desk. "Would you believe that the guy had the audacity to die on me? Goddamn liver failure! How rude of that son-of-a-bitch, you know?" He chortled whole-heartedly.

"Let me guess, the man was a lush, right?" Chill replaced his pen inside of his coat pocket.

"Yeah, it was a horrible and protracted death, too. Hell, in his last days, his entire body turned yellow from jaundice due to the accumulation of toxins that his liver had failed to process. Manual may have drank too much, but, he made me the filthy rich pig that I am today. So, I'm thankful. God, I miss him!" he uttered wistfully.

"Of course, Michael, it's understandable." Chill nodded.

"Yeah, good old, Manual," Michael continued, and then cleared his throat as he brought his attention back to the task before him. "Anyway, Willie, you strike me as a man with a keen appreciation for money. It's no doubt about that. So, let me tell you that if you can process these credit reports for this small amount right here," he said, as he pointed to the credit-cleaning fee that Chill had written on the report. "It would be more than helpful. And this fee right here will feel paltry, compared to the humongous sums that we will be dealing with through my investment people, as well as my stock clientele."

At that very moment, the surge of adrenaline hit Chill like a powerful force, and he hoped that he was able to conceal his excitement.

"Oh really?" he asked, with forced ease.

"Man," Michael sighed, and leaned over the desk for emphasis. "This could make both of us multimillionaires!" He retreated back to his chair and rested his elbows on his cherry wood desk. "Money is what I am. I live, breathe, eat, and yes, crap money. I deal with other like-minded people also, who share my motivation. I know a million dollar opportunity when it knocks on my door. So tell me, Willie, are you ready to get paid?" he questioned. He appeared to be quite careful with his words.

"Yes, I am!" Chill calmly reached out to shake Michael's hand. "That's for sure." He glanced at his Rolex. "Look Michael, I don't mean to sound rude, but I have an impending appointment that I must attend, so, if you don't mind, shall we get down to business here?"

"Oh yeah, man, don't be ridiculous! I know that I've already talked your ear off! So let me go and get that $9,700 in cash for you." He rose from his chair and left the office.

Chill pumped his fist triumphantly and whispered, "Yes!"

At 2:36 that afternoon, Chill was sitting across the desk from the president of Macklin's Income Tax Service, in Chatsworth, California.

Fred Macklin, the 62-year-old African-American sitting opposite from him, sounded desperate. He really wanted to meet with Chill after business hours, to get his personal credit cleaned. Chill however, had other plans for the evening and seemed a bit hesitant, as he explained, "Fred, man, I don't normally do this, because I've got responsibilities at home. You know the wife and kids? On the other hand, since it is you, I'm willing to make this a onetime exception. I mean, I have to make sure that my Income Tax Consultant is happy, right?"

Fred smiled. "That you do, Son."

"Well, you need to make sure that you're ready to roll when the time comes. I really don't want to be waiting around outside of the restaurant for you."

"I promise that I won't keep you waiting, man. I'm going to have the credit reports and the $6,500, plus an extra grand for your valuable time, of course."

"That sounds cool to me, Fred. I'll see you at Charlie's tonight at eight o'clock sharp, my man. I'll be right outside of Charlie's right on Ventura Boulevard."

"I know where it's at. I got you, Chill. Don't trip," he replied, standing as well. "And thank you my brother, you're the best. You can't imagine how much I appreciate you doing this for me. I've got a lot of tax issues that I need taking care of. They're killing my credit report!"

"Fred, trust me, I know. I also know that you're going to love me."

Chill knew that he was totally in control of things.

"Going to?" Fred exclaimed. "Hell, Chill. I love you all ready, baby!"

Chill smiled as he left the office.

Two weeks had passed and Chill had considered himself to be one of the new kings of credit. He confidently felt as though he had mastered all of the major aspects involved in the illegal enhancement of an individual's personal credit report.

He was smiling as he drove south-bound in his Mercedes-Benz on Topanga Canyon Boulevard. He had recently left a profitable meeting with a credit client at his insurance office in Porter Ranch, California.

"Let me see what this fool Jo-Jo is up to?" he said, while "*A Woman's Got to Have It*", by Bobby Womack played smoothly from his stereo. He lowered the volume and fetched his cell phone on the center console.

"This boy better answer his goddamn phone," he whispered, while he carefully watched the road ahead of him and scrolled downward through the phone book. He initiated the call, once he located Jo-Jo's entry, and pressed the phone against his ear.

Within Jo-Jo's master bedroom, inside of his Tarzana Hills home, the portable phone on the nearby nightstand began to ring. The room was thick with the stench of rock cocaine smoke, and Jo-Jo and his wife were heavily intoxicated.

The two of them were totally nude and drenched in perspiration in their king-sized bed. A pornographic movie was playing on the big screen television in the corner of the plush, second story bedroom.

"Yeah," Jo-Jo uttered, as he exhaled an obscenely large cloud of cocaine smoke from his glass pipe.

He looked at Lena. "Here, baby," he mentioned, as he handed her the pipe and a disposable cigarette lighter.

She nearly dropped them, as her hands shook uncontrollably. The drug's results were quite evident, he noticed, as he carefully watched her struggle to align the flame with the end of the pipe, which dangled from her chapped and blistered lips.

After she finally made sufficient progress, she greedily inhaled the smoke. At which point, he slightly felt comfortable enough to reach over to the nightstand and answer the phone, without failing to carefully observe her every move. He didn't trust her very much when it came to her handling his cocaine. As it turned out, on more than a few occasions, Lena had stashed some rocks in between the mattress on her side of the bed.

After glancing at the caller I.D., Jo-Jo became irritated once he observed who was calling.

"Damn, babe!" he rasped. "It's that fool, Chill!"

Lena was so startled by Jo-Jo's announcement, that she dropped the red hot pipe between her legs and watched it as it instantly began to burn through the black silk sheet.

"Oh shit!" she yelped, and frantically groped for the pipe. "Ouch!" she screamed, as she mistakenly grabbed it by the hot end and flung it across the room. "Fuck!" she blurted, and then stared at her fingers. She noticed that the pipe had taken with it a thin layer of skin from her fingers as it shattered against the wall.

"Calm the fuck down, Lena! Damn! Now, shush!" he demanded, while placing his finger against his mouth. "I got to take this call, woman!"

Lena whimpered and rocked back and forth as Jo-Jo answered the phone.

"Mister Bruce, I presume?" he gurgled. "What's happenin', boy?"

"There ain't nothin' happenin'! I'm just checkin' these bucks!" Chill boasted, feeling as if he was in fact, the true king of credit. "I've just been busy raking up all this money that these folks been laying on me, that's all."

Jo-Jo observed as Lena fled into the bathroom. He suddenly heard her rifling through the medicine cabinet.

He shook his head. "How many fish you done hooked now, Chill? Because I've noticed you've been cleaning clocks ever since I let you loose on Los Angeles."

"Man, I couldn't stop the money from rolling in if I wanted to! Hell, Jo-Jo, I've done hooked four more clients this morning! I tried to call you, but you weren't there." He sighed. "I don't know, man. It seems to me like you've been tripping lately."

"Trippin'?" Jo-Jo scowled. "I heard the hell out of that!" he said roughly. "It ain't tripping when a man's trying to get a little peace and quiet for a change. This phone gets to ringing nonstop sometimes. So, with that in mind, I decided to turn the motherfucker off."

Chill smirked. "You did, huh?"

"Hell yeah, I did! "You watch, Chill. When you get to the point where I'm at in this credit game, you're going to do the same thing."

"Your phone is ringing all day and all night, huh?" Chill grinned.

He seemed doubtful as he pulled the car into a convenience store parking lot and stopped in a stall near the entrance.

"Yeah, like I said, man. These cats don't have no kind of consideration for other folks, especially while they sleeping!"

"My phone's already ringing a lot," Chill admitted candidly, as he stepped out of his Mercedes and approached the store.

When Jo-Jo finished a violent coughing fit, he came back on the line. "You ain't seen nothing but the tip of the iceberg, Chill. You wait until things really get to rolling for you. You'll see what time it is. These folks will drive you crazy!"

Chill stopped on the walkway right outside of the store's double glass doors.

"Jo-Jo, what in the hell you choking on over there, man? Are you all right? And what's up with your voice, boy? It sounds like you got a load of snot stuck up in the middle of your neck. Like it's all rattling in your throat! It sounds disgusting man, and that's for real!"

"There ain't anything wrong with my voice, boy! I'm just a little hoarse, that's all," he lied, as he observed Lena return from the bathroom with a bandage on her hand.

"Your voice is messed-up, man!" Chill pressed on. "Whatever, Jo-Jo. Just know that your voice sounds fucked-up, that's all."

Jo-Jo glared at Lena, as she began to gather up some Rock Cocaine crumbs from the shards of glass on the floor, where the pipe exploded.

He placed his hand over the receiver and yelled at her to get away from the glass!

She quickly cowered and returned to the bed and then rocked back and forth once more. She finally interrupted him and begged him for some more drugs and another pipe, but he shoved her away.

"Come on, Joseph!" she blurted, persisting to bother him.

"Chill, man, hold on a second!" he scoffed, and then dropped the receiver on the bed and screamed, "You damn dope fiend! Leave me alone, Lena!"

"Fuck you, then!" she yelled back, and jumped off the bed and proceeded towards the bathroom.

"Come here, girl!" he hollered, as he jumped off the bed and grabbed her by the arm.

Chill heard the sounds of screaming, hitting, and slapping ensuing for a few, long seconds.

He yelled Jo-Jo's name into his phone several times, and then he barely made out the unmistakable sound of Lena's audible sobbing.

"Jo-Jo!" Chill shouted again, while a uniformed police office exited the store.

The officer eyed him with a passing interest, and then he walked around the corner and stepped out of view.

Jo-Jo finally snatched up the receiver and screamed, "Shit, Chill! I'm right here, nigga'! Quit all of that goddamn hollering!"

Chill looked appalled. "What the hell am I supposed to do? I hear the phone drop, and then you and Lena gets to fighting and trippin' and shit! Man, Jo-Jo, what the hell kind of madness you two assholes got going on over there?"

"Nothing, man! Ain't nothing going on, nigga'! Goddamn!" he blurted, seeming out of breath.

"Nothing?" Chill sighed. "I heard the hell out of that! Nothing, my ass! That's some straight bullshit, Jo-Jo! Someone done got the dog-shit slapped out of 'em! I heard it myself! You and Lena done went straight crazy over there!"

Jo-Jo sighed, while he held the palm of his hand against his left eye.

"I'm telling you, Chill. This bitch of mine done got way out of line, man! Her nutty ass is the one who started this shit in the first

126

place! Fuckin' crazy ass Cambodian! You know that she had nerve enough to cold-cock me in my goddamn eye!"

Chill broke out in laughter. "She did?"

"Yeah, nigga'! Jo-Jo chuckled.

"That's crazy, man!" Chill chortled.

"Tell me about it, shit. My eye hurts like a son-of-a-bitch, too!"

Chill laughed uproariously. "Man, that's yawls business," he continued. "Anyway, check this out. I'm hauling a gang of cash in the trunk right now."

"Is that right?" Jo-Jo grinned, while his head began to throb.

"Yeah, man. I've got it hidden up under the spare tire. I've also got a check for $5,600, too. On top of that, I'm picking up some more money from a new client of mine at eight o'clock this evening. So I'll swing by your crib afterwards, between nine and nine-thirty. Is that cool?"

"Yeah it is, boy. I'll see you then."

"Okay. I'm out, fool," Chill replied.

"Later," Jo-Jo said, as he hung up the phone and stared at Lena, who was slipping into a red silk robe.

He pointed and shouted. "Where you going, girl?"

"Fuck you, Joseph!" she yelled, and then stormed out of the room.

He leaped from the bed in the nude, and then walked over to the bedroom door and locked it. "Fuck you too, bitch!" he screamed through the door while he pressed his palm against his blackened eye.

"Kiss my ass, punk!" Lena yelled back, as she stomped down the stairs.

"Punk ass!" he muttered, and then went into the bathroom to retrieve another glass pipe, and some more rock cocaine that he had in a plastic bag, which was concealed in his secret hiding spot under the sink.

He then proceeded to the bed and placed his back against his headboard. "To hell with that bitch," he whispered, and then sucked on the cocaine pipe while he watched the pornographic movie. Eventually, he started to masturbate.

Meanwhile, Chill was standing inside of the store and wondered what was happening with Jo-Jo. It was quite obvious that drugs were the problem to him.

127

"They've got to be messing with some dope or something," he mumbled as he headed for the soft drink refrigerator.

Chapter 13

"This boy is straight balling!" Chill mentioned, as he eased his Mercedes-Benz into the intricate Cobblestone driveway of Jo-Jo's ostentatious, two story, Spanish-style home.

Jo-Jo's black, late model Range Rover and Mercedes-Benz were parked in front of the four-car garage. Near the Mercedes was a customized "Hog." It was a Candy-apple red, 1951, Pan-Head Harley-Davidson motorcycle.

Beautiful machine, Chill thought, as he carefully parked behind it. He admired the Harley for a few long seconds before he stepped out of the car with two manila envelopes in his hands.

He locked the car doors and armed the alarm with his key-fob remote. The Mercedes-Benz chirped once in compliance, as he proceeded to the double door entrance with the utmost caution.

The porch was eerily dark and it made him a little uneasy, as he quickly began searching for the illuminated doorbell button.

Inside of Jo-Jo's master bedroom, the cocaine smoke hovered thick in the air a few feet above the floor. It was almost as if it were some kind of an unusual type of morning fog. It managed to irritate the matching black-eyes of Jo-Jo and Lena, who were both lying underneath the ruined silk sheet with their backs resting against the velvet headboard.

Jo-Jo's black-eye however, was by far the worse of the two. Lena had taken notice of it, and assumed that she had done a pretty good job on his face. *"Yeah mother-fucker, that's what you get!"* she mused with an evil grin,

They watched, *"Cock-Lover's Yacht Charter."* It was a popular pornographic movie, starring a beautiful Caucasian woman named, Christina Cock-Lover.

He kept the end of the pipe lit as Lena inhaled the noxious fumes.

"Yeah, baby. That's right. Keep on sucking on it. Suck it nice and slow for me. Yeah, that's right," he murmured, when suddenly, the doorbell rang.

Apparently, it must have sounded like a shotgun blast to Lena, because she screamed and convulsed violently, and then flung her arms about and accidently launched the pipe against the wall, where it once again exploded.

"Goddamn, bitch!" he shouted.

"Fuck, Joseph!" she blurted. "Who in the hell is at the door?" she continued, as she hoped out of the bed and scampered around the room like an animal fearing for its life.

Jo-Jo whispered forcefully, "Calm your ass down, Lena! Scary ass! And if you break one more of these goddamn pipes, I swear to you, I'm cutting your ass off! You understand?"

She began to whimper and sob as she rocked on her knees on the carpet. "Who's at the door?" she screamed with eyes wide open. She quickly began to bite nervously on her fingernails.

"Lena, you need to know when to be satisfied! You're too goddamn greedy, girl!" he mentioned, and then checked the time on his Rolex on the nightstand. "It's just after nine, woman! It's probably Chill's ass with my money and some paperwork that he's got for me." He slipped the heavy timepiece onto his wrist. "So quit tripping and calm the fuck down! You need to take your ass to sleep, that's what you need to do!"

He gulped from a bottle of cognac on the nightstand, and then licked his lips and examined Lena.

"Girl, you look like you're the only survivor in a goddamn airplane crash!"

He shook his head as Lena continued to rock back and forth on her knees. He observed that her tongue was swollen, and that it protruded out of her mouth from her consistent dehydration.

"Look at your crazy ass, girl!" he exclaimed. "You're sitting in there looking like a guppy-mouth fish! You've got your tongue all hanging out your mouth an' shit! You're crazy as all outdoors, Lena!" he said, shaking his head. "Just wait in here while I go deal with Chill's ass." He pointed sternly towards her. "Don't you go anywhere, and don't you do nothing! Just stay your weird-lookin' ass up in here until I come back. You hear me?"

Lena's response was a low, guttural, animal-like growl.

He shook his head and slipped into a black, silk robe and some black leather house slippers. He stared at her for a long moment, obviously disgusted, and headed down the stairs as the doorbell rang again.

Lena screamed, "Hurry, Joseph!"

As Jo-Jo reached the foot of the stairs, the doorbell rang once more. Suddenly, he heard the sound of broken glass, as it filtered downward from the master bedroom.

"Crazy ass, bitch!" he muttered, and shook his head as he stared upward at the ceiling.

Finally, he yanked open the front door and said, "Man, why in the hell are you living on my goddamn doorbell button?"

Chill scoffed and blurted, "Because nigga', you didn't answer!"

"I knew that you were coming, Chill! One ring is enough! Jesus!" Jo-Jo said, as he closed the door and embraced Chill, and then led him into his posh living room.

Chill caught sight of Jo-Jo's black eye and immediately started laughing. "Holy shit, dawg! She really touched you up, huh?"

"Yeah man, that old crazy-ass broad of mines. Boy!" Jo-Jo sighed. "She's way outta' line, man! That's all I could say about her slanted eyed-ass!"

Chill had some difficulty processing the fact that Lena, who was 5'-3" and weighed 128 lbs. could have so easily blackened Jo-Jo's eye, because of the fact that he stood at 6'-4", and weighed over 230 lbs.

"You mean to tell me that she actually hit you?" He scowled.

"Hell yeah, she did!" he admitted sheepishly.

"Is she wasted or something?"

"Yeah, Chill. She's got a real problem with rock cocaine. She doesn't know when to say when, you know? The broad done messed around and went crazy! You know what I'm saying?"

Chill shook his head in disbelief. "Both of you two are crazy!"

He looked up at the ceiling when he suddenly heard some rapid thumping sounds coming from upstairs. It sounded as if somebody was running.

"Jo-Jo, what in the hell is she doing up there?"

"The hell if I know!" he replied, as a low moan quickly rose to the scale of a blood-curdling scream. The noises sustained for more than a few seconds, and then they were immediately followed by the sound of Lena scampering down the ornate, spiral staircase. She reached the bottom of the steps and stood there in her red-silk robe.

"Just look at that weird-ass bitch, Chill!" Jo-Jo blurted, as the two of them observed her grinning wildly from ear to ear.

"I see her, man. But what the fuck is she doing?" Chill mentioned.

"I told you that the woman done lost her goddamn mind, didn't I?" Jo-Jo blurted, as they observed Lena commence to slap her left hand against her pubic area. She began to laugh while she swayed her body from side to side. Her eyes, one of which was blackened, appeared to be glazed over.

Chill and Jo-Jo appeared bewildered as they looked at one another.

"You see what I'm saying, man?" Jo-Jo finally uttered.

Chill had an expression of disbelief on his face when he answered, "Yeah man, I see what you're saying. But I've got to tell you, Jo-Jo. You and Lena's about two of the weirdest motherfucker's that I ever met in my entire life! Now I know why it took you so long to answer the fuckin' door."

He shook his head and scowled at Lena. "Damn, Lena? Are you okay, girl?"

Lena hissed loudly at Chill, and then ran back up the stairs and slammed the bedroom door behind her.

Jo-Jo made some circular motions with his hand, as the sounds of broken glass filtered down the steps once again.

"The bitch is wacko, huh?" he chuckled.

Chill laughed. "No shit! Did you see that bullshit?" he asked, as they made their way to the black leather couch.

Jo-Jo sat down. "Yeah, I saw it." She's trippin'. Anyway, have a seat. What you got for me?"

"Here, nigga'." Chill dropped the manila envelopes on the glass coffee table in front of Jo-Jo. "Man!" he blurted, and then walked over to the light switch near the front doors. "Why don't you turn some goddamn lights on in this place, man," he said while he flipped on the living room lights.

Jo-Jo covered his eyes and protested, "Man, Chill! Why'd you have to do that?"

"I did it so that we can see for more than a foot in front of us, fool! You've got it all dark and creepy up in here!" he replied, as he took a seat next to Jo-Jo.

Jo-Jo laughed as he dumped the contents of one of the envelopes onto the coffee table. A large stack of $100 bills plunked onto the table along with a personal check. He smiled to himself as Chill upended the second envelope onto the table and exposed a pile of credit reports.

"Yeah, Chill. You done did real good, boy," he rasped, while he pointed to the cash, which was wrapped in a red rubber-band. "Is all the cash here?"

"What the hell do you think?" Chill snapped, appearing mildly offended. "Of course it is nigga'! It's a total of $8,400 dollars in cash, and a check for $5,600. That's $14,000 dollars total, right?"

Jo-Jo seemed lost in ponder for a moment, and then mentioned, "It's all here, right?"

Suddenly, Chill felt butterflies fluttering around in his stomach. "Jo-Jo, are you okay, man? We just talked about this here, remember? I've got $8,400 dollars in cash. And I've got a check for $5,600 dollars," he repeated slowly, as if he was speaking to a toddler. "We do accept checks, don't we?"

"Yeah, we don't trip on checks at all. Because if we ever get a stop-payment on a check from a client whom we done already perform the work on, I'll simply undo the cleaning work and slap a bankruptcy, or civil judgment on their credit report. That'll fix their scandalous asses."

"Damn," Chill whispered.

"Yeah Chill, we can do that as fast as anything else. These folks that we deal with know the business. That's why we never trip on accepting their checks. They know that it would be all bad for them, if they tried to get slick on us, you dig?"

Chill nodded. "Yeah, I hear you. It's harsh, but necessary, I guess. But yeah, Jo-Jo, I dig what you're saying."

"You damn well better," Jo-Jo mentioned between coughing fits. "Now, let's settle up and get you your money, all right?"

Chill rubbed his palms together. "That sounds cool to me." "All right, then," Jo-Jo said, as he grabbed the wad of money from the table and counted out forty $100 bills. "Here you are, boy." He handed Chill the cash. "That's four thousand bucks for you, my brother. That's some pretty good money for only one day's work, don't you think?" he asked gruffly.

"Hell yeah, it is!" Chill agreed emphatically.

"It's only going to get greater for you, you watch. Just stay on board with me and you'll see what I'm talking about. The money's out there for you, Chill. There's plenty of it."

Chill smiled. "Believe me, man. I plan on sticking around. I ain't going anywhere!"

"Yeah boy, that's what I'm talking about! Keep on paying attention to me, and make sure that you stay as focused as you can. Also, try your best to keep your mind on nothing but, credit, credit, and more credit!" he crooned.

"Yeah, Jo-Jo, I understand. Anyway, boss. Seeing as it's Friday night, and I ain't got shit to do, I was thinking about taking Jen to Las Vegas for the weekend. I mean, if it's okay by you?"

Jo-Jo laughed and immediately had another coughing fit. "Sure. That's not a problem. You take your woman to Vegas. Y'all enjoy yourselves. You two deserve it. It gives y'all a chance to take a break from the family, you know?"

"No shit!" Chill blurted. "We'll drive back on Sunday night," he said shaking Jo-Jo's hand.

"That sounds good."

"You know, man," Chill began, while he shook his head. "Lena needs to get her ass some kind of help. Matter of fact, you both need to talk to somebody. I mean, she came down here screaming like a goddamn mad woman! Come on, man! What the fuck was all that about?"

Jo-Jo shrugged his shoulders and chuckled, "The hell if I know!"

"Man, that whole episode on the steps was weird! You and Lena's got some crazy shit going on up in this joint! I swear! I ain't lying, neither! On top of that, you've got this whole house stinking from that rock cocaine shit. Not to mention that both you guys have got those nasty-ass black eyes! You need to put a Porterhouse steak on the motherfucker!" he laughed.

"Fuck you!" Jo-Jo chuckled.

"I'm serious, man!" Chill resumed. "I mean, I just care about you guys. You two are my family, man."

Chill seemed frustrated as he slid the money inside of his pants pocket.

"Chill, you ever tried cocaine?" "Yeah I did. It was only once, though. I didn't like it, made me too paranoid. I sold enough of that shit, that's for sure. That stuff is for suckers and weak-minded motherfuckers, Jo-Jo! The dope can't be that goddamn good!" he exclaimed, absolutely disgusted.

"Rock Cocaine makes you feel like you're Superman or something. And that ain't no joke!"

Chill laughed. "Yeah, man. That is, until that kryptonite shit called reality gets a hold of your black ass. And then before you know it, you'll come crashing down to Earth like one of them meteorites. Besides Jo-Jo, I've witnessed way too many folks mess their lives off behind that bullshit. Good folks, too! Like I said Homie, I use to sell that crack shit like I had a license. It was fast money, too. But I woke-up one day, and I told myself to get my ass out the game."

"Why?" Jo-Jo asked curiously.

"One of the reasons was... I thought about how I was ruining people's lives who lived around me. You know, selling that shit to my homeboys' families an' shit."

Jo-Jo seemed to ponder while he nodded. "Yeah, Chill. I could see your point."

"Yeah, I'm sure that you can. The other reason was... I wanted to get my black-ass up out of the game before fools got to snitchin'. You know, the way they are now."

Jo-Jo thought about Chill's words for a moment, and then nodded. "I know exactly what you mean. Because these Nigga's today are trying to get themselves up out of those jail-house cases, rather than do their time."

Chill sighed. "I heard that!"

Jo-Jo paused, and then bragged, "You know that I've been up for about three days now, don't you?"

Chill sneered. "Yeah man, it looks like you have, you big dummy! It's written all over your face. You know, you guys trip me the fuck out, dawg'!" he admitted, shaking his head.

"Don't trip, baby boy. Because I'm what the drug treatment world calls, a 'Functioning Addict'. I'm totally in control of this here. You can best believe that!"

Chill chuckled. "That's a motherfuckin' lie, Jo-Jo! You're not in control of anything! All that you are is a goddamn crackhead! That's plain and simple. The only thing is… you seem to handle this shit a little better than most folks do. But your woman, man," he sighed, while shaking his head. "She's up stairs bouncing off the walls! I don't know, Jo-Jo. I hope that this crack shit don't interfere with the business that you and I have got going on. I mean, if I'm going to rob somebody. Believe me, it's going be with a pistol. I ain't trying to rob nobody by gaining their trust. That's some con-man shit. And that ain't cool at all," he said, as he stood to his feet.

Jo-Jo stood as well. "This cocaine that I'm smoking ain't got anything to do with the business that you and I have got going on. I swear! You can trust me on that, Chill!"

"I hope that it don't interfere with our business, man. Because that crack smoking that you guys are doing ain't cool at all! And you and Lena are smoking that shit like y'all some goddamn fools! It's almost as if it's the 1980's or something!" He scowled. "You're sitting here talking about that you been up for three days! Three days, my ass! I heard the hell outta' that, man! That ain't anything to be bragging about! That's crazy! Matter of fact that's just plain stupid if you ask me!"

Jo-Jo smirked. "Well, it's a good thing that I'm not asking you about my life. Because Chill, whether you know it or not, I'm a drug connoisseur. I only smoke the best shit!"

Chill laughed half-heartedly, "You're burnt the hell out, man! That's what you are!" He gave Jo-Jo some dap, and then continued, "But seriously fool, you and Lena need to get some kind of a drug intervention or something, because this cocaine smoking that you guys are doing is real bad for business, man! And that's for real!"

"I know, Chill," Jo-Jo admitted.

Chill shook his head in disappointment. "I'm outta' here, Jo-Jo," he said, as he left the house grumbling, "Stupid asses!"

The following night, Chill had returned to his Las Vegas hotel suite and was feeling in pretty good spirits. He had won $3,200 in poker chips on the Texas Hold 'em tables.

The song, "*For the Lover in You*," by Shalamar, was gracefully playing from a clock/radio on the nightstand, which he enjoyed, as he sat in bed nude underneath the sheet with his back up against the headboard.

The television on the wall displayed a popular gourmet cooking show, as he was speaking into his cell phone to Michael Leon, who was lounging in his home in the San Fernando Valley. "That's not a problem, Mike. We'll deal with that issue bright and early on Monday morning. I promise," he said, gazing out the window at the impressive expanse of the Las Vegas Strip. "I'll be heading back to Los Angeles tomorrow evening. I'm out here in Vegas right now with my wife," he paused, "Yeah, man. It's pretty nice out here right now. Although, it was hot as fish grease earlier today!" He paused again. "Yeah, no shit. I know how hot that 'Vegas get. But I did get a chance to meet a few new contacts at a Mortgage seminar today. I also won a few bucks on the poker tables. But anyway, do me a favor and hold onto that money for me. I'll see you Monday morning."He paused once more. "Yeah, Mike, that's not a problem at all my man. Later, dude," he said, before closing his cell phone.

Suddenly, Jen entered the room from the shower with some black bath towels wrapped around her head and her nude body.

Chill smiled. *Gorgeous*, he thought, as she walked over to the dresser and removed the towel from her head and draped it over her shoulders. He watched her as her beautiful, strawberry scented hair drape down her back.

Jen knew that she was heavy on his mind, as she decided upon a favored brush from the dresser, and then moved to the floor-to-ceiling mirror, where she began to thoroughly and sensually brush through her luxurious locks.

She smiled as she noticed him eyeing her in the reflection.

Chill bit his lower lip and uttered, "Mm!"

Jen giggled and asked, "So how'd the phone calls go, babe?"

Chill smiled, as he picked up the phone from the nightstand and turned it off.

"It went all right, Momma'. But I think that Mike's call will be the last one that I'm taking as long as we're here in Vegas. What do you say about that?"

She smirked. "I'd say that it's about time that we enjoyed our little vacation without your damn phone driving us crazy!"

She placed the brush on the dresser.

"What?" he blurted.

"You heard what I said!" she chuckled, while she sprayed on some Far Away perfume. "Just like I said it!" she smiled and walked over to the other side of the bed. "What, do you want me to repeat myself?" She slid underneath the sheet next to him.

Chill smirked. "Hold up a minute, Momma'! Time out here! Aren't you the one who agreed with me, when I told you that I wish that my phone would start ringing off the hook like Jo-Jo's phone be ringing all the time?" He arched his eyebrows and awaited her response.

"Of course I agreed with you, dear. And your phone is ringing a lot, now. And that's a good thing, I guess. I mean, in your new line of work it is. But babe, you have to take a break from business every now and again, right? Otherwise, you might go insane."

Chill nodded. "True that. True that," he said, as he leaned over and began to run his fingers gently through her hair. "That's what I love about you, baby. You're a very smart cookie. That turns me on, too!"

Jen smiled. "Daddy, do you really want to know what turns me on about you, other than your looks and your capable anatomy?"

"Do tell, dear. Enlighten me."

"What turns me on about you is your ability to flip a script from your neighborhood lingo, and speak like a college professor whenever you choose to. That really makes me all dizzy and hot!"

"Is that right, baby?" he blurted, and then hopped out of the bed and assumed an arrogant stance in the middle of the carpet. "You mean like this? Your verbose proclivities engage a particular aspect of my physiology, such that the exchange of fluidic ally housed genetic material is imminent! Is that what you're referring to?" He chuckled.

Jen's mouth was wide open for a moment before she broke it down for him in simple terms.

"Okay, Willie, so, what you're telling me is that you're completely turned on by the fact that I enjoy big words and, umm, it makes you want to make love to me? Is that your point, dear?"

"That's correct-o-mundo, sugar," he admitted and then jumped onto the bed.

Jen screamed as he dove on top of her. "Stop, babe!" she blurted, while he acted like he was a monster and gobbled at her legs, stomach and neck. He laughed as he continued childish play, and when he reached her face, he kissed her passionately and looked her straight in the eyes.

"You know, Momma', your golden brown skin tone is so beautiful." He watched her blush. "Yeah baby, it is!" he continued, and kissed her softly on the lips. "It's so tropical, and exotic. And you really don't need to wear any make-up at all."

"Yeah, right!" she smirked.

"I'm telling you the truth, Jen! I don't know why you even bother to put it on. All you need is a little lotion, or maybe some baby oil or something, and that's it."

"Jen smirked again. "Why nigger, are you saying that I'm ashy or something?"

"Of course not!" he chuckled. "All that I'm saying is that you look like one of those beautiful Polynesian models. You know, like you're from Hawaii or someplace exotic like that."

"Yeah, but I'm not from Hawaii! She smirked. "I'm from Cambodia, dear."

"I already know this, girl!" He leered. "I'm just saying that you're very beautiful. That's all. You do know that, don't you?" he whispered.

"Of course, I do!" she blurted snobbishly, catching him totally by surprise.

"Oh, no you didn't!" he laughed.

"Oh yes I did!" she giggled, and then arrogantly ran her fingers through her hair, as if she were an egotistical supermodel. "I was just wondering when you were going to take notice of how beautiful I am!"

Chill laughed and shook his head, "Sugar, you know, sometimes you just ain't right!"

"This is true, Willie, but I'm always right for you. And I'll always be your sugar," she told him, as he kissed her again.

She seemed to ponder momentarily, before saying, "You know, babe, coming out here for the weekend turned out to be a really good idea. I mean, we really needed to get away from the kids for a couple of days, because sometimes they drive my mom and me crazy."

"I know they do. But we needed to take a break from the hectic rat-race also, let alone, the kids. I mean, I love them to death, and I know that you do, too. But this quietness is nice, don't you think?"

"It certainly is, my love." She kissed him on his chest.

139

"Besides, when was the last time that we were able to kick back together and walk around butt-naked, without having to worry about the family? Not to mention being able to spend some quality time with each other?"

Jen pondered for a moment. "I don't know, dear. I'll have to consult with the fossil records if you want the exact date." She smiled.

"You see what I'm talking about?" He scoffed. "That's the kind of shit that I've got to deal with! You ain't right, baby, with your sexy, slant eyed ass!" he exclaimed, as he quickly began to tickle her all over her body.

"Ha-ha-ha," she giggled uncontrollably and screamed, "Stop it, Willie!"

"That's right, Momma'!" he growled. "I've got that ass now!" He smacked her softly on her buttocks.

"Baby, you've got my ass, my heart, my liver, my brain, and everything else for that matter."

"I know I do, so tell me, about how long do you think that you and I are going to be together? I hope its forever."

"I hope so, too," she whispered, and then kissed him softly on the lips. "But at our wedding, you remember? You and I solemnly swore to one another that we were going to stick it out through thick and thin, until death do us part, didn't we?"

"Yes we did, baby. But that sounds like a long time away. I mean, it could easily be more than eighty years from now, you know? I'm talking about at least eighty-plus!"

"I pray that it's eighty-plus. Okay then, I'll tell you what, Willie!" she blurted. "Eighty-plus it is then, because I couldn't stand to be without you."

"Ditto, my love," he replied.

"Now, give me some of that magic stick," she said, and then kissed him passionately.

"It's all yours, baby." He smiled, and then with practiced elegance, he positioned himself on his back and allowed her to straddle his form.

"I know it's all mine. It'd better be! Otherwise, I'll cut it off, nigger," she whispered.

Chill scowled. "Ouch! Not the dick!" he exclaimed.

She smiled sensually, "Yes, my dick," she said, as she granted his manhood an easy entrance.

The two of them moved together in an easy rhythm that was neither fast nor slow. Finally, after a prolonged period of time, they climaxed simultaneously and cuddled in each other's arms, appearing breathless and satisfied. There they napped for almost an hour.

Jen awakened first and kissed him softly on the lips. He instantly regained consciousness with a yawn and a pleasant smile. "Hello, my love," he whispered.

"Hi baby. My God, Willie that was absolutely fantastic!" she mentioned, just inches away from his face.

"Only because you made it so," he smiled.

Jen planted kisses all over his face, head, and neck. "I love you, baby," she whispered.

"I love you, too, momma. You are my Cambodian Queen, you know?"

Jen smiled. "I know, dear. So, tell me how it went over Jo-Jo and Lena's place the other day."

He sighed, "It was a mess, babe! I didn't give you the whole rundown about what went on over there, because I didn't want for you to get to worrying. You know how you get to acting sometimes."

Jen smirked. "Whatever!"

Chill chuckled. "You know, girl. But anyway, Jo-Jo and Lena are crazy! I mean, they are off the chain!"

Jen frowned, "What do you mean by that? What happened over there?" She sat upright and waited for him to continue.

"Baby, when I got there Jo-Jo had a black eye. The place was dark and creepy. And then Lena's weird-ass came screaming down the staircase. She was looking like she was a part of a freak show or something. She had a black eye, too!"

Jen couldn't believe what she was hearing and appeared shocked. "What?" she blurted, and then shook her head.

Chill grinned. "It wasn't that bad, though. Not like Jo-Jo's eye. His eye was fucked-up!" he chuckled.

Jen laughed. "What the hell are they tripping on?"

"Shit, I don't know! But the whole place smelled like that rock cocaine bull-shit."

"That's a shame!" She smirked.

"I know." He shook his head. "I'm telling you, babe. Those two fools have lost their goddamn minds. That stuff is eating them up. You should see them. It's sad."

Jen shook her head for what seemed like an eternity. "I can imagine," she finally uttered, while she toyed with her Diamond Wedding ring. "First and foremost, Willie," she mentioned, and looked him in the eyes. "I want you to know that you can talk to me about anything. I trust you, babe. You need to trust me as well. Okay?"

He tried to argue, "But Jen, I do-" She immediately cut him off before he could go on.

"You don't have to justify anything, Willie. Just know that. Okay?"

He nodded and then kissed her on the lips. "Okay," he whispered, and then lovingly embraced her. As he did so, Jen continued to ponder the situation.

"You know, sweetheart," she began, breaking the silence. "It sounds to me like those two are on a downward spiral."

"Yeah, that's true."

"And as far as addicts go, I think that Lena and Jo-Jo will have to hit rock-bottom before they will even try to seek some help. Hopefully, it'll be sooner rather than later, you know."

"Yeah, I know. I already talked to Jo-Jo about that last night. But he ain't listening, though. That boy's got a hard head."

"Well dear, you need to be real careful in dealing with him, then. I mean, at least while he's sucking on that rock pipe. You never know. He may start to slip really badly. And once that ball gets to rolling down hill, it'll take everyone down with it. That includes you, dear. Not to mention the rest of your loved ones."

"Yeah, I totally agree with you. Man," he sighed. "I love it when we can talk to one another without fighting." He smiled.

She smiled back. "That's only for this weekend, dear," she replied, with a sparkle in her eyes. "And, it's only because you were so exceptional in this bed right here!" She patted the bed softly.

"I know, huh?" He boasted.

"That's without a doubt, babe! My gosh, Willie! You were all into it! It's almost like you were starving!"

"Shit, I was!" They both burst out in laughter. "Damn girl, I'd better do what I did to you a lot more often, then!"

"It would be the smart thing to do, sweetie!" She smiled beautifully.

"Is that how you feel, girl?" he blurted, and then began to tickle her again.

"Stop, babe!" she exclaimed, and then made a token effort to escape from his overpowering grip. He finally relented and relaxed next to her on the bed.

"Damn," she murmured, as she began to rub her neck with a pained expression on her face. "Babe, I've got an awful crick in my neck. Would you be a dear and rub it for me, please?" She rolled over on her stomach.

"With pleasure, my love," he told her, and then bounced out of the bed and made a bee-line for the dresser. "Yeah, this should do it," he mentioned, while he grabbed a bottle of baby oil and returned to the bed.

He smiled, while he gazed at her well maintained buttocks. "I'm going to hook you up really well, dear," he continued, while he poured the oil in his palms, and then warmed it up by rubbing them together. "Okay, momma', here we go," he resumed, as he began to massage her neck, shoulders, and her back.

"Yes, my love," she moaned in pleasure, as she felt her muscles relaxing under the influence of his expert touch. "You are the best masseur that I've ever had, Daddy. I'm serious."

"You like it?"

"Of course I do! You're hands are like magic. You could easily get certified and have your own massage business if you wanted to."

"That's an interesting idea, baby. But I'm sure that you wouldn't want for me to be rubbing on some other woman now, would you?"

"Hell no, I wouldn't! You know, I didn't even think about that," she smirked as he continued.

"I know you didn't. Besides baby, I'm a cook."

"You're a cook?" She scowled, and turned her head and looked into his eyes.

He noticed that she appeared quite curious, and continued, "Yeah, baby. Just what I said, I'm a cook."

"Since when?" she blurted.

He smirked. "I've been cooking shit ever since I was a kid, baby. Shit, I cook dope and everything!" He chuckled.

Jen burst out laughing. "You're a nut, Willie!"

"I know," he chortled, as he continued to massage her for another thirty minutes.

When it was time for him to stop, he asked, "So, how was that my queen?"

Jen was snoring loudly.

He smiled and whispered, "I couldn't have been paid a higher compliment. Thank you, baby."

He eased the sheet over her nakedness, and then slid himself off the bed and onto a nearby lounge chair. He picked up the remote and turned off the television.

Chill pondered hard about Jo-Jo. He felt as though he really could not trust him anymore. Because, he thoroughly understood that even with family, a drug user could not be trusted, under any circumstances!

He became conflicted, although, he still needed to deal with Jo-Jo to be able to get his money, as he had been doing. He wished that he could quit worrying, but the uneasiness quickly overcame his thoughts and soul, almost like when water overwhelms the earth's surface, never stopping.

He would have done well to have taken up the practice of meditation, which had been rumored to be an effective palliative for anxiety and restlessness. However, Chill knew that he would never, at least not in this lifetime, have the patience to correctly practice the ancient remedy. He stood up and walked to the window and gazed out at the main Las Vegas Strip. Even at the late hour of 2:36 a.m., he noticed that throngs of people were easily coming and going from the myriad of fine dining and gambling establishments.

He knew that for some people, gambling was like baseball, the great American family past time. He took in a slow, deep breath, and then exhaled it slowly while he nodded. Suddenly, he was startled when Jen placed her hand on his shoulder.

He turned his head towards her and mentioned, "I thought you were sleeping, baby."

"I was. But you were thinking so loud to a point, to where I had no choice but to awaken."

He smirked at her, "You've got some crazy-ass, bionic hearing then, girl!"

She giggled, "I know. Are you okay?"

He nodded slowly. "I think so. I was just going over some stuff in my head. Anyway, onto a lighter note, you know that Jo-Jo

144

mentioned that as far as the house thing goes, we'll be out of escrow procedures and into our new home by the middle of next month."

Jen nodded. "I know that you're looking forward to it, and don't get me wrong, babe, I'm looking forward to it, too. But I need to know, are you sure about this new house thing? I mean, can we really afford $3,200 a month for a mortgage on top of the rest of our bills?"

"That ain't no problem, we'll be able to handle it, so don't trip. And you're going to love it! Just trust me."

"You know that I trust you, Willie. But... with the kind of work you're doing and all. Well, that's what I'm having my doubts about."

"I don't know what else to say to you, that I haven't already said. Everything is going to be great, baby. Believe that!"

Chapter 14

Monday morning in his posh office suite, Nick Crane sat at his desk smiling while he gazed out of the window into the clear Blue Yonder. He was pondering the possibilities of his new found success in a business, which he had not so long ago, thought was hopeless. On his desktop was a thick stack of $100 bills and several credit reports neatly placed near his computer monitor. He adjusted his office phone's cordless headset, and said, "Yeah, that's correct, Willie. I've got the cash that you require right here in front of me. I'm looking at it right now. I can even smell it. It's a total of $11,700 dollars, just as you instructed." He leaned back in his executive chair and kicked his black Alligator boots up on the desk, as he continued to stare out of his second floor window which overlooked Ventura Boulevard.

Meanwhile, Chill was standing in a Studio City gasoline station along Laurel Canyon Boulevard. He was observing morning traffic that cruised by him while he pumped fuel into his Mercedes-Benz. "So, Nick, how many reports do you have over there for me?" he mentioned into his Bluetooth earpiece.

"Here's the deal, my man. I have six reports in all. But one of them belongs to a friend of mine named Johnny Delany. He has eighteen derogatory entries. Needless to say that his credit score is abysmally low."

"The hell, you say!" Chill blurted sarcastically. "I mean, goddamn, Nick! With eighteen derogatory statements, I would usually expect nothing less than an A-1 credit rating!"

"I see that you've got jokes, huh? You must be wide awake this morning!" Nick chuckled, and was obviously amused by Chill's apparent excitement.

"I keep a joke or two in my stash. I've got to keep it light, man. Otherwise, a motherfucker might lose it, you know?"

"Yes sir, Willie. I know exactly what you mean."

"Anyway, about this Johnny D. character, damn, did dude ever pay a bill in his entire life?"

Nick chuckled. "Well, it's obvious that he may have missed a few."

Chill laughed. "He may have missed a few, my ass!"

"You're very funny, Willie."

"I know. But so is your Johnny Delany friend, with his eighteen derogatory entries!"

"Anyway," Nick smirked playfully. "I know that it's going to be expensive. But I hope it's not too much trouble for you," he said, as Chill's cell phone informed him of another incoming call. "I'll tell you what, though," he resumed. "As farfetched as it may seem, Willie. Johnny is one of my best clients. After all, with my help, he's been able to acquire numerous properties in the Canoga Park area."

Chill mused over the situation while he nodded. "It sounds workable, Nick. Don't trip. But listen buddy, I've got another call coming in. So I'll swing by your office a little bit later. Let's say, around 1 o'clock this afternoon. Is that okay with you?"

"That sounds good to me, sir. I'll see you at 1 o'clock then."

"See you soon, Nick." Chill pressed a button on the phone and answered the other call.

"Al, baby!" he blurted, as he slid into the seat behind the steering wheel. "What's happening, man?" he asked jovially, while he closed the door and fastened his seatbelt.

Al sounded excited as he sat in his office at his car lot. "You asked me what's happening, Willie? I'll tell you what's happening, young man! You know that I've got a shit-load of people wanting to get their credit cleaned, don't you?"

"I'm sure that you do," Chill responded casually.

"Yeah buddy, I do. And I need to see you, pronto! Because, I have the money for your fees right here in my desk," he concluded, breathless, it seemed.

"Is 2 o'clock all right with you?" Chill asked, as he started his car and revved the engine a couple of times. "I'd be there sooner Al, but I've got a couple of prior engagements with some prospective clients. I hope you understand."

"Of course I do, my friend. Absolutely! I mean, I can't expect to be your only client, now can I?"

"Yeah, man. I do have quite a few clients, you know?"

"Yes sir. Now, 2 o'clock is perfect with me, Willie. But listen man, you're going to want to hire an armed guard to escort you home after you leave here!" he cackled. "Because, you'll definitely be loaded down with cash, pal."

Chill chuckled. "I'm always heavy laden with cash after I part ways with my clients! Al, I'm one of the kings of this shit, baby!"

"Well now, forgive me for making assumptions, will you?" He joked.

Chill pulled out of the station and turned right onto the Boulevard. "You're forgiven, my man!" He chuckled.

Al laughed as Chill's phone indicated that he had another incoming call.

"Al, stud, forgive me, but I've got to cut this short. I'll see you at your car lot later on, because I've got to take this call. It's about money, man."

"No problem, buddy. See you soon, Willie."

"Yep," Chill said, as he checked the caller I.D. "Big Mike's ass," he mentioned, and then pressed the green call button and answered with, "Well now, if it ain't Mr. Michael Leon!"

"I'm the one and only!" Michael blurted.

"How in the hell are you, bud?" Chill asked, as he proceeded to drive into the on-ramp to the north-bound Interstate 101.

Michael was ecstatic. "I feel like a million dollars, champ!" He yawned and stretched his arms out, while he gazed admiringly out of his office window at the expanse of Woodland Hills. "We're going to make a killing off this credit cleaning shit! I'm telling you, Willie, this is good stuff that you've got going on here!"

"You can say that again!" Chill chuckled.

"Well. It's Monday, my man. So tell me, when can I expect you over here? I do, of course, have all of the essentials that we discussed previously."

Chill smiled. "That's excellent, Mike. I'm happy to hear it," he replied, while he was driving past the Woodman Avenue off-ramp. "Now, I know that I told you that I would meet with you early this morning. However, I do apologize, but as it turns out, my itinerary had to unfortunately accommodate a couple of emergencies that required my immediate attention."

"I understand."

"I know you do," Chill said, respectfully. "Would you mind if I showed up casually late, at let's say, 3 o'clock this afternoon?"

"Willie, that's not a problem at all. Shit happens, as they say. But I'll look forward to seeing you around 3 o'clock, then."

"That's great, Mike. Thanks a lot, buddy. I'll see you then."

"Okay, bud."

"Peace out." Chill ended the call.

Later that morning, he was seated inside of an executive office at the Capital Mortgage Resale Corporation, conveniently located in Los Angeles' Mid-Wilshire District. He was there meeting with Tony Kin, the overweight, 32-year-old Cambodian cousin of his wife, Jen.

On the desk was a small pile of credit reports situated near the telephone.

Chill noticed that Tony seemed to be quite desperate, as he pleaded, "Come on Chill, man! You got to help me out here. I'm dealing with the Lacy Camp! "The Family," man! Those crazy-ass Nigga's ain't playing, neither!"

"I know they're not, fool! I know them cats!" Chill blurted, while he mused over the situation.

As it turned out, he had gone to grade school with the youngest brother, Izzy Lacy. He knew that he was a cold-hearted gang member from a local Crip neighborhood. He knew of the other brothers as well.

"I know you know 'em, too, Chill. But damn, man. I've got to have these eight credit reports processed within the next ten days." Tony knew that without a doubt, "The Family", as people referred to them, was a group of eight, merciless African-American male siblings, who were residing in South Los Angeles. "The Family" had acquired a nice sized fortune from the heavy sales of rock-cocaine in the early 1980's. Legend has it "The Family" was also known to commit a homicide or two when things didn't go as planned. With that in mind, Tony continued, "Otherwise, Chill, my deal with "The Family" is off, and it's my ass that's on the line here. I'm serious, man! "The Family" ain't fucking around! Please help me out, will you?"

"Goddamn, Tony! What the hell is going on here? You know how them fools get down! Why are you even dealing with them cats?"

Tony shook his head and spread beads of perspiration all over his desk. "I already know how they operate, man. But, I can't get into that shit right now. I will tell you this though, I've got to do something! It's a hell-of-a-lot of money involved in this transaction. I mean, it's some dangerous shit that I'm dealing with here."

Chill nodded. "It sounds like it is."

"I'm happy that you agree with me!" Tony smirked. Although he seemed relieved that Chill appeared to be leaning towards helping him out with his dreadful predicament.

He pointed at Chill. "And that's why I really need your help on this one. Face it, Chill. I don't know who else to turn to. I really don't. I mean, you are one of the kings of credit, right? Ain't that what you told me? You said you would never turn a credit cleaning job down? You even said that you could straighten out anything."

"Don't screw with me, Tony!" Chill blasted in a no-nonsense tone. "You know the business, man! All this rushing shit, that's a no-no, buddy! You already know this, fat-ass!"

Tony chuckled, "Listen man. I already know your policy. I know how you don't like being rushed. But please Chill, I'm begging you! Help your family out, dawg."

"Okay, Tony. Goddamn!" he blurted. "But miss me with all that family shit that you're talking about, this is business, family ain't got anything to do with this."

"Okay, okay, Chill. I'm sorry, man," he pleaded. "Jesus, thanks a lot though. I know that it's kind of on a last minute notice. But could you please make sure that all the files have got a Triple-A credit rating?" he requested, breathless.

"Yeah, Tony, but calm your big ass down, okay? I don't want for you to drop dead on me. Because it looks like your fat ass is way out of shape. You need to work-out or something."

"I know, huh?" Tony grinned, sheepishly.

"Now, the Triple-A credit rating isn't the problem here. What is the problem, fat boy, is the time allotment that you're working with. I can't stand being rushed and you know damn well that sixteen days is the minimum for a deal like this one. Sixteen days, Tony, no sooner, man! I mean, we're talking about some thick-ass files here. Eight of them, no-less," he informed, sternly.

Tony sighed. "I know. But check this out. I'll pay you four times the regular fee for your services. How does that sound, family?" He grinned.

Chill's eyes flew wide open, as he whistled in disbelief. "Four times my regular fee?"

Tony smiled. "Yep! I'll even turn you onto some other things that I've got going on."

Chill smiled as he reached across the desk and shook his hand. "Of course now, nothing is written in stone here. But boy, Tony…" He shook his head. "You really are in some deep shit, aren't you, boy?"

"Yeah, man. I'm in some deep, deep shit, man!" he sighed. "You just don't know."

"Oh, yes, I do. Okay, yeah, I'll get them done. I'm telling you, though. Your ass is getting taxed on this one. But yeah, I'll do it."

Tony's body went slack, as he released an enormous sigh of relief. "Thank you, Chill. Thank you very much, man. You're saving my life, you do know that, don't you?"

"Yeah, man. Because you're dealing with some goddamn fools! Those cats don't be fuckin' around, but anyway, don't thank me yet. I need that money, fool, and I mean, I need it right this minute!"

Tony blinked, seeming stuck for a moment. "Oh yeah, Chill, the money. Of course, man. It's right here," he said, as he opened a drawer in his desk and placed four stacks of brand-new $100 bills on the desk top. Each stack was wrapped with the original bank strip, which read, "$10,000, U.S.D."

Chill seemed shocked. "Holy shit, Tony! Where'd you get this money?"

"Don't ask, don't tell," he winked.

Chill smirked. "You're killing me today, man. You know that, right?" he mentioned, as he began to remove the paper strips from the money. "This cash better not be traced either, you fucker," he whispered, while he loaded his attaché case with the loose bills, and then rested it on the corner of the desk.

"Don't trip, Chill. I wouldn't do you like your old scandalous ass partner, C-Dub, did me and my homeboys when we were in the Pen."

Chill grinned. "Fuckin' C-Dub!"

"Yeah, man. Fuck that nigga'! That fool really fucked us over on the yard back in Placerville that one time."

"He was scandalous, huh?" Tony sighed. "Tell me about it. That fool stole our dope. You're damn right he's scandalous, that bald-headed, black motherfucker!"

Chill chuckled. "Yeah well, you're still sitting here trippin' off of that situation. But it seems to me, that you failed to remember that it was I who paid you slant-eyed gooks for my man's actions!"

Tony drummed his fingers together and smiled while he stared at the desk. *What an embarrassing moment*, he thought.

Chill immediately recognized Tony's discomfort and continued, "I'm sure that you remember how you charged me for that shit, don't you, Tony? You charged your own people! So don't come at me with that 'family' bullshit, hell, you're the scandalous one!"

"I apologize for that, Chill. But you're the one who stepped up to the plate and offered it to me. So, I had to accept your money."

"No shit, you did, fat boy!" Chill chuckled.

"Besides, it wasn't all my investment in that deal. There were two other homeboys involved in that buy. However, that was just business, Chill." Tony smiled.

"Business, my ass." He scowled.

"But anyway, dawg'," Tony began, and pointed towards Chill's attaché case. "That money right there in that case is as untraceable as Jimmy Hoffa's dead body."

"It'd better be, asshole."

Chill paused for a moment, as he reminisced about his buddy, C-Dub. He suddenly grinned. "Yeah, man. But good old C-Dub's ass is probably through with money by now."

Tony laughed. "That's right! I heard a little something about that kidnapping charge that he was facing from my cousin."

"Which cousin?"

"Chandy, the skinny one. He told me that he was in the county jail with that nigga' a short time ago. He said that C-Dub was looking all stressed out, like he was really going through it. He said that he lost a whole lot of weight. I wonder what ever happened with that case."

"I don't know." Chill wondered about C-Dub himself, as he had not heard anything about him in a while.

"Anyway, Tony. I'm only doing this one time favor for you and that's only because you're a part of my wife's family. If you were anybody else, I would tell you to take that pile of cash back to the cops who gave it to you. You dig what I'm saying?" Chill mentioned, and then opened his suit coat and displayed a holstered 9mm semi-automatic pistol.

"Whoa, Chill!" Tony exclaimed. "There's no funny shit going on here, I swear to you, man!" He waved his hands in the air in front of him.

Chill closed his suit coat and smiled. "Don't trip, Tony" He playfully reached across the desk and slapped Tony on his shoulder. "Because if I thought that you were doing me dirty, I'd blow your goddamn brains out."

"Dude, what the hell happened to your arm?" he asked, as he pointed to a dirty bandage that Tony had wrapped around his left wrist.

Tony sighed and lifted his coat sleeve. "You mean this?" He exposed the injured area.

"Yeah, fool, what the hell happened?"

Tony sighed again. "Man, Chill. It was some weird-ass shit! I mean, I was minding my own damn business in the club one night. I was just starting to get at this Mexican broad, when suddenly this fucking black dude jumped up and stabbed me in the arm. The motherfucker did it for no reason at all."

Chill laughed. "He stabbed your fat ass for no reason, huh?"

Tony chuckled, "Yeah, man. I'm serious, Chill! I didn't do anything to that dude. He tripped out on me for no reason. I swear he shocked the hell out of me."

"Yeah, Tony, I bet he did," Chill laughed. "And I remember what you told me that happen to you last month, too. You said that this guy punched you in the eye inside of a video store. I guess that was also for no reason at all, huh?"

"Hell yeah it was. I didn't do anything to that dude. I was just checking out some porno."

Chill laughed. "I don't know, Tony. If you ask me, you might want to leave that liquor alone. The alcohol seems to be your main problem. That's why you keep getting into all of this bullshit."

Tony sighed, "Why doesn't anybody believe me, man? Damn, I didn't do anything to that cop. That goddamn police just punched me in the eye for no reason at all. Just all out of the blue, you know?"

"Yeah, Tony, I know," he chortled.

"You're laughing an' shit! But I'm serious, Chill. I was minding my own damn business!" He quickly became visibly upset by Chill's nonstop laughter. "Chill man, this shit ain't funny! I've been going through this ever since I can remember," he pleaded.

Chill's eyes were filled with tears, as he struggled to regain control of himself. "Tony, you are definitely in denial. I ain't talking about a river in Egypt, neither!"

Tony shrugged his shoulders. "I don't know anything about any rivers in Egypt. But I do know that I need a drink."

Chill shook his head as Tony reached inside of his desk drawer and produced a large bottle of cognac and two shot glasses. He placed a glass in front of Chill, who politely declined.

Tony shrugged his shoulders and brought both glasses before him. "Are you sure you don't want a drink, man?"

"Yeah Tony, I'm good, man!" Chill blurted, waving him off dismissively.

"Okay, if you say so."

He filled them up until they overflowed and then gulped them both.

"Damn fool!" Chill whispered.

Tony repeated the process, and then burped rudely. "Mm, much better," he slurred.

Chill shook his head. "Tony man, I know that it ain't any of my business. But you're my folks, and what I'm seeing right now worries me. You're at work, you goddamn douche-bag. What the hell are you doing getting drunk, you idiot?"

"What I'm doing is controlling my emotions. That's what I'm doing. It's all chemistry, Chill. You sure you don't want a shot?"

Chill shook his head. Not as an answer to Tony's question, but as a reaction to his pathetic state. "Man, Tony!" Chill exclaimed and crinkled his nose. "Something sure smells funky up in this joint. Jesus! Is that you?"

He jumped out of his chair and approached Tony and smelled him.

"Goddamn, man!" he blurted, and then he stopped suddenly and pinched his nose. "Fuck!" he mentioned, as he retreated several feet and gagged. "What the hell, Tony? You smell like a shit pizza with extra mozzarella!

Tony blinked. "Whatever, Chill! I don't stink! Your ass is trippin'," he laughed.

"You're a damn lie! I ain't trippin'. I'm serious, man! You smell like a goddamn pigeon-coop, Tony! I can't believe that your co-workers haven't mentioned anything to you! Because you are funnn-key!"

Tony sighed. "Actually, two of them did say something, but those two knuckleheads enjoy hating on ballers. They live to say things that get into my head. It's like fucking terrorism."

"Man, when was the last time that you scrubbed your stinking ass?"

"This morning, asshole! I take a shower every day!"

"Damn! Well, you need to take another one! And use some soap this time. You need to scrub your fat ass with some Tide or something!"

"Fuck off, Chill!" Tony laughed.

"I don't know what to say, dawg'. 'Cause it smells like you found something this morning, did you grab a dirty diaper up out of the trash can and swallow the motherfucker!"

Tony continued to laugh. "Shut up, Chill! You're an asshole, you know that?"

Chill smiled. "Yes, I've been told."

"Anyway, man," Tony resumed, "I really appreciate your help on these reports. I mean, these Lacy cats are serious folks!"

Chill stopped pinching his nose and looked at Tony pityingly. "I know this. But tell me, Tony, what in the hell happened to you, man? I mean, this is not the Tony Kin that I came to know and like. What the hell is your malfunction, dude? Because it looks to me like you're losing it."

Tony had an uncomprehending expression on his face. "So, you'll be able to get these credit profiles finished in less than ten days, right?"

Chill suddenly appeared upset and jabbed a finger at him. "How many times do I have to tell you not to use that word?"

"What word, Chill?"

"Profile, man! Can't you comprehend? That's like going into a Head shop and asking the salesman for a goddamn cocaine pipe! Shit, you'll be lucky if you only get your ass kicked out of the store and never allowed back in! You get what I'm saying, man?"

Tony nodded, while Chill continued, "This stuff is serious, Tony! Stop saying that word, especially when you're talking over the telephone!"

Tony placed his palms above his shoulders and pleaded, "I'm sorry, Chill. I'm a little slow sometimes and I forget stuff. Please, allow me to rephrase that. So, you'll be able to finish those credit reports in less than ten days, right?"

"Yeah, Tony, shit! Man, why did you get yourself in such a messed-up jam like this in the first place?"

Tony Kin was silent, as he stared at a photograph on the wall of him and his wife, Ruth, Jen's 29-year-old, Cambodian friend.

He suddenly remembered how wasted he was on that hot summer night. He was dressed in a black suit and had tomato and fish sauce all over his white dress shirt. His smile seemed to be forced, as he sloppily draped his arm around Ruth's shoulders. He could only remember bits and pieces of that evening at one of his relative's wedding reception, which was hosted at La-La's Asian Restaurant and Banquet hall, in Long Beach, California.

"Anyway, Chill, do we have a deal, or what?" he finally asked.

"Shit yeah! For forty grand, who wouldn't solidify a deal?" he said, as he reached across the desk and shook Tony's hand.

"That's what I'm talking about, man!" Tony smiled, and then let out a huge sigh of relief. "You don't know how much this means to me."

"I already know, Tony. But, do me a favor, though."

"What's that?" he asked curiously.

Chill chuckled. "Try to keep your face out of shit, okay?"

Tony smirked. "I'll do my best. That's scout's honor, I promise," he replied, holding up two fingers.

"That sounds good. Also Tony, I want for you to try to back up off the liquor. I mean, especially while you're at work, you dip-shit!"

Tony scoffed. "Shit, that'll be a cold day in hell if I do!" He chuckled. "Because I needs my juice, you know." He burped.

Chill laughed and reached across the desk to shake his hand, but Tony suddenly appeared to be nauseated. "Oh, shit!" he exclaimed.

"What's the matter with you, man?"

"It's my stomach, man!" He gagged, and then made a mad dash out of the door in route for the employee's restroom.

Chill laughed and shook his head and let himself out of the office.

Three weeks and two days had passed, and it was a beautiful Saturday morning in the hillside city of Tarzana, California.

Down the street at the end of the block from Jo-Jo and Lena's house, was a Hauler's moving truck parked in front of the Bruce's new two-story, five-bedroom home.

Two very hard-working Caucasian men employed by the company, were unloading the truck and gingerly carrying its contents into the house.

Chill had his Mercedes-Benz, along with Jen's brand new black 2005 Cadillac Escalade parked in the open four-car garage.

The Haulers' employees were a father and son team by the name of Carl, age 47, and Ralph, 20 years old. The men were in the process of carrying a brand new, white-leather couch down the truck-ramp. "I've got this end, dad. You watch your step there," Ralph advised, as the two of them carried the couch through the front double doors.

Jen was smiling while standing in the middle of the living room, and politely directed the men to place the couch against the wall across from the fireplace.

Chill was enjoying the sight of his wife's happiness, as he observed the men with his arm draped around Jen's shoulders.

"How's that, Mrs. Bruce?" Carl asked, and moved so she could view the furniture setup.

"That's perfect. That's very good, Carl. I want to thank you guys."

"You're welcome, ma'am," the two of them said in unison, and then headed back to the truck.

"Is my queen satisfied with her new castle?" Chill asked, as the two of them surveyed their new contemporary furnishing.

"Well, it's really too big for us, dear." She turned toward him and hugged him tightly. "My God, we've got all of these big rooms in here! We're going to have to rent some of them out!" she snickered. "But, to answer your question, Willie, yes, I love this house. I also love you, very, very much, dear."

"I love you, too, Momma'," he mentioned, and kissed her passionately.

Chapter 15

On August 22, 2005, the charming seven-bedroom, Claremont Cordova Ranch home of Jesse "Boss-Hogg" Braxton, seemed normal and peaceful during the mid-day hours. The grounds keepers, a family of male Koreans were busy manicuring the property when suddenly the atmosphere was disturbed.

The father of the family noticed it first and warned his sons, as four drab-colored Crown Victorias loaded with dangerous-looking men; all Caucasian, crept up the extended black-top driveway in route to the mansion.

The family observed the words, "U.S. Government", that was printed on the license plates, as the Federal Secret Service agents drove past them and stopped in the circular section, directly in front of the main house.

Meanwhile, inside of the home, the spectacle was being witnessed through the front window by a rather frightened Boss-Hogg, an overly obese, 52-year-old African-American male, and also a full-time credit defrauder.

Vicky, his corpulent, 50-year-old Hispanic-American wife, stood near his side in a state of panic.

The two of them were staring dumbfounded as three tall men emerged from two of the cars and walked toward the front door.

"Who in the hell are these guys?" Boss-Hogg asked nervously.

"I don't know, Jesse. But they look like they could be some F.B.I. Agents. But why would they be here? What in the hell is going on?"

"The fuck if I know!" he snapped.

Supervising Special Agent, D.W. Dobbs, the 65-year-old field commander, along with two of his lesser agents approached the front door and rang the doorbell.

Boss-Hogg caught sight of the white, 10-Gallon-cowboy hat that Dobbs wore. He noticed the official law enforcement badge which hung from a thin silver chain around his neck.

He suddenly felt nauseated. "Dear God, Vicky! It's the Secret Service!" he whispered, visibly shaken.

Vicky gasped and covered her mouth, and began to pray in Spanish.

The doorbell rang again and was followed by heavy, prolonged knocking.

"Damn!" Boss-Hogg whispered, as he and his wife moved to the door and peered through its glass window.

"You've got to open it, Jesse," she pleaded.

He nodded. "God help me," he whispered and put on his best, cordial and relaxed face before opening the door. He attempted to fake his surprise upon the sight of the three men on the porch. "Oh, my God!" he blurted. "Good afternoon, gentlemen! How may I help y'all?"

Agent Dobbs glared at him while the other agents drew their weapons simultaneously and stormed into the home.

They began barking orders for Boss-Hogg and Vicky to lay face-down on their waxed, teakwood floor in the center of the foyer.

Agent Dobbs handcuffed Jesse Braxton, and then when he saw that his hysterically crying wife was also similarly secured, several more agents charged through the house in different directions.

After a short time, one of them shouted, "Clear!"

Agent Dobbs holstered his sidearm and the other men followed his lead.

The two terrified homeowners were ordered to remain lying face-down on the floor.

Boss-Hogg finally broke the silence when he shouted, "What the hell did I do? And why are you guys doing this to my wife and me? You all are trippin'!"

160

Agent Dobbs crouched down near Boss-Hogg's head and looked over at his wife.

"I'm supervising agent, D.W. Dobbs. I'm employed by the U.S. Secret Service, ma'am," he said, as he tipped his Stetson hat to Mrs. Braxton, who quickly began to sob with sickening, heaving and sucking sounds.

"I don't give a shit!" she yelled.

Dobbs smiled. "I know you don't, ma'am. But anyway, we came all the way out here to the boondocks, just to see y'all and make sure that y'all are getting along all right. I see that y'all haven't been going hungry out here! It doesn't look as if y'all have been missing any meals, I can see that," he chuckled."

Boss-Hogg struggled vainly against his restraints. Dobbs noticed this and uttered, "But really y'all, I'm here to execute a federal arrest warrant on you, Mr. Braxton. You sir, are under arrest for credit fraud and a whole slew of other securities violations."

"I ain't done any of that shit!" Boss-Hogg yelled.

Agent Dobbs smiled. "Clearly now, Mr. Hogg, you may explain all of that information to the Federal Magistrate himself. His name is Thomas L. Bradshaw. You'll be visiting him real soon, son. I guarantee you that."

Dobbs turned his attention to Agent Velar, a middle-aged man. "Velar!" he exclaimed.

"Yeah Boss?" he replied, and stepped forward.

"Unhook the lovely wife here. We're not charging her with anything, as of yet, anyway. She's free to eat some more, if she likes," he chuckled.

Agent Velar found his comment humorous while he removed Vicky's handcuffs and helped her to struggle to her feet.

"Y'all ain't right for treating my wife like that, man! She ain't done nothing, either!"

Agent Dobbs tipped his hat to Mrs. Braxton again. "Please accept our sincere apologies, ma'am. You see, it is our standard operational procedure. We have to secure anybody and everybody until we work out the who's-who and what's-what, you know?" he explained.

Vicky hollered, "You bastard!"

"I know, ma'am. You enjoy the rest of your day Mrs. Braxton." He laughed as he tipped his Stetson and proceeded to escort Boss-Hogg toward the back of the nearest Crown Victoria in the driveway.

Vicky trundled down the steps behind them and shouted," Don't worry, Honey! I'm going to call your attorney and tell him what the hell is going on out here! I love you, Papi!"

"Yeah sweetheart, call Larry Pearlstein! And quick! Otherwise, I'm fucked!"

Agent Dobbs looked over his shoulder at Mrs. Braxton. "I have to tell you ma'am. Attorneys don't do any good for cases as airtight as this one."

As they approached the rear door of the Crown Victoria, Agent Dobbs told Boss-Hogg, "And for the record, fat boy, you were right about one thing- you are fucked!"

He doubled over in laughter as agent Velar secured Boss-Hogg inside of the car.

Two days later, the space was quiet and gloomy inside of the Federal Metropolitan Holding Center's interviewing room. Boss-Hogg was upset with a massive headache, as he sat anxiously at a steel table in the middle of the room.

He sighed and whispered, "Damn," as he shook his head and stared blankly at his personal cell phone on the table in front of him. The time on the phone indicated 9:41 a.m., and attached to it was a high-tech, digital tapeless recorder. Also in front of him was a cold cup of coffee, a half-pack of Menthol filtered cigarettes, and a burning cigarette in a full astray, which permeated the room.

He was dressed in a two-piece, beige khaki uniform that was saturated with sweat. He knew that he was in serious trouble.

Agent Dobbs entered the room with a big smile on his face.

Boss-Hogg smirked when he noticed his black business suit, which was neatly pressed.

Dobbs positioned himself near the tape recorder on the other side of the table. He seemed to be in deep thought with one of his arms folded across his chest and his right hand placed against his chin. "Mr. Braxton," he began, shaking his head, "it's obvious that you're far from being a stupid man. However, for some strange reason or another here lately, you've been making some extremely stupid decisions. Oh, wait." He nodded. "I think I know why. Yeah, it's probably because you're fat, lazy, disgusting, and a greedy asshole!" he shouted. "Yeah, that's got to be it!" he blurted, as he slammed his palm down against the table.

Boss-Hogg appeared startled.

Dobbs smiled. "Lordy, big fella', you were lost, but now, thanks to me and my influence with the United States government, you have the opportunity to be found. I must warn you, though. You have only this one chance to prove yourself, Mr. Braxton. Just one chance."

Boss-Hogg scowled. "What do you mean I have one chance to prove myself?"

"What I mean is, fat ass," Dobbs snapped, "is that you've got to prove to me exactly how bad that you want your liberty. And then maybe, just maybe, I'll save your Black-ass from serving a shit-load of time in Federal prison!"

He observed as Boss-Hogg pondered his no-win situation.

"Yeah, Jesse, you get my point." Dobbs smiled. "Therefore, you're going to call your so-called, protégé, Mr. Joseph "Jo-Jo" Milton. And you're going to tell him about what you and I previously discussed. Otherwise, as old as you are now, your hefty ass will never get out of prison."

Boss-Hogg dropped his head and squeezed his eyes shut.

"Yes, that's right, fatty!" Dobbs clapped his hands and rubbed them together. "We've been onto you for four long years now. And you can thank your partner, Mr. Joseph Milton for that."

Boss-Hogg looked him straight in the eyes and blurted, "What in the hell do you mean by that?"

"What I mean is that, because of Jo-Jo's loose and drunken tongue, we know everything there is to know about you and your little credit-cleaning operation," he gloated.

"Holy shit, that loud-mouth, out-of-pocket asshole! I'm so fucked!" he blurted, while he shook his head and lit another cigarette.

Dobbs noticed how badly that his prisoner's hands trembled, as he grabbed the cup and gulped down the rest of the coffee.

"You need to slow down, lard-ass!" he snapped. "Jesus man, take some time to enjoy the coffee!"

Boss-Hogg sighed as he sat the cup back on the table.

"Now, calm your ass down, man, because, you won't be as fucked as you think you are. Not as long as you do what the hell that I tell you to do."

He shot Boss-Hogg a sinister look and continued, "Mr. Hogg, I've been looking forward to this day right here, with you in this room, for an awfully long time now. Yes sir. Because I know that

163

you're the real king of credit. Hell, everyone knows that you're the middle-man, the true liaison between the streets and the programmers who work inside of the credit companies. It's no secret that you've got them all dancing in the palms of your chubby, monkey-ass hands. Trust me, there are no more secrets. We know all there is to know about you. Probably more than you know about yourself."

Boss-Hogg shook his head as his mind raced at a thousand miles per hour.

"We've got the complete work-up on all of your associates as well, all of them. I thought that you would want to know that. I'm talking about the ones that you've got working in three different states, no less," Dobbs chuckled.

"Man," Boss-Hogg sighed.

Dobbs snickered, "You're absolutely proud of your work, aren't you? Anyway Boss, you'll recall what I mentioned to you in front of your lawyer, the eminent, Mr. Larry Pearlstein, Esquire, don't you?"

Boss-Hogg nodded reluctantly.

Dobbs smiled. "Yeah, I know how you feel, man. But yeah, I've got to give you credit, though. Because what you had going on was a clever little scam. It was, indeed. Although, I've got to tell you,… I've encountered better, much better. But that's neither here nor there." Boss-Hogg scoffed.

Dobbs grinned. "Yes, Mr. Braxton, I'm sure that you do. We know all about your little street representative, Mr. Milton. And compared to the average street thug, he's excellent at what he does. But to me and my boys in the Justice Department, he's nothing but another street punk. Shit, he's certainly no match for us, not at all. Not the Federal government." he continued, as he watched Boss-Hogg stare blankly at the table with his head hung in shame. "Did you know that he was a crack head?"

Boss-Hogg blurted, "Nah, man!" He lied. "That's news to me."

Dobbs chuckled, "I seriously doubt that, Mr. Braxton. You're a liar!" he shouted, as he verified the connection between Boss-Hogg's cell phone on the table and the tape-recorder. "But that's strange that you would deny that. I mean, because Milton shows all of the clinical signs of substance abuse. It seems to me that a man as sharp as you would've noticed that."

"Man, if I had known that Joseph was still fucking with that bullshit, I would've cut his sorry-ass off a long time ago!" he admitted, shaking his head, and then stared agent Dobbs in his eyes. "Would you believe that I've been babysitting that boy for years now?"

Dobbs smiled. "Yeah, I know, Jesse. It's been eight long years, to be precise. Mister, Godfather!" He laughed.

"Godfather?" Boss-Hogg scowled, seeming surprised.

"That's right, fuck-head! I said, Godfather. Oh, what? You seem a bit taken aback that I would know this information," he laughed.

"Actually Dobbs, yes, I am. How'd you know that?"

"Come on, Jesse, It didn't take Sherlock-fucking-Holmes to find that out. It was quite elementary, really," he quipped. "The investigation was aided, ironically, by Joseph Milton himself. You see, he loves to boast and run his fucking mouth. On top of that, if you mix in some strong hooch, and perhaps, a little cooch, boy oh boy, he'll tell ya' everything you ever wanted to know. He's terrible at handling his liquor."

He paused while he analyzed Boss-Hogg, who seemed to be fuming.

"That's right, fat-ass, get mad, go on!" he shouted. "Anyway, Mr. Braxton, one of our female operatives, she's a gorgeous little number," he said, shaking his head. "Beautiful creature, I tell ya'!" He smiled. "Man, she's got these stunning baby-blue eyes, and this long, golden blond hair. Man!" He blurted, and shook his head again. "I believe that she stands about 6 feet tall. Somewhere there-a-bouts, I'd say. She's amazing!"

"I get it, Dobbs! Just tell me about Jo-Jo's punk ass!"

Agent Dobbs glared at him. "Okay, Jesus! Anyway, it was at a New Year's Eve celebration, 2000, matter of fact. She was looking lovely, too! She had positioned herself near Mr. Milton, while she sipped on her cocktail. I forget the name of the nightclub, but it was located in Beverly Hills somewhere. Anyhow, the shit that Joseph bragged to her about, man," he sighed. "It was some things that most people in your line of business, would only divulge at gunpoint. I mean, up under extreme pressure! Some torture, you know?"

"What kind of things did that nigga' talk about?" Boss-Hogg blurted.

Dobbs snickered. "Man, Joseph flaunted on and on about him being the king of credit. About how he had a fat-ass Godfather named, Jesse "Boss-Hogg" Braxton. Yes, according to him, you had some loyal insiders working for the credit companies, presumably in Dallas, Texas, who were employed on you all's payroll. He bragged about how someone could have their credit report purged of all their negative information. He even mentioned something about how some new, positive credit accounts could be easily added on." Agent Dobbs shook his head. "Hell, he even mentioned to her that during the past seven years, he had never had a single dissatisfied client. On top of that, do you know that clown even had the audacity to proposition our charming female operative?" Agent Dobbs laughed for a long time, while Boss-Hogg scowled at the table.

"The nerve of that arrogant asshole!" he resumed. "He even invited the foxy lady to join him at his home with his cute little Asian wife."

"Lena," Boss-Hogg grinned and shook his head.

"Yes, Lena, with her cute little self," Dobbs continued. "That dude had promised our agent a wild night of cocaine and let me see how that butthead said it", he mentioned, as he glanced upward at the ceiling. "Ah, yes," he smiled and pointed at Boss-Hogg. "He invited her to a fabulous-fantastic-fuck-fantasy, that's the combination of words that he used."

"That's Jo-Jo's ass for you! He always thinks with his dick. Fuckin' asshole!" he sneered.

"Tell me about it, fat boy!" he chuckled. "I've got the whole video right here. See it for yourself." He reached inside of his coat pocket and removed a small digital video recorder. "Check this out," he said, as he placed the recorder on the table near Boss-Hogg's cell phone.

Boss-Hogg glared at the small camcorder. "What the fuck is that?"

Dobbs smiled. "This here is your boy, Jo-Jo, running his goddamn mouth! As always," he commented, while he positioned the display screen in Boss-Hogg's line of sight. "Are you ready to see this?" he grinned.

Boss-Hogg scowled. "Just play the goddamn thing, will you?"

"Okay, fat-ass!" Dobbs chuckled. "I'll play it. You just pay attention, and learn something! Now Jesse, here we go."

He smiled, as he pressed the play button on the camcorder. "Watch closely now, asshole!" he blurted, and then stood there with his arms folded across his chest. He seemed to be enjoying the sight of Boss-Hogg's frown, while he glared at the viewfinder screen.

It was a chilly New Year's Eve, December 31st, 2000. The ostentatious Beverly Hills' Le' Hot Club on Kindle Lane was crammed with well-to-do intoxicated party-goers. The digital clock on the wall behind the extravagant liquor bar indicated: 11:59 p.m., and every one of the well-dressed partiers was filled with excitement, as the countdown to the New Year was about to begin.

Special agent, Brittany Casey, the 31-year-old and statuesque blond, was dressed in a black business suit and matching pumps. She was enjoying the evening as she sat on a stool in front of the bar, and was nursing a non-alcoholic Shirley Temple beverage. She was deftly eyeing the clock, while she sipped from her cocktail and awaited the three seconds to pass before time struck Midnight. "Fifty-seven! Fifty-eight! Fifty-nine! Happy New-Year's!" she yelled, along with everyone else in the club. She looked over her shoulder and saw that the crowded dance floor had quickly turned into an array of hugs and kisses. She tilted her glass towards the excitement, and then turned and faced the bar.

Jo-Jo was eyeing her from a short distance away, and decided to approach her with great interest, "Hello, darling, and Happy New Year's to you," he announced smoothly, but somewhat intoxicated, and with a glow of confidence.

"Hi. Happy New-Year to you, too," she mentioned rather dryly, appearing uninterested, as she turned and stared in the other direction towards the end of the bar.

Suddenly, the middle aged Caucasian woman that was seated next to her stood up and walked away. "Good-looking out, sweetie," Jo-Jo whispered to the lady as she passed him. He snapped his finger in the air and captured the attention of Dino, the 30-year-old African-American bartender, "Bring me another cognac, Dino! And bring this lovely lady right here whatever it is that she's sipping on, too! Please, sir!" He slurred over the noisy bar.

"Sure Jo-Jo!" the man yelled back, and resumed his business.

"Anyway, Ms. Lady," Jo-Jo continued to agent Casey, who turned to face him.

"Anyway, what Mr. Man?" she smirked.

"Wow!" He chortled, enjoying her sarcastic response. "I know that somebody has got to be happy." He smiled.

She thought about his comment for a moment, and then smiled. "Really?" enjoying his originality. She hadn't heard that particular pick-up line before. She inched herself closer to where they were practically shoulder to shoulder, and said, "Pardon me? What was that? What'd you say again?" Jo-Jo took a sip of his cognac and repeated, "I said I know that somebody has got to be happy! That's what I said, love."

She sneered, "And how would you know that? You don't know anything about me."

"Shit, look at you, baby! If I had you in my life, I'd be happy. I know that much!"

Agent Casey smiled. "That was kinda' cute. I kinda' like that line. It seems to be original."

"Oh, but it is, Ms. Beautiful. What's your name, honey? You're kinda' cute," he asked, as Dino placed their drinks on the bar and then tapped the counter twice.

"There you are, Jo-Jo, enjoy," he said, walking away.

"Good-lookin' out, Daddy-O! I got you, Dino! Put it on my tab!" he blurted over the noise.

"I know you do, Jo-Jo!" he responded over his shoulder, and then waved his fist above his head, "Handle your business," he continued, while he moved toward an attractive Black woman who was seated at the end of the bar in a sheer red dress.

Jo-Jo looked at Brittany and said, "My name is, Jo-Jo, dear."

He lifted his glass and touched it against her glass.

"I would assume that," she chuckled and then sipped from her glass.

"Anyway, sweetheart, happy New Year to you," he uttered, while they clicked their glasses once again.

"And Happy New-Year to you, too, Jo-Jo," she smiled.

"So, tell me, lil' Momma', what's your name? And what's your story this evening?"

"Well, my name is Brittany, and I'm in the mortgage business. That's what I do."

"Oh, really?" he blurted, seeming surprised.

"Yes, that's my name. And as I said, that's what I do for a living. I work hard all week long, too. Other than that, I have a drink every now and again. And that's about it. And that, Jo-Jo, is my story."

"Well darling, that's an awfully good story that you've got there. What is it that you do in the mortgage business?" he asked curiously.

"I'm a real-estate agent. What do you do for a living? What's your story?" She smiled, and then made certain that she positioned herself, so that her middle suit coat button (which was actually a Microphone/Camera transmitter) could easily record her subject.

"I work for you, baby. That's my story, and that's what I do for a living." He smiled back.

"And your point is?" she smirked, but appeared very sensual.

"My point is… I clean credit. That's what I do. I work for hundreds of hard-working folks, just like you. They all love me, too, because I'm the king, darling!"

"The king, huh? The king of what?"

"The king of credit, Sugar!"

She laughed. "I've heard that line before."

"I'm sure that you have. But you've never heard it from me."

"Well, Jo-Jo, how do you clean credit? What makes you so special? Do you clean it like everyone else?" She shrugged her shoulders. "What, you send dispute letters to the credit bureaus?"

Jo-Jo scoffed. "Hell nah', Brittany! Of course not, darling! That shit's for squares!"

"It's for squares, huh?"

She smiled and glanced at her middle-aged Caucasian partner, agent Carlton. He was recording the entire scene at the bar from his slim-line pen-camera at a nearby table.

"Yeah, baby, that's for squares, just like I said. I'm the bull's-eye king! I hit my target on the first shot. Every time, I might add. I don't play around with dispute letters and shit. I get shit done. All the time! I've got a Godfather, his name is, Jesse. He has some folks who work inside of the credit bureaus," he mentioned, as he sipped from his glass again.

"Really? You said the bull's eye, huh?" Her eyebrows rose.

"Yeah, momma'! I'm one of the kings of this credit game! My folks, Boss-Hogg, he ain't no joke! Not at all."

"Jesse?" She sneered. "You mean, Boss-Hogg? I've heard of him. Damn, it's been a while, though. But yeah, he's good! I've heard a lot about him. What's his last name?" She seemed to ponder. "Damn, I can't remember. It's right on the tip of my tongue, too," she said, as she suggestively ran the tips of her manicured fingernails across his left hand.

He looked at her delicate hand and smiled. "It's Braxton. Jesse Braxton. Why, you know him or something?" he asked, appearing disappointed.

"No, not really. I mean, I haven't actually had any dealings with him personally, but my girlfriend, her name is, Cindy. She has. She told me that he is the best in the west, at what he does. But unfortunately, she lost contact with him some time ago. She told me that he was the guy who made it possible for her to start her own business. And she's very wealthy now! I wish that I could get in contact with him. I'm telling you, Jo-Jo, I've got plenty of work for him. I mean a whole bunch of files to be cleaned!"

"Is that a fact?" he slurred, appearing unimpressed.

"Yeah. I've got at least twenty-three files on my desk for him right this minute. Could you hook me up with him? I would really appreciate it if you could."

"Why do you need to hook up with him, Brittany? Hell, you've got me, sweetie! I'm all that you need! Fuck Boss-Hogg's fat ass! I'm the new Sheriff in town, shit!" he slurred.

"Is that right? But are you as good as Boss-Hogg was?" She smiled and sipped from her drink.

"I'm better than him, Baby. The same way that he could, I can delete any and all negative information from anybody's credit report, and that's guaranteed! I wouldn't give a shit what kind of information that your clients have on their credit report! I can also add some positive accounts onto 'em, too! That's easy, for me. Hell, I've been working with Boss-Hogg's punk-ass for the past eight years now. I can do this shit myself! Believe it or not, Brittany, I haven't had one disappointed client, either!" he bragged.

"You don't seem to care for Boss-Hogg too much, do you?"

"I'm kind of pissed off at him right now. But that's neither here nor there."

"You must have your reasons, I guess."

"That's without a doubt, Brittany. I do, sweetheart."

"Anyway, Jo-Jo, what I need to know from you is… can you straighten out some credit reports as fast as Jesse could? Because my girlfriend told me that he processed her work quick. I think that Cindy mentioned that it took him something like, two weeks, from start to finish."

Jo-Jo laughed. "Lil' Momma', I could do it in one week! Fuck Boss-Hogg! I'm the king of this shit! Boss-Hogg can kiss my black ass!"

Agent Casey chuckled. "In that case, Jo-Jo, hurry up and give me your number then. I could definitely use your services, and that's for sure," she said playing the role, while she easily held her hand out to him, palm upward.

Jo-Jo reached inside the breast pocket of his suit coat and pulled out one of his business cards. "Here you are darling." He handed her the card. "Make sure that you don't lose it now."

"Because I'm telling you, if you do, you'll be sorry." He shook his head. "Because, I'm definitely one of a kind, love. They broke the mold when they made me, and that's no bullshit."

Agent Casey chuckled. "You sure don't have a problem with insecurity!"

"I never have, sweetie," he replied.

"I won't lose it, Jo-Jo, I promise."

He watched her as she slid the card down inside of her black lace brassiere under her suit coat, which he seemed to appreciate.

He smiled. "Brittany, now that's about as safe a place as any for my card to be, nestled right up against your tits." He winked.

"That's because this particular number is important to me. It's secured. I won't lose it," She winked back.

"I'm sure that you won't lose it. Not where it's at, anyway." He paused for another sip of his cognac. "So, Baby, do you have a man in your life? I mean, not that it would make any difference to me. Because I look at it like this... what he doesn't know, won't hurt 'em."

She chuckled, "No, not at the moment, I don't. I'm single. Unlike you, though," she mentioned, and pointed to his Platinum and Diamond wedding ring.

"Yeah, well," he blushed. "Ah, this here old thing ain't nothing but a ring to me. That's all. But yeah, you're right I do have a wife at home. However, she likes what I like. And if I like you, then she would undoubtedly like you, too. And I'm digging you like a great big pile of cash!"

"Is that right?"

She smiled as she nonchalantly glanced at her partner again.

"Yes, it is true," he continued, followed by another sip. "And I love money, sweetheart! So Brittany, what would you say to a little fun this morning, you know what I mean?"

"No, not exactly," she smiled, while she sipped from her glass. "What do you mean?"

"Well, for starters, we could have a nice little blow. You know, some fine powder cocaine, and some champagne an' shit. And then,

171

you, my little Asian bitch an me, we could have a wild time, you dig? I'm talking about us having a fabulous-fantastic-fuck-fantasy, just the three of us, Baby. Nobody else has to know. It'll be our business. And I promise you that I won't tell!" Agent Casey smiled. "So, what do you say, baby?" Jo-Jo resumed. "My crib is right up in the hills. It's only twenty minutes away from here. Are you down with us? We'll be nice. I promise you that."

Boss-Hogg was fuming as he shoved his finger towards the Camcorder and shouted, "That worthless piece of shit! Fucking no-good-ass-son-of-a-bitch!" he blasted, and then slammed his fist against the table and accidently knocked the camcorder onto the floor.

Agent Dobbs was instantly amused as he chuckled heartily while he picked up the camera and turned it off.

"Needless to say, Mr. Braxton," he said, as he placed the recorder back inside of his coat pocket. "Our lady operative graciously declined Mr. Milton's decadent invitation. Don't you wish that you had done your homework on this asshole, Milton? If you had viewed the results of his psychological evaluation, the kind that are a prerequisite to a career in law enforcement, you would have been able to see his chatty-Kathy type tendencies. He runs his mouth too much."

"No shit!" Boss-Hogg scowled.

"I'm glad that you agree. Therefore, alas- Boss-Hogg, chalk it up to one more poor choice on your part. Hindsight is always 20-20. Believe that! But, I digress. Anyway, the worst thing about Jo-Jo is his pompous disregard for our system of law, which I for one, value. He's the worst white-collar criminal that I've ever encountered in my thirty-six years in law enforcement. The worst, I tell ya'!" he blurted and spat on the floor. "And if I had it my way, Mr. Braxton, I'd have him declared as an enemy combatant and transferred over to the custody of the military. An indeterminate sentence in a place like Guantanamo Bay would scare the shit out of him! You see, Mr. Hogg, to me, all of you criminals are essentially terrorists. And it's my opinion that you guys do not deserve the benefits of our legal protections."

"That bullshit doesn't scare me, Dobbs!" Boss-Hogg yelled. "I'm an American Citizen! Not only that, I ain't done no terrorist shit! So you can kiss my ass with that shit you talking!"

Agent Dobbs smiled calmly, as he pulled a manila envelope out of his suit coat pocket and slapped it down on the table. Boss-Hogg looked at it and then stared quizzically up at Agent Dobbs.

"Read it, asshole!" Dobbs boomed.

Boss-Hogg complied and opened the envelope and began reading the documents within. Suddenly, he felt his stomach fall to the floor. "What the fuck is this shit, man?" He screamed, discovering a Somalia passport displaying his photograph, as well as a Somalia identification card and a birth certificate bearing the name, "Mooloof Al-Tahiri." He scowled at agent Dobbs while his hands shook uncontrollably. "I was born in Whittier, man!"

Dobbs shook his head. "Not anymore, Mr. Al-Tahiri. Please, read on," he continued, and grinned mischievously.

Boss-Hogg began reading what looked like some vital statistics. Displayed before him were his fictitious hometown, his political affiliations, (rumored to be a high-ranking Al Qaeda operative in deep cover, residing in the Los Angeles area) and, some intricately detailed plans for the assassination of the Los Angeles Mayor, Sam Pinkerton.

There were also itemized diagrams for blowing up the regional Los Angeles F.B.I. field office, which was located exactly one city block to the north of the holding center.

"These plans of course, will be found in your ranch house somewhere. And you can rest assure, that a full supply of C-4 plastic explosives will accompany them. Not to mention, some other juicy favorites of ours."

Agent Dobbs could not stop laughing as Boss-Hogg began to panic.

"But it'll be easy to check my name, my Social Security number, my life, man!" he shouted. "You can't do this shit to me! I'm an American fucking citizen, for Christ sake!" he blasted, as his eyes began to water.

Agent Dobbs spat on the wall. "Not any more, you fat son-of-a-bitch! You're a citizen of hog shit, Hogg! That's what you are! Hell, you thought that you were a hot-shit business man with your little altering personal credit bullshit?" He laughed. "Why, at the touch of a button, I will make you a Somalia member of the Al Qaeda! You fucking ass-hole!"

"Al Qaeda?" Boss-Hogg screamed at the top of his lungs.

"Yes, sunshine," he whispered directly in Boss-Hogg's face, and then smiled as he continued, "One who happens to be residing here on an expired Visa, no doubt. I'll then have your trifling-ass transferred into the custody of the United States Military. I mean right now, with just one phone call. Not two calls, Jesse, just one. It's really that simple, pal. Try me, if you like. I dare you!" he shouted. "I'm the real king of this shit, boy! You'd better recognize!" He cackled maniacally, while Boss-Hogg began to weep.

"Jesus Christ, Dobbs! You're a fucking monster!"

Agent Dobbs found that statement to be particularly amusing, and laughed for a full minute.

"A monster? Moi?" He pointed to himself. "Really now, Mr. Braxton, that's quite harsh, don't you think? Or should I call you, Mr. Al-Tahiri?"

"I ain't no goddamn, Mooloof Al-Tahiri, man! My name is, Jesse Braxton!" he screamed.

Agent Dobbs smirked and waved him off dismissively. "Anyway, Mr. Al-Tahiri, I am not a monster at all. Matter of fact, I am not anything of the sort. I am however, a good-natured person. As far as I know, good goals require planning and patience. Unlike you, I have all these qualities, and I utilize them to achieve my goals, as you can see."

"But what if I refuse to cooperate with you people? What would really happen? Because all that I'm hearing from you right now is talk," Boss-Hogg blurted defiantly.

Agent Dobbs stared Boss-Hogg in the eyes for a long moment.

His meaning was clear- *don't fuck with me*!

He smiled. "That's up to you, sir. I mean, if you choose to make that choice. It would be the worst one imaginable. I'll tell you that, Mr. Al-Tahiri. Heck, if that's the way you feel, I'll simply make a phone call to my youngest nephew, Archie. He happens to be one of the big-wig's over in the Department of Homeland Security. Knowing him the way that I do, he will, in turn, dispatch contingent forces to transport your fat, lousy ass into the custody of the United States Military."

He shook his head and smirked. "And before you know it, you'll most likely be interrogated immediately, and perhaps tortured, if necessary. Afterwards, I'm sure that you will then be taken into the custody of some other top-secret organization, which will in-turn,

174

torture you some more, just to get their jollies off. Afterwards, you'll definitely be flown to Cuba to your new residence. I'm sure that you'll enjoy your accommodations there." He chuckled. "You'll undoubtedly be in legal limbo forever. Legal counsel would be definitely out of the question. Not to mention any form of contact with the outside world."

"That's crazy!" Boss-Hogg shouted.

Dobbs laughed heartily as he slammed his hand against the table and grinned evilly, just inches away from Boss-Hogg's face.

"You say "that's crazy," fat-boy? Well, tell me how does this sound as being crazy? Picture yourself residing in overcrowded, dank cells, with shit for food, and piss for your beverage. The floor, well," agent he chuckled. "That will be your restroom facilities. I'm sure that you'll enjoy those accommodations, won't you? You'll surely be abused by the servicemen there, perhaps, even murdered." He shrugged his shoulders." Who knows?"

"That's fucked up, Dobbs!"

Dobbs smiled. "I know it is, Mr. Braxton. I know. But, how do you like me now? You see, I really can be a monster. That is, if you force me to."

"That's some bullshit! Because all that I would have to do is speak in perfect English, and they'll know that I'm not a fucking terrorist from Somalia!" Boss-Hogg protested sheepishly.

Dobbs stood up and stretched and yawned. He then shadow boxed a little and stretched again, before whispering, "Do you actually think that you're the only deep-cover spy that I created, who supposedly had plans to defile our great land? Of course you speak English- specifically. It's the regional dialect of the area in which you were infiltrating. Stupid! Of course you would be fully versed in the customs and general facts that every American citizen knows." He leaned against the table and peered in Boss-Hogg's eyes. "Mister, do you think that a person like you, trying to explain your plight to the officers during your flight to Cuba, will be received well?"

He scornfully smacked his lips. "Nigger, please!" he whispered and waved him off dismissively. "Before you utter two words, Mr. Al-Tahiri, you'll be beaten, force-fed valium, and then muzzled." He grinned sadistically.

Boss-Hogg closed his eyes and began to weep silently while he shook his head.

Agent Dobbs nodded satisfyingly. "Yes, it's a hell of a thing, Braxton. I mean, for a man like me to be able to do that sort of a thing to a scum-bag like you. Just take away your entire identity, and force an awful fictitious one upon you, just like that." He snapped his fingers. "It's a hell of a thing, I tell you!"

"It certainly is, sir." Boss-Hogg admitted in surrender, and then blew his nose loudly in a paper napkin that he yanked from his uniform's shirt pocket. "I'm ready to do whatever you want, Mr. Dobbs. Just please, don't do me like that! I'm not a terrorist, man."

Agent Dobbs clapped his hands enthusiastically. "Bravo! Bravo!" he blurted. "I know you're not, Mr. Braxton. But I've got to tell you... I was beginning to get worried there for a minute. Because I thought that I was actually going to have to make that call to my nephew. I mean, I would hate to have done such an awful thing to you. The fact is, Mr. Braxton, I kind of half-way, chicken-shit like you, you know. And I want to thank you for not placing me in that sort of a position."

"Now," he continued, as he yawned and stretched his arms out. "Let's get down to business. Because, by making this here phone call, you will be spared the previously mentioned horrors, and instead, you will be spending only a few minor years in a minimum-security Federal prison."

He watched as Boss-Hogg stared at the table. Obviously in deep thought.

"That's right, my man. Think long and hard about it," he resumed. "Because you see, you'll be living in some comfortable conditions in your own spacious cell. You'll even have complete access to a microwave oven. They'll be fresh popcorn, and a nearby telephone for you to use daily, if you like. Now tell me, how's that sound for starters? Are you willing to accept that proposal, or what, Mr. Braxton?"

Boss-Hogg nodded emphatically.

"Now that's very good, my man! Very good indeed." He smiled. "Job well done, Son, you are a wise man after all, Mr. Braxton. But before you make that call to Mr. Milton, you've got to calm yourself down. Because man, you're shaking like a snitch at a gangster's party," he chuckled. "It looks like someone just shot two bullets at you, and missed!" He laughed loudly.

He grabbed the cup from the table and shook out the coffee residue onto the floor. "You need a drink, Mr. Braxton, Jesus! You need it to calm your terrible nerves, man."

He pulled out a silver flask from within his suit coat pocket and held it up in front of Boss-Hogg. He smiled as he shook it lightly and caused the liquid inside to slosh.

Boss-Hogg licked his lips. "What's in the flask?" he asked curiously.

Agent Dobbs continued to smile. "It's cognac. It's y'all's favorite. At least according to our research it is."

He grinned and poured a small amount of the liquor into the Styrofoam cup. "Here you are, Boss," he mentioned, as he handed him the cup.

Boss-Hogg raised the cup to his lips and then hesitated. "Wait a minute, man!" He sniffed the contents in the cup. "How do I know that this shit ain't poisoned?"

Dobbs rolled his eyes and snatched the cup out of Boss-Hogg's hand. "Goddamn, man! Pay attention, dip-shit!" he blurted, and then upended the contents into his mouth, and swallowed loudly as he did so.

He rubbed his lips with his coat sleeve. "Yes, now that's the shit!" he exclaimed as he refilled the cup.

"Here, stupid!" he continued, and handed the cup back to Boss-Hogg, who greedily gulped it down.

"Ah, that's good," Boss-Hogg told him, and then held the cup out for more.

Dobbs laughed and handed him the flask. "Enjoy, fat-boy," he chuckled, and then watched him as he tipped the flask up and swallowed the cognac until he received the very last drop. Boss-Hogg seemed out of breath as he wiped his mouth with his uniform sleeve.

Dobbs pointed to him. "Remember this, man. Whatever you do, don't tell my boss, Boss." He laughed.

Chapter 16

Wednesday, later that day, Chill was speaking on the office phone to his client, Fred Macklin, while he relaxed in his and Jo-Jo's shared Westwood Office. He smiled and uttered, "Thanks for the recognition, Fred. But it's normal for you to feel the way that you do, I have to admit that. But after all, you're working with one of the kings of this shit, Baby!" he boasted and then he kicked his black suede loafers up on his desk.

"I have to agree with you on that one, Chill," Fred said, as he appeared to be filled with appreciation.

Chill smiled. "Fred, isn't it obvious by now that I'm second to none, man? Because who do you know in the entire country who can do what I do, as fast as I can do it?"

"No one can do it the way that you get shit done, not that I know of, anyway."

"You're goddamn right, man! Because my folks are the only ones who can do it the way that we do it! Nobody else can. No where!"

"Chill, you guys are definitely the best! The top dogs, matter of fact."

"You're motherfucking right, my friend!" he boasted.

"And that's no, doubt," Fred replied, and was beaming from ear to ear, as he lounged in his Income Tax office in Chatsworth, California.

"Au contraire, Fred," Chill resumed. "For without my clients, you, I have nothing."

Suddenly, the office door exploded inward and a haggard, and frightened Jo-Jo barged into the room.

Chill, who was slightly startled, kept his eyes on Jo-Jo while he said to Fred, "I'm sorry man, but something recently came up which requires my immediate attention. Let me call you back, Fred, okay?"

"Sure thing, kiddo', but make it A.S.A.P., okay. It's about money, you know?"

"Will do, sir," Chill said, before he hung up the phone and stared at Jo-Jo, while he wondered what was going on.

Jo-Jo appeared to be exhausted, as he stood there in his heavily soiled velour black sweat suit. He had a black suede baseball cap draped over his messy hair-cut, and on his feet were a pair of dirty black and white leather tennis shoes.

In an unsteady hand, he held a brown paper bag, protruding from which was the neck of what looked like a 40 oz. bottle of Malt Liquor. Chill heard him utter a string of unintelligible obscenities, before Jo-Jo dropped himself into his chair.

Jo-Jo burped and farted loudly, and the putrid stench of human digestion quickly filled the office. Chill scowled and gagged, while he covered his nose and mouth and pushed his chair as far away from Jo-Jo as he could get.

"Goddamn, Jo-Jo!" he blurted, and then immediately began to wave the stench away with a copy of Sure Finance magazine. "Man, Jo-Jo!" he said, and then jumped up from his chair and stood with his back against the wall, while he continued to wave the recent issue.

"My bad," Jo-Jo chuckled.

"What the hell, Jo-Jo?" he exclaimed. "Look at yourself, with your trifling ass! You're looking like a black-ass vampire! On top of that, you keep farting and shit! It smells like something done crawled up your ass and died!"

Jo-Jo laughed as Chill sat the magazine back on his desktop and then plopped himself down in his chair. "Smelly-ass nigga'!" he stated, as he rolled the chair back near his desk and studied Jo-Jo's demeanor. "Joseph man, what's up with it?" He finally asked.

Jo-Jo burped again and opened his glazed-over, mildly blackened and bloodshot eyes. He scowled and said, "What?" before he took a long swig from the bottle and gagged, nearly vomiting.

"I said, what's up, homie? Goddamn!" Chill scowled. "What's happening with you, man?"

"The only thing that's happening is some madness, dawg'. Some crazy-ass bull-shit, that's all!"

"That's interesting," Chill mentioned, as he rested his elbows on his desk and drummed his fingers together. "Damn, Jo-Jo, you look like you done just run away from a bunch of mad-ass grizzly bears."

"I look that bad, huh?" Jo-Jo chuckled.

"Hell, yeah you do!"

"Well, I really can't argue with you about that statement, because that's how I'm feeling about right now." He farted again.

"Damn, Jo-Jo! Can't you at least say *'excuse me'*?"

"I'm sorry, Chill. Excuse me, nigga'. I mean, really. Excuse me. But I'm pretty messed up right now, you know."

"Yeah, I know. And you're messing up the oxygen in here, too, with your nasty-ass farts."

"Sorry, dawg'," he mumbled.

"You're sorry my ass!" He shook his head. "Just stop it!"

Jo-Jo began to massage his throbbing temples and tired eyes. "I'm telling you, Chill. If it ain't one thing, it's another. Man, that seems to be the story of my goddamn life."

Chill looked on with concern. "If you got a problem, Jo-Jo, you know that you can tell me about it. Hell, I might be able to help you to solve it. So, tell me what's up? What's bothering you?"

Jo-Jo sighed heavily. "Man Chill, we've got some major problems, dawg'."

Chill scowled. "What kind of problems?"

He noticed that Jo-Jo's hand shook badly as he tipped the bottle in the bag to his lips again, allowing some disgusting gulping sounds to issue from his throat, which filled the room.

"Goddamn, Jo-Jo, slow your ass down! You're going to mess around and drown, fool!"

Jo-Jo wiped his mouth with his jacket sleeve. "Well, when I tell you what I got to tell you, you're going to want a drink, too."

"Nope! That's wrong, man. What I'm going to do is… stay sharp and clear-headed, so that we can best deal with this problem. That's what I'm going to do. Now man, what's happening with you?"

"All right then, listen to this, Boss-Hogg was arrested two days ago at his house in Rancho Cordova."

Chill was shocked, as he felt wave after wave of anxiety wash over him. He tried his best to keep it hidden. "Why did it take so long for you to find this out?"

Jo-Jo sighed as he clanked the bottle against the desk a few times.

"Apparently, his wife, Vicky, she had left a bunch of messages on my voicemail. But I didn't receive them. I guess it's because I had my phone turned off the whole time. I was busy, you know?"

Chill smirked. "Yeah, I know. You were busy, my ass! I heard the hell out of that! Do you know that I've been trying to get a hold of you ever since yesterday morning? I guess that you and your woman were too busy smoking on that bullshit."

Jo-Jo scoffed. "Come on, Chill. I really don't feel like getting into that mess right now. Lena's butt is at home sleeping right this minute. I hope she is, anyway. She was when I left the house. Anyway Chill, Vicky called me about an hour ago from her mother's house in San Fernando."

He sighed heavily. "Man, she told me all about how some Secret Service agents forced her to get off their ranch property earlier this morning. She said that they were seizing the property or something like that."

Chill couldn't believe what he was hearing. "You mean the United States Secret Service? Holy shit, Jo-Jo!" he blurted.

Jo-Jo smirked. "Yeah boy, the Secret Service. Why, you've got some partners in there or something?"

"Hell nah', motherfucker! Fuck you!" Chill chortled.

Jo-Jo chuckled. "Anyway, it's the one and only Secret Service, Chill. And those fools ain't playing around. They mean business." He shook his head. "No shit!" Chill agreed. "Man, Jo-Jo, what the hell happened?" he asked curiously.

Jo-Jo shook his head. "I don't know. I can't tell you for sure. But I do know that some strange shit is going down. Because something crazy happened right after I hung up the phone with Vicky."

"Something crazy like what?"

"I'm not sure. But that fool Boss-Hogg called me from his cell phone, somehow, I don't know." He shook his head. "He told me that he was calling me from the Metropolitan Holding Center, downtown."

"You mean, M.H.C.?" Chill nodded. Yeah, Jo-Jo, I've heard of that joint."

"Well, whoop-dee-do! That's nice to know," Jo-Jo smirked, before he swallowed the remainder of the beer and placed the empty bottle into a nearby wastebasket.

"Fuck you, Jo-Jo!" Chill blurted, and then looked at him with extreme concerned. "Anyway, so what did Boss-Hogg have to say to you?"

Jo-Jo rubbed his burning, bloodshot eyes, and replied, "He gave me the whole rundown about how the Secret Service allegedly ran up in his ranch house, and he mentioned some shit about how they forced him and Vicky onto the floor, and what that they found on the property. And then he explained where it was that he was being locked up, et cetera. I think it's all a bunch of bull-shit, if you ask me."

"It might not be, though," Chill replied, shaking his head.

"I know. But then, check this out... the fat motherfucker mentioned something about things ain't looking too good, "for me.""

Chill pointed towards Jo-Jo's chest. "Ain't looking too good, for you?" he exclaimed. "What the hell did he mean by that shit?" he questioned, while his anxiety was mounting.

Jo-Jo shrugged his shoulders and shook his head. "The hell if I know! I'm still trying to figure that out. But that's another strange thing, Chill. Because when I asked him about what in the hell did he mean by that statement, the goddamn phone hung up! I mean, just all of a sudden, you know!"

"All of a sudden!" Chill exclaimed with disgust.

"I know. That shit was weird, huh?"

"You're damned right it's weird!"

"Tell me about it," Jo-Jo continued. "But dig this here. So, I tried calling his cell phone back, but the thing went straight to his voicemail. It's like it was turned off or something."

"All of a sudden, the phone gets turned off! Just like that!" Chill scowled. "That's crazy! That's some weird-ass shit, Jo-Jo!"

"Tell me about it!" Jo-Jo sighed, while he massaged his temples.

"I tell you what, though," Chill resumed. "I may be new at this credit cleaning business. But I'm a master when it comes to committing crimes. Hell, I've been committing crimes most of my life. I know the codes of the game, man. And one of the main codes is to do your own time and keep your mouth shut! No snitching allowed, you know? And I ain't the smartest nigga' in the world, neither. But Jo-Jo, I damn sure ain't the dumbest! And I ain't ever heard of no jail where they allow you to make personal calls on your own goddamn cell phone! So I hate to say it man, but it sounds to me like your boy Boss-Hogg is in cahoots with the Feds, man. Like he's shacking up with them alphabet boys."

"Alphabet boys?" Jo-Jo asked, confused.

"Yeah, man. The Feds. You know how they're always using them alphabets like D.E.A., F.B.I., C.I.A. and shit. It sounds to me like your boy is snitchin'."

"Fuck!" Jo-Jo yelled, and slammed his palm against the side of his head. "I can't believe that I didn't see it coming myself! I mean, right in front of my face at that! Man!" he sighed. "Boy, do I feel stupid! Chill, if it was raining pussies, I'd be the only man in the world to get hit in the head with a dick! A big one at that, with my bad-ass luck!"

"Look here, man. We need to be prepared for the high likelihood that Boss-Hogg is working for the Feds now, and that he's trying to drag us down underneath him to soften the fall."

"Man Chill, tell me about it. Because I believe now, that he can't hold his water for nothing!" He rubbed his face. "Man, that fat sucker's gonna' roll over on me. I know he is!"

He stood up and nervously paced around the room.

He stopped suddenly and grumbled towards the floor," I ain't going back to the joint, man. Fuck that shit! I'll blow my own brains out first! Hell nah! I'd rather die than go back inside!"

Chill couldn't believe what he was hearing. He stood up and walked over to Jo-Jo and yelled directly into his face, "Look at me, nigga'!"

Jo-Jo half-heartedly forced his head up, but his eyes were still downcast.

"Joseph Milton, I said look at me, God-dammit!" he shouted.

The shame in Jo-Jo's eyes was palpable, as he finally looked into Chills' eyes.

"All right, Jo-Jo, good!" Chill continued. "Now you listen to me, fool! You're talking crazy! You done messed around and lost your rabid-ass mind! You're thinking too goddamn much, that's what you're doing! You're standing in this office talking about taking your own life! You're talking like some soft, wimpy-ass dude, blood! You must've forgotten that you and I are some soldiers, nigga'! You've got the game twisted, Jo-Jo! Because there's one thing that we soldiers never do- commit suicide! We don't get down like that! You understand?" he blasted, pointing his finger in Jo-Jo's face.

"That's all well and good, Chill," he replied reluctantly. "And I love and respect you for trying to put my ass in check. But make no mistake about it, man. I am not going back to the penitentiary. Not for nobody! Not alive, anyway," he admitted, staring at the floor.

Chill pondered the situation while he looked him straight in the face. He was tempted to slap him across his head, but thought otherwise.

He finally figured out what kind of a person that he was dealing with. It was the kind that he never respected.

Chill believed that God would tolerate a lot from His children. But the taking of one's own life was not accepted! Cowardice! Selfish! And, hell-bound was the end result.

He mused about how self-centered Jo-Jo appeared.

How could he do such a thing? What about his wife, and the rest of his loved ones who depended on him? A punk-ass mother-fucker! That's what he is, Chill thought.

Chapter 17

Joseph "Jo-Jo" Milton wasn't always considered to be one of "The kings of credit." Matter of fact, in his hometown of South Jackson, Mississippi, he had to make ends meet by working wherever minority high-school dropouts were hired.

At the time he wasn't enjoying himself or life very much. He envied those who had more than he did. He envied most people in general. Growing weary of the daily grind, living to work and working to live, he longed for something on a grander scale. It was perhaps, inevitable that he would procure a .38 Smith & Wesson, snub-nosed 6-shot revolver. He found a nice one and purchased it from Pug, an African-American childhood associate of his. He had run across Pug at a local labor maintenance job placement center. It was one located on the end of the block down the street from his deceased parent's home. They had passed away in a head-on collision with a drunken tow-truck driver nine months earlier.

Jo-Jo paid $100 for what Pug had promised to be a mighty fine weapon. He quickly took it home and felt its weight in his hand. *It felt so right*! *It felt like destiny.*

He pointed the weapon at the small black-and-white television set. He had it perched on top of a couple of milk crates in the corner of his room.

He pulled the trigger several times. "Pow-Pow! Pow-Pow-Pow!" he exclaimed.

Yes, it felt excellent. It felt as if he held the collected powers of the world in the palm of his hand. *It was his choice, whether a person lived or died. His only.* "I could do this shit! No problem. And I'll pull the trigger if I have to. And pow! The last shot. Dead-man, motherfucker!" he blurted, as he slid the pistol inside of the waistband of his black denim pants. He made certain that it was concealed underneath his black sweatshirt.

Jo-Jo never was a man whom was prone to consider the consequences of his actions. Because, when he walked into a local convenient store one morning wearing a black ski-mask with his gun in hand, the middle-aged Pakistani clerk screamed. He quickly began trembling and sobbing, and then he threw up his hands to heaven and began to pray in Hindi.

In the store also was Boss-Hogg, who was purchasing a bottle of cognac and a pack of menthol cigarettes. He was smiling at Jo-Jo, and appeared to be totally relaxed, even amused, it seemed. Jo-Jo, who was nearly hyperventilating and sweating profusely, pointed his gun at the smiling man's face.

"Hey, fat-ass!" he shouted. "What the fuck are you smiling at?"

Boss-Hogg shifted his weight and introduced himself. "The name is Jesse Braxton, son. And God knows, I think that my prayers have just been answered," he continued to smile.

Jo-Jo shot a quick, paranoid glance over each shoulder and jammed the gun up under Boss-Hogg's chin. "You're a real weird-ass dude, you know that?"

"That's your opinion, son. And opinions are like assholes. Everybody has one," he explained, and continued to smile calmly.

"No shit, dickhead," Jo-Jo blurted.

His hand shook nervously, as he pressed the revolver harder against Boss-Hogg's neck. "Why don't I just pull this trigger? It will be one less weird, fat-ass motherfucker out here in Mississippi."

"Son," he began, calmly. "I want for you to come and work for me. I'm already rich. But I can make you rich, too." He smiled. "Of course, while you're making me richer, that is."

Jo-Jo was intrigued by Boss-Hogg's boldness, and how he seemed so fearless in the face of his own violent death. "What the hell are you talking about, fat-boy?" he asked calmly, with the gun still pressed under his chin.

"Please, youngster. My friends call me, 'Boss-Hogg', and I'd appreciate it if you would do the same."

"Man," Jo-Jo said, as he quickly surveyed the store. He spotted the security camera near the ceiling on the wall behind the counter. "Aren't you worried about saying all this shit in front of this scary-ass clerk?"

He removed the gun from under Boss-Hogg's chin and pointed it directly at the clerk's head.

"Please don't kill me!" The man shouted, and quickly began jabbering in his native tongue, clearly scared to death.

"Shut the fuck up, slurpy!" Jo-Jo screamed.

Boss-Hogg held up his hands. "Look here son. All that you're facing right now is a simple armed robbery. You'll be out of prison in about five years with good behavior, of course. "

"Now, if you kill that poor man, who is simply doing his job and trying to provide for his wife and six kids, the State of Mississippi will lock you up and throw away the key. That is, if they don't electrocute you. I promise you that! Now kid, you asked me why I speak so freely in front of this man." He glanced at the clerk. "Well, I happen to know that his memory is very short, because I've known him for many years now. So do the smart thing and put the strap away. I'll take you for a ride in my automobile, so that you and I can talk," he said as he pointed to his brand new 1997 Corniche Rolls Royce. He had it backed into a parking stall across the lot.

He glanced suddenly at the car. *That's a nice dark-blue paint job he's got on that ride*, "That's a clean car, man."

He focused his attention back to Boss-Hogg and the frightened clerk.

"Thank you, my man," Boss-Hogg replied, smiling. "That's my Baby."

Having found himself at the end of his rope this morning, Jo-Jo was desperate for anything which promised him deliverance from his material poverty. He was still far from trusting this strange man, however.

Boss-Hogg glanced at his gold wristwatch and said, "You'd better decide now, Son! Because the clerk has already pressed his silent alarm button about ten seconds ago. Now, depending on the speed at which the police department responds, some patrol units could be arriving here at any minute. Therefore, I suggest that you keep your ski-mask on until you walk out of this store. That way, the clerk and the cameras won't see your face. Now the parking lot is clear, boy!"

Jo-Jo briefly considered killing the clerk, but it would have only added to his problems. He pocketed the pistol as Boss-Hogg hurried to the front glass doors and blocked Jo-Jo from the view of anyone who might have entered the parking lot. "Let's go!" he blurted and then pushed open the right-side door and exclaimed, "Now boy, pull off your mask and walk casually over to the Corniche! Do it slowly!"

Jo-Jo's heart was pounding harder now than when he first entered the convenient store intent on robbing it.

The Corniche was the only car in the parking lot, besides the clerk's black 1992 Honda Civic.

Boss-Hogg, who moved surprisingly fast for someone so sickeningly obese, waddled around to the driver's door and impatiently motioned for Jo-Jo to get in, which he did.

"I thought you said to do it casually, man, shit!" Jo-Jo whispered, breathless.

"Shut up, kid! I have to speak to my vehicle!"

Jo-Jo blinked, quite baffled. "You got to what?" He scowled.

"Silence, I said!" Boss-Hogg snapped, bringing instant quiet to the luxurious light-blue leather interior. He then mentioned toward the polished wood dashboard in a soft, comforting voice, "Hello, Vicky. It's Jesse, darling. Start the engine, now," he continued, and was quickly rewarded by a series of electronic beeps, which were followed by the soothing, 8-cylinder hum of the fabulously crafted motor.

Jo-Jo, seemed totally amazed at what he had witnessed, as Boss-Hogg eased the vehicle out of the parking lot and onto Rest Haven Highway, heading south.

"Whew," Boss-Hogg sighed. "That was close, young man." Jo-Jo glanced over his left shoulder. "Damn," he whispered, while he stared at a team of light-brown police cruisers, as they sped into the convenience store's parking lot. He turned back around and trained the sight into the side-view mirror. "But damn, Jesse, you're on that camera for sure, man!" he stated nervously.

188

"I'm always on that camera, boy!" he snapped. "Shit, I've been going to that store for years now."

"Yeah, but when the cops question that clerk, he's going to snitch on you for sure. I know he is! "

Boss-Hogg snapped, "The man ain't going to snitch on me! It's being taken care of as we speak. He knows who I am and what it is that I do. He's already one of my, how should I say this- beneficiaries. Yes, that's it, beneficiary. Anyway, Fahood is a good man. And one of these days, I would like for you to properly apologize to him for scaring the shit out of him."

Jo-Jo remained silent for some time. He finally turned towards Boss-Hogg and asked, "Who in the hell are you, anyway?"

Boss-Hogg brought the Rolls Royce to a gentle stop at a red light. "I should be asking you that question, young man. Because it seemed to me that you forgot your manners, when I introduced myself to you back inside of the store."

"I'm sorry about that bullshit, G. But my name is Joseph. Joseph Milton. But nobody calls me by that name any more. Everyone calls me, 'Jo-Jo'."

Boss-Hogg laughed. "Jo-Jo, huh? You mean, like Jo-Jo the clown?"

Jo-Jo scowled. "Nah, man, just Jo-Jo! That's it."

"Well, Jo-Jo, it should be Jo-Jo the clown. Because that's the way you looked, as well as the way that you acted back there in that place of business."

Jo-Jo suddenly appeared to be very upset. "You know, man. You sure are mighty casual with me, seeing as I'm the one who's holding the gun and all."

Boss-Hogg ripped the car over to the side of the mostly empty highway. "Oh yeah?" he said, as he placed the vehicle in park. "I don't think that you'll do it, tough guy! I don't think that you're a killer at all. If you were, you would have blown both mine and the clerk's head off back there in the convenient store. But I tell you what. Here's a perfect opportunity for a much better lick, Joseph. You can kill me and take my car," he mentioned while pulling out his wallet and then opened the center console, which revealed $70,000 in brand new $100 bills.

"Goddamn!" Jo-Jo exclaimed.

"Yes young man. Including the cash, that's about a $320,000 robbery in all, son. So?" He shrugged his shoulders. "What in the hell are you waiting for? Kill me! Go ahead! I dare you, motherfucker!"

Jo-Jo couldn't believe what he was witnessing. *"This Nigga's insane!"* Boss-Hogg displayed the same uncanny level of Zen calm that he had witnessed back inside of the convenient store.

"I don't think that you have it in you, Son," Boss-Hogg resumed. "Shit, I've seen and been around some real stone-cold killers in my days. And believe me, young man, they move in the shadows. They're soulless and dead. But I don't see that heartlessness in you, Joseph, not at all. It's not too late, though. Why don't you give me that pea-shooter that you've got there, and get rich with me? You see, I recognize a little game in you, Son. I'm willing to teach you all the necessary game that you'll ever need to know. All you have to do is trust me, youngster. Just trust me."

Jo-Jo mused-over the situation for a long moment, and then blurted, "I ain't no weirdo, man! And I ain't about to do no funny-ass, freaky shit with you neither! That's for goddamn sure! I like women, period!"

Boss-Hogg cackled. "Man, do you really think that I rescued you from serving the rest of your life in prison, just for some sort of sexual gratification?" He scoffed and smacked his lips. "Nigga', please!" he blurted. "Joseph, I am a happily married man. To a woman, I might add!" he concluded with a chuckle.

Jo-Jo relaxed a bit and reached into the pocket of his black flight-jacket. He removed the revolver and suddenly experienced an extremely brief period of indecision. He exhaled a deep breath. "Here man," he mentioned and handed him the gun, handle first.

"Thank you, Jo-Jo." Boss-Hogg smiled, as he patted him gently on his left shoulder.

"Yeah, Boss-Hogg, man," he muttered.

Boss-Hogg immediately opened the cylinder and removed the bullets, and then placed the items into his sport coat pocket.

"Young man, these are not the tools of business. No self-respecting businessman carries one."

"Yeah, that's easy for somebody who never grew up in the 'hood' to say. Because I'm from the bottoms, man. Having a piece can mean the difference between life and death."

"Believe me, Joseph. I understand what you're saying. I can relate to your situation, because, originally I am from, "the bottoms". I was born in Whittier, California. But I grew up in Watts, in L.A., to be exact. And if that ain't, "the bottoms", then I don't know what is. But from this point on, son, you no longer have to live in, "the bottoms". I'm taking you to your new home, if you choose for it to be."

They drove in silence for quite some time, passing the city limits and entering the more rural and agricultural areas. *Nice places*, Jo-Jo mused.

Gigantic horse ranches were spread along either side of the road and the beasts were either resting or playing. The foul odor of horse dung and manure filled the car. Jo-Jo couldn't take it any longer and he finally opened his window. The onslaught was so overwhelming to him that he quickly closed it.

Boss-Hogg laughed. "Don't trip, Joseph. You'll get use to it. Besides, that odor that you're inhaling is the smell of money, son."

Jo-Jo flashed Boss-Hogg a crazy look and blurted, "The smell of money!"

"You heard me right. It's the smell of money, man. I say that, because there's millions of dollars that is flowing through these cattle ranches. It's a damn good business!"

They finally left the ranch zone and the road wound through a series of lush green valleys and gently rolling hills. Boss-Hogg finally came upon a T-Junction in the road and then proceeded to its right. They were now traveling on a well-paved driveway. The road dipped suddenly, revealing a spectacular, triple-level white mansion with Greco-Roman columns, which framed the entrance.

Behind the mansion was a majestic lake, whose present occupants were a lovely pair of swans. The water birds appeared to be in no particular hurry, as they paddled around and occasionally dunked their heads.

Jo-Jo absolutely enjoyed the view. "Damn, Jesse, this is a nice crib that you've got here."

Boss-Hogg smiled. "Thank you very much, Son."

He pulled the Corniche around the driveway which passed several feet from the front doors, and then it curved around an enormous fountain in the center of the roundabout.

"My wife, her name is Vicky, and she's away for a couple of weeks at her mother's home in California. We have no children. Well, not anymore, anyway," he admitted, sorrowfully. He sighed and after some time, he beckoned Jo-Jo out of the car.

In the main living room on the second floor of the estate, Jo-Jo was sitting in a comfortable green-leather recliner. He was resting his feet on a matching ottoman, while Boss-Hogg lectured to him about the world of credit cleaning.

The large fireplace crackled loudly, as Boss-Hogg stood near it with his arm resting on the mantle. Beside him on the mantle was a gold-framed 8" X 10" photograph of his late son, Melvin. He marveled at exactly how much that Jo-Jo and Melvin resembled one another.

"You know, Joseph, I had a son, once. He looked exactly like you. In fact, the two of you could have been identical twins who were separated at birth," he chuckled, causing his pendulous belly to jiggle. "Melvin had everything going for him. Although, he wasn't at all satisfied with what he called, "the square life." Well, to make a short story shorter, he tried to rob an old gas station/convenience store. It was named, 'Sam's Mart.' From what the police informed my wife and me, the clerk had shot him in the back of his head. The guy said that he did so as my son was attempting to make his getaway with the petty-ass change from the register."

Boss-Hogg paused as he attempted to keep his emotions under control.

"Joseph, you can be so much more than that, man. I guarantee you that! You see, I'm very fond of you, and I'm going to teach you the proper tools of the trade. In a sense, you'll be in effect, my apprentice. In return, I ask nothing of you, except perhaps, that you never pull a gun on anyone, ever again- unless it is clearly in self-defense."

Jo-Jo nodded his head. *This dude wants to make me his son. He's trying to replace the one that he lost. He also wants to make me rich! Shit, it sounds to me like a win-win situation,* he thought. Yet, there was still a nagging question that he must ask.

He rubbed the back of his neck and said, "Mr. Braxton, you could have picked anybody out there to work for you. What made me so special?"

Boss-Hogg moved away from the mantle and sat down in a matching recliner across from Jo-Jo.

"Well son," he began and then pointed directly towards Jo-Jo's chest. "In that convenient store in town, you demonstrated mettle and an extreme willingness to attempt to fix your current situation. I admire that. Because not everyone can point a loaded weapon at another human being! No sir." He shook his head. "But you, you have heart. That's without a doubt. But it happens to be a wild heart, one that appears to be prone to rash actions. But I also chose you, for one reason."

"And that one reason is?"

Boss-Hogg smiled. "Son, I saw in you the raw material that I would need to mold you into becoming one of the great kings of credit."

Jo-Jo mused while he stared at the white marble flooring. *This man seems a bit batty, but otherwise, harmless. Besides, if worst came to worst, I could simply jump ship and go back to my old life. I could then take this motherfucker for all that he is worth in the process. Yeah, I could definitely do that.*

Boss-Hogg stood up and walked over to a small walnut cabinet in a corner. He opened it and removed a bottle of cognac. He marveled at it for a moment. "Good choice," he mentioned, as he carried it back to the glass table in between them, on top of which, two iced glasses were waiting.

"I hope that you enjoy cognac," he asked with a slight twinkle in his eyes. "I'm sure that you do," he continued.

"Of course I do, Mr. Braxton."

"Just as I figured," Boss-Hogg uttered, before he filled both glasses, and then motioned for Jo-Jo to pick his up.

Jo-Jo enthusiastically snatched up the glass. "You figured it right! Cognac's the bomb!"

Boss-Hogg smiled and nodded as he raised his glass and then gave a toast.

"Here's to you, champ. The future is yours to enjoy."

Jo-Jo nodded as they tapped their glasses together. The men took healthy draughts from their glasses and savored the fine flavor.

"Hey, uh... Mr. Braxton, sir?" he said, staring at the floor.

"Yes, son, what is it?" Boss-Hogg looked fondly upon him.

"All this stuff that you're doing for me, I know that I don't deserve it."

"Nonsense, boy!" he snapped. "As far as all this stuff is concerned, don't dwell on what's deserved and what's not. Just say, thank you." He smiled warmly and sipped from his glass.

Jo-Jo looked up at Boss-Hogg with tears streaming suddenly down his face, and said, "Thank you, Mr. Braxton."

Boss-Hogg chuckled and placed a comforting hand on his shoulder. "You do deserve it, son. You deserve it all." His eyes began to water as well.

Chapter 18

Six months later, Jo-Jo was a federal fugitive cruising through the streets of downtown Jackson, Mississippi. He was deftly piloting his pride and joy. According to him, it was the best car that he had ever owned. Two weeks prior, he had acquired a brand new 1998 jet-black Bentley Azure. It was absolutely beautiful. However, due to his current predicament, he soon expected to lose it, along with his liberty, once the federal authorities were to catch up with him.

It has been said that, "the love of money is the root of all evil, and that greed is the fool's vice." It is highly unlikely that Jo-Jo had ever heard these maxims, and, even if he had, he never took them to heart.

Suddenly, the eerily quiet cabin of the Bentley was filled by the jarring, electronic ringing of his cell phone. Jo-Jo cursed and slammed his fist against the steering wheel repeatedly, before he finally grabbed the phone from the center console and glanced at the caller- I.D.

"Damn! It's Boss-Hogg," he whispered, confirming what he had already knew- Boss Hogg was desperately trying to get in contact with him.

Jo-Jo had discovered the joys of rock cocaine exactly one month earlier, and it had been that long, since he had last seen or spoke with Boss-Hogg.

Three weeks prior, he had taken advantage of his stellar credit score to obtain several high-limit premium credit cards- including a platinum card.

He was never used to having a large amount of wealth at his disposal therefore, he used the cards indiscriminately on drugs, women and lavish hotels. Not to mention, myriad electronic devices. But now, he was on the run.

His A-1 credit rating and his sudden credit-card splurging had attracted the attention of the United States Secret Service Agency, who was blatantly tipped off by the credit company itself.

Jo-Jo was heavily intoxicated when he swerved to avoid colliding with the red 1964 convertible Mustang in front of him.

He felt like he was on the verge of having a nervous breakdown as he pulled the Bentley into a shopping center's multi-level parking structure.

After a moment, he located a relatively secluded corner parking spot on the 3rd level.

He backed the vehicle into the stall and shut down the engine. He pondered his situation for a moment before he finally released his grip on the steering wheel and pulled out from his black suit coat pocket, a disposable cigarette lighter, a small glass pipe and a large plastic bag of rock cocaine. He loaded the pipe with an obscenely large chunk from the bag and brought it eagerly to his lips.

His eyes widened as he began to inhale the smoke, while he brought the lighter's flame to the rock on the other end of the pipe. The characteristic crackling sound given off as the rock rapidly melted, filled the interior of the car.

Jo-Jo leaned back in his seat and then lowered his window a bit, before he exhaled the addictive cloud out of the window.

"Now for a little sounds," he mentioned and then turned on his stereo and listened to, "The Whispers" song, "*My Heart, Your Heart*," which played smoothly from a popular Jackson, Mississippi jazz station.

The relaxing music flowed soothingly throughout the car, while he smoked the remainder of what was left on the pipe, and then he reloaded it with another hefty rock. The process continued for a long while.

At one point, Jo-Jo found himself using some tweezers to pop some pimples on his face that did not exist. He would stop for a moment, and then his hands as if by magic, would fly back to his face and continue to pick at the invisible pimples. The lack of sleep had begun to make him hallucinate.

Suddenly, he was struck with a massive migraine headache, as a loud, high-pitched tone suddenly filled his ears. He turned the radio off, but the sound was unchanged and constant.

He squeezed his eyes shut tight and doubled over at the waist and screamed.

As fast as the burdens came, the headache, along with the piercing tone vanished completely.

Jo-Jo opened his eyes and wiped the rivulets of perspiration from his forehead, when suddenly, he was aware of a presence which caused every hair on his body stand up.

He looked to his left, but the reality seemed to be running in slow motion.

He sighed and uttered, "Man," as he loosened his pink-silk tie and gazed at what appeared to be the *Grim Reaper*. He noticed that the thing had on a black hooded robe, as well as a grungy scythe clutched tightly in his hand.

"I can't wait to come for you, Joseph," the figure whispered in the deepest baritone voice imaginable.

Jo-Jo became inquisitive, as the voice seemed to have come from within the middle of his head, which made his eyes water and his teeth rattle.

He had never had an experience quite like this one before. His natural reaction, which was supposed to be stark-raving terror, had failed to manifest. He was instead, filled with an intense curiosity. He scowled and asked, "Are you for real, man?"

The Reaper burst out in laughter, which made Jo-Jo's head ache even worst.

"I'm as real as you are, Joseph," he blared.

"But why are you here? Am I about to die or something? Are you going to take me to whatever comes after this life? What is the plan?" he asked nervously, while his hands shook beyond control.

The Reaper pointed towards Jo-Jo's chest. "Whatever gave you that idea, Joseph?" He continued, sarcastically. "Joseph, you do not know what you're doing to yourself, do you? Why don't you stop bullshitting around, and blow your brains out with that pistol that you've got hidden in your glove box?" he said, as something clanged loudly inside of the glove compartment.

"Who... or what, are you?" Jo-Jo screamed with his eyes wide open.

"The truth is way beyond your present ability to comprehend. I appear to you as an ancient archetype, processing height, width, depth and temporal span. I appear in this form, so that your nervous system can correctly process me. Otherwise, you would die from a heart attack, for sure."

"But why me? Why do you care?"

"Again, the truth is far beyond your grasp. You would do well, Joseph, to question less and listen more."

"But... why now? Why can I see you right now?"

"Because, Joseph, you altered your brain chemistry in the same way that you would change the channel on your television. Let's say that you're on Channel 8 most of the time. Well, now you're brain is picking up Channel 99 right on top of it. Your brain is an antenna, Joseph. It picks up and it sends out. Be mindful of both. That is all."

At once, reality snapped back to normal, the Reaper had disappeared and the fear began hitting Jo-Jo in waves.

He suddenly flung open his door and vomited on the pavement. Afterwards, he shut the door, grabbed his cell phone and immediately called his mentor, Boss-Hogg.

Boss-Hogg was lounging in his backyard staring lovingly at the beautiful swans and nursing a glass of cognac.

He began to weep upon hearing Jo-Jo's voice. "Man, Oh my God, Joseph! Where in the hell are you at, boy? Are you all right?"

Jo-Jo explained everything that had recently happened to him, and Boss-Hogg's heart sank. He thought that Jo-Jo was losing his mind, but didn't dare tell him that.

"Son, you need to know something."

"Know what?" his anxiety began to rise.

Boss-Hogg sighed. "Well, the authorities are after you. They informed me that they have a warrant for your arrest. They've been seeking your whereabouts for some time now."

"I know, Boss. That's why I haven't contacted you."

"I figured as much. But I've got to tell you, man." He sighed again. "You did exactly the opposite of everything that I taught you not to do. And naturally, son, this is usually the end result. So listen to me. Hear what I'm saying, because you need to come home and detoxify yourself. Right this instant. And you need to turn yourself in to the police."

Jo-Jo became outraged. "I need to do what? Turn myself in? What the fuck, Jesse? Do you call this looking out for me? Shit!"

Boss-Hogg sighed, and then continued, "Son, get rid of the drugs and the gun, otherwise, you'll get twenty years. As it stands right now, you're only looking at around sixteen months in a Federal facility. Do you know how lavish those Federal prisons are? The minimum-security ones are nice, especially where you'll be residing."

"Man, Jesse, you're talking like I'm already in the joint!"

He sipped on his cocktail and then sat the glass on the table nearby. "You go on in and do your time, boy. And then when you get out, I'll have my contact that happens to be in a very high position in the United States Federal Task Force Agency, to erase your Federal felonies."

"Man, Jesse, it all sounds good until we get to the actual doing time in Federal prison part!"

Boss-Hogg smacked his lips and blurted, "Just dump the gun and the dope and come on home! That way, we can speak face-to-face. Will you do that for me, Son?"

Jo-Jo surrendered as he hung his head. "Yeah Mr. Braxton, I will," he grumbled.

"You're sure that you're okay to drive now?"

"Yeah, I think so."

"Then you get your ass on over here, right away! You hear me, Joseph?"

"Yes sir. I'm on my way."

"That's very good, son. Just make sure that you drive careful while you're en route over here. I don't want for you to speed, don't make any illegal lane changes, and don't attract the attention of the police. Because we're going to have you turn yourself in on our terms, not theirs. I want for you to be able enter the jail through the front door, not the back door."

"Okay Boss, I'm going to get rid of this gun and the dope right now, sir. And then after that, I'll be on my way home, okay?"

Boss-Hogg breathed a sigh of relief. "That sounds good to me, Joseph. I'll call Vicky at her mom's house and let her know that you and I finally spoke. I'm sure that she'll be happy also. So you make sure that you drive carefully. I'll see you soon, boy, okay?"

"All right, Mr. Braxton."

Jo-Jo closed his cell phone and pondered for a long moment. He finally opened the glove box and removed the full magazine from his Glock-21, 9mm pistol. He then pulled back the slide and removed the last round.

A short time later, he was back inside of the third-floor den in Boss-Hogg's lavish Estate.

Jo-Jo was mumbling his frustration as he paced back and forth, while Boss-Hogg, who was hunched over in his recliner chair, was clearly aggravated with Jo-Jo's resistance to seeing things his way.

"Jesse, man," Jo-Jo began, with his arms folded across his chest, "I really don't want to turn myself in to the cops. Shit! Did Jessie James turn himself in? Hell nah, he didn't!" he blurted, answering his own question and shaking his head. "I really don't want to go to Federal prison, man! I don't care if it is lavish!"

"Jo-Jo, you've got to realize that you've made a terrible mistake, as we all sometimes do. However, we face the consequences of those mistakes, and we face them as men."

"Jo-Jo," he resumed, "Sixteen months is a far cry from serving a lengthy sentence in prison. Just try to look at it like this... you'll have a good job, your own room, even. You don't have to play those prison politics games if you don't want to. Just mind your own business, and keep your nose clean. Do your own time, as they say. And I don't want for you to worry about money. You know that I'll make sure that you have plenty of it in your account for your commissary. Hell," he chuckled. "I don't want for you to get sick after eating that inmate-prepared slop. You know, that shit that they call, food."

Boss-Hogg laughed as Jo-Jo cracked a wry smile and shook his head.

"Mr. Braxton, man, I'll bet that you're the only person on this Earth, who can make doing time in prison sound good!"

Both men laughed.

Later that day, after Boss-Hogg had telephoned the Speedy taxicab service, for Jo-Jo's ride to the downtown Jackson Police station, a car horn was heard blaring outside in the driveway.

Boss-Hogg walked over to the window and peered through the green venetian blinds.

"It's your ride, Jo-Jo," he uttered over his shoulder. "You'd better get a move on, son," he continued, and then opened the front door.

He had promised Jo-Jo that he would keep up the $1300 monthly payments on his Bentley Azure, which was being stored in the garage. Jo-Jo was happy to hear that he had someone who loved him in his corner. Especially while he was to be locked away in somebody's prison.

Boss-Hogg gave Jo-Jo a quick hug and pat on the back. "You call me as soon as you can get yourself to a phone, you hear me, son?" he mentioned with a stern point of his finger.

Jo-Jo nodded and exited the mansion. He waved goodbye and climbed into the rear of the blue and white checkered cab.

Within the downtown Jackson, Mississippi Police station, the atmosphere was one of cold efficiency. Jo-Jo approached the desk Sergeant, a gruff, middle-aged, mustached Caucasian who scowled at him. His nameplate read, "Sgt. Miller."

"Can I help you, boy?" Sgt. Miller asked in a very sarcastic manner.

"Yeah, man. I'm here to turn myself in. My name is, Joseph Milton. I'm wanted by the Feds."

Sergeant Miller paused for a moment, seemingly stuck, his mouth was wide open and his eyes were narrowed.

In the next moment, before Jo-Jo could realize what happened, he was ordered to lay on the ground at gunpoint.

The other officers in the building, although confused at first, converged on Sergeant Miller and tackled his suspect, kneeing and punching him in the process.

"Goddamn y'all!" Jo-Jo yelled. "Is all this shit really necessary?" he said, as Sergeant Miller handcuffed him and yanked him painfully to his feet. "Fuck, all I did was got some goddamn credit cards illegally! Y'all crackers treating me like a red-headed stepchild! Damn, like I done took a shot at you honky son-of-a-bitches!"

Sergeant Miller placed him in a secured headlock and whispered into his ear, "Shut the fuck up, nigger-boy! If you lie, you'll steal. If you steal, you'll kill! So shut your black-ass up, you fucking porch-monkey!"

"Fuck yourself!" Jo-Jo screamed, while he resisted against his restraint. "And let me go, you red-neck, hick, motherfucker!" he shouted, as twenty other Caucasian officers angrily stood nearby.

"No, fuck your mammy, boy!" Sergeant Miller roared, while he harshly escorted Jo-Jo to a dank, empty holding cell at the very end of the dim corridor.

He released the handcuffs and shoved him in the cell before he slammed the door shut behind him. "Now, you sleep tight, nigger-boy!" he uttered, breathless.

"Kiss my black ass!" Jo-Jo blurted, as he paced around the tight, chilly cell.

Sergeant Miller pointed towards Jo-Jo's face and blurted, "You can kiss the magistrate's ass when you see him, motherfucker! You'll be in front of him in the morning, in the Downtown Jackson, Mississippi United States Courthouse, asshole! So have your black-ass ready, you fucking coon!"

"I've got your coon, mother-fucker! It's hanging right down here by my nuts, peckerwood!" Jo-Jo yelled through the bar door, as the Sergeant disappeared down the corridor.

The following morning, Jo-Jo was locked inside of the inmate holding room in the United States Southern District Courthouse, which was located on Beauregard Road, in the center of Downtown Jackson, Mississippi.

He was speaking with Mr. Larry Pearlstein, Esquire, who was a prominent, 67-year-old attorney who was hired for him by Boss-Hogg.

Mr. Pearlstein was a pleasant and helpful Caucasian gentleman, who was at present, answering questions from his client, and giving Jo-Jo the best advice that he could, regarding his terrible predicament.

"So, Larry, what happens now?" Jo-Jo asked, seeming highly disappointed.

"Well son, my staff submitted a motion to Judge Crabtree, and also one to the prosecutor, Allen Jacobs. The motion stated that you are willing to plead guilty to one count of Federal credit card fraud. In return, Son, you'll be sentenced to sixteen months flat. No more than that. I guarantee you that. Is that okay with you, champ?"

Jo-Jo reluctantly nodded. "Yeah," he muttered.

Pearlstein smiled. "Anyway Joseph, I heard through the grapevine that you had an interesting moment with good old Sergeant Miller and his welcoming committee yesterday. Is that true?"

Jo-Jo scoffed. "Fuck that pink motherfucker!"

Pearlstein chuckled. "Yeah well, son. I'm pink, too. But, that's neither here nor there. However, I must inform you that he mentioned the same thing regarding you."

Jo-Jo shrugged his shoulders and said, "Whatever. Fuck that cracker!"

"Yeah, anyway son, I've got to get out there in the courtroom and take my place at the defendant's desk. So, you'll be joining me soon, okay?"

"Yeah, Pearlstein, I'll see you out there.

Okay, Champ." He shook Jo-Jo's hand.

Moments later, Bailiff Phillips, a hefty African-American man, announced the arrival of the elderly Caucasian Judge, Mr. Henry J. Crabtree. He was a tall and handsome man, who served proudly as a battlefield Captain in World War II. Mr. Crabtree seemed as though he was not at all enthused about being in his courtroom on this particular morning.

A long silence occurred, as he perused the many documents on his bench that were related to Jo-Jo's case.

He suddenly peered over his gold-framed reading glasses at Jo-Jo, who was sitting nervously at the defendant's desk.

He pointed an accusing finger towards Jo-Jo, and said, "Mr. Milton, you do realize why you are present in my courtroom this morning, don't you?"

"Yes, sir, I do," Jo-Jo responded. His heart was racing. *Was this all a big mistake?*

Judge Crabtree nodded, and then looked down at the documents spread out in front of him. After a moment, he stared at Jo-Jo. "Okay Mr. Milton, very well, then. It is to my understanding that you wish to plead guilty to one count of Federal credit-card fraud. Is that correct, sir?"

Jo-Jo nodded. "Yes, sir, it is."

His Honor nodded, "Okay, son, Let me ask you this…were you in any way, forced by the authorities, or coerced by anyone, for that matter, to enter this guilty plea today?" he asked slowly.

"No, sir, I was not," Jo-Jo replied, but failed to mention Boss-Hogg's considerable influence.

"Okay, Mr. Milton. Let's proceed."

He gazed around the courtroom. "Let's see here," he uttered, as he directed his attention to the United States Attorney, Mrs. Lydia Harris, a middle-aged Caucasian woman sitting patiently at the Plaintiff's table.

"Okay, Mrs. Harris. Do the plaintiffs have any objections to this guilty plea today?"

She smiled and shook her head. "None what-so-ever, your Honor."

Judge Crabtree sighed and looked at Jo-Jo again. "Very well then, by the authority vested in me, young man. By the great government of the United States of America, I hereby find you, Joseph Milton, guilty of the charge of Federal credit card fraud. I, therefore, remand you to the custody of the United States Bureau of Prisons. This will be for a period of time, not to exceed 485 days from today's date."

The crack of the Judge's gavel echoed in Jo-Jo's mind, as he was being escorted in between two Caucasian bailiffs back to his holding cell underneath the courthouse.

Later that evening, inside of his cell at the Downtown Jackson Federal holding facility, Jo-Jo was picking uneasily at his meal, which happened to be a dismal affair. It consisted of some very small, over processed soy and chicken parts, as well as an assortment of tasteless, rubberized vegetables.

While he placed the unwanted tray by the door, he was surprised to see the smiling face of Larry Pearlstein.

"Hey there, Joseph!" He blurted, with a wave of his hand. "How are you holding up in here, son?"

Jo-Jo sighed and shook his head. "I ain't doing well at all, Larry. Shit, I'm on my way to prison, man."

"Not just any prison, son. You'll be residing at Tom Loc. In fact, it's in good old sunny California! Home of the so-called, 'Chicks with dicks!" He chuckled.

Jo-Jo scoffed. "I don't fuck around, Larry!"

"I believe you, son. But seriously, Joseph, you're going to love it out there! I mean, for being incarcerated and all."

Jo-Jo smirked. "Shit, me, lovin' prison? I heard the fuck outta' that!"

"Anyway, son, Boss-Hogg wanted me to mention that to you. It's a very nice facility, you know. You shouldn't have any problems there."

Jo-Jo smacked his lips, "That's easy for you to say, Pearlstein!" he exclaimed.

Larry placed his face right up to the glass and said sternly into the tiny holes, "You've got a real problem with gratitude, son. You might want to express some of that gratitude towards Mr. Braxton, the next time that you speak with him. Hell, he pulled a dozen or so strings, just so you wouldn't have to spend twenty years of your life in prison for the shit that you pulled off, but didn't get away with." Larry jabbed his finger up against the glass, which seemed to shock Jo-Jo.

"Oh," Larry grinned. "Joseph, you mean to tell me that you didn't know how much prison time that you were facing? I'd say that you're blessed, son."

He softened up a bit, and smiled. "Listen to me, kid," he continued. "Everything happens for a reason. But what's done is done. Therefore, keep your eyes and your ears open, and your mouth shut especially if you're not versed, or familiar with something. Because, it's better to be thought of as a fool, than to open your mouth and remove all doubt, as the Good Book says. So, educate yourself, Joseph. I want you to read, son. You need to read everything that you can get your hands on. I'm talking about, everything, Joseph!" he whispered and nodded.

He snapped his fingers and blurted, "Oh yeah. I almost forgot to tell you something, son."

"What's that, Larry?"

"Mr. Braxton specifically wanted me to inform you, that you need to surround yourself, with the best and the brightest minds available while you're in there. If you don't, you'll never get the opportunity to un-fuck yourself."

Jo-Jo blinked. "What do you mean, "un-fuck myself?"

"Yes, my man, exactly what I said, un-fuck yourself. That's some smart advice that he's giving you, son. You need to use it well, okay?"

Jo-Jo chuckled. "Thanks a lot, Mr. Pearlstein. I appreciate you and Mr. Braxton. I really do, man."

Larry smiled. "I know you do, Joseph. And you're welcome, kid. Listen, when you get to the Tom Loc facility, give Mr. Braxton and I a call, will you?"

Jo-Jo nodded. "I will. That's without a doubt. So, you take it easy, Larry."

"You too, son," Larry replied, and then knocked once on the door and left the holding area.

Six months later, Jo-Jo was counting down the days. He was exactly ten months away from being released from Federal prison, and his freedom was the only thing that was on his mind.

He was working- ironically, as a librarian clerk in the main library at the Tom Loc Federal prison. It was in this library that he would learn a very hard lesson about respect.

It happened to be a Saturday morning and Jo-Jo was the only inmate in the library, besides the main librarian, named, Martin. He was a short, 58-year-old Caucasian man with a bland sense of humor. He was employed on the institution's "Free-Staff" committee, and lived in the nearby community of Surf, California.

Jo-Jo had developed a high-level of care and concern for everything that was involved in his job. He was prone to work for Martin, off-hours, cleaning up, painting and even repairing and varnishing the check-out counter.

It was after a particularly strenuous book-moving session that he was approached by Shelton Hines, a truly bizarre Caucasian man in his late twenties.

He was serving a six year bid on the charge of transporting stolen liquor bottles across the State lines.

His social skills completely matched his personal hygiene - nonexistent. There was even speculation that he was an 'in the closet' homosexual.

It was not the sound of his approach which tipped Jo-Jo off as he stood behind the check-out counter, but the smell of the God-awful-stench, which came from the man who did not appear to have the common sense to bathe.

As Hines closed the distance between them, Jo-Jo gagged and quickly backed up a few steps. "Whoa! Goddamn, Homie!" Jo-Jo blurted and scowled. "What the fuck is up with you, man! Did you take a bath in some shit this morning?"

Something so simple could have such drastic consequences.

Hines seemed for the briefest of moments to be on the verge of tears. He suddenly smiled at Jo-Jo, waved goodbye, and then turned around and walked out of the library at a leisurely pace.

Jo-Jo sat there shaking his head and pondering about what an imbecile this guy seemed to be, as he watched him stroll out of the library door. The following Monday, Jo-Jo was busier than normal. He happened to be processing an unusually large number of literatures and seldom got a chance to look up at the faces of the inmates as they checked out their books.

It was therefore unsurprising that he was able to see Hines' shank, as it flew suddenly in front of his face.

In an instant, Jo-Jo felt some hot liquid gushing out of his neck. He screamed in a state of panic, while he held his neck wound tightly. Although large amounts of blood continued to pump out through his hand, spilling all over the book that Hines had placed on the check-out counter. It was called, "*Bleed to Death*," by Grazie Franco.

After twenty-seven sutures and three pints of transfused blood, Jo-Jo was lucky to be alive. The doctors at a nearby hospital had informed him that the laceration had barely nicked his left jugular vein, and had it fully penetrated, there would have been no way that the fast-responding prison triage team could have saved him.

Hines was satisfied with the work that he had performed on Jo-Jo, which caught himself an attempted murder charge. Needless to say, the local government was more than willing to pick up the case and prosecute him.

Given his criminality, along with the premeditated nature of the offense, Hines was sentenced to a "Dark-Day." A "Dark-Day" meant life imprisonment, by Federal prison's statutes.

Hines was immediately transferred to the Stern Island Federal Prison facility, located in San Juno, California. The prison officials reported that he was murdered shortly thereafter. Apparently, while he was lifting weights one day on the exercise yard, a small group of White Supremacists, in response to the unwanted tension that he had caused amongst the other races, had ordered a "hit" on Hines.

The murder was to be carried out by a 300 lb., veteran Caucasian convict, who was also sentenced to a "Dark-Day." Reportedly, his name was, James "Mad-Dog" Youngblood.

Mad-Dog appeared to be in pretty good spirits, as he casually approached the area where Hines was lifting weights on the stationary bench press unit near the wall. After a short and friendly conversation with Shelton, Mad-Dog glanced around the vicinity at the other inmates, as well as a few of the prison guards, which were scattered about the yard.

"Now is the time," he whispered to himself, before he nonchalantly dropped a 110 pound iron dumbbell, directly on Hine's forehead, which crushed his brain instantly.

He grinned evilly as he casually strolled away from the scene, leaving Hines' dead body to lay motionless on the bench in the eastern corner of the yard. He was eventually locked-up in the segregation housing unit by the prison staff. It was due to the testimony of "Precious," his 30 year old, Caucasian homosexual cellmate.

*****

"Well, man," Jo-Jo continued shamelessly, as he and Chill stood near Chill's desk inside of their Westwood office. "I mean that, too! I'm not going back to the joint for anybody! I'm not going back alive, anyway!"

Chill stood there staring at his brother-in-law in complete disappointment. "Jo-Jo, you're crazy!" he blurted.

"I know. But, what can I say?" Jo-Jo continued, as he rubbed his hand gently against the horrible scar that Hines had created on the left side of his neck, which marked him for life.

"Boy oh Boy, Jo-Jo," he grumbled, shaking his head. "You need to see a professional, man. I mean, you've got some serious issues. As for me homeboy, I couldn't shoot at a mirror with my own reflection in it, let alone take my own life, shit," as he pounded his hand against his chest. "I'm a gangster, nigga'! And gangsters don't get down like that! That's what suckers do!"

"I hear what you're saying, Chill. But that's you, man. I can't deal with that shit again," he admitted, as he continued to massage the violent scar on his neck. "I guess that God made me different. I don't know." He shook his head.

He dropped his gaze back to the floor as Chill returned to his seat behind the desk. *He wanted to tell Jo-Jo that he was indeed different. A weak, soft, punk-ass mother-fucker! One who couldn't control his emotions. An emotional gangster, so to speak.* However, he would never say such things to his loved-one, unless he was prepared to harm him, and he had too much love for him to do that.

In his frustration he waved Jo-Jo off dismissively, and said, "Yeah Jo-Jo, whatever, man."

He gave up trying to help him for the moment, and instead, chose to focus on fidgeting with his blue silk necktie.

"Anyway Jo-Jo, let's stop tripping on the things that we can't change for right now."

Suddenly, Jo-Jo threw Chill totally off guard, when he sprang to life, appearing energized and excited.

"Look here, Chill! I'm flying out to Texas today. I really need for you to roll with me. It's about business, man."

"Fly to Texas? Why, what's up?"

"What's up is... we need to take care of some business. I'm telling you, we won't have a business, if we don't satisfy our clients. We'll be dead in the water. Therefore, we've got to hurry up and find our own inside contact. We've got to come up with a computer programmer who works inside of the credit company, and then we've got to put his or her ass to work. We're already backed up with files that need to be processed as it is, and we can't wait any longer. Time is money, Chill. We can't afford to waste it. So, are you going to roll with me, or not?"

"Hell yeah I'm rollin'! Let's roll out, partner! But tell me something?"

"Tell you what?" Jo-Jo asked, as he sat on the corner of his desk.

"How in the hell are we going to come up with this, 'inside contact'? I mean, at the drop of a hat?"

"You know, boy. You ask way too many questions, kinfolks. Just watch me, and I'll show you Daddy-O! Just pay attention to your boy!"

Chill's head was still spinning. Although, he had to give Jo-Jo a lot more credit in spite of him. "Jo-Jo, you really trip me the fuck out sometimes, man!" he blurted.

Jo-Jo laughed and beckoned him out of the office.

Chapter 19

At 5:56 p.m., their flight out of L.A.X. had landed uneventfully at the Dallas-Fort Worth International Airport. Upon disembarking, Chill and Jo-Jo made their way to the baggage-claim area. There, they were cheerfully greeted by Dick Rosenberg, a 55-year-old Caucasian chauffeur. He was dressed appropriately in a black business suit and held out in front of him, a white placard bearing the name, "Mr. J. Milton."

Rosenberg grabbed a hold of their carry-on bags, and then he loaded their check-in luggage items from the carousel onto a push-cart. He then guided them toward a gleaming black 2005 Lincoln Town car, which was parked across the street in the multi-level parking structure.

"Here we are, gentlemen," he said with a pleasant smile, and then held open the rear passenger door until they were properly seated inside.

He proceeded to carefully load their luggage into the trunk, and then pushed the hand-cart against the nearby wall afterwards.

He finally climbed into the driver's seat. "Welcome aboard," he said, as he adjusted his rear-view mirror until he was able to see them both in the back seat.

"We're happy to be on board," Jo-Jo replied.

"Okay," he continued, as he started the engine and turned the air conditioner up to its maximum. "I've taken the liberty of stocking the coolers with some chilled bottled water, some soft drinks, and some fine champagne. That is, if you gentlemen would care to indulge?"

"Cool! Thank you, my man," Chill mentioned.

"You're welcome, Mr. Bruce." He used his right thumb to point over his shoulder. "They're conveniently located in the door panels."

"You must've read my mind, Mr. Rosenberg. I'm parched!" Jo-Jo admitted, as he opened the panel and grabbed the Champagne, but quickly changed his mind. Instead, he pulled out two bottles of Mountain Spring water and handed one to Chill, while Rosenberg faced forward and proceeded to whisk them away from the airport.

"I figured that you guys would be thirsty in this scorching heat out here."

"You figured right, sir. Thank you very much, Mr. Rosenberg," Chill said, after he gulped down half of his bottle.

Rosenberg smiled in the rear-view mirror. "Don't mention it, Mr. Bruce. You're quite welcome. And please, call me, 'Dick', if you don't mind," he mentioned, as he proceeded towards the Dallas, Texas county line.

"No problem, Dick," Chill answered.

Jo-Jo showed Chill his water bottle, and uttered, "You see, boy? Some water."

Chill smirked and shrugged his shoulders. "Uh, yeah, and? It's water, Jo-Jo. So?"

"Man, Chill! Can't a brother ever get some kind of praise from you, instead of this negative, critical-ass stuff that you've been on lately?" he asked playfully.

Chill shook his head and smirked again. "Way to go, brother. Keep up the good work. I'm proud of you." He smirked again.

Jo-Jo grinned. "Now, that's what I'm talking about, boy! Was that so hard for you to say, brother-man?"

Chill rolled his eyes and smirked again.

Jo-Jo laughed and turned his attention to the driver. "So, Dick, you know the way to the Credit Company of America building, right?"

"I absolutely do, Mr. Milton. By the way, sir, it's actually within walking distance from the Kingston-Palace hotel. From my understanding, that's where you'll be residing. Therefore, you shouldn't have any problem at all getting there in the morning. But if you like, I can swing by the company on the way to your hotel. You know, so that I could show you gentlemen its location."

Jo-Jo smiled. "That would be outstanding of you, Dick! Thank you, sir."

"You're quite welcome, Mr. Milton. And by the way, if there's anything else that I can do for you fellows that I haven't already thought of, please, don't hesitate to let me know."

"That's good looking out, but we're fine. Thank you anyway, Dick," Jo-Jo concluded.

A short time later, the chauffeur parked the town car at the curb in front of a modern, six-story and mirrored-glass office building. The passengers noticed that the adjacent concrete parking structure was equally massive.

"And that right there gentlemen, is the Credit Company of America," Rosenberg announced, pointing to the building. "I believe that they will be open for business at nine o'clock tomorrow morning," he informed them, as he surreptitiously looked at them from the rear-view mirror while they gawked at the building as though it were a *beautiful woman*.

"Dick, you said at nine a.m., right?" Chill asked, gazing at the building's entrance.

"That's correct, Mr. Bruce. If it's not open at nine a.m. exactly, it should open for business shortly thereafter, sir."

"I've seen enough, Dick," Jo-Jo told him, as he casually sipped some water and leaned back in his seat. "If you could sir, please continue on to the Kingston Palace hotel now."

"It would be a pleasure, Mr. Milton. It's right down the street in the next block, sir."

He pulled back into the mild traffic along Lone Star Boulevard and proceeded to the hotel.

After his arrival to the driveways circular entrance, Rosenberg placed their baggage on a brass luggage rack that was being attended by the bellhop, a 25-year-old Hispanic female.

"Gentlemen?" he began, shaking their hands while standing near the town car, "It's been a pleasure to chauffeur you guys. I hope that you'll enjoy the Kingston Palace experience. It's amazing, to say the least."

Jo-Jo smiled and shook his hand. "Thank you, Dick. I'm sure that we will. And thanks again for showing us the credit company, too."

"You're very welcome, Mr. Milton. It was certainly my pleasure. As a matter of fact, sir, I would be more than willing to chauffeur you gentlemen back tomorrow morning, if you like?"

"That's unnecessary, Dick." Jo-Jo continued, while he peeled off three $100 bills from a thick roll of currency and handed him the money. "That's a little something extra for your impeccable service."

Rosenberg appeared grateful. "Thank you very much, Mr. Milton," he said, as he slipped the money into his pants pocket.

"You're welcome my man," Jo-Jo mentioned, as he flashed him a pair of peace signs.

Dick smiled and returned the gesture to the both of them.

"May peace be with you gentlemen too, you guys enjoy the rest of your evening." He shook their hands again.

"You also," Chill and Jo-Jo mentioned, and then turned and began to walk into the Kingston Palace hotel, while the dutiful bellhop proceeded to push their luggage cart behind them.

Rosenberg smiled to himself as he observed them walk away. He then advanced around the rear of the town car to the driver's door. He grabbed a quick moment to un-button his suit coat, before he stepped in behind the steering wheel and drove easily towards the end of the driveway. He smiled and nodded. "300 bucks. That's a nice tip," he mentioned, as he made a quick right turn onto Lone Star Boulevard and parked the vehicle neatly against the curb.

Soon afterwards, Special Agent Dick Rosenberg, who happened to be under the employ of the United States Secret Service Agency, removed a small digital audio recorder from within the inside breast-pocket of his suit coat.

Agent Rosenberg, the consummate professional that he appeared, had given absolutely no indication to Chill and Jo-Jo as to his true identity.

He turned the recorder off and grinned as he placed it next to himself on the passenger seat. "Clueless bastards," he uttered, while he unclipped a cell phone from his waistband and placed a call to his supervisor.

Agent Velar was busy driving Dobbs in his Crown Victoria along Ventura Boulevard in the city of Sherman Oaks, California, when suddenly Dobbs' cell phone on the seat near him began to ring. He immediately snatched it up and looked at the caller I.D.

"It's Rosenberg," he mentioned, before announcing into his Bluetooth earpiece, "Dobbs here."

"Hello sir. It's Dick. Dick Rosenberg."

"What'd you get, Dick?" he asked, while he held onto a foot-long Submarine sandwich and a large bottle of root beer. Rosenberg smiled. "I've got juicy bits of intelligence for you, sir."

Dobbs glanced at his partner and grinned. "Oh yeah, Dick? Juicy bits, like what?" he asked, before he bit into his sandwich.

"Well sir, apparently, according to the front deskman at the Kingston Palace, Joseph Milton accommodated two adjacent rooms-numbers 618 and 619. Milton also requested that I drive him and his cohort, Mr. Bruce, to the Credit Company of America building."

Dobbs seemed suddenly surprised. "Oh really?"

"Yes sir and I obliged them of course, before I dropped them off at the hotel about two minutes ago," he reported energetically.

"You said that you drove them by the credit company?"

Rosenberg smiled, as he figured that Dobbs would enjoy this particular field report.

"That's affirmative, sir," he continued. "Mr. Milton specifically requested that I take them there."

Supervisor Dobbs laughed for a long while. Agent Rosenberg politely joined in, although, he saw nothing funny about this investigation. "One more thing, boss."

"What is it, Dick?"

"I hope that it's all right, but I took the liberty of recording their entire in-vehicle conversation. I mean, for what it's worth. I just figured that you should know this."

"Good call there, Dick!" Dobbs blurted. "You know that it's always better to record something which turns out to be useless or inadmissible than to ignore some valuable information that would ensure us a conviction. Now, you're doing an excellent job there, son. Keep up the good work, and keep me informed, will you?"

"Ten-four, sir," Rosenberg replied, as he grabbed the digital recorder and placed it inside of his coat pocket.

"All right, agent Rosenberg. Touch bases with agents Smith and Niles. I believe they're checked into room 603. It's directly across the corridor from Milton's rooms."

"I will, sir. Oh, one more thing before I go."

"Yes? What do you have for me?" the commander asked, as agent Velar continued to chauffeur him into the Encino area.

"Milton checked into the Kingston Palace with a credit card, sir."

"A credit card?" he said, seeming clueless. "I fail to see the significance, agent Rosenberg."

"It was a Platinum card, boss."

Dobbs chuckled briefly. "I am not surprised. His arrogance is completely unsurpassed. Anyway, meet up with Smith and Niles as soon as possible, okay?"

"I copy that, sir. You have a good evening."

"You do the same, Dick. And oh, don't work too hard." He joked.

Both men laughed before hanging up. Rosenberg finally placed his cell phone in his coat pocket with the recorder.

Chapter 20

Later that night, Jo-Jo was clad in his black silk pajamas and was laughing hysterically.

The television was displaying a reality T.V. program, as he was resting in his bed with his back against the headboard in room 619.

Chill was seated in the chair near a small round table by the curtains. He seemed playfully upset, as he exclaimed, "I can't believe that you're over there laughing an' shit! This is serious business, Jo-Jo! You know I'm right! Because you and your woman need to leave that bullshit alone! Both of you guys are crazy! Man, just look at what it's doing to poor Lena! I mean, the other day when she came down the stairs, she was acting like she was high off some bunk-ass P.C.P., and some Acid! I'm telling you man, her brain ain't handling that crack shit too well. On top of that, both of you nuts have got those goddamn black-eyes. I mean, damn man, how much more of a wake-up call do y'all need? How many more chances do you think you're going to get? Because you keep rolling the dice with your life, and sooner or later, you're going to hit snake eyes. Trust me!"

Jo-Jo was pondering Chill's statement, but instead of responding when he knew that Chill was right, he decided to ignore him by staring at the television.

"Yeah, nigga," Chill continued. "You're acting like you don't hear me. But I know that the truth hurts like a motherfucker!" He folded his arms across his chest and asked, "Why in the hell are you guys messing with that stuff anyway?" What does it do for y'all?"

Jo-Jo grinned and shrugged his shoulders as he used the remote to change the television channel

"You know, Chill. I really don't know, man. I wish that I could tell you, but I really don't know my damn self!" he replied lamely.

Jo-Jo stopped changing the channels when he landed upon a re-run segment of a hit comedy show. "It's just something to do, I guess." He shrugged his shoulders again. "I don't know."

Chill glared at him in outrage. "You said it's something to do? I suppose that you can make you melting your brains into a national fucking pastime! And that's just, "something to do," huh?" He smirked.

Jo-Jo chuckled, "Fuck you, Chill!" and then he flipped him off with his middle finger.

""Fuck you, too, boy!" Chill chuckled, and then asked, "Do you know what that stuff does to your nervous system?"

Jo-Jo smirked and smacked his lips. "Nah, fool, but I'm sure that you're going to enlighten me."

"Yes I am, you damn smartass!" Chill sneered. "Anyway, it doesn't happen all at once. It adds up, little by little. You know, every time that you smoke that shit. Man, you're setting yourself up for Parkinson's disease, and all the rest of that wonderful shit, Jo-Jo! And then pretty soon, you'll start twitching and jerking, almost as if you can't control your own muscles."

Jo-Jo suddenly appeared bored and smirked. "I already know all that!"

Chill scoffed. "I seriously doubt that," he chortled. "Otherwise, you'd stop. But anyway, once all of that happens, it's permanent, dawg'! There's no cure at all. It's no turning back, man. And then after a while, you won't be able to get as high from smoking what you were used to smoking. So, you'll have to smoke more and more, just to chase the same high, which you'll never reach, I might add. And then you know what most junkies do when that happens, don't you? They start shooting it up inside of their veins. That's when

217

they done graduated, jack! Yes sir! Now you're rolling with the big dogs! You're putting so much of that poison up into your head, to where you'll start seeing and hearing things that ain't even there. At first Jo-Jo, you'll know that it's not real. But after a while, you don't know what's real and what's not anymore. They call that a Stimulant-Induced Psychosis. For many of these stupid-asses, their minds get stuck in la-la land. Stuck on stupid, you dig?"

"I know all this shit, Chill, goddamn! What, you think that I don't?"

"I know you know what I'm saying, fool! But listen, Joseph."

Jo-Jo scoffed and continued to stare at the television.

Chill glared at the side of his face and continued, "Like I told you before, nigga', I'm only saying all of this because I got a lot of love for you. If you weren't family, I'd let you go on and kill yourself. Just try looking in the mirror, man!"

Jo-Jo looked up at the mirror on the dresser and immediately turned away.

Chill shook his head in frustration as he watched him hang his head in shame.

"Man!" he blurted. "That's real fucking sad, Jo-Jo! You can't even look at yourself in a mirror, dawg'! You need to look in the damn thing more often. Because you look like you're shot the hell out! And to tell you the truth, you smelled like shit this morning when you came into the office!"

"You're burnt the hell out, Chill!" Jo-Jo chuckled.

"I'm just sayin' man, that stuff that you're smoking ain't cool at all. And it definitely ain't what gangsters do!"

Jo-Jo smiled. "That's what I always loved about you, Chill. You always keep it real with me, no matter what. You're a straight talker. I admire that. But you shamed me so bad today I took my ass home and grabbed an hour-long shower this morning. I think that I washed up about three times, and then I sent my clothes off to the dry cleaners."

Chill looked outraged. "You did what? Oh my God! You mean to tell me that you actually made someone else have to smell your funky ass? Man, you really are low, Jo-Jo! You and Lena need to check yourselves into a drug rehab'. That's for real."

Jo-Jo smacked his lips, turned over and quickly fell asleep with his back to Chill.

"Crazy ass fool," Chill whispered, as he tried his best to make himself comfortable by propping his feet up on the table with a blanket covering him.

He yawned and glanced at the digital clock on top of the nightstand in the darkened room, which read 2:08 a.m.

He sighed and stretched his arms out. "Man", he whispered, and then threw off his blanket and stood up. He stretched his lower extremities and restored the blood flow to his body. The blood that was lost long ago, apparently by the prolonged contact with the uncomfortable chair.

He channel surfed for a while, finding nothing that interested him. He finally glanced over enviously at his peacefully sleeping brother-in-law.

Chill toyed briefly with the idea of laying out his blanket and sleeping on the floor, but ultimately decided against it, on account of not having any extra blankets.

Jo-Jo began to snore loudly and smacked his lips unconsciously.

Chill looked on lovingly and thought, "Yeah, asshole. You look real good right now, getting some sleep, fool!" He yawned and stretched, before he finally forced himself to watch a late-night talk show.

Chapter 21

Thursday, the following afternoon, a black late model B.M.W. 750 Li, was parked amongst similar vehicles across the street from the Credit Company of America complex.

Secret Service agents Smith and Niles, both middle-aged and healthy-looking Caucasian men, occupied the front seats, while agent Rosenberg sat in the rear.

The agents were engaging in the clandestine observation of Chill and Jo-Jo, who were both wearing dark business suits and dark designer shades.

Their subjects were sitting on a concrete bench along a paved walkway, which led to the building's main entrance a short distance away.

Agent Rosenberg checked the time on his silver-toned wristwatch and cursed, "It's fucking hot in this car! Jesus! Good grief! I really hate these damn stakeouts! We're getting hazard pay right now, aren't we?"

Agent Smith laughed and wiped the sweat from his face.

Agent Niles blurted, "Come on, Rosenberg! Haven't we gone over this nonsense before? Man, don't you know that they've got to take us out and shoot us in the chest before we can qualify for hazard pay? You know how this madness works!"

"Well, hell! Why couldn't we at least start the damn engine and run the air-conditioner for a few minutes?" Agent Rosenberg complained, as he wiped some perspiration from his forehead with his white shirt sleeve.

"Are you on dope or something, Dick?" Agent Niles asked sarcastically. He smirked. "Sure, let's just start the damn engine and attract attention to ourselves. That's a great idea you've got there, genius!"

"Fuck you, Niles! You're a fucking smart-ass, you know that?" Rosenberg snapped, while he sulked in the rear seat.

"No, fuck you! You incompetent, unprofessional asshole!"

Agent Smith interrupted the argument. "All right, ladies! Knock it off already! Quit acting like children, you guys!"

"But he started it!" Rosenberg shouted.

Agent Smith chuckled. "I know that it's hot in this car, and we're not used to these high-heat details, guys. But we're sworn servants of the United States Government for Christ sake! And we're engaged in a duly appointed task here. So let's conduct ourselves with dignity, shall we? I'll tell you what… I'll buy us all cold brews and pizza afterward. That is, if we behave ourselves."

The interior quickly became quiet. "All right," Agent Smith resumed. "Let's get back to the task at hand, you guys."

Agent Rosenberg nodded and asked, "Any ideas about what these assholes are up to?"

"Well, they're not trying to collect money for the homeless, that's for sure!" Niles offered sarcastically.

Rosenberg scoffed. "Asshole," he muttered, and then checked the time on his wristwatch. "It's twelve-oh-four p.m."

Agent Smith sighed loudly and used his binoculars to survey Jo-Jo and Chill on the bench. He observed that the two of them seemed to be talking and laughing loudly.

"These guys are having lots of fun over there," he mentioned acidly. The others offered no response.

From his position behind the steering wheel, Agent Niles said, "It's a fair assumption that those two are waiting to speak with someone who works inside of the credit company itself. I would guess that it's probably in an attempt to procure their own inside man. Especially, now that Jesse Braxton's in custody," he resumed, while they continued to watch their subjects in front of the building.

Agent Rosenberg replied, "It makes sense to me," as he snapped several more photographs of their subjects, using a professional, 30-megapixel digital camera. "However, Milton's no dummy. That's for sure," he concluded.

Niles smirked. "And what makes you so sure?"

"Because, dickhead, he purposely made no mention of any of this to his partner while I was chauffeuring them in the town car yesterday."

"You're a dickhead, butthole!"

"Anyway," Rosenberg continued, rolling his eyes. "It's obvious to me that given the circumstances of this case, luring in some poor sap who works inside of that building is precisely what he's doing. Someone who can be bribed to illegally alter personal credit profiles."

"Do you think that they'll be able to find someone, Dick?" Agent Niles asked.

Rosenberg laughed and shook his head before going back to his camera, and snapping another photo. "Do I think that they'll be able to find someone who isn't opposed to breaking a little old white-collar, Federal law? Not to mention, getting paid exorbitantly in the process? Hell yes, I do! I would be surprised if they haven't already found the greedy rotten scoundrel!"

Niles laughed. "But you've got to at least recognize and appreciate Milton's genius ways. He's unparalleled in what he does."

"I absolutely do, Niles. That's why he must go down!" Rosenberg blurted.

Agent Smith cut in. "He will go down, Dick. Because, you of all people, know that there is not a team of criminals on this Earth, who can ever match-up to the full force and tenacity of the United States Government."

"I'll drink to that," Rosenberg said, and then he raised his thermos in a toast. The other agents did the same.

Meanwhile across the street, Jo-Jo yawned and said, "Man," as he was standing next to Chill. He seemed to be in a cheerful mood. He also appeared to be well rested as he stretched his arms out. "I feel like a champion today, Chill! I mean, this is the best I've felt in a long time! That's for real!"

Chill yawned, appearing fatigued. "That's how you suppose to feel when you have got yourself a good night's sleep for a change," he smirked. "I know that you ain't ever knocked out cold in bed at 8:30 p.m. before. I was trippin', man. Because you was sleeping so good to where I got a little jealous. I think that the television is what actually woke you up around one something in the morning."

"Yeah," Jo-Jo smirked. "It did. But you know that you didn't have to sleep all night in my room, in that hard-ass chair like you did. You could've slept in your own room. I'm a grown-ass man! I don't need a damn baby sitter, especially way out here in Texas!"

Chill scoffed. "The hell if you don't! This is one hot-ass joint, too, Jo-Jo. And they sell cocaine rocks out here like it's the thing to do. The same as they do back in Los Angeles. And you're one rock-smoking, crack-head-ass nigga'! So I had to post up near your dope fiend ass!"

Jo-Jo burst out in laughter. "You're crazy boy!"

Chill stood to his feet in a mock outrage. "You mean to tell me that you have the audacity to call me crazy! Man, look at how you're looking right now! Shit, you were walking around out here in Texas trying to hide that black eye up under those sun glasses! And look at how you been acting lately. You're talking about how you're a 'functional drug user.' Not to mention that your woman looked like she done lost most of her goddamn mind. On top of that, you were picking at the flesh on your face like a common crack head!"

"Man, I had some pimples on my face to deal with! I popped them! So?" Jo-Jo shrugged his shoulders.

"Yeah right, fool!" Chill laughed. "I heard that! All of a sudden you had some pimples on your face so bad, to where you had to remove them with a potato peeler and a goddamn cheese grater!" He chuckled.

Jo-Jo burst out laughing again. "You're lying, boy!"

"Man Jo-Jo, your face was looking like some fire had been burning on it, with all of them holes in it!"

"Fuck you, sucker!" Jo-Jo exclaimed.

"Nah' man, you need to speak with your wife about all that freaky shit. Because all I'm doing is trying to look out for your big-eared, Dumbo-looking ass!"

"Shut up, Chill!" Jo-Jo blurted, while he playfully launched his right fist towards Chill, who quickly parried the blow and backed up a couple of feet.

"Man, Jo-Jo, you're about one big-ass heavyweight, boy!"

"What, you thought I wasn't?" he replied, and appeared as if he was ready to throw another blow.

Chill however, remained ready to block his punch, if necessary. "For real, man." He chuckled. "Jo-Jo, you ain't no little-bitty dude, boy!"

"You better recognize that, fool. I hit hard, too," he said, holding up his over-sized fist. Both men laughed.

"But all bull-shitting aside, man," Chill continued. "You do understand why I stayed in your room last night, don't you?"

Jo-Jo rubbed his face and sighed. "Yeah, I know why."

"It's like this, dawg'. The way that I see it, somebody's got to watch out for your ass. You know, just to make sure that you ain't out here running amuck in these deadly-ass streets all night, searching for that poison."

"Goddamn, Chill! You make it sound like I'm Blackula or something, running around in the streets all night." He chuckled.

"You ain't far from being Blackula, boy. Trust and believe that! But anyways, that's the reason why I stayed up most of the night in that damn uncomfortable-ass chair. I just wanted your big scary ass to know that!"

Jo-Jo smiled. "I love you, too, dawg'."

He shook Chill's hand and pulled him in for a brief embrace, and then he kissed him on the cheek and glanced at his Rolex. "It's twelve-oh-nine right now," he mentioned, as he stared at the glass entrance to the Credit Company.

"Yeah Chill, they should be just about getting ready to go on their lunch break at any minute now," he said, and eagerly rubbed his palms together.

Chill also began looking expectantly at the entrance. "Man, I'm still tripping off this shit, though," he uttered, shaking his head.

"Tripping off of what?"

"I'm tripping off the fact that, we're supposed to approach just anyone who pops up out of the door?" He smirked. "That seems kind of risky to me, man."

Jo-Jo laughed and patted Chill on his back. "It is risky! It's very risky! But so is life. You got to know what to do, how to do it, what to say, and yes, how to say it!" he explained, when suddenly, the front doors to the Credit Company opened.

The two of them silently observed as a steady stream of suavely dressed employees of all ethnicities, exited the building in a hurry to eat lunch, presumably.

"And they're off!" Jo-Jo announced in a melodramatic voice.

He straightened his gold silk necktie against his white cotton shirt. "Let's boogie, baby!" he exclaimed, as a throng of employees began passing them by on their way to their cars in the parking structure.

"Show me what you've got, then," Chill challenged, as the employees continued to exit the building.

After a moment, the two of them caught sight of what they assumed would be their potential inside contact. He was a 26-year-old athletically built, African-American man, who was casually approaching their vicinity. Jo-Jo noticed that he was wearing an inexpensive, navy-blue business suit.

"I think that we hit the jackpot with this young brother right here," he mentioned, and nonchalantly lifted his head toward the guy. "Do you see him, Chill?"

"All I see is a young brother in a blue suit."

Jo-Jo chuckled, "A young brother in a trifling, cheap-ass blue suit at that," he whispered, and then he studied the man as he closed the distance between them. "I'll bet you a rack on it right now that he's the one. He's our man. You want to bet a thousand dollars on it?" He held his hand out for Chill to shake.

"Hell nah! I ain't betting on that! But how do you know that he's the one?" Chill said, as he was trying to see something that he could not make any sense of, Jo-Jo's confidence.

"Because this fool looks like he's hungry and broke to me. And you know that it's a known fact that broke Nigga's make the best crooks. And he looks like a poor nigga' from the ghetto to me, the same as you and I. And, game recognizes game. Now Chill, pay attention to your boy. Watch how a real professional get down," he whispered, as he and the man made a certain eye contact with one another.

Jo-Jo raised his hand discretely towards the guy. "Excuse me, black man."

The guy stopped abruptly close by and seemed a bit uneasy. "What can I do for you brothers today?" he asked apprehensively.

Jo-Jo, in response to the guy's obvious discomfort, smiled and effortlessly displayed two peace signs.

"First of all, my brother," he said, and then gestured towards Chill. "My brother-in-law right here and I would like for you to know that we come to you in the name of peace. Secondly, I know that you're a busy man. It's obvious, but we would really appreciate it if you could give us a moment of your time. It won't take long at all. I promise you this."

The guy checked the time on his inexpensive gold-toned wristwatch.

"Okay, brother, you've got it. But I'm really in a bit of a hurry, though. I'm on my lunch break right now. You know what I'm saying?" He offered a polite smile.

Jo-Jo smiled in return. "Of course I do, my brother." He lifted his coat sleeve and made an exaggerated display out of checking the time on his Presidential Rolex. He made certain that the man took notice of it as well, along with the gold letters, J.M., which was neatly monogrammed on the French cuff of his white long-sleeve shirt. The guy recognized it and seemed to appreciate the clear signs of wealth, as Jo-Jo continued, "Far be it from me to keep a man from his lunch break! I totally understand. Believe me I do. And the good Lord knows that a brother's got to eat! With that all being said, I have something very important that I would like to tell you. The best part is that, it won't take long at all. And, it won't cost you one dime either. That's my promise to you. Besides, you'll begin to reap the rewards of our little chat, right away! So, what do you say, brother?"

The guy seemed to muse for a moment. "All right, my brother." He smiled. "Let's hear it. What you got? What are you brothers selling?"

"We're selling time and conversation, brother. That's it," Jo-Jo mentioned, as another stream of employees exited the building. "Please, allow me to introduce myself. My name is Joseph. Joseph Milton."

He extended his right hand to the man, who shook it briefly and firmly. He then indicated to Chill. "And this here is my brother-in-law, and my business partner, Willie Bruce."

"Good afternoon, sir," Chill offered, and shook his hand as well.

"Okay fella's. My name is, Chris Darrington," he replied, and then noticed an attractive Puerto-Rican woman. She was wearing a red-lace dress and was moving towards them. "Hi, Chris," she smiled and waved.

"Hey Karen, have a good lunch," he said, and then observed her walk toward her gray mini-van in the parking lot.

He finally looked back at Jo-Jo, who was also watching Karen proceed toward the parking structure. "She's pretty nice, Chris."

Chris smiled, "She damn sure is," he replied and stole another glance at Karen's gluteus.

"Well, anyway Chris," Jo-Jo resumed, while agent Rosenberg's camera across the street inside of the B.M.W. continued to photograph the scene. "It's a pleasure to meet you, man. I've got to tell you, though. My man Willie and I, we flew out here all the way from Los Angeles to speak with you."

He seemed duly impressed. "Damn! You guys came all the way out here from, 'Boss' Angeles?" "Yes sir. All the way from the City of Angels," Jo-Jo answered.

"And to what do I owe to the pleasure of your presence?"

Jo-Jo smiled. "Well, sir. I understand that you're on your lunch break, and that you've not yet had a chance to dine. But I'd like to, at my expense of course, be given the opportunity to discuss a possible business venture with you. Maybe we could dine at that fine-looking establishment over there," he told him, while he pointed towards the French's Tenderloin restaurant across the street.

Chris and Chill both looked in the direction of the restaurant.

"So, Chris, what do you say? Are you hungry?" Jo-Jo concluded, as Agent Rosenberg frantically snapped photos of his subjects, who were suddenly looking in his general direction.

Chris' seemed surprised. "You mean, French's Tenderloin? I've always wanted to eat at that joint."

"Well, now's your chance, Chris," Chill told him.

Chris chuckled. "Yeah, but I've been told that it's very expensive."

"My man, money's no object," Jo-Jo boasted.

"Shit, in that case, Mr. Milton, I am hungry. But you're sure that you want to eat in there?"

"Chris, my friend, it's my treat. I'm picking up the tab. So, let's eat. Don't worry about the cost. I just want for you to enjoy yourself."

"Okay," he smiled.

"Very well, then," Jo-Jo nodded. "However, before we continue, I'm required to ask you a rather awkward, but necessary question.

So please, don't take offense. Everyone is asked this same question, okay?"

Chris appeared puzzled. "Yeah brother, what's your question?"

"Okay, sir. Are you now, or have you ever been employed, or otherwise involved with any form of a law enforcement agency, whether it be local, State or Federal?"

Chris seemed to take a mild offense. "The answer to your question, it's a categorical, 'no'! Of course not! Why, do I look like a cop or something?"

He self-consciously inspected his own clothing before opening his suit coat and displayed the lack of any guns or badges.

"Mr. Darrington, you never can tell. Looks really can be deceiving. Now listen, I really do appreciate your honesty. By the same token, I must inform you that Willie and I are not, nor have we ever been, employed by, or otherwise involved with any form of law enforcement, local, State, or Federal. So, are you ready for lunch, sir?" he asked, and shook his hand. "Absolutely!" Chris answered eagerly.

Jo-Jo smiled and gestured with his arm out toward the restaurant. "Let's do this," he said, as he began to walk toward Lone Star Boulevard with Chris beside him.

"Damn, this crack-head-ass Jo-Jo is one smooth player," Chill whispered in admiration, before he suddenly realized that he was falling behind. "Oh, shit!" he whispered, and then briskly caught up with the men.

From his position in the rear seat, agent Rosenberg snapped nine more photos of his subjects as they were moving through the crosswalk on their way towards the restaurant.

Rosenberg seemed a bit annoyed, as the other agents steadily complained about how miserably hot the interior of the car was.

He scoffed. "You guys get on my damn nerves!" he blurted, before he and his co-worker's observed the trio disappear behind French's Tenderloin's, ornate brass and stained-glass doors.

His partners offered no response, while he wiped some fresh perspiration from his forehead with his shirtsleeve and said, "I'm telling you, guys, this seems like a by-chance encounter to me. And, I think that we'll all agree on one thing. It's pretty damned interesting, and it's worthy of our continued attention."

"No shit!" Smith scoffed.

He cocked his head at Smith and exclaimed, "Yes, asshole! No shit, because we could very well be onto something big here," he added, as he sat the camera on the seat near him.

He wiped some more sweat from his chubby neck, and then resumed, "That's without a doubt, guys. And I wouldn't be at all surprised to learn that this skinny Black kid turns out to be their new inside man."

"I concur," Agent Niles agreed, as he gulped the rest of his coffee, and then placed the empty Styrofoam cup in the center console's cup holder.

He looked over his shoulder at agent Rosenberg. "My God, man, just look at your flabby ass!" he blurted, noticing that Rosenberg was drenched in perspiration, and appeared as if he had recently finished a fully clothed shower. "Jesus, man! You weren't kidding about the car being hot! Are you all right back there, Dick? You're sweating like a hog!"

Rosenberg scowled. "I'll be fine and dandy, once I get some goddamn air in here!" he shouted.

"Okay, shit!" Niles blurted, and then started the engine and allowed the air-conditioning to finally cool down the black leather interior.

He looked at Rosenberg in the rear-view mirror. "This is what I was thinking, Rosenberg. Let's say that Smith and I hurry up and position ourselves inside of French's Tenderloin . So that we can see what's going on with these Bozo's. Because, I'm telling you, man. This little investigation is getting really good." He grinned and rubbed his palms together.

"That's a great idea, Niles. Meanwhile, before I die from a fucking heatstroke, as well as asphyxiation, I'll get some information from the Credit Companies human resource department, as to exactly who in the hell this alleged contact is. So, I'll meet up with you guys back here," Rosenberg added glumly.

"Okay, Dick. Smith and I will maintain radio silence until you make contact with us," Niles mentioned. "Roger that," Rosenberg replied, as he grabbed his black suit coat from the passenger's headrest, which was hanging behind the seat. "I'll see you guys soon. That is of course, unless I keel over in the street and die from this fucking heat exposure! Shit, it's hot out here!" he blurted.

Agent Smith observed Niles roll his eyes and smirk, as agent Rosenberg climbed out of the car.

The two of them seemed to enjoy agent Rosenberg's mishap, as he staggered the first few steps away from the car, and then headed toward the Credit Company of America building.

Chapter 22

French's Tenderloin Bar & Grill provided an authentic Cajun dining experience. The atmosphere was cozy, yet posh. The dim lighting seemed to invite intimate, interpersonal encounters. Indeed, French's was designed with lovers in mind.

Situated around the classy, candle-lit tables sat an assorted bunch of couples, small business groups, and even the occasional solo diner.

Its patrons understood that enjoying some fantastic gourmet Cajun cuisine does not require company.

The two-story, red-brick structure, housed a 1920's-contemporary motif, which included an illuminated black and white linoleum tile dance floor.

The period black-velvet wallpapering design, with red-rose prints featured dozens of priceless and unique black and white photographs, which were mostly of old-school entertainers. Neatly placed, were works of art, ranging from the majestic Louis Armstrong, to the insurmountable, Mr. Duke Ellington. The graceful Mrs. Lena Horn's image, happened to bless the settings as well. The live entertainment was superb, and was provided daily between the hours of 11:30 a.m., and 10:30 p.m.

Fabulous Fast Eddie, along with his eloquent, contemporary jazz quartet, expertly performed on the stage near the exclusive liquor bar.

The arduous investment of the time and pride was given by Mrs. French, Mrs. Helen Simpson's grandmother, a stunningly beautiful Creole woman from Lake Charles, Louisiana. French, together with her dedicated husband and business partner, Mr. Harry Simpson, opened the establishment in 1920. Harry was certainly the quintessential, African-American gentleman.

Jo-Jo, Chill and their mutual guest, Chris Darrington, were relaxing comfortably in a secluded booth, which was nestled in between the bar and the French glass doors to the immaculate Chefs' kitchen.

Employed were eight full-time gourmet Chefs, which were hand-picked by the descendants of French Broussard herself who prepared the delightful meals for everyone to enjoy.

Spread out on the table before them were French's world-class Cajun meals. Included were ornate goblets filled from a bottle of fine champagne. The spirit was nestled in a bucket of ice that sat in the center of the table.

Jo-Jo was absolutely lost in gustatory delight. "Mm-Mm! Man, this steak is the bomb, Chris!" he exclaimed, while he chewed on a piece of well-prepared steak. It was known as '*French's flaming Cajun fillet.*'

He wiped some perspiration from his forehead. "It's hot as hell! But it's good," he mumbled, before he grabbed his goblet and tossed back a large amount of champagne.

"You can say that again," Chris agreed, as he savored a mouthful of dirty rice. Chill wiped his mouth with a black cloth napkin and added, "Man y'all, I'm sweating like a dog! This food is hot! But it's good as a mothafucka'!" he continued, and then swallowed some champagne and sat the goblet back on the table. "Would you guys care for some more champagne?"

"Yeah," the fella's responded, and held out their glasses.

Chill expertly topped off his own glass and then refilled the others.

Jo-Jo held out his glass. "Gentlemen, I'd like to propose a toast." Chill and Chris raised their goblets. "Here's to all of our real friends," he uttered, and clinked his glass against the others. "And to all the fake friends, well, may they all burn in hell!"

"I heard that!" Chill agreed, and toasted Jo-Jo's glass again.

"Man, brother. That was some powerful stuff," Chris stated, as he toasted Jo-Jo's glass and then the three of them sipped from their goblets.

As the trio enjoyed their entree's, champagne and conversation, they were totally oblivious to the fact that they were under the tenacious scrutiny of the Federal agents, who were discretely seated in a booth on the other side of the dimly lit dance floor.

Using a small video recorder, agent Niles managed to capture the action at their subject's booth, while agent Smith provided cover for him across the table, by holding open a current issue of a local newspaper, and occasionally sipping on some hot coffee.

Jo-Jo placed his fork down on his plate and wiped his mouth. "Anyway Chris, I want to make sure that I heard you correctly. So basically, what you're telling us is that you have total and unlimited access to virtually anyone's personal credit information. That is... anyone within the Continental United States, of course. Did I get that right?"

"That's right, Joseph. You see, all day, every day, all I do is program and transfer folks credit information. That's my job. It's what I do. I'm good at it, too."

Jo-Jo shot Chill a wink and a smile, and said, "That is fantastic, my brother. That's good enough for me. Now, I hope that you don't mind me asking you this, but I'm curious. What exactly do they pay you at the credit company for your loyal services?"

"I'm doing pretty well, actually! I rake in about fifteen dollars and fifty cents an hour," he stated confidently.

Jo-Jo scowled. "Wow, Chris! You make fifteen fifty an hour?" he blurted in mock surprise.

"Yep," Chris boasted, obviously missing Jo-Jo's sarcasm. "That's what I make." He smiled. "Fifteen fifty's not bad, huh?"

"Yeah, for a square-ass job, it's not," Jo-Jo exclaimed, seeming disappointed. He shook his head. "What a shame, man." "That's a terrible thing, man."

"That's just plain awful!" Chill added.

Jo-Jo nodded. "No shit, Chris. I'm sorry to hear about that. Hell, I'm sure that you deserve to be raking in a whole lot more money than that. That's plain insulting!" He smirked.

Chris seemed suddenly dejected, and stared at his plate.

Chill sneered and glanced at his Rolex. "Yeah, Chris, that's really a shame, my brother. I mean, for what they're having you do in there, you should be raking in at least five times that much! It just ain't right, man! It ain't right at all!" he mentioned, and looked at Jo-Jo. "Shit Joseph, that's slave wages, if you ask me."

"I'm inclined to agree, folks." Jo-Jo replied.

Chris became defensive all of a sudden, and responded with, "Fifteen fifty an hour is the most money that I've ever made!"

Jo-Jo chuckled, "Well Chris, I'm sorry about your luck," as he and Chill exchanged some sarcastic looks before sipping some more of their champagne.

Jo-Jo shook his head as he set his goblet on the table and resumed, "Trust me Chris, I'm sorry to hear about all of this. I really am, man. But you see, there comes a time in a man's life when he must face the facts. And the fact of you being paid fifteen dollars and fifty cents an hour, is that you're only making a petty-ass, one hundred and twenty-four bucks a day. That's chump change! And as my brother-in-law said, that's slave wages. Besides, that's what you're making before taxes, I'm sure. Am I correct?"

Chris thought about it for a minute and sighed heavily. "I'm afraid that's the truth, Joseph."

Jo-Jo smiled. "Chris buddy, you have just met the silver lining in your dark financial cloud! I'm here to rescue you, man. Now, how would you like to be raking in nine, or maybe even ten grand a week? Does that prospect appeal to you in any way?"

Chris shook his head rather quickly, while his mind raced dangerously fast. "Wait a second!" he exclaimed. "You're serious, man? You said nine or ten thousand dollars a week? That's a lot of money, Joseph!"

Jo-Jo shrugged his shoulders and smirked. "It's okay, I suppose. So, are you interested?"

"Hell yeah I'm interested! Only a fool wouldn't be!" Chris blurted.

Jo-Jo stared unconsciously at Chill before he lifted his goblet and stared into its clarity. He then began to slowly rotate it by the stem between his thumb and forefinger.

"Chris my man, that's beautiful, brother," he mentioned, as he continued to examine the imperfections in the goblet.

He smiled as he continued, "I admire and respect a man who's about pulling in some money. I'm all about my money, too, as you can see. And I firmly believe that if it don't make dollars, it don't make sense."

As Jo-Jo continued to stare into the refracting light from his champagne glass, he suddenly relived a vivid memory of an exchange that he had with his mentor, Boss-Hogg.

It was two years earlier, and the summer afternoon was sweltering in the back yard of Boss-Hogg's, Rancho Cordova ranch house. It happened to be a mandatory Sunday ritual that Jo-Jo and his wife spend some quality time with Boss-Hogg and Vicky.

They would always meet in their fashionable and casual attire, and then enjoy a soothing day of rest and relaxation, along with some delicious back yard B.B.Q. Not to mention a complete arrangement of mouth-watering soul food. As a gesture of his appreciation, Jo-Jo would always insist on bringing along with him, a few bottles of their favorite spirit, cognac. During their stay, if he and his wife were to become too intoxicated, Boss-Hogg would always insist on them spending the night at his home. Jo-Jo could not recall the number of nights, which he and Lena were forced to sleep in one of Boss-Hogg's guest bedrooms.

The time was 2:07 p.m., and Jo-Jo and Boss-Hogg were relaxing on the patio in some lounge chairs, which Boss-Hogg had situated near the poolside.

The two of them seemed to be multi-tasking, as they casually chatted while monitoring the brick B.B.Q. pit, which was blazing in the distance.

With cognac glasses and expensive Cuban cigars in hand, the men appeared to enjoy the sight of their wives frolicking around in the swimming pool.

Boss Hogg, who was somewhat tipsy, caught himself staring directly into his glass.

He smiled suddenly, and said, "Oh yeah, Jo-Jo," he held up his glass. "It's one more thing that I want for you to pay attention to, while you're out there in the field acquiring some new credit clients."

Jo-Jo tipped his cigar ash in the tray on the glass table in between them. "What's that, Boss?" he asked curiously.

"You see this glass of cognac right here?"

"Well, yeah!" Jo-Jo replied sarcastically. "Sure I see it." He chuckled. "Boss-Hogg, are you all right, man?"

"Yes I'm all right, goddammit!" he slurred. "I'm trying to teach you something here, boy! So please, pay attention, will you?"

Jo-Jo appeared to be slightly embarrassed. "Sorry about that, Boss. All right, yeah. I see it. It's a glass of cognac."

Boss-Hogg nodded. "You're right. That's exactly what it is. But tell me, what is cognac?"

"Its alcohol, Boss'," he responded oddly.

"Exactly, Joseph. It's alcohol." He took a gulp from his glass and grimaced, and then sat the glass down on the table.

"Now, remember this bit of gospel that I'm about to bless you with. I'm sure that it will help you to avoid some terrible trouble in the future. Okay now, picture this. You're out there in the field meeting with some new prospective clients." He picked up the glass and took another sip and then winked. "This is some good shit right here, boy."

Jo-Jo silently nodded as Boss-Hogg continued, "Anyway, as I was saying. You're out in the field meeting with some new folks, and suddenly, you develop a bit of doubt about him or her, as to whether or not they're the Feds. If this ever happens, I want for you to try your absolute best, to get them to have an alcoholic drink with you. Or, just try to get them to take a toke from a marijuana joint that you may possess. If they do, it is virtually guaranteed that they're not associated with any sort of a law enforcement agency, because cops can't drink- or at least they're not supposed to, not while they're on duty, anyway. They're especially not going to smoke marijuana. "Also, beware of those folks who claim to be a recovering addict, or alcoholic, but, even worse, someone who claims that they've never had an alcoholic beverage in their life."

Jo-Jo nodded. "I see your point, Boss."

"Yes, I'm sure that you do. But, my advice to you is to politely excuse yourself, and leave these types of people behind. They're few and far between, but you'll definitely encounter them sooner or later."

He pointed his finger directly towards Jo-Jo's face. "They may not be cops, but you can bet your black ass, that half of them will report you to the authorities, mainly to recognize themselves as doing the right thing. How sickening that is!" He scowled and shook his head.

236

Jo-Jo smiled as he noticed that Boss-Hogg had worked himself into a complete frenzy. "Yeah, bossman. That makes a lot of sense to me."

"Of course it does, boy!" Boss-Hogg snapped. "And it works, too. So always remember what I told you while you're out there working. Hell, you never really know who in the fuck these assholes are, or whether or not they can be trusted. Do you understand where I'm coming from?" he asked, looking Jo-Jo straight in the eyes, but seemed impatient as he waited for his response.

"Yeah, Boss-Hogg, I understand," Jo-Jo continued, nodding. "I'll remember what you said. Thank you, man."

"You're welcome, son," he slurred, as he reached over the table and patted Jo-Jo on his shoulder.

"This is ground control! Captain Bruce, calling Joseph Milton! Come in, Joseph!" Chill said, with his hands cupped over his mouth, while he playfully imitated the sounds of some airport radio communications. When his antics failed to rouse Jo-Jo from his fugue, he snapped his fingers near Jo-Jo's face, which slightly startled him.

Jo-Jo looked briefly at Chill, and then continued with his previous fascination with the champagne goblet in his hand.

"I'm here, Willie." He smiled. "I heard you gettin' your clown on. I was just lost for a moment. I was reminiscing about something that fat boy had told me."

He returned his glass to the table, and then locked eyes with his prospective inside man. "So, Chris, you mess around with that chronic, brotha'?"

Chris chuckled, "Hell yeah, I do! Shit, I've got a freshly rolled Blunt in my car right now. If you brothas wanna' get high, come with me! I'll take care of you. That's the least that I could do for you guys!"

Chill and Jo-Jo were easily amused by Chris' sudden outpouring of enthusiasm.

"Thanks for the offer, Chris, but I was just checking, you know?" Jo-Jo mentioned, and then winked at Chill.

Chris laughed. "Oh, I get it now. You're just bull-shittin' with me, huh? You were testing me. Well, did I pass the test, brotha'?"

Jo-Jo grinned. "Yes, Brotha', you did. As far as I'm concerned, you've passed the test with flying colors my man."

Chris smirked and whispered, "I told you guys that I wasn't a cop, didn't I?" "Yes Chris, you certainly did. But in this game, it's better to be safe than sorry as they say. There's no such thing as being too careful." Jo-Jo reached across the table and shook his hand. "Welcome aboard, Chris'."

Chill followed Jo-Jo's lead and reached across the table and shook his hand as well. "I'm happy to have you with us, Chris'."

"Thank you, Willie. I'm honored, man."

"You're welcome," Chill replied.

"It's going to be all right, Chris," Jo-Jo continued, and then patted him on his back. "The honor is ours, my man," he told him, and then removed a 3-page credit report from his coat pocket. "Check this out, if you will," he said, as he handed him the documents.

"Sure," Chris mentioned, and then he silently perused the three-page document.

"I'm sure that you're no stranger to these sorts of documents," Jo-Jo told him, while he cut a piece from his Cajun fillet and began savoring it.

"Yeah, I'm far from being a stranger to these sorts of documents. After all, they're exactly what I deal with all day at work."

Jo-Jo nodded. "That's right. I assumed that you did. So tell me, Chris, do you happen to have a fax machine at your home?"

"I sure do," he answered, and then sipped some more of his champagne. "It's a brand new fax machine. In fact, I haven't even touched the thing. To tell you the truth, I'm kind of wondering why I even bought it. It's got about a half-year's worth of dust on it."

"Damn," Jo-Jo chuckled lightly. "Well, wonder no more, my man. When you go home, whenever that is… I want you to dust it off, plug it in and get it ready to operate. Because my friend, your life is about to change for the better."

Chris smiled. "Is that right?"

"That's guaranteed, brotha'." He toasted Chris' glass. "As soon as Willie and I return to our Los Angeles headquarters, my dedicated staff will commence to faxing you credit reports, much like this one that I've shown you here today."

"All right then, Jo-Jo." He nodded. "I'm ready to do this shit, man. I'm telling you!"

Jo-Jo looked at Chill and smiled. "What did I tell you, boy?"

Chill seemed confused. "What?" he asked.

"I told you that Chris was just a poor nigga' from the ghetto, just like you and I, didn't I?"

Chris smiled. "That I am, Joseph. And you can believe that! I'm straight up out the 'hood, dawg'!"

Chill grinned and nodded his approval as he gave Jo-Jo some dap. "You called it, Jo-Jo." "I guess you can say that Nigga's are the same all over the world, huh?"

Jo-Jo grinned. "You're mother-fuckin' right! You can take the nigga' out of the ghetto. But you can never take the ghetto out of the nigga'."

He pointed to Chris, who was savoring champagne. "Ain't that right, Chris?"

He chuckled. "Yep, that's true. You ain't lyin' about that Joseph!" "Tell me about it," Jo-Jo chortled. "But anyway Chris, my staff will be sending you some detailed and fool-proof instructions, which will accompany each report. So, there will be no confusion at all for you. It's real easy, man. Hand me that document, will you?"

"Sure," he mentioned, and then handed Jo-Jo the credit report.

Agent Smith was holding open the newspaper, and desperately attempting to crane his neck as much as he could, so that he could see their subjects, without drawing un-wanted attention to himself.

He finally asked agent Niles, who was sitting across the table from him, and was obviously irritated, "Can you see what the hell those papers are that they're all so fascinated by?" Niles took a deep breath before whispering, "Hell no I can't, Smith! Shit, my super powers aren't working, you douche-bag!"

"Piss off, Niles!" he whispered.

"No, you piss off, idiot!" Niles shot back. "It's not my fault that this fucking camcorder doesn't have a goddamn telescopic lens, so that I can see around that fucking news paper!"

Smith scoffed. "Dick-head!"

"Yeah, you too," Niles jeered, before saying, "You know, ass-hole, it would have helped us out a lot, to have been seated a little closer than a mile away from those no-good-ass law-breakers!"

Niles was upset, apparently, because at their present distance, they were unable to resolve the level of detailed intelligence that they needed to render a conclusion as to what, precisely, their subjects were all examining.

Smith flipped him off with, "The Finger."

Niles returned the rude gesture and chuckled, "Fuck you, too!"

239

"Fucking wuss!" he muttered, and then flapped the newspaper angrily.

Niles scoffed and placed his palms against his head. "Goddamn Smith, could you please keep that newspaper still! Otherwise you'll compromise the whole operation, stupid!"

Agent Smith pursed his lips tightly and complied.

Niles picked up the camcorder and positioned it in an area of optimum concealment, while at the same time, trying hard not to limit their line-of-sight to their subjects.

He cut his eyes at Smith and muttered, "And you call yourself a professional!" he mocked. "A professional, my ass!" he snickered, as he began recording and nonchalantly examining the video viewfinder.

He finally looked at Smith and winked. "Now rooky, given what we know about this ass-hole, Joseph Milton, I would say that it's reasonable to infer that they're not reading a list of library books," he commented sarcastically.

Smith snickered. "I've got more seniority than you!"

"Yeah, butt-wipe, by three whole days. Wow!" He smirked and rolled his eyes. "Whoop-de-doo! Anyway, moving on. No, Smith, I'd say that it's most likely a credit profile of some sort. And if that is the case, it's equally likely that this new Black kid is, in fact, their inside man."

Agent Smith was fuming as the camcorder continued to record the trio on the far side of the restaurant.

He shook his head and smirked. "Niles, why must you be so condescending?"

Niles shrugged his shoulders and chuckled, "Yeah, and why must you be so dense?"

Chapter 23

Later that evening, after returning from their fruitful trip to Dallas, Texas, Chill and Jo-Jo made their way through the Los Angeles International Airport with their baggage, to the parking structure where Chill had parked his Mercedes-Benz.

He aimed his car-alarm Fob at the vehicle and pressed the unlock/disarm button. The vehicle dutifully chirped, and the door-lock mechanism could be faintly heard.

They loaded their luggage into the trunk and approached the front doors.

"So Chill, how do you like your new wheels, boy?" Jo-Jo asked, while he and Chill grabbed a hold of the door handles.

Chill smiled. "Man, this isn't like any other car I've ever had. This ride is the bomb!"

Jo-Jo chuckled and nodded. "What about that eloquent time-piece that you're sporting oh so suavely?"

Chill laughed. "This watch is so heavy. It's probably because there is so much detail to it. It feels valuable just being on my wrist. I have never seen any watches with a continuously rotating second-hand."

"That's right, player. That's because it's a Rolex, boy. It ain't no good to have some cash and you can't spend it!"

He opened his door and slid into the passenger seat. Chill quickly followed suit.

"This is only the beginning, Chill. It's the tip of the iceberg. If you stick with me, you'll be rich. Whether you know it or not, I'm the king of a vast empire, and fortune has placed you in my path. You're going places, boy! But never forget where you came from. Now, let's roll."

Chill gave him some dap, and started the vehicle and pulled out of the Airport complex.

Moments later, he managed to maneuver the car onto Century Boulevard, when suddenly, a low tone sounded from the dashboard, which displayed the red icon of the fuel pump.

"Damn!" he sighed. "We're all out of gas, Jo-Jo! Shit!" he blurted. "I could've sworn that I topped the gas' tank off before we parked the goddamn thing!" Jo-Jo laughed. "Yeah, boy, it looks like your car done caught you slipping, dawg'!"

"No shit, fool," Chill smirked, as he suddenly felt the engine began to cough and sputter. "Damn, Jo-Jo, we're riding on fumes, man! Where's a goddamn gas station at?"

Jo-Jo pointed towards the windshield. "It should be one right up here on the right. There it is, Chill. It's right on the corner of Aviation Boulevard," he said, while he pointed to a gasoline station on the south-west corner.

Chill allowed the Mercedes-Benz to coast the last one hundred feet into the station, which was thankfully empty, and was before the intersection on the right side of the street. He stopped in front of a bank of gasoline pumps.

"All right, Jo-Jo. Do you need anything from the quickie mart while I'm in there?"

"Nah man, I'm all right. You go on and handle your business. But try to hurry up, because time is money, you know?"

"Yeah it is. I'll be right back."

He exited the vehicle and proceeded inside of the store, which housed the sequestered and shielded gas-station attendant. Although, the man, a middle-aged Pakistani, could not be properly called, 'attendant', Chill felt, since the guy rarely left the cocoon of his office.

Jo-Jo watched Chill enter the store and then he began to admire the interior of the vehicle.

"This is a nice whip," he thought as he began to gaze around at its upholstery.

He pondered about how clean it appeared, but no, nothing like his S-600 Mercedes-Benz, which was parked at home in his garage.

He turned on the radio and tuned it to 105.9 F.M. "So Fly," by Baby Bash was playing. "Yeah, this is a tight-ass song right here!" He turned up the volume and began singing along.

After a moment, he flipped the visor down and opened the vanity mirror, where he suddenly stared at his reflection. He smiled and seemed impressed by what he saw, except for the black-eye, of course, thanks to his wife.

He then began making funny clown faces, when suddenly, his reflection was replaced by the face of his drug connection, "Square Will." The baritone-voice of the 50-year-old African-American gentleman began to speak to him.

"Why don't you give me a call, Jo-Jo? You know that you want some of this," the apparition mentioned, and then held up a large sandwich bag that was filled with a white, powdery substance. *Cocaine,* Jo-Jo noticed, and then immediately began to smacking his lips together and fidgeting around in his seat.

"Man, Square Will," he began. "I owe you $22,000! There ain't no-way in hell that you're going to sell me anymore dope!"

The man tilted his head back and laughed uproariously.

"I'm your friend, Jo-Jo! Don't you worry about the money that you owe me. I understand what you're going through, believe me. I understand that shit happens. I want to help you out, that's all. You know how we do it, my nigga'! You'll see. Just pick up your phone and give me a call! I'm here for you, man!"

The figure in the mirror vanished, and was quickly replaced by Jo-Jo's reflection.

He threw open his door and jumped out the car.

Chill observed him as he was exiting the store with a white plastic grocery bag in his hand.

"I hope that this nigga' ain't trippin' again," he blurted, while he walked toward the gasoline pumps.

He seemed concerned at Jo-Jo's sudden behavior, which, in the last five minutes since he had pulled into the gasoline station, had definitely taken a turn towards bizarre, he thought, as he watched him walk away from the car.

He noticed that Jo-Jo's Bluetooth ear set was in place, and that he was dialing a number into his cell phone.

Chill shook his head. "Yep, he's trippin' again," he whispered, as Jo-Jo dropped the phone back into his pants pocket.

"This motherfucka'!" he muttered, as he observed Jo-Jo brush his hands over his head and face.

Chill knew Jo-Jo well. And he knew that when he displayed a certain look of trance-like edginess on his face, he definitely had the need for cocaine on his mind.

"Goddamn dope fiend!" he blurted, as Jo-Jo approached the intersection on the sidewalk.

He shook his head in frustration, as he began to pump the fuel.

Square Will seemed upset, while he was sitting in the living room of his Encino Hills home. "Is that you, Jo-Jo?" he mentioned into his land-line telephone.

"Yeah, Square Will, it's me, man," Jo-Jo replied nervously. Silence occurred.

"What the fuck you want, nigga'?

"Man, Square Will. I was calling you to see if you could sell me a little dope?" he asked, shyly.

The man scoffed, "You called to see if I could sell you a little dope, huh?"

His voice on the other end of the line sounded absolutely incredulous.

Jo-Jo stuttered nervously, "Yeah... yeah...Square Will. Na... not too much, though. Jus... Just a Q.P., Okay?"

"A quarter pound of dope, nigga'?" he shouted. "You want for me to sell your lousy, lame, no-good ass a quarter pound of my yayo, Joseph? You must be out of your rabid-ass mind! Where's my goddamn money, mother-fucker?" he yelled.

"I'm gonna' get it to you real soon, man. I promise."

Square Will scoffed. "You owe me over twenty thousand dollars! I tell you what, Joseph; you got balls, man, you fucking bastard! You bring me my money, tonight, and I promise you that I won't blow your goddamn brains out the next time I see you! How does that sound, Jo-Jo?"

Jo-Jo appeared panicky, as he began making strange arm movements, and striking odd poses.

"Come on, Square Will!" he begged, as he was trying to negotiate the sale of a quarter-pound of cocaine from a man who actually wanted to kill him.

"Come on, my ass!"

"Big fella' look," Jo-Jo said, trying his best to sound calm. "I know that I owe you a lot of cash, and I want for you to know that there is absolutely no excuse on my part. None whatsoever, man. However, I have recently been having a dry spell in my line of business, as you already know. But you know how I am. I'm all about the money. Therefore, I have recently corrected the problem. I can promise you that in one week from now, I will have your $22,000, plus 10% extra, for your troubles, and for your understanding, you know? All I need is for you to work with me here. I need a little more time. One more week, and that's it. So, what do you say to that?"

"Jo-Jo, I'd say that it sounds good, but you really messed up by not telling me what was up with that money you owe me. If you're going to be late with my money like that, just tell me! Don't leave me hanging in the air like that! That's a very dangerous and stupid-ass thing to do."

"I know it is, Square Will."

"Boy, do you know how close that I was to sending out a couple of my assassins to wax your ass?"

Jo-Jo was now past the intersection at Century Boulevard and Aviation. He placed a hand on his chin and pondered, while pointing towards the sky with the other hand.

He had realized that he had to think of something quick.

"This is what I'm going to do for you, Square Will," he finally said. "Now, you know that I'm one of the kings of this credit game! Well, what I'm going to do for you is, I'm going to clean up your personal credit report, and then I'll add on a few favorable items, which will substantially raise your credit score. Of course now, being the businessman that you are, I'm sure that you'll appreciate the value of not having to spend one cent on these outstanding improvements."

Square Will laughed. "Jo-Jo, you really are a smooth-ass talker, you know that? Boy, oh boy, you're good," he sighed. "I tell you what I'm going to do for you. Not only will I give you a week to pay me back my money, but, as a gesture of faith and goodwill on behalf of this new promise that you've made to clean my credit, I will sell you a full pound of the deadly dust- at cost. Now, you better at least have the cash for that. Because you're not getting any more credit from me until you pay me off, you dig?"

Jo-Jo laughed. "Man, Square Will, I could kiss you!" he blurted, and then wiped some perspiration from his face with his shirt-sleeve.

Chill had finished topping off his gas tank and was beginning to wonder, *what the hell was taking Jo-Jo so long to return?*

He assumed that he was sitting at the bus-stop enclave at the corner, since that is where he was when he had first disappeared from view.

He replaced the gas pump and closed the car's fuel port. "This boy gets on my goddamn nerves!" he exclaimed, as he began to walk briskly toward the bus stop.

When he saw that the bus stop was unoccupied, he cursed under his breath and began looking up and down the street.

"This crazy-ass, dope-fiend-ass nigga'!" he blurted, as he spotted Jo-Jo standing on the sidewalk. He was at least a whole City block past the intersection.

Anger and confusion quickly swept over Chill. "Look at this motherfucka"!" he said, as he observed Jo-Jo doing what looked to be jumping jacks- without the jumping, though.

"This stupid-ass son-of-a-bitch!" he continued, and then jogged back to his car and entered it. "Goddamn fool gets on my nerves!" he ripped out of the gas station.

He was heated as he headed eastbound on Century Boulevard. He hit the brakes briefly at the red light, before he punched the accelerator and flew through the intersection. He passed through Aviation Boulevard and somehow avoided a collision with a black, Ford cargo van. He cursed as he pulled over and stopped at the curb alongside Jo-Jo, who was facing south, away from the street.

He angrily looked on, as Jo-Jo engaged in what seemed to be a high-speed Tai-Chi demonstration. Chill thought that Jo-Jo was crazy, while he stood there on the sidewalk with his arms and legs flailing about in a crude choreography.

Chill lowered his passenger window and tapped his horn a few times, but Jo-Jo did not respond. He finally slammed his hand against the horn button for several seconds.

"Hey, nigga'!" he shouted, as he threw the gearshift into 'park'.

He finally threw open his door, jumped out of the car and then walked around the front of the Mercedes to the sidewalk.

"What's up with you, mother-fucker?" he yelled, as he approached within 3' ft. of Jo-Jo, who was obviously on an important call and did not wish to be disturbed.

Chill observed him smacking his lips, and then he turned around with his arms fully extended, facing Chill, who blurted, "What the fuck, Homie?"

Jo-Jo rudely waved him off and continued his telephone conversation. "All right, Square Will. I'm telling you now, you can count on me! I'm serious!"

"Okay, Jo-Jo," He sighed. "Bring your ass on over here. And remember that you owe me."

"Yep, okay. I'll see you then. And thank you."

"Whatever, Jo-Jo!"

"I'm out, Square Will," he said into his ear set, and then hopped into the Mercedes without saying a word to Chill.

Chill stood there on the sidewalk with his hands on his hips, and was angrier than he was before. He eventually walked around the car and got in behind the steering wheel. "What the hell is up with you, man?" he shouted, while he gripped the steering wheel tightly.

"There ain't nothin' up with me, Chill. Take me home, player," Jo-Jo uttered calmly.

Chill scoffed. "Take you home? Really? I mean, just like that? We go to get some goddamn gas, and then your weird-ass just up and disappears. It was like some goddamn aliens had beamed you up to their ship, and then did some crazy-ass experiments on you, you ass-hole! That shit ain't cool, Jo-Jo!"

Jo-Jo laughed. "You're crazy, Chill! But I knew you'd find me. Everybody knows that you're my Guardian Angel, man!"

He patted Chill on his shoulder.

Chill jeered. "Jo-Jo, you're a cold piece of work, man! You burnt the hell out, too!"

Jo-Jo chuckled, "Come on, dawg'. I got some business to attend to. So take me back home!"

"Sir, yes sir!" Chill exclaimed, and then saluted him with his right hand. "I know what kind of business that you got going on, nigga'!" he blurted, as he placed the car in gear and gunned it away from the curb.

He was soon speeding at 80 Miles per hour down Century Boulevard. He looked mad as hell while he headed eastbound towards the northbound 405 freeway.

Chapter 24

It was Saturday Morning, two days later, and Chill was bored while he was sitting in his Mercedes-Benz. He was listening to some music and tapping his palms against the steering wheel, while he was waiting in the parking lot of a popular Beverly Hills donut shop.

He began to tap his hands against his thighs, as the perennial "Pink Floyds' classic song, "*Money,*" was playing from his stereo system, and easily filling the car.

Suddenly, he saw Michael Leon's late model black customized Porsche 911 zip up into the parking lot. He smiled to himself, as the car came to a stop in a stall in between his Mercedes and a pair of Los Angeles Police motorcycles.

"Rich mother-fucker," he whispered, as Michael immediately exited his vehicle holding a large manila envelope, and then made a bee-line for his Mercedes.

Chill laughed as Michael practically jumped into the front passenger seat and slammed the door shut.

"Goddamn, Chill, what's up with all this five-o shit? All these goddamn cops?" he asked, seeming out of breath, as beads of perspiration dotted his forehead.

Chill chuckled, "Mike, I don't know! Those donut eating pigs is probably hungry, I guess." He pointed at the manila envelope sitting in Michael's lap. "Is that all the files that you've got for me?"

"That's correct, my man." He handed him the envelope. "There's a total of twelve reports, which comprises sixty-one non-public record derogatory statements. One guy had all of his restaurants cooking equipment repossessed from two of his failed Miami Beach establishments. I won't mention his name right now. But you'll recognize it when you see it. He's a very suave legend, and, an extremely gifted actor."

"Who is it?" Chill blurted.

Michael smiled. "You'll see."

"Okay, I'll check it out. But hold up for a minute. I have to tally up the damages," Chill said, as he retrieved his pocket calculator from the pocket of his red sweat-coat pocket. He then removed a gold pen from his matching pants pocket, and then eased back into his seat.

"Mike," he began, as he laid the envelope on the armrest between them. "You did say that it was sixty-one non-public record items, right?"

That's correct, Chill. That's also at a figure of $650.00 a pop, isn't it?" he asked, as Chill keyed in the computations.

"Wrong, my man. It's $750.00 each, for non-publics, you know that!"

Michael smirked. "I was just making sure."

"Yeah, right," Chill chuckled. "Okay, Mike. That figure comes out to be, $45,750."

"That's correct, sir," Michael agreed.

Chill wrote the figure down on the manila envelope and said, "Okay, man. We've got the two public-record items, the restaurants equipment repossessions, and those are $1,850 each, for a total of $3,700." He jotted the new figure below the first one.

"Correct again, Chill." Michael smiled, as he reached into his suit coat pocket and pulled out a folded manila envelope, which was wrapped in a thick red rubber band.

"Now, that brings us to a grand total of $49,450, my man," Chill continued, as he tapped his pen on the final figure on the envelope, and then replaced his calculator and the pen inside his pockets.

"That's precisely what I came up with," Michael stated, and then handed him the envelope. "That's $49,500. I thought that an extra $50.00 would round things out nicely for you."

"It does indeed, Mike. Thank you, buddy. It's greatly appreciated. Now, I don't have to count it, do I?"

"You can if you want to. But I wouldn't do it in this hot-ass, cop infested parking lot. Not in broad day light, anyway," he said, while he stared at the officers enjoying their coffee and donuts inside of the busy donut shop.

Chill laughed. "No kidding, huh? I'll take your word for it."

Michael placed the envelopes on the center console. "Besides, Mister Bruce, my word is my bond. It's all I've got, and I stand behind it one hundred percent."

"That makes two of us, Mike." Chill reached over and shook his hand, and then glanced at his Rolex. "It's ten twenty-four. I'll fax these reports over to our headquarters later on this evening when I get home. I would do it right now, but I've got seven other clients who are expecting me. So, I'm going to be out of the office pretty much all day."

Jesus, Chill!" Michael chuckled. "You're serious about this credit cleaning stuff, aren't you?"

"I've got to be serious, Mike. That's mandatory. I've got too many mouths to feed, you dig? Hell, I'm providing for my whole family. I ain't got no time for games, or bullshit. So let me get the hell up out of here, before these cops get to trippin'."

"Yeah, I'm with you on that one, buddy. Take it easy, Chill."

"Will do. You do the same."

He shook Michael's hand before he opened the door and stepped out of the car.

Later that evening, in the living-room of Chris Darrington's Dallas, Texas apartment, the digital clock on the breakfast bar displayed 8:09 p.m.

Chris seemed to be in a pleasant state of mind while he was speaking to Chill on his cordless phone.

The nightly news was in progress as he relaxed on his leather loveseat and sipped from an ice-cold bottle of beer.

"Okay now, Chill. Let me get this straight," he began enthusiastically. "For every non-public record item that I remove from someone's credit report, you're going to wire-transfer me, $100.00, right?"

"That's right, my man. You'll get $100 a pop. That's our arrangement," Chill informed him, as he was lounging in his home-office in Tarzana Hills.

Chris squirmed excitedly in his seat and exclaimed, "And for the public-record entries, I get paid $300.00 each?" "You got it, Daddy-O," he chuckled. " Goddamn, Chris! You're all excited over there!"

"I know, man. But this is a lot of money that we're talking about here. "I'm cool, though."

"Yeah, I hope so. But anyway, that's our payment system," Chill said, while he was preparing to fax a multitude of credit reports to Chris' fax machine.

"And you're faxing me twelve reports, with sixty-one non-public record items, and two public record accounts, correct?"

Chris was extremely happy. His hands were shaking terribly, as he finally shot out of his loveseat and rushed over to his fax machine. In the process, he dropped the beer on the carpet and knocked his digital alarm clock onto the floor, which broke into several pieces.

"Damn!" he muttered, as he rushed to unplug what was left of the clock from the wall as it popped loudly.

"Is everything all right over there, Chris?"

"Yeah, Chill. I got it all under control. It's nothing, man."

"I'm glad to hear that," Chill chuckled. "Now, are we ready to roll, or what?"

"I'm almost ready, dawg'. I'm turning on my fax machine right now." He powered up the device. "Okay Chill, it's ready to go now." He took a seat on a wooden barstool near the breakfast counter and stared intently at his fax machine.

"That's good to hear, man. Now, I'm going to wire you $6,700 to your bank account. I'll be doing that first thing on Monday morning. It should be showing up there, no-later than nine-thirty. I'm faxing those twelve reports to you right now, though. I want for you to call me back right after you receive all thirty-six pages, okay?"

"You said thirty-six pages?" Chris was somewhat surprised as he picked up a pen and a writing pad from the counter.

"Yeah, Daddy-O, it's thirty-six pages in all."

"I got it, Chill." He wrote down the number on the pad.

"About how long will it take you to complete this job? I need to know, so that I'll have something to tell my clients, you see?"

"*Hmm*," he pondered, while he tried his best to clean-up the spilled beer and the bottle. "Let me have about four days from start time to finish. That's three reports a day. I'll start working on them first thing Monday morning, okay?"

"That's fantastic, Chris." Chill began loading the pages into his fax machine on the file cabinet behind his desk. "This goes without saying, Chris, but make sure that you're aware of your surroundings while you're doing this stuff. I want for you to check over your shoulder often. Watch out for people who suddenly start acting funny around you. Remember this, man what we're doing is illegal as hell."

"Yeah, I've got you. Thanks for the warning, brother. I know what time it is, though. I ain't trippin."

"Yeah, baby boy, as long as you know what you're dealing with. Make sure that you check with your bank account around 9:20, on Monday morning. You'll be in the game by then. That's for sure. Make sure that you call me back when you get all of the pages I'm sending, okay?"

"Will do, Chill. I'm on it, brother."

"Cool. I'm out, then. I got some other things to do."

"Later, man," Chris said, and then turned his phone off and placed it on the counter.

Exactly eleven seconds later, the phone rang once, and the fax machine came to life and began printing out the credit reports.

"Cool!" Chris whispered, as he sat at his cubicle desk inside of the Credit Company of America building. The time was 10:14 a.m., on Monday, and he knew that he had to get busy on the files that Chill had faxed to him, while at the same time, not compromise his job position behind the felonious act itself.

After verifying that the money had landed into his bank account, he stopped by a greasy spoon restaurant and treated himself to a moderate breakfast, consisting of 2 scrambled eggs, 2 beef sausages, hash-browns and grits. He furtively reached into his black-leather attaché case on the floor and pulled out one of the credit reports. He was nervous, but sure of himself.

"Okay, Chris. Here we go, boy," he mentioned, and casually placed the report on top of his cubicle's desk.

He nonchalantly glanced over his shoulder and then pulled up on his computer terminal, the personal Credit report on Marie Vega-Martin, a 47-year-old Hispanic woman.

Marie was 90 days late on her Las Vegas Condominium mortgage, which was financed properly through the, Jacobs, Fagin & Slater Financial Group, located in Henderson, Nevada.

He typed in a series of keystrokes which highlighted the offensive entry. His finger hovered over the delete key for a moment of indecision before striking it.

Like magic, the late-payment notation vanished from his screen. "It never existed," he whispered, as he more confidently highlighted the next delinquency to be erased from Mrs. Vega-Martin's report.

Two weeks later, Chill was busy counting out a stack of $100 bills, while Al observed him from his desk inside of his trailer office at his car lot, Universal Sales Automotive.

"That's eight, nine, ten, eleven, and the last one makes, twelve thousand, Al," he uttered.

"That's twelve thousand dollars on the nose, Chill," Al smiled. Yep. Twelve gees," he replied, as he stuffed the stack into a large manila envelope and then fastened the clasp.

He sat it on top of another manila envelope on the desk, which contained six neglected Credit reports. "I'll forward these reports to our headquarters later on today when I get back to my office. Give me about a week to complete them. I'll tell ya', Al, my new folks in Texas is kicking ass like ninety going north, man!"

Al laughed and nodded. "Yep, at least that's what my cousin told me," he mentioned, before he bit the tip off of a Cuban cigar.

"Michael Leon's a good Client. He takes care of business. No funny shit. That's why I like him."

Al sighed and lit his cigar with a gold-plated lighter. "My cousin's an arrogant, elitist asshole! That's what he is. But he's a good kid, you know? He informed me of those twelve reports that you had processed for him." Al appeared impressed.

"That's right. Can you believe that it was sixty-three items in all?"

"Yeah, that's what he told me."

"That was about two weeks ago. This new crew that we've got, Al, they knocked those negatives entries straight out of the ball park. And when it comes to public records, my team is unsurpassed. They're killing 'em! The best part about it all, is that once we clean up a credit report, those derogatory statements ain't ever coming back! It's D.O.D. baby."

"D.O.D.?" Al asked, curiously.

Chill smiled. "Yeah man, D.O.D. Dead on Delivery, you dig?"

"Oh, okay," Al chuckled. "I get it. But, what if it does come back?" He exhaled a thick cloud of smoke up toward the ventilation system in the ceiling.

Chill sighed. "Man, in the off chance that something so astronomically rare, actually did pop back up, we'll knock them off again, for free. And that's our assurance, because your clients have already paid for our services. And their satisfaction is our guarantee, or they'll get their money back. No funny shit. That's how we get down, Al!"

Al nodded his head thoughtfully. "Chill my man, that's good enough for me."

Chill stood to his feet and picked up the envelopes from the desk.

"You can bank on it, Al." He reached across the desk and shook Al's hand.

Al stood up as well. "Tell me something, Chill."

"What's that, my friend?"

"How do you guys do it?"

Chill smiled. "How do we do what, Al?"

Al came out from behind his desk and walked to the door. "What I mean is... how do you guys do what you do with this credit-cleaning stuff?"

Chill grinned. "Al baby, if I told you, I'd have to kill ya'," he chuckled, and saw a bit of apprehension overcome Al. "Al, I'm just bull-shittin' with you, man!" He laughed and quickly shook Al's hand again. "But seriously, my friend, I can tell you this." "

Let's hear it," Al said in nervous anticipation, as he opened the office door leading down the steps to the car lot.

"Our methodology is sound. And that's about all that I can lace you with, pal!"

Al smiled. "You can't fault a guy for asking, can you?"

"That's without a doubt, my friend. You know what they say? A closed mouth, won't get fed, right?"

"That's what they say," Al mentioned disappointedly, and then walked through the door and down the steps, with Chill close behind him.

The two men stopped and faced each other near Chill's Cadillac Escalade. "With that all being said, I'm going to have to leave you hungry, Al. Sorry, buddy."

Chill shook his hand, and then he moved around the Cadillac Escalade and opened the driver's door.

"You're a cold man, Chill," Al blurted with a grin.

He saluted Al and then he climbed into the vehicle and started the engine. He smiled as he lowered the front passenger window and exclaimed, "It's not personal, Al! It's only business, baby! So, keep your head up!"

Al smiled and waved as he walked back up the stairs to the office.

An hour later, Chill entered the front door of Angel Aslanian's Downtown Los Angeles Jewelry shop. The time was 11:06 a.m., according to the Antique Grandfather Clock which stood in a corner.

Angel, the chubby and hairy-chest, 67-year-old Armenian jeweler, was standing behind one of the many glass display cases containing expensive jewelry and other artifacts.

He wore a huge grin when he looked up and saw Chill standing there. "Chill, friend!" he blurted, while Chill was admiring the fine pieces being displayed prominently throughout the store.

"Hey, Angel," Chill said, as he walked over to Angel and shook his hand. "Well, it's about fucking time that you paid me a visit!" Angel exclaimed.

"So, how the hell are you, man?"

"Well, I'm doing all right. It's a little slow this morning." He walked out from behind the display cases and hung the closed sign on the door. "But, I expect for business to pick up around one this afternoon."

He returned to where he was and observed Chill admiring a beautiful collection of gold women's Rolex watches in the case between them. "That's some nice jewelry, huh?"

"Hell yeah it is," Chill agreed.

"Anyway, I was told that it's pretty slow around here at this time of the morning. They say that it has something to do with the distribution of foot traffic in this location of Los Angeles, supposedly, between the hours of ten and five. At least that's what my mathematician friend tells me."

Chill nodded and pointed at a women's gold Oyster Perpetual Rolex in the case.

"This is a nice watch right here. How much would that hit me for?"

Angel smiled. "Ah, for you my friend, let me see." He placed his palm against his chin and pondered. "Well, as it turns out, I've been dealing with you since you were a junior in high school, yes?"I'm sure of it. It seems like ancient history, huh? What was that, when you were about seventeen years old? Surely, you weren't any older than eighteen!"

"Yeah, I was seventeen when I first met you, Angel."

"That's right!" He laughed and opened the case, and then carefully removed the Rolex and handed it to him. "Man, Chill, I will never forget that Friday afternoon in 1987. It's like it was only yesterday," he chuckled. "I'm telling you, kid, I still find myself laughing every now and then. That was some funny shit. Because, when you and your young cohorts waltzed in here like you guys owned the place, with not one, but two pillow cases filled with stolen jewelry, I couldn't believe my eyes. All that I could think of at the time, was how bold that you youngsters were."

Chill laughed, as he admired the watch. "Yeah Angel, the homeboys and I had robbed a jewelry store near Long Beach earlier that morning."

"I know! I remember. Because the jewelry shop owner was all over the news that day. He looked like a fucking raccoon with those matching black eyes that you all gave him!" He laughed.

"That dumb bastard had more than that coming, truth be told." Chill rested the Rolex on a black velvet pad on the case. "That fool had the nerve to try to grab Lil' Devil's .38, so I broke his goddamn nose with my 9-millimeter. What'd you expect, Angel? He should've been thanking us on the news for sparing his punk-ass life!"

"Well," Angel chortled, "I couldn't complain, that's for sure! Hell, I made out like a bandit that day, thanks to you and your friends," he admitted, as he lovingly wiped the Rolex with a black microfiber cloth.

Chill locked eyes with Angel and stood up straight. "You sure did, you asshole! Hell, we brought your lousy-ass at least a half million dollars worth of jewelry that day!" he blurted, and stared him straight in the eyes.

Angel laughed. "It was a hell-of-a-lot more than a half a million dollars, son! And I paid you guys exactly what you wanted, remember?" He unflinchingly met his stare. Chill smirked. "Yeah, Angel, I remember. You paid us exactly what we asked for all

256

right." He smiled. "That's true. But now that I think about it, you worked us over real good, man! Because sixty-thousand dollars between three men wasn't nothing!"

"Ah," Angel smiled. "Don't you mean sixty-thousand dollars between three kids? And that happened way back in 1987. Economy was a lot cheaper then. Doesn't that count for something?" Angel replaced the Rolex onto the velvet pad. "Chill, you seem to keep forgetting the fact, that you yourself were the kid who mentioned the sixty-thousand dollar figure, not me. You were the one who was in charge of your little group. All that I did was ask you kids how much you all wanted for everything in the pillow cases? You spoke up on it, not me. I faithfully paid you boys, right then and there. I gave you youngsters exactly what you asked for. With no questions asked, I might add."

"That's true, Angel," Chill admitted. "But the fact remains, that you worked us like a bunch of Hebrew slaves that day!" Chill cracked a grin at Angel and began to examine the women's Rolex once again.

Angel laughed. "You youngsters sure did get worked that day! Hell, I had to gage myself just to keep from laughing in your faces when you told me sixty-thousand!" he chuckled. "I made a total of two million and three-hundred-thousand dollars off that deal. And thank you, by the way!" He continued to laugh.

Chill pointed directly toward his face. "You damn bastard!" He blurted. "You ain't even right, Angel! You ain't right at all, man!"

"I know," Angel chuckled and held his belly. "Okay, cry baby. I've got a proposal for you."

"And what is that, asshole?"

Angel picked up the watch and proudly held it up in front of him. "Since I can't stand to hear a grown man whine, I'll do this for you. You go ahead and give this six-thousand-dollar Oyster Perpetual Rolex to that beautiful wife of yours. She deserves it, don't you think?"

Chill gasped. "Yeah Angel, she does indeed."

Angel smiled and gingerly handed him the Rolex. "Now, all of that stuff that happened back in 1987 is a dead issue, right?"

"It's dead and buried my man. It's gone," Chill agreed, as he coveted the Rolex.

"Good. Very well then, let's get down to business, shall we? I'm going into the back to my office for a moment to fetch you those

257

credit reports, along with the cash that you requested, and also a box for you to put your wife's watch in."

"Okay, Angel. And thanks a lot, man." "No, Chill," Angel chuckled. "Thank you!" he replied, and then he burst out laughing.

"Fuck off, Angel!" Chill laughed, as Angel headed into the back room laughing hysterically.

Chapter 25

Chris Darrington was sipping from a bottle of chilled beer and singing along with "50-Cent's" song, "*Heat*," which was blaring from his brand new home stereo system.

"Get money, baby," he crooned, as he dutifully watched the credit report pages in his fax machine pile up in the tray.

He took a long sip of the beer and shouted, "Cha-Ching!" while he moved his body in rhythm to the music. After a moment, he glanced at his newly purchased designer wristwatch. "It's eight-forty p.m. Let me call this fool, Chill."

He sat the beer on the breakfast counter and picked up his cell phone and pressed in Chill's number.

Meanwhile, Chill was wearing his black pajamas in the home office of his Tarzana Hills home. He was faxing the last page of a credit report to Chris, when suddenly; his cell phone on his desk began to ring. He flipped it open and acknowledged the caller's name. "It's Chris' ass," he said, and then pressed the call button as he placed the phone against his ear. "Chris, my man!" he blurted.

"What's up, dawg'?

"Money baby, that's what's up. You should be receiving the last page coming through right now. I've sent you a total of eight reports. Its thirty-eight pages in all. What do you have over there in your fax machine?"

Chris gazed at his fax machine. "I've got the last page coming in right now," he reported, while he watched excitedly as the fax machine dropped the completed page into the tray. "I've just received the thirty-eighth page, Chill."

"That's excellent, man. Now, check it out, throughout those thirty-eight pages are two hundred and twenty-eight derogatory statements."

"Ah shit!" Chris whistled and cracked his knuckles.

Chill chuckled. "Damn, boy! That's right get excited about getting your paper, dawg! Now dig, all but twelve of them are non-public record items."

Chris made a poor attempt to suppress his exhilaration. "All but twelve, Chill?"

Chill's reply was casual. "Yeah, that's right. It's two-hundred and sixteen non-public record entries, and twelve public records in all. With the public record entries, you'll be dealing with four state tax liens, four federal tax liens, and four luxury vehicle repossessions."

Everywhere that Chris looked inside of his apartment, all that he could see were dollar signs. "Man!" he whispered, as he hastily groped for his fiancée's calculator inside of the utility drawer near the kitchen sink.

"You said that it was two hundred and sixteen non-public records, and twelve public records, right?" He frantically keyed in the computations. In doing so, he accidently stepped on a piece of shard from the destroyed digital clock's plastic housing. "Ouch!" he yelled, and then dropped his cell phone on the carpet and howled in agony.

He finally grabbed a broom from the utility closet and shoved the sharp pieces away from the area where he was standing.

He examined his foot for a long moment. It was not bleeding, but it *hurt badly*, he thought, as he picked up his cell phone and placed it up to his ear.

"I'm sorry about that, Chill. But I messed around and stepped on something sharp in my goddamn kitchen!"

Chill's eyes were wide open on the other end of the line, as he poured himself a glass of cognac on the rocks.

"Man, Chris, that's kinda' jacked up, dude! You better make sure that you clean your foot real good. Because, if you mess around and get an infection up in there, it could be all bad for us all! Because I need for you to be able to get to work, you know?"

Chris was breathless, and his pain was still intense. "I know what you mean, Chill. There ain't no blood, though. Not any that I can see, anyway. I don't think the piece even penetrated the skin. But still, it hit a nerve or something! I mean, it hurts like a mother-fucker!"

Chill found the whole ordeal to be too funny for words. "Chris man, you need to calm your ass down, you know? You're over there acting like a little kid on Christmas day! Take it slow, and be thoughtful, man. Hell, I call you up to give some work and I hear shit breaking, things popping, snapping sounds coming over the phone! It reminds me of some of that damn electrical shit out of one of those Frankenstein movies! You're the insider, Chris. The buck stops with you, man. Without you, I have no business, at all. I can't afford to have no clumsy-ass members on my team! That's a liability, dawg'. Now, I'm glad that you're okay, but try and be more careful in the future, all right?"

"Yeah, Chill, I will. I guess I got a little excited, you know?"

"Yeah, man, I can tell! Hey, don't get me wrong, getting excited about money is all well and good, but there is a time and a place for that, all right?"

"'All right, Chill. I hear you brother. You've got a good point there."

"Most certainly, I do! Anyway, back to business. According to my calculations," Chill continued, as he slid into his recliner. "Your total payment for this particular job is thirty-five thousand, two hundred dollars. Does that match up with what you figured?"

"It sure does. That number is right on the money- so to speak." Chris placed the calculator back in the drawer.

"That's good. Okay, sometime tomorrow morning, I need for you to go by the mailing joint that we talked about. You should have received the bouquet of flowers that I sent you by then. The cheese is hidden under the soil in a plastic protection bag. Please Chris, don't drop the pot and break the mother-fucker, at least not inside of the business, or outside in the parking lot, for that matter."

"I won't," Chris assured, as he continued to massage his aching foot.

261

"Please, dawg! Because all that we need is for some square-ass, nosy package worker, seeing what time it is with that cash in the bag. So don't be clumsy, man!

"Don't trip, Chill!" he chuckled. "I've got this here. I'll remember what you said, though- take it slow, and be thoughtful. I'll stop by there first thing tomorrow morning. I need for you to give me about a week to have those reports completed. I'll start knocking them out in the morning as well," he said, as he gathered up the credit reports from the tray in the fax machine.

"Okay, Mr. Darrington, we'll shoot for a week from Wednesday, then. Let me know when you get your roses. I hope you like red ones?" Chill said in an effeminate tone of voice, as his wife entered the room and plopped down in his lap.

Chris laughed. "You're scaring me, Chill! But of course I like red roses. Especially when they come chocked full of 'cheddar'! Thanks, man."

"No. Thank you, Chris. Oh, for your information, I was only playing earlier. I ain't funny, Homie. I'm a happily married man, with five kids no doubt. So don't trip."

"Yeah, I kind of figured that you weren't."

"Anyway, Chris, I'll holler at you tomorrow. Later, man."

"Peace, Chill."

"Peace out, brother."

Chill ended the call and placed the cell phone on his desk. He turned to his wife and gave her a soft kiss on the lips. "So, my love, do you like your new Rolex?"

Jen smiled briefly. "Yes, I love it. Not because of what it is, but because of the spirit in which you gave it to me. Although it could've easily been a fifty-dollar watch. It wouldn't have changed how I feel about things. You know how I am, babe? I don't trip on material stuff, like a lot of other people do. But, I'll always cherish and love you for your care and concern."

"I'll always cherish and love you, too, Momma." He planted a passionate kiss upon her lips.

The next morning at the Credit Company of America building, Chris Darrington was seated in front of his computer terminal.

He nonchalantly glanced over his shoulder, and then marveled at the ruined credit score information of one of Al's clients that was displayed on the screen.

"Man, this douche-bag has straight fucked over his credit score!" he whispered. "Mr. Limmie Little's. He's a Black man, age 48. He has thirty-six negative inquires. Damn, brotha'!" he sighed. "That's real bad, Homie," he whispered, as he typed in a now familiar key sequence.

His efforts were rewarded as the entire block of inquiries were suddenly highlighted in bright yellow. He pressed the delete key without hesitation, this time. "Adios, amigo," he chuckled and checked over his shoulders again. "Now, let's get to the rest of this bullshit."

He scanned the report for more derogatory items, which he found, highlighted, and then erased them with the ease and speed of an expert playing a simple video game.

Chapter 26

On Wednesday morning, Chill was sitting at his desk in the Westwood office that he and Jo-Jo shared. Sixty-nine thousand dollars in $100 bills were placed on top of a manila envelope, which was filled with five Credit reports. Nick Crane was seated comfortably in the chair opposite him.

"So this particular package is guaranteed to raise the credit scores, right?" Nick asked.

"Nicky, baby, this package is fool proof. It's been tested and proven," Chill assured him, and then he produced a couple of credit reports from a desk drawer. "Check these out, if you will." He proudly placed them on the desk in front of him. "Here's a before and after snapshot of our work. It's self-explanatory."

Nick picked up the reports and began reading them. "Okay, Chill. We've got a Mr. Martin Phillips here- what a sorry bastard, eh'?" He shook his head. "His credit score is a 449. He has at least forty negative inquiries, two repossessions, three Federal Tax liens and three judgments against him. He also has all of these goddamn late payments." He silently counted them. "He's got sixteen of them, no less!" He looked at Chill. "It looks like this cat would have benefitted from a bankruptcy!"

Chill smiled. "Martin was very close to filing for bankruptcy, before he was introduced to me, of course." He leaned back in his chair. "Don't stop reading, Nick! Continue on. Check out the other document; the after report. I'm sure that you'll find it very interesting."

"All right, Mr. Bruce." Nick picked up the "after" report and began perusing it. "Holy shit, man! Jesus! This same guy has a credit score that is out of this world, now!" He looked up at Chill, who was grinning.

"Yeah Nick, I know." Chill laughed. "Please, read on and become enlightened as to why we are the best in the business."

"Man, you guys really are good!" He seemed impressed as he began to read more of the report. "The guy has two late-model Mercedes-Benz'. They were both financed through the Merriam Brothers Financial, in Atlanta, Ga. Both cars are valued at $110,000 each. They're both totally paid off and were never once late on a payment, according to this report." His eyes followed his finger as it cruised down the page, stopping suddenly on a particular item. "Son of a bitch!" he blurted. "This guy now shows as owning a paid-off home in Atlanta, valued at four hundred and fifty thousand dollars! Motherfucker!"

"It gets better, my man. Keep reading."

Nick shot him a confused look. "How could this possibly get any better, Chill?" he asked, as he scanned further down the sheet. "This guy has no debt, whatsoever. Ah ha! He's got a platinum credit card with a $100,000 limit, and another gold card with a $50,000 limit. "Jesus," he whispered.

Chill smiled. "You can't find a single blemish, can you?"

Nick seemed impressed. "I've searched this entire credit report. This guy doesn't have a single derogatory statement."

"What'd I say to you before, Nick? I told you that we don't be playing around. We're the kings of this empire."

Nick sighed as he placed the credit report back on the desk. "Chill, man, don't get me wrong, but if I doubted your abilities at all, that stack of Benjamin's wouldn't be sitting on your desk, and I wouldn't be here in your office."

"Nicky baby, I know this already." Chill moved the cash aside from the manila envelope and opened it. "The proof is in the pudding, as they say. And I can prove everything that I say to you," he continued, as he pulled out five credit reports.

He spread them neatly out on the desk before him. "Okay- first of all, you already know that your client's credit reports are totally trashed. These dummies couldn't finance a damn thing, let alone, qualify for a median-priced home loan. But this is all about to change, as you already know."

"I knew you'd say that." Nick smiled, as he leaned back in his chair and folded his arms across his chest.

"I'm one of the Kings of this Credit Empire, man! As I previously promised you, I'm going to clean up these five credit reports at absolutely no cost to you. For free, zilch! This would normally cost your clients over $27,000! Keep in mind that this figure only applies to the deletion of the derogatory entries. However, we have what we call, the "add-on" package. If you need some positive credit information added on, we can do that, too. But my friend, it's going to cost you. Because we charge $4,600 for each item that we add onto the reports. However, our "add-on" packages have a three-item minimum."

Nick whistled. "That's pretty pricey, Chill!"

"I know it is. This stuff ain't cheap! But it's well worth it to have these enhancements on your credit report. And you know it is, too. Especially when you take into consideration, all of the things that you can do, once they're established onto your report. Besides, when you buy our "add-on" package, we'll throw in an A-1 credit card that's in good standing- at half the price."

"At half the price, huh?" Nick appeared interested.

"You heard me right, Daddy-O. Why don't I give you the whole rundown on our "add-on" packages, okay?"

"Yeah," he nodded. "Break it down for me, if you will," he requested, listening intently.

"The first of the three "add-ons" are always a $450,000 home. It shows as being paid in full, without any late payments. That's $4,600."

Nick nodded. "That sounds good."

"I know it does. Now, the second of the three add-ons is always a late-model luxury vehicle in the $100,000 price range. The same as the house, it's shown to be paid in full with no late payments. It's also $4,600."

"Are you talking about a new Mercedes, a B.M.W., Audi, or some other luxury vehicle like that?"

"That's not important. What is important are the dollar amounts, and the fact that there are no late payments. Now, the third and last "add-on" item is a premium credit card with a $50,000 limit. So, three times $4,600 is $13,800. That's our total price for the "add-on" package."

"What about the half-price deal?" Nick asked curiously.

"When you purchase the "add-on" package, you can acquire an additional premium credit card at half the price."

"So that's an additional $2,300, correct?"

"Yeah, Nick. And that's peanuts compared to what you can rake in with a credit score of 800 or higher. I mean, if you know what the hell you're doing!"

"Shit." Nick laughed. "800 is overkill for a person like me! Hell, you'd be surprised what old Nicky-boy here can do with a 640!"

Chill shrugged his shoulders. "Yeah, that is, if you don't have any derogatory entries. Otherwise, it's nothing special."

"That's true, Chill." He nodded. "That's true. You're definitely the man!"

Chill smirked. "Yes, Nick, I've been told that a lot lately." He placed the money into his desk drawer, and then looked at Nick and assumed a serious posture. "Now, man, make sure that your clients know that they don't actually own the physical items that we're adding onto their credit reports. This stuff is only useful to somebody with half a brain. This gives them the ability to qualify for loans and other financing. It is our association's expertise which does the actual whispering into the ears of the banks and the other financial institutions, saying, 'trust him- he pays his bills on-time. He also has money to spend. Lots of it!' So Nick, don't jeopardize us all by sending us some lame-brained suckers. You know, cats like this young, rich-ass crack cocaine-dealing fool up out of Los Angeles. Man!" He sighed.

"Check this out," Chill continued. "I was introduced to this young Black dude by an associate of mine named Tony. I finally met up with the dude at a restaurant in Ladera Heights, not too far from L.A.X. The fool called himself, "Chucky Mack." He shook his head.

"You say the guy's name was, Chucky Mack?" Nick chortled.

"Yeah, man!" Chill sighed. "So anyway, I had a second meeting with this fool a couple of days later in this small, lousy-ass clothing shop over on Century Boulevard. He claimed to be the owner of the joint. This little slick-ass sucker wanted me to crank up his credit score to reflect a "900." He was talking about how he wanted to purchase a sixty unit apartment building over on Western Avenue, right down the block from his momma's house."

Chill paused to take a sip from his iced tea on the desk.

"Anyway, Nick," he resumed, while he placed the styrofoam cup back on his desk. "I checked his eyes out to see if this stupid-ass 23-year-old brother was smoking on some cocaine rocks or something. So I said to him, you want me to hook your young ass up with a 900 Credit score?" He says, "Yeah," like he was all sure of himself an' shit. I couldn't help but to burst-out laughing right there in his face."

"And what did he do?" Nick grinned.

"He started looking at me like he was all butt-hurt. So, he called himself mad-dogging me like I was a little punk or something. So I said, look, you idiot, the first time that you try to use that "900" credit score, you're not going to see it, but all of these goddamn alarms, bells and whistles and shit are going to start sounding off like it's the Fourth of July or something. The next thing you know, a bunch of Federal agents are going to descend upon you, chew your young-ass up, and then spit your sorry butt into the Federal prison system. This will be done so fast it'll make your head spin. By then, you'll have snitched on everyone and everything that you know and love on this planet. So, you know that my Black ass wouldn't stand a chance with you. That's what I told him, Nick."

"This story's getting good! What happen next? Did you have to beat him up or something?" Nick smiled and sat straight up with his elbows resting on the desk, extremely curious.

"Not at all, Nick. If that was the case, I would've just shot his punk-ass in the head. Fuck all of that fighting! I'm getting too old to be getting my knuckles all bruised up."

"So what happened next? Finish the story!" He chuckled.

"I'm trying to, if you let me!"

"Okay, okay, Chill. I'll let you finish your story. Continue on, my good man."

"Are you sure?" Chill grinned.

"Yes sir. Continue, please."

"Okay. So dig, this kid fires back with some shit, like... I ain't a snitch! 'Cause snitches are some bitches, and I ain't no bitch! He said some punk-ass, square-ass phrase like that. Man, Nick," he chuckled. "Chucky Mack was a cold piece of work. I'm telling you, so, anyways, I tell him this, you might not be a snitch right now, youngster. Not right this minute, anyway. But you'll get to snitchin' on your own momma. You'll tell them Federal boys shit that ain't even true, just to get them up off of your weird, Gonzo looking ass!"

Nick managed to speak between bouts of laughter. "Did the dumbass have anything else to say after that?"

Chill held back his laughter. "Nope, he just stood there looking stupid. But I could feel the idiot eyeballing the back of my head, as I got up and walked the hell away from him and his trifling, raggedy-ass little shop." Nick continued to laugh. "Anyway to make a long story short, please, don't bring me any dumb-ass suckers like that. Leave the Chucky Mack's of the world outside of the door where they belong. Please man! I'm begging you, Nick."

"Well, since you asked me so nicely," Nick said, as he suddenly lost all control of himself with laughter. Chill held back his emotions as Nick's tears began to stream down his face.

"Goddamn, Nick! Are you all right over there, man? That story wasn't that goddamn funny!"

Nick struggled to regain control of his laughter. He wiped his eyes and face and said, "I'm sorry, Chill. I know that I got a little out of control there. But, I haven't laughed that hard in years, man. You're a funny guy, you know that?"

"Yeah, man. I'm not that funny though," Chill continued. "'Cause you've done shown your ass in here today, I'm telling you anyway, my point is this, keep it intelligent, will you?"

"Undoubtedly," Nick mentioned, as a partial laugh managed to blow through his lips. He reached across the desk and shook Chill's hand, and then the two men stood to their feet.

"Anyway, give me about eight, but no more than nine days to get these credit reports washed-up and polished for you."

"That sounds great to me. Oh, by the way, let me know when it's okay for my clients to begin with their escrow procedures."

"I will, Nick. But in the meantime, go ahead and advise your clients, that they must not do anything at all with their Social Security number, until I give you the green light. It's a must, because until I finish doing my job, they can't be applying for stuff. You know, drawing unnecessary attention to their Social Security number and to my people on the inside. That would be, how can I say this- catastrophic, for all parties involved."

He shook Nick's hand and mentioned, "It's important that trust exist between us. The work will be done- they can trust and believe that! But for a lot of the working-class folks, pouring their hard-earned cash into something of this magnitude for the first time can be a little uneasy. I totally understand this. Your clients may feel the need to check on their credit report to see if I've done anything to improve their situation. I repeat, Nick, for them to do this would spell certain disasters for them, as well as for us. Therefore, you must do what you have to do to keep them up off of their blue-chip until you instruct them to precede, understand?"

"Yes, sir." He shook Chill's hand again before checking the time on his wristwatch. "It's almost lunch time. Are you hungry? Let's do lunch. It's my treat."

"I would like to take you up on your offer, Nick. I am hungry! But, I've got to pick up some files from my associate, Tony Kin. He's the guy that I was telling you about, the one who cut me into that Chucky Mack fool. But thanks, anyway."

"Tony Kin? He's Chucky Mack's guy, right?" Nick laughed.

"Yeah," Chill snickered. "That asshole!"

"Very well, bud'. Oh yeah, Chill. What the hell is a blue-chip?"
"A 'blue-chip' is what we call the Social Security card."

"Okay, cool. I'll have to be sure and take a note of that."

"Yes, please do so, because I try not to use the words, Social Security, especially when I'm talking over the phone."

"Okay, I've got your point. But anyway, let me know when my clients can start looking into their blue-chip."

"Very good, Nick. You're getting hip now. You'll be the first to know that information. And I'm sure that you'll remember to go over with your clients everything that we discussed, right?"

"Absolutely, my man." They shook hands.

"I'll be in touch," Chill told him, as he led him to the office lobby.

Chapter 27

The time on the faxed copy was 1:02 P.M. Al pulled it out of the credit-report machine in his office at Universal Sales Automotive and then began to read it. He suddenly became irate, and blurted, "Holy shit, Chill! What in the hell is this bull-shit?"

Chill remained seated and wondered what could have made Al so angry. "What's wrong, Al? Talk to me." He pleaded curious.

Al walked around his desk to where Chill was seated and dropped his weight in an adjacent chair. He took a long, deep breath, and when he let it out, it sounded like a huge deflating balloon. For some reason, this sound gave Chill the chills. "Check this out!" he exclaimed, and tossed the credit fax onto Chill's lap. "We're fucked, Chill! We're totally fucked, pal!" He sighed.

Chill picked up the report and his eyes quickly came upon the word, "DECEASED," which was plastered in big-bold letters across the top center of the document. He gasped and whispered, "Oh shit!"

"Now you can see my point, can't you? This Johnny Moore clown on this report is dead as a fucking doornail! What's up with this shit, Chill?"

Chill scratched his head. "Damn, Al! I don't know, man!" He shrugged his shoulders. "Man, I should have known better than to trust Tony Kin's scandalous ass!"

Al went back to his desk and plopped down into his chair. "Who the hell is Tony Kin?"

"He's an associate of mine! He's in the mortgage game. That stupid asshole gave me this blue-chip, and asked me to run a make on it and get back at him with my credit cleaning fees." He dropped the report on Al's desk.

"At the very least, you need to call this punk and tell him about the shit storm that he's started over here! I'm telling you, man. Those assholes from the Social Security office are going to be here crawling all over me and my goddamn car lot! Man!" He sighed. "They're going to be on my ass like flies on shit, Chill."

"Damn!" Chill whispered, while shaking his head. He finally jumped up from his seat and grabbed his black suit coat from the hanging rack near the exit door.

"Hold up a minute, Chill." Al said, as he reached in one of his desk drawers and pulled out an automobile application and placed it on his desk. "Sit down for a minute."

Chill hesitated, but sat back in his seat. "This is all bad, man. The Feds could be on their way over here right now, as we speak," Al resumed nervously.

"Holy shit, Al! You mean to tell me they work that damn fast?"

"You'd better know it! Those pricks have nothing else better to do, and they have unlimited funds to do it with. So, if and when they do show up here in their cheap suits and drab four-door sedans, asking questions like, why in the hell was a corpse here at my car lot purchasing a vehicle? We're going to hedge our bets here. Therefore, I need for you to fill out this vehicle application with as much of this schmuck's personal information that you have, and fast! But first- are you right or left-handed?" He quickly produced a pair of clear latex gloves and a pen from his desk drawer and placed them on the desk in front of Chill.

"I'm right-handed, man. Why?"

"All right, I need for you to fill out this vehicle application with your left hand then. But first, slip on these gloves."

"Why must I fill it out with my left hand?" he asked, as he pulled the disposable gloves onto his hands.

Al sighed. "Because, Chill, if the Feds go so far as to use a handwriting specialist, he won't be able to match what's on this application to you. Look, we're only trying to be on the safe side here, okay?"

"I hear you, man." Chill grabbed the pen and began filling out the car application, all the while, he was thinking of some not-so-nice things that he would like to do to Tony Kin.

The next day at 11:28 a.m., he was at Jo-Jo and Lena's house explaining the details of what happened at Al's automotive business, while he stood directly inside of the master-bedroom door.

He seemed very upset, as he used a manila envelope filled with credit-reports to ward off the thick rock-cocaine smoke that billowed in his direction. Jo-Jo found it amusing, while he and Lena took turns exhaling it.

Lena appeared to be highly intoxicated, as she sat nude in the bed with her back against the headboard. She seemed to be convulsing underneath the sheet, which she had drawn up to a point above her breasts. She wore a deranged grin, as some thick white foam issued freely from her mouth and nose. Chill thought that she was crazy, as she gleefully gouged out small chunks of flesh from her sunken cheeks with her bare hands.

She flicked a piece of flesh toward Jo-Jo, who sat on the edge of the bed in his black silk boxer shorts. Chill shook his head as he watched Jo-Jo suck greedily on the glass cocaine pipe, for dear life, it seemed.

"Damn, Lena! That's nasty! Stop flicking your damn pimples on me, girl!" Jo-Jo yelled.

Lena growled and gurgled, and clapped her hands together wildly.

"Goddamn, Lena!" he shouted, as she continued to pick at her bleeding face.

He looked at Chill and mentioned through a thick cloud of smoke. "I'm sorry about this bullshit, man. But she can't stand pimples, that's all," "Apparently, you can't either!" Chill smirked. "Man, Jo-Jo, you've got her looking like that crazy-ass bitch from the Exorcist! Look at her, man!" he exclaimed, pointing at Lena's face. "She's picking at her face like she's done gone crazy or something! Man, she's bleeding now! Are you seeing the same shit that I'm seeing?"

Jo-Jo shrugged his shoulders. "Yeah, Chill, I see it. But, I've got this, all right?"

Chill nodded. "Yeah, I give up man. If y'all want to take the express train to hell, that's on you guys. I'm just here to talk some business with your weird ass!"

"Now you're talking!" Jo-Jo chuckled.

Chill spent the next few minutes recounting all of the drama relating to the dead man's Social Security number. "I checked that sucker, too! Tony had me so hot I damn near socked his stupid ass in his face!"

Jo-Jo nodded thoughtfully. "You did what I would've done. Man, what kind of idiot would try to build up a dead man's Social?"

"Tell me about it!" Chill sighed and waved away a rapidly approaching cocaine cloud. "I knew that fool had a driver's license hook-up in L.A. somewhere. But I found out that he was just waiting on a cool blue-chip."

"Yeah," Jo-Jo snickered. "That blue-chip he had was about as cool as a corpse, too!" He and Chill laughed.

Lena howled and began spreading drops of blood from her face all over her breast.

"So tell me, Chill, where did the dead cat's blue-chip information come from?" "Well, Tony said that he got it from that dope-peddling-ass, 'Chucky Mack fool."

Jo-Jo suddenly observed Lena lose interest in her face and began jamming a pair of tweezers into her nostrils. He scowled. "Damn, Lena!" he blurted, while he shot her a menacing look. "Girl, why don't you stop that shit!"

Lena giggled, "I ain't gone eat no more boogers, Daddy. I promise," she said, as a light stream of blood began to flow down the tweezers and onto her hand.

Jo-Jo scoffed and exhaled some smoke. He quickly began coughing violently and finally recovered enough to rasp, "That punk-ass Chucky Mack!"

"Yeah, man, the one and only Chucky Mack. I'm telling you, Jo-Jo. That fat-ass Tony Kin fool is starting to get on my goddamn nerves! Family or not, I'm ready to get off in his ass. You know what I'm saying?"

"Of course I do, that's why I dumped him off on you." Jo-Jo laughed. "I got tired of him, too," He cackled wildly, as Lena began to bang her head against the headboard.

Chill shook his head and whispered, "Damn." He found it disgusting that Lena's bloody nose began to drip onto the sheet.

Jo-Jo grabbed her and gently patted her shoulder. "Listen, baby," he mentioned, as he held her out in front of him. "You need to calm your ass down! Do you need a band-aid or something?"

Lena's pallor seemed noticeably paler since Chill arrived, and her facial and nasal wounds showed no signs of clotting. She meowed in response to Jo-Jo's question.

Chill seeming exasperated, stood near the door shaking his head. "Jo-Jo, she needs a lot more than a goddamn band-aid! And I don't think that there's a plastic surgeon this world, who could fix that chunk of bloody Swiss cheese that she calls a face. If I were you, I'd take her to the hospital, you damn idiot!"

Jo-Jo sighed. "I told you Chill, I got this, boy!"

"You ain't got shit, man!" Chill blurted. "And thanks a lot, by the way." He smirked.

"Thanks a lot for what?" Jo-Jo asked, as he continued to hold onto his wife.

"Thanks for dumping a stupid ass client like Tony on me, nigga'! Good looking out, I really appreciate that!"

Jo-Jo began to dabble at Lena's face with a black bath towel. "Don't forget, man, I gave you a lot of good clients, too."

Jo-Jo held the bloody cocaine pipe up to Lena's twitching lips, which Chill thought was absolutely *repulsive*.

"Yeah, nigga', you did. But damn, Jo-Jo. Why'd it have to be somebody like Tony? He's more trouble than he's worth. Man, you know damn well that one bad apple spoils them all." He shook his head, and observed as Lena suddenly experienced a mild seizure.

Jo-Jo gently laid her down on the bed and continued to dab at her deep facial gouging.

Chill scowled. "Your dumb-asses done lost your minds!" he exclaimed. "You guys need to leave that shit alone, smash those goddamn crack pipes against the wall and check yourselves into a rehab'! That's what you need to do! I know I told myself that I was going to mind my own business. But this stuff is sick, fool! He pointed to Lena lying naked on her back. "Do you see what I'm saying? Man, just look at that poor girl!" he continued, while he noticed that she was suddenly snoring and twitching every few seconds.

Jo-Jo nodded and exhaled another plume of smoke in Chill's direction.

"You've got it all wrong, Chill! I know that it's hard for you to see things the way that my baby and I see it right now, but it's true man. I'm at my best right now. I'm unsurpassed even. I mean, you think that you're the only nigga' in the world with a big-ass vocabulary? Well, I'm as sharp as a razor, too, and there ain't anybody on this earth who can mess with me. Nobody will, either! Because if they do..." He pointed to his Glock- 9mm handgun that was hanging from his coat-rack behind the door.

He made sure that Chill saw it too. "I'm serious!" he said, as he blew some more smoke in Chill's direction, which he quickly waved away with the envelope.

"Jo-Jo, you ain't going to shoot shit!" Chill blasted. "You ain't no killer! Now, as far as you being sharp as a razor," he chuckled. "That's some straight bullshit! You're dull as a butter knife, man!" He paused. "How long have we been back from Texas now? It's been damn near a month already! And what the hell have you been doing with your time? Nothing! Nothing at all, but sucking on that cocaine pipe like it was oxygen or something. Every day, man! And look at this little wretch of a woman that you've got right here." He pointed at Lena snoring on the bed. "She can't handle that crap, and your crazy ass can't even see it!" He scoffed. "Man, Jo-Jo, this cocaine shit that you've got going on in here ain't nothing but evil, pure evil. That's plain and simple."

Chill walked over to the sliding-glass doors and ripped open the curtains. Suddenly, the brilliant morning sunlight flooded the entire room.

"Goddamn, Chill!" Jo-Jo yelled, and then used his body to shield Lena from the light. His face contorted into terror while he held his hands up in front of his face and protested, "Close that shit, Nigga'!

"Hell nah'!" he blurted, and pointed past the sliding-glass door toward the magnificent morning outside.

"Come on, Chill! Close the motherfucker!"

Chill shook his head and grinned. "Nope, I'm not. I can't believe that you would rather be in here in the bed, wallowing in Lena's blood and sucking on that poison, than to be outside taking some breaths of clean, fresh air!" He pointed to Lena. "Just look at Lena's face, man. It's fucked-up! To tell you the truth, she looks like she's working as an actress in a goddamn horror flick! Hell, she's already wearing her costume!"

"Jo-Jo chuckled, "You're a nut, fool!"

"I'm serious, Jo-Jo! Because both of you two weirdoes look like some damn vampires! You got yourselves all locked up in this coffin with no lights on!"

Jo-Jo laughed, and then he took another toke from the cocaine pipe and exhaled it toward Chill. "You're stupid, boy!" He chuckled.

Chill shook his head and waved the smoke away. "Nah' brotha', you're the stupid one!" "You're trying to put that label on me. I don't want it. You keep it, dawg. I want that money, man. That's what I want."

Jo-Jo smacked his lips and pointed towards Chill's face. "And you're going to get it, Chill, trust me."

"Yeah," he smirked, appearing unmoved and disappointed with Jo-Jo and his drug usage. "Man, do you know that you've got clients who are about to knock down your door to give you their money? But you're sitting here acting like you're just cool as a motherfucker! I don't think that you understand what's about to happen here. You're about to make more money than you ever made in your entire life. But no, just look at you, man! You're sitting in this coffin and smoking that shit like this planet's about to blow the hell up!"

Jo-Jo laughed. "Where in the hell do you be coming up with some of this bullshit that you're always saying?"

Chill shrugged his shoulders. "The hell if I know. But what I do know is that you're hiding something from me. Is there something going on that you know that I don't? Is there some kind of big-ass asteroid that's about to smash into this planet or something?"

"Nope," Jo-Jo chuckled. "Not that I know of, anyway. I'm just minding my own business, you dig? I'm kickin' it, Chill," he rasped, as he placed his pipe and the lighter on a plate resting on the bed.

"The only thing you're kicking is the bucket, sucker!" He nodded toward Lena. "Lena's damn near dead from the looks of her! You better take her ass to a hospital! On top of that, you need to get your black-ass back out there in the streets with that "kings of credit" shit that you used to boast about!"

He checked the time on his Rolex.

Jo-Jo began to shake his head. "Check this out, dawg', my black-ass is staying right here in this house where I'm safe with my sweet, sweet schnookums." He lovingly caressed Lena's oozing, frail, and once beautiful face.

She jerked violently and moaned. Jo-Jo smiled and whispered, "That's right, Lena baby. You know that you're my precious, sweet and beautiful angel."

He looked up at Chill, who was smirking and shaking his head. "Chill, man, now you understand? I've got to be here for her, man. These streets out there are way too crazy for us right now."

"Jo-Jo, you need to see a goddamn head shrink! Where'd you say that y'all were from?" He snapped his fingers. "Oh, yeah, it was planet weirdo?" Chill sighed and checked the time on his wristwatch again. "I can't believe that it's almost lunch-time, and your ass is still lying up in this bed, like you're cool as a mother-fucker or something! You act like you don't have a care in the world, Jo-Jo!"

"You're right, Chill! I don't. You're the one who's always on a schedule. Not me."

He picked up his pipe and loaded it with a fresh rock of cocaine. Chill held his hand over his nose and blurted, "You use to give a damn about what really mattered! Lena, money and all that other good shit that goes into a normal lifestyle."

Jo-Jo scoffed. "I heard that," he said, and then he smoked up the entire rock and held it in for a short moment. He finally exhaled the smoke towards Chill, who quickly waved it away with the envelope again. Chill scowled. "Goddamn, Jo-Jo! Why don't you blow that shit somewhere else!" he blurted.

"Whatever boy," Jo-Jo said, and waved him off dismissively. "Anyway fool, I want you to think about this, since you're such an intelligent young nigga'. What kind of sense would it make for me to be out there in the streets right now, talking about how I'm one of the Kings of Credit? Don't you remember that Boss-Hogg's fat ass got cracked by the Feds? Man, who knows what that corpulent cocksucker done told them good old boys about me. Hell, all that they would have to do is deny his lard-ass some food for a day. Not even for 24-hours. I'll bet you that he would squeal on his own wife. Chill, I truly believe that, that fat bastard can't be trusted now."

"You're delusional, Jo-Jo! You're talking crazy, man! It's probably because you've been sucking on that glass pipe too long. You probably haven't had any sleep in a month, neither!"

278

"First of all, Lena and I both had a cool night's sleep just a few days ago. Secondly, what about the fact that Boss-Hogg called me from the Federal jailhouse from his own goddamn cell phone? Is that being delusional, nigga'?"

Chill sighed and rubbed his head. "They probably forgot to search him."

Jo-Jo shot up from the bed and yelled, "And you say that I'm delusional! Man, you are something else, Chill! But you know what?"

"What, crack-head?" Chill snickered.

"I really shouldn't be doing this after all of the bull-shit that you been talking lately. But here it goes anyway. Listen up- everybody in this credit game knows who I am, unlike you. After all, I really am, the king of this shit. As it stands right now, I've got a line of credit that's worth a couple million dollars in my own name, and for me to be out there in that traffic like that, all up in the mix, campaigning about what I'm able to do, that would be pure and utter foolishness. Especially after what that lame-ass Boss-Hogg fool done got himself into. I know you know what I'm saying."

Chill shook his head. "You're crazy, Jo-Jo."

"No I'm not. And Lena and I ain't starving at all," he admitted, while he lovingly looked upon Lena's rigid, supine body. "So this is what I'm going do from now on," he continued. "Chill, your name is about to start ringing as one of the new 'Kings of Credit'. So, consider this here your coronation, boy!"

Lena moaned in her sleep and rolled over, facing away from the open curtains. Jo-Jo looked at her and smiled, and then he walked back over to her and whispered some sweet nothings into her ear.

Chill looked on, shell-shocked. "You've got some serious issues, man." He sighed. "Anyway, what about your boy Chris Darrington in Dallas, Texas? Also, what about all of your clients, and the future clients that they might know? You're going to leave them hanging in the air like that?"

Jo-Jo smirked. "What do you think, boy?" He blew some more smoke in Chill's direction. "I made you the new king, baby. You're the new liaison. You're the one who's going to deal with them. That includes all of my clients as well. It's going to be fifty-fifty between you and me from now on. We're going to split the profits right down the middle, you dig?"

Chill appeared reluctant to shoulder such a burden so suddenly and completely. "It's you and me now, Chill," Jo-Jo said, as he stroked her hair.

Chill smirked as he placed his back against the wall near the big-screen television and folded his arms across his chest.

"Yeah, Jo-Jo, if you say so. Whatever, man."

"Boy, I'm trying to explain to you that it's got to be like this, Daddy-O. Because it's getting crazy with that Boss-Hogg fool getting his greasy ass locked up like that. Man, I wouldn't put it past him to get to cozying up with them Federal boys. That is, if he hasn't already!"

Jo-Jo's eyes widened, as he lit the pipe again, and then while inhaling the smoke he suddenly broke out into a spastic coughing fit.

Chill sighed and was obviously frustrated with his foolishness. "Whatever, Jo-Jo," he mentioned, as Lena suddenly began to flop around on the bed like a fish. Her limbs flailed around as if she were drowning.

Chill shook his head. "You motherfuckers are stupid! You've got your money for Nick's add-on package, and I've got my cut. So I'm about to shake this spot. That shit that you're smoking is nasty! Here's the damn credit report from Nick." He tossed the manila envelope onto the bed next to Lena and scoffed. "You guys are tripping!" He glared at them for a moment while shaking his head. "I'm out, nigga'!" he blurted, and walked briskly out of the house.

Meanwhile, parked against the curb down the street from Jo-Jo's house was a nondescript, newer-model mobile-home. The vehicle was in actuality, a Secret Service surveillance/ command post.

Agents Rosenberg and Smith manned the opposing consoles of the ultra-high-tech, state-of-the-art audio-visual and espionage equipment.

One of the four high-resolution video monitors depicted Jo-Jo completely in the nude. He was sitting on the edge of the bed with his hand between Lena's legs, and was attempting to coax her out of her stupor by blowing cocaine smoke into her face. She finally sat up and appeared to be zombie-like.

In the corner of the room near the sliding glass door was a pornographic movie playing on their big-screen television.

"Well, Smith," Agent Rosenberg said, while staring at the monitor, "It looks as if there's a new so-called king, who is taking over the old credit throne."

Agent Smith blinked several times and then he gave Rosenberg a condescending look. "That's right. And, it looks like you're the new king of stating what's painfully obvious!"

"Asshole," agent Rosenberg scoffed.

Smith grinned mischievously. "No, Dick, but thank you anyway. I would take you up on your offer, but I'm married. Sorry."

Rosenberg's face quivered with rage and turned blood red.

Smith pointed. "Be careful now, Dick. I wouldn't want for you to sweat to death like you almost did back in Dallas!" He laughed.

Rosenberg scoffed. "Fuck off!" he mentioned, as he suddenly concentrated on the live video feed, which depicted Lena with her eyes rolled in the back of her head.

The agent's noticed how intoxicated she appeared, and the fact that Lena could not seem to hold her head up straight. Nonetheless, she managed to kiss her husband passionately.

"Hot damn!" Smith blurted, staring hard at the monitor. "It's about time that we had some real live entertainment up in here!"

"No shit!" Rosenberg chimed in, as he and his partner eagerly watched Lena climb on top of her husband and expertly insert his erect penis into her vagina.

"Oh baby," Rosenberg crooned. "Joseph boy, you'd better get your fill of that pussy right now. Because where you're going, there isn't anything but dicks!"

"He'll probably end up switching teams anyway, if you know what I mean, Dick?" Smith Chuckled.

"That may be true. I do know that he'll have more than enough time on his hands to get used to it. That's for sure!"

Both men laughed heartily.

Chapter 28

At 8:39 that evening, Chill was lounging on his couch in the den wearing his red-silk pajamas and speaking to Chris Darrington in Dallas, Texas. The nightly news was in progress on his plasma television.

"So, Chris, you received a total of ninety-eight hundred, right?"

"That's right, my brother," Chris said. He seemed excited, as he sat in the living room of his new apartment. "Man, Chill, as soon as you told me that the money was there, I hurried up and got my ass down to the postal joint and picked it up. That really helped me out a lot. Thanks, man."

"Look here, brotha', it's nothing personal, just business. You earned every penny of that money. But you're welcome. Now, did you receive all of the credit reports that I faxed to you?"

"I sure did, Chill," as he aimed the remote at his big-screen television and changed the channel. "I got all of them late this afternoon. They were waiting in the tray for me when I got home from work."

"That's cool. How long do you think that it will take for you to process them?"

"I hate rushing things, especially things this important. So, I'd say, give me about four, or maybe five days. I'll have those puppies all cleaned, pressed and starched for you."

Chill sounded impressed. "Five days?"

"That's right. They'll all be taken care of by Monday afternoon at the very latest."

"Damn, dawg'! Five days? Wow! I'm impressed, Mr. Darrington, You go, Daddy-O."

"Hey, it's really nothing, you know?" He smiled and channel surfed until he landed on a local news channel, and placed the remote on his glass coffee table.

"Okay, Chris. So I know that I've got all of this right. You're telling me that you will have those credit reports straight by Monday afternoon, right?"

"That's right, Monday afternoon. However, don't be surprised if you hear back from me sooner. I've got the particulars for each report right here, the homes, the luxury vehicles, and the credit card information to be added onto each of the accounts. So, don't trip. I'll start working my magic on them tomorrow morning, player."

"Please, don't forget to clean off the derogatory statements first, "Chill said, as he picked up a glass of cognac from his coffee table.

"Come on now, Chill. I know how this thing goes! This ain't my first rodeo! I've got this shit down pat!"

Chill snickered. "Please, forgive me, master! It all sounds good. So let's go on and get this cheddar."

"Say cheese!" Chris exclaimed.

"Cheese!" Chill blurted humorously.

*****

The popular Stone Hills Mall in Culver City, California was teaming with noontime shoppers roaming about the many extravagant stores, boutiques and specialty eateries. Included was the World Famous Chocolate Cookie Company on the second level in the center of the mall, which was bristling with people who were eager to get their sugar fix before continuing on about their business.

Standing near the balcony railing was a 37-year-old Caucasian Secret Service Agent dressed as a casual civilian. Her attention was trained on the optical store across the mall in her direct line of sight.

She noticed that there were less than a handful of people in the store. She observed Chill, along with the portly, 50-year-old Korean owner of the store. The two of them walked out of a door towards the rear of the shop and appeared in the optical display area.

The agent surreptitiously began recording the encounter with her ultra high-tech, 20-megapixel, slim line telescoping video camera which was unavailable to the public. She managed to capture the exact moment, when the store owner stepped behind the counter and passed a black attaché case to Chill near the cash register.

"It looks like we've got another contact, people," she said into the microphone on her wrist which was hidden underneath her shirt sleeve. "Most definitely," she said, as she continued to record.

Later that afternoon, Chill was enjoying a lunch meeting with a 40-year-old Caucasian woman. The two of them were seated in a booth nestled in a corner of Carol's Lobster House in Marina Del Rey. The establishment was filled to capacity.

Sitting clandestinely at a table in the opposite corner was a 39-year-old Puerto-Rican Secret Service Agent. He used his high-resolution digital camera to snap photos of Chill and the woman. The man smiled when the camera recorded the lady pushing a large manila envelope across the table.

"Guys, Mr. Bruce is a very busy man," he whispered into his wrist microphone, after he observed Chill glance briefly at the cash inside of the envelope, and casually place it inside his attaché case on the seat near him.

The next morning, in the Holdings International Bank parking lot in Sherman Oaks, California, Secret Service Agent, Rudy Morales, a 49-year-old Hispanic male, sat behind the wheel of a black 1999 Ford Mustang. "The subject has exited the bank with one male Caucasian, people," he spoke into his handheld radio transceiver, and immediately began to snap pictures. He managed to capture photos of Chill, who spoke in hushed tones with the 45-year-old man, near the bank's rear door.

He noticed the two of them seemed to be having a lively and friendly conversation. Obviously a crime partner, agent Morales assumed. He observed them as Chill and the guy shook hands and parted ways.

Later that evening, Jo-Jo was lounging in a steamy bubble bath in his master-bathroom. His eyes were fatigued and blood-shot from a week without any sleep. Although, he tried his best to sound up-beat, while he spoke into his cordless phone to Chill and simultaneously watch a pornographic movie that was playing on his laptop computer which sat on top of the closed toilet seat nearby.

Chill recognized that Jo-Jo's voice sounded raspy, as he exhaled a cloud of cocaine smoke and slurred, "Are you for real, boy? You mean to tell me, Chill, that you done collected seventy grand, in one day?"

"You're goddamn right I did!" Chill boasted into his Bluetooth earpiece, as he drove his Mercedes-Benz westbound on Pacific Coast Highway, in Malibu, Ca.

"Get your money then, dawg'!" Jo-Jo rasped.

"Man, Jo-Jo, what else you think I been doing, while you've been sitting in the house on your ass, and tripping with that bullshit? You think I've been jacking off or something? Man, I've been out here in the streets hustling and campaigning, and passing out my business cards."

Using a cheap disposable lighter, Jo-Jo burned the tip of his pipe and inhaled some more smoke. "Well, well, well," he smiled, while concentrating on the computer monitor. "You need to hurry up and get your good hustling-ass on over here and bring me my goddamn money, then, and make it quick, boy, before I mess around and fall asleep!"

"Now that's a good idea, man. Because you would look pretty good, if you caught yourself a couple days sleep for a change. Anyway, I'm on my way, man."

"Chop-chop, boy, Jo-Jo said, "And stop by a fried-chicken joint and bring me and Lena something to grub on. Also, pick me up a fifth of that cognac, too."

Chill laughed and shook his head. "Man, what in the hell do I look like, Benson or somebody?" he blurted, as he continued to drive up the coast towards Topanga Canyon Road.

"Nope," Jo-Jo laughed. He reached down and grabbed another piece of rock cocaine from a plate on the floor next to the bathtub. "You look like that square-ass dude, Jeffery, nigga'! Now, get your good hustling-ass on over here already," he placed the rock on his pipe.

As the rock began to melt, the cheap plastic brackets which held in place the spring, the flint and the cylinder mechanism, also melted, which caused the hot flint to shoot off of the lighter and down into Jo-Jo's throat, sizzling its soft tissue fibers on impact.

Suddenly, Chill heard what sounded like a woman screaming, after which, the telephone line went dead.

Damn, he wondered. "What in the hell is going on over there?" He sighed. "The devil is busy at their house tonight, boy!" he immediately re-dialed Jo-Jo's landline telephone number.

Jo-Jo had leapt out of the bathtub, naked and drenching wet, and was hunched over the sink, his nose running, as he coughed, gagging and cursing out loud. All the while, he totally ignored the ringing of the cordless phone.

He quickly cupped a handful of water from the sink and drank it. Immediately, he began to cough violently, and eventually expelled the flint which had lodged in his throat.

He plucked the flint out of the sink and held it directly in front of his face, staring at it dumbfounded.

"Son-of-a-bitch!" he blurted, and then picked up his laptop and lifted the toilet seat. "Cheap-ass cigarette lighter!" he exclaimed, as he threw the flint inside of the bowl and flushed it. He finally closed the lid and replaced the laptop, which he noticed was no longer playing his pornographic movie. He peered at it for a long moment, and observed that the display monitor was dark, as though it were turned off.

He tried rebooting the system, but there were no signs of life, whatsoever.

"Mother-fucker!" he yelled, and slammed the computer as hard as he could onto the bathroom floor. "Damn!" he whispered and rubbed his hand over his face, wondering what his next move should be.

He finally glanced around the bathroom and yelled, "Ain't this about a bitch!", when he suddenly discovered the shattered plate on the floor that once held his cocaine rocks. He panicked as he rushed down on his hands and knees and desperately searched for the rocks.

Very quickly and completely, he developed the notion that he had dropped the rocks inside of the toilet bowl. He turned around and scampered to it, and flung open the lid with such force, that it bounced off of the water tank and immediately slammed shut.

Again, moving more slowly, he lifted the lid and looked inside, seeing nothing but water. Jo-Jo knew that he had to move quickly before the cocaine rocks dissolved. Drastic times called for drastic measures.

The toilet itself had to be removed, and the plumbing had to be inspected. This was a must!

The dope must not be lost! He pondered, while he squatted down in front of the toilet and gripped it tightly along the base, almost as if it were a long-lost lover that he was finally reunited with.

"I've got to get my shit!" he blurted, and began to tug and pull at the toilet, completely nude. The scene itself could have easily been mistaken for some sort of obscure German fetish pornography.

Indeed, either as a result of an exertion, or because of some bizarre erotic impulse, he developed an erection right before the toilet broke free from the floor, accompanied by the sounds of the snapping teak wood paneling.

Jo-Jo found himself lying on his back with the toilet resting on top of his chest, nestled in his arms. He quickly cast it aside and admired his handiwork when he noticed that a small fountain of water was steadily flowing out from where the toilet used to be.

Jo-Jo knew that he had to turn off the water before a full and proper inspection of the plumbing could be possible. He smacked his lips and waited for the voices to tell him what to do. They always did.

It's amazing what someone is willing to do for- and in the name of- rock cocaine.

Jo-Jo splashed through the flooded bathroom floor and stood in front of the mirror. He painfully admired his diminished physique, as well as his rapidly lightening skin tone.

Suddenly, the mirror went totally black, and out of the darkness, issued a mechanical voice. "What is required, Joseph?"

"I need to find my goddamn rocks, man!" he blurted, while pointing at the toilet. "I tore out the toilet like you told me to, but there's water everywhere. I can't look in the damn pipe, man! It's too much goddamn water flowing all over the place! Help me out, shit!" he shouted, desperately.

"Use your head, Joseph. Go and turn off your main water valve. It's just that simple. Think," the emotionless voice instructed.

"Man, I can't believe that I didn't think of that shit!"

"Oh, but you did."

"What do you mean, I did? You're the one who told me to do it!"

Strange laughter filled the master bathroom, which gave Jo-Jo goose bumps.

"Who do you think I am, Joseph Milton?"

Jo-Jo swallowed hard. "I thought you were an alien or some shit."

The water began flooding into the master bedroom.

"We're not aliens," the thing said.

"What are we, then?"

"There is no, 'we', Joseph Milton, there is only you."

"You mean to tell me that you are me?"

"In a way, yes, I am. However, you are unable to fully understand what is going on at this moment in time. Suffice it to say that you have damaged a good portion of your brain. When you do drugs, stuff like this happens."

"I feel like I'm stuck, man."

"That's why I'm here, Joseph. Go now. Run to the main water valve in the garage and turn it off. Then you will be able to find that which you seek."

"Thanks, dude."

"Don't mention it, Joseph Milton. Remember, use your head."

The mirror returned to normal, but Jo-Jo was out of the bathroom so fast that he never saw the change. He seemed completely out of breath as he bounded down the stairs and proceeded into the door that connected the garage and the house.

Chapter 29

Chill pulled up to the Milton residence an hour after he had last spoken to Jo-Jo, the fact that he was unable to get hold of either Jo-Jo or Lena, after continuous calling led him to suspect some very grim possibilities.

He parked his car and brought his .45-caliber Glock along with him in the pocket of his brown suit coat.

He tried calling Jo-Jo once more, but there was still no answer.

He racked the slide on the Glock and chambered a round. He felt the familiar rush of adrenaline, accompanied by a gloomy fear that if somebody did something to his loved ones, they were more than likely far away by now. Nevertheless, he had to know and help his family if he could.

He got out of the car and began to make his move towards the house, when suddenly, he noticed an obese Caucasian woman staring at him, as she was walking her long-haired Chihuahua along the sidewalk.

"What the hell are you looking at?" he blurted.

The woman remained quiet and issued him a dirty look. Chill stared oddly at her, and said, "Keep it movin', lady!"

The woman scoffed and glared at the dog. "Come on, Precious!" she snapped, and practically dragged the dog past him.

For some strange reason, Precious suddenly became enraged and charged at Chill and swiftly chewed on his Achilles tendon. The pain was so fierce that it brought him to his knees.

Chill reached out with the pistol to strike the dog, but the owner quickly snatched the animal up in her arms and hurried away.

"You fucking bitch!" he yelled.

The lady looked back laughing hysterically as she quickly moved on.

"Fuck you, and your punk-ass dog!" he yelled, as he carefully inspected his wound. He was thankful that the skin was not broken.

Chill marveled for a moment at everything that had happened. He couldn't help but smile to himself. He definitely respected the fact that the tiny dog had the sense and the skill to bring him to his knees. He just didn't know why.

He jumped up to his feet and, while walking was painful, it wasn't even close to the pain that he had felt at other times in his life as a gangster. "Stankin' ass mutt!" he muttered, as he continued on foot with a slight limp towards Jo-Jo's home.

As he approached the front door, he noticed that there were no lights on in the house, at least none that he could see from where he stood a few feet away. His fingers were only inches away from the doorbell button, when suddenly his entire body froze.

"What the fuck?" he whispered, staring hard at the front door.

He aimed his Glock at the door. His other hand he used to turn off his cell phone. He looked at the door which was open no more than an inch. The sliver of darkness beyond it didn't tell him anything that he wanted to know.

He gently and slowly opened the door until it made contact with the adjacent wall. He then took a tentative step into the house. "What in the hell is this?" he said, after he brought his shoe down onto the foyer carpet, which made a squishing noise.

His first thought was that it was the blood of either Jo-Jo or Lena, the victims of a home-invasion robbery, and possibly, an assassination.

He quickly crouched down and sunk his fingers into the rug. It was wet. Dripping in fact; but as he held his fingers up to the light of the doorbell, he could instantly see that it wasn't blood, and when he smelled his fingers, he realized it was most likely water. He whispered to himself, "But, from where?"

Meanwhile, Jo-Jo was struggling in the darkened garage with the main water valve. He was totally exhausted from his earlier exertions with the decommissioned commode.

He was hunched over the water valve, nude and breathless, hungry, thirsty, and borderline psychotic.

He tried once more to rotate the large iron ring which regulated the flow of water into his home. As he did so, he let out a loud primal grunt, after which, he picked up the nearest heavy object that his groping, fumbling hands could grab, in this case, a crowbar. He picked it up with both hands and brought the instrument crashing down several times on the metal valve.

Chill was halfway up the stairs when he heard the distinctive sound of metal impacting metal, accompanied by what sounded like a man's nonverbal vocalizations of anger and exertion. When he heard the blaring clang, he was so startled by it that he almost fired off a round from his Glock into the drywall. He quickly regained control of his composure, and squished across the flooded rug and proceeded back down the stairs.

"I'm going to kill me a mother-fucker tonight," he muttered, and walked in the direction of the banging and grunting. He found himself standing outside of the door to the garage, his gun at the ready, his adrenaline and heart rate, *red-lined*.

He placed his hand near the light switch panel, took a deep breath, flicked on all three switches, and then bashed through the door, screaming!

What he saw was hard to believe.

Jo-Jo was naked and holding a crowbar high over his head. "Oh, shit!" he screamed, and squinted from the sudden onslaught of light in the room.

"Jo-Jo, what the fuck is you doing?" Chill yelled, as he lowered his gun and observed Jo-Jo drop his crowbar, which clanged loudly against the garage floor. "What in the hell have you got going on in here, man? I thought that you were being killed or something! Oh, damn, dude! Put some clothes on, for Christ sake!"

Jo-Jo shrugged his shoulders. "Let's go into the living room, Chill. Did you bring my cognac and the chicken with you?"

Chill was slack-jawed. "Hell no, Nigga'! I was about to get all that stuff that you wanted, until I heard you scream like a woman!

Man, I thought that you was being murdered or something! Then you hung up the phone and I couldn't get a hold of you or your wife. So, I thought that checking up on you two was a little more important than picking up some goddamn chicken wings and cognac! You know what I'm saying, you fucking naked ass clown?" He hollered, clearly upset.

Jo-Jo scoffed, and silently led Chill through the door and into the house.

"I'll be right back," he mentioned, and ran up the stairs, squishing water the entire way.

Chill stood there wondering, *exactly what did Jo-Jo do to flood his entire house?*

Jo-Jo soon came trundling back down the stairs in his signature red-silk robe. He seemed to be totally oblivious by what had recently transpired. As he stood there before Chill with his lips puckering and his face smug, Chill had to exercise an incredible amount of willpower to avoid knocking Jo-Jo across the room.

He sighed deeply and removed a manila envelope from his coat pocket, which contained $70,000. "Here, fool!" he said, as he tossed it at Jo-Jo, who caught it and then smiled brightly.

"Yeah, Chill, now that's what the hell I'm talking about! Hey dawg, you really don't need the gun right now, you dig? You're kind of making me nervous, man."

Chill blinked and realized that he had been holding his gun down at his side. He slowly pocketed it without a word, as Jo-Jo continued, "Are you going to get me my cognac and chicken, or what?"

"Yeah man, sure. Whatever." Chill scowled, as he looked around the living room. "Whatever you want, man! But are you going to tell me what in the hell is up with all of this goddamn water?"

Jo-Jo grinned suspiciously. "Don't trip it, Chill- I got it."

Chill sighed. "What happened in the bathtub that made you scream like a woman, and then you hung up the phone earlier?"

"Nothing, man. I was chillin'." He sat down on his sofa and cradled the stack of money between his legs.

"You was chillin'?" Chill blurted. "What the hell does that mean, chillin'?"

Jo-Jo sighed and smacked his lips. "Just what I said- I was chillin', Chill! Goddamn! I was taking a bubble bath and watching my laptop computer."

"And what else?" Chill chuckled.

"What else?" He sighed. "I was checking out some fine-ass Asian broad. She was getting the shit fucked-out of her by some big-dick black dude. He was the same mother-fucker that's always wearing that black baseball cap. Besides that, you old nosy-ass nigga', I was sitting in my tub, smoking my dope and jacking my dick off in some hot-ass water! Since you just gotta' know! Is that what you want to hear, you old Sherlock Holmes-ass motherfucker!"

Chill laughed and shook his head.

"Now Chill, is there anything else that you want to know before I get to cleaning up all of this goddamn water in here, detective Bruce?" He asked sarcastically.

Chill snickered and shook his head as he pointed at the carpet. "Yeah, sucker! I want to know what the hell happened in here with all this fucking water, you goofy-ass pervert," he blurted, but he really wanted to ask him about the episode in the garage.

Jo-Jo inhaled sharply. "I got this, baby boy. Don't trip. Just get me my vittles, man!"

Chill shrugged his shoulders. "Jo-Jo, you go fuck yourself! You nasty-ass, Bozo-looking nigga'!"

Jo-Jo smiled. "Yeah fool. I love you too, Chill. Now, can you please go and get me my cognac and some chicken, before you make me mad?" He laughed.

Chill smacked his lips. "I'll be back, dick-head!" he grumbled on his way out of the house. As he approached the front door, he stomped his foot and splashed some water out onto the front porch.

Against the curb down the street from Jo-Jo's property, the Secret Service mobile-command surveillance unit remained parked and unsuspected.

Within the clandestine vehicle, agents Rosenberg and Smith continued to observe the four television monitors, which displayed certain sections of Jo-Jo's home.

One of the monitors had especially captured their interest. It depicted Lena lying nude in their bed with a sheet covering her body up to her neck.

Her eyes were closed, but every few seconds she would briefly open them, and her eyelids would flutter before falling closed again.

Suddenly, Jo-Jo entered the room and sat beside her. After a quick moment, he appeared to be trying to rouse her. She finally opened her eyes and wrapped her arms around his neck, and pulled him in closer.

The two of them began to kiss each other fiercely, as Jo-Jo removed the silk sheet covering her body.

The agents smiled simultaneously, while a pornographic movie continued to play in the background on the big-screen television.

Agent Rosenberg turned to agent Smith and said, "Can you imagine that? This kid, Chill, made seventy fucking grand in one day! Christ almighty, Smith! That's absolutely obscene. It's crazy, isn't it?"

Agent Smith sighed and shot a frustrated look at his partner. "Indeed it is, Dick."

The agents suddenly observed Lena exhale some cocaine smoke towards the ceiling as Jo-Jo licked on her breast nipples.

Agent Rosenberg continued, "I've got to admit it, man. These two characters are really some professionals."

Smith looked upon him with utter disgust. "That's some bullshit! Because if they were so 'professional', we wouldn't even know of their existence! What in the hell are you talking about, Dick? These two lame-brains are nothing more than a pair of common thugs. They just so happen to have one foot in the door of high finances. That's it! But," he said with a smile, "that foot is about to be chopped completely off," as he used his hand to simulate a chopping motion, just inches away from Rosenberg's flinching face. "They're going down, I tell you!"

Agent Rosenberg cleared his throat before saying, "I'd have to agree with you there, Smith, thanks to Mr. Braxton and his confession."

Smith smirked. "Oh, was that the break in this case? Gee, Dick, I thought that an alien spacecraft had landed on the White House lawn and gave the President all of the details of this case," he scoffed.

Rosenberg snickered. "You're a real grouch, you know that, Smith?" He blurted, and then turned away and sulked.

Smith laughed. "That reminds me of something that I've marveled at for some time here. You know, while we've been dealing with these two idiots."

"And what's that, Mr. Smith?"

Smith grinned. "It's the flawless chemistry between these Jo-Jo and Chill characters. I mean, when they're together, it's like some comic genius or something. Well," he chuckled. "I mean, when they're not trying to kill each other, most black people are fairly amiable amongst themselves."

Agent Rosenberg scoffed. "Smith, not only are you a dimwit, but you're also a racist, to boot!"

Smith refused to bite into his comment. "Anyway, Dick, I'm sure that the D.E.A. will be grateful for the scraps of information that we're going to toss them once we complete our investigation."

Rosenberg smiled. "Now, that's finally something that we can both agree upon, huh?"

Smith scowled. "Rosenberg, you make me sick!"

Rosenberg scoffed, and then suddenly, the two of them observed on the monitor, as Lena closed her eyes and opened her mouth, while Jo-Jo's head disappeared between her legs.

Chapter 30

Chill was dressed in some sharp business attire when he pulled his professionally detailed Mercedes-Benz out of his driveway at 10:04 the following morning.

"The Love I Lost," sung by "Harold Melvin and the Blue-Notes," featuring "Teddy Pendergrass," was playing in the car stereo as he drove down his street near Jo-Jo's house.

Shortly after passing the house, he began to admire the Mobile Home/Secret Service surveillance unit, which was parked against the curb.

He suddenly marveled at the dark tinted windows, and wondered, how much would something like this cost for me and my family?

He eventually accelerated away, but continued to stare at the superbly manufactured vehicle in his rear-view mirror.

Later that afternoon, Chill was in such good spirits as he was leaving Al's office at the Universal Sales Automotive, that he descended the steps from the trailer two at a time.

He carried in his hand two manila envelopes, one of which contained twenty-seven thousand dollars in cash. The other filled with five credit reports- one requiring the 'add-on package', which was designed to provide the client with one of the best credit scores possible.

He checked the time on his Rolex, noting that it was 12:05 p.m. "My next appointment is Teddy B. at Money Solutions," he said, as he walked toward his car. As he approached the driver's door, his cellular phone began to ring.

He suddenly appeared irritated as he yanked it from his belt and opened it, seeing only, "incoming caller', where the name or number of the caller was usually displayed.

He smacked his lips and smirked. "Damn, another incoming caller! I can't stand these mother-fuckers!" He pressed the green "call" button and placed the phone to his ear. "Hello, S.H. Financial services. Willie Bruce speaking, how may I help you?" he mentioned in his best professional voice.

"What it do, boy?" The caller's baritone voice bellowed into his cell phone.

The man was sitting in an old rocking chair on the rickety porch of a single-family home. It was a dilapidated house located in a low-income residential district in South Los Angeles.

Chill, uncertain of the caller's identity, asked, "Who is this?" as he sat the manila envelopes on the hood of his car.

"Oh, Chill baby," the caller murmured, very evenly and sure of himself. "I can't believe that after all that we've been through, you done forgot about me already, Mr. Willie... Chill... Bruce!" C-Dub mentioned, and laughed uproariously.

Chill suddenly felt as if he had been shoved out of an airplane that was flying at a cruising altitude of 35,000 feet.

Upon hearing C-Dub's old familiar voice, he had to struggle to catch his breath. His heart seemed as if it was about to jump out of his chest. "C-Dub is that you, man?" he asked, uneasily.

"What, Chill, you thought that I was a goner, didn't you boy?"

"To tell you the truth, 'Dub, hell yeah I did!" Chill answered hoarsely. His throat was suddenly parched. "Because I called the jail that same night, and some woman cop had told me that you were facing a shit-load of serious charges- two kidnap for ransoms, two robberies, and a bail that was like, four million dollars! I think that she told me something about an attempted murder charge, too. So yeah dub, I really didn't think that things looked too good for you, you know?" he replied, while he picked up the envelopes and stepped into his car and started the engine.

"Man, Chill, I've been locked up for almost nine months now. So I assumed that you had forgotten all about me." He stood up and leaned his buttocks against the chipping white paint on the porch railing. "Was that the case, youngster?" he asked, as he began to watch some teenage boys that were playing tag football in the middle of the street.

"Nah, nigga'!" Chill blurted, after collecting enough of his nerves. "I didn't forget about you. But 'Dub, you know damn well that I wasn't about to go downtown to the county jail for nobody." He nervously lit a mild cigar. He finally got it lit and opened his front windows and the sunroof.

"Yeah, my friend, I already be knowing," C-Dub said, sounding upset.

Chill blew smoke out of his side window. "Anyway, 'Dub, where in the hell are you at? Are you still in the county jail? Or, you in the pen' now?"

C-Dub laughed. "Nah man, I ain't locked-up no more. They cut me loose early this morning about six o'clock."

"What happened? I mean, how'd you get out?" Chill brought the cigar to his lips and realized that his hands were shaking badly.

"They released me due to lack of evidence. My case was dismissed in court yesterday morning. God Bless America, eh! But anyway, young blood, you and I need to have a little chat, and I mean, A.S.A.P. you dig?"

C-Dub relished in the moment. He knew that the punishing words that he was pounding into Chill's ears were placing him ill at ease.

"What do you mean '*a little chat*'?"

Chill flicked the cigar out of the sunroof and onto the pavement near the passenger side of his car. "Chat about what, man?" he asked defensively, understandably unsure about what C-Dub's intentions were.

"Why, about you of course, Mr. Bruce." C-Dub said, and struggled to contain his laughter. He could almost feel Chill's fear on the other end of the phone, as he returned to the rocking chair.

Chill felt goose bumps shoot down his spine. "Chat about me? What about me, man? I ain't done a damn thing! So what the hell do you need to chat with me about?"

"Well," C-Dub began, leaning back in the chair and crossing his legs. "Let's just say that you've got some serious problems, man. And I'm talking about some major ones, Daddy-O."

Chill leaned his head back against the seat and stared blankly at the Boulevard's heavy mid-day traffic, passing by the car dealership.

"What kind of problems, C-Dub?" he asked, as he closed his eyes and began to rub his temples in response to his rapidly developing migraine headache.

C-Dub smiled gleefully. "I'll run shit down to you when you get here. So hurry up," he said, before hitting the "mute" button and cackling for several seconds.

Chill finally opened his eyes and watched the traffic again. "And where in the hell would that be?" he finally asked. "Get a pen, nigga'," C-Dub replied, as he continued to rock in the chair and stared out at the kids in the street enjoying themselves.

Two hours had passed and the atmosphere was tense within Chill's new black 2005 Cadillac-Ext. He had a lot on his mind, as he drove slowly along 109th street in search of C-Dub's address. Jen was equally saddened, while she sulked in the passenger seat beside him.

He lowered the volume on the stereo system, which had been playing, "*Sunshine*," by "The Enchantments."

"The house should be right up in here somewhere," he began to call out the numbers on the addresses as they appeared. "That's 824, 826, 828. Here it is, babe." He pointed.

"That's the address," Jen told him, as he pulled the vehicle over and stopped at the curb in front of a dingy white, run downed single-story house on the right side of the street.

"Damn, babe! That's a triflin'-ass house," he said, as he and his wife stared at a dirty piece of cardboard. "Look at that bull-shit," Chill said pointing at the cardboard that was duct-taped to a broken window near the battered rocking chair on the porch.

"Damn, Charlie is living in there now?" Jen said, as she examined the unkempt shrubbery and the brown neglected lawn, which was over-ran with crabgrass.

Chill smirked and rolled his shoulders. "I guess so. C-Dub told me that while he was in the jail downtown, he had lost everything he owned."

Jen suddenly appeared surprised. "Damn babe, he lost everything?"

"Yeah momma', he said that he lost the car wash and everything else he had. At least that's what he told me, anyway. He said that he was staying with some crack-head woman named Brenda. I guess she lives in that house." He shook his head. "Damn, what a dump!" he blurted, while he looked on pityingly at the property.

Jen looked around at some of the other homes in the vicinity, noting their similar conditions. "It sure is a dump. He's obviously doing really badly now."

"No shit, momma. It looks like he's doing beyond," he said, as he glanced up and down the street at the pitiful array of dilapidated houses. "Damn," he whispered, and took a deep breath and tapped his car horn three times consecutively. The two of them watched as suddenly, a very unhealthy looking C-Dub exited the house wearing a thick wool sweater, some dirty denim jeans, and some worn out white leather tennis shoes.

"Here comes this nigga'," Chill uttered bitterly. "Damn, this fool done got sucked the hell up while he was locked-down!" he muttered, appalled by C-Dub's physical degeneration.

"Tell me about it," Jen said, as C-Dub stepped off the porch and proceeded along the broken cement pathway, towards her side of the vehicle. "Oh my God, Willie! He looks awful!" she whispered.

"I heard that," he agreed, while he lowered the passenger side window.

"What's up, y'all?" C-Dub exclaimed, as he approached the car with a wide toothy grin plastered across his face.

"Not a goddamn thing, nigga'," Chill said, as C-Dub shook Jen's hand.

"Hi, Jen! Long time, no see! How've you been?" he asked, with an obviously forced smile which revealed several missing teeth.

She smirked. "Other than the kids driving me crazy, I've been all right, I suppose.' She shook her head. "But you- you don't look so good."

"You can say that again, momma'," Chill cut-in.

He pointed at C-Dub's mouth. "Man C-Dub, you look like one of those Jack-o-Lanterns, dawg'!" He chuckled. "What the hell happened to your grill, man?"

C-Dub snickered. "I see you got jokes, huh? Ha-ha, very funny, motherfucker! Very funny indeed," he laughed, as he flipped Chill off with his middle finger. "Anyway, I'll tell you how I lost my front teeth. I was downtown in the County jail, as you already know. I guess that it was about three months ago. I was gambling in the two-thousand block in the back of Baker tier. It was with some fools from out of the bottoms, you know? Well, one of them got to cheating. I caught his ass cuttin' the dice on me."

Jen scowled and asked curiously, "What does cutting the dice mean?"

"It's when a nigga' brings some crooked dice to the game."

She nodded her head and pondered. "Oh, okay. I get it."

"Babe, that type of stuff happens all the time," Chill explained.

"No shit, Chill, but anyway y'all," C-Dub resumed. "So, I called him on his cheating shit. The next thing I knew, we were fighting. When I finished beating his ass in the corner by the back of the tier, this other nigga' named, Reno, from the Swans. That fool busted me in the mouth with a metal mop ringer."

"Oh my God, Charlie!" Jen cried out, as she sat up in her seat. "That had to have hurt!"

"Hell yeah it did, Jen! It hurt like a son-of-a-bitch!" C-Dub replied scornfully.

Chill found his story hilarious. "I know that fool, too. Reno, he's a reputable from up out of them eight-nine boys on the eastside. He's solid folks, though."

C-Dub shot him an icy stare for a brief moment, and then grinned.

"Yeah well, I can't wait to catch up with his reputable-ass, the next time that I see him. But anyway," he said, as he glanced at Jen's Rolex on her wrist.

"Jen, that's a nice wristwatch you got there. Is that a Rolex?" He blurted, while he checked out Chill's Rolex as well.

"Yeah, my beautiful husband right here got it for me not too long ago."

C-Dub smiled. "It sure is nice," he mentioned, as he continued to stare at Chill's watch on his left wrist.

Chill nonchalantly flaunted the notable time-piece, while he comfortably gripped the polished wood steering wheel.

"Thank you, Charlie," she continued. "It's all right, I guess. It's only a watch." She leaned back in her seat.

"That's not just a watch, Jen, that's a Rolex," C-Dub explained.

"Anyway y'all," he resumed. "I'm all right. I mean, other than some missing teeth! They finally cut my ass loose from the county jail earlier this morning. My case was dismissed yesterday on some kind of technicality, thank God!" he sighed, appearing relieved.

"Yeah, I heard," Jen uttered dryly.

She had some reservations about C-Dub, and was sure that he was up to something shady, but she wasn't sure what it was.

C-Dub took a couple steps backwards and admired the 22" chrome Asante rims, which were cradled within the low-profile tires on the customized S.U.V.

He returned to Jen's window. "Damn, Chill! What in the hell have you been up to, boy?"

Jen nonchalantly cut her eyes at Chill. *Babe, watch what you say to this dude,* was her secret message, which Chill quickly got the hint.

"Shit, 'dub. I ain't been up to nothing much. Just a little bit of this, and a little bit of that, that's all."

"You've been up to, just a little this, and a little that, huh?" C-Dub smirked.

"Yeah, man, that's about it."

"I heard that!" C-Dub replied scornfully, as he continued to stare at the rims. "Man, what you got on this car, some dubs?"

"Nah', big dawg'!" Chill blurted. "I ain't got no twenty inch rims on my whip, man! These rims right here, they're some deuce-deuces that I've got on this bitch!" he boasted, and glanced at Jen, who rolled her eyes and smirked.

C-Dub chortled. "Well now, some twenty-two inch rims, huh? Excuse the hell out of me! That's not bad at all. So this is yours, I gather?"

"Yeah, dub. I bought it a few days ago," Chill informed him, and then he used his right thumb to point over his shoulder to the rear seat. "Now, go on and hop in the back, so we can roll up outta' here."

He pressed a button on his door panel and unlocked the doors.

"Yes sir, Mr. Willie Bruce," C-Dub blurted sarcastically, before he entered the vehicle and sat in the rear set directly behind Jen.

A moment later, Chill pulled his vehicle into a gasoline station on the corner of Century Boulevard and Vermont Avenue, and then backed into a parking stall at the rear of the property.

He noticed that there was an unoccupied pay-phone booth near the right rear-end of his car.

He decided to leave the engine running and turned up the air-conditioning in the vehicle. He finally moved his seat all the way back and turned himself around, because he wanted to make sure that he was able to easily look C-Dub directly in the eyes.

"Man, C-Dub!" He scowled. "Aren't you hot in that big-ass sweater that you got on? I mean, goddamn, man! It's the ass-end of August, dawg'! It's probably the hottest day of the year, too."

C-Dub appeared to perspire across his forehead, while he uncomfortably flashed a dentally deficient smile. "Nah, Chill. Actually, man, I'm freezing right now."

"Freezing?" Chill scowled.

"Yeah, dawg'. I'm cold!" He suddenly shivered. "Because while I was in that hell-hole, I messed around and caught myself one of those jail-house colds a few days ago."

"Oh, okay, 'dub. I get it now. I knew that it had to be something." Chill grinned. "Yeah, I know all about those county jail colds."

He looked at Jen. "They're real hard to shake, babe. Mainly because we're forced to constantly be around a bunch of foul, dirty, nasty-ass dudes. I'm talking about some straight bums!"

"That's terrible," she uttered, shaking her head.

"Tell me about it," C-Dub agreed.

"But other than that, Dub," Chill continued, "Are you straight? I mean, are you all right?" he asked, peering directly into C-Dub's eyes.

"Yeah Chill. I'm cool, man," he answered nervously, as he continued to perspire profusely.

The sweat was suddenly dripping from his face and onto the black wool sweater he wore.

Chill observed his shaken demeanor and thought, *this nigga' is hiding something. This ain't the C-Dub that I know.*

"Nah', Charlie!" Chill barked, and gave C-Dub an icy glare. "What I'm asking you is... are you straight, homie?"

If looks could kill, C-Dub would be dead.

C-Dub suspiciously averted eye contact with Chill, and instead, began to stare out of the side window at the telephone booth. "Look here, Chill," C-Dub began apprehensively, as he glanced back at Chill's powerful gaze. "I've got nothing but love for you, man. I would never in my life do anything to hurt you, and you should know that," he mentioned. He appeared to be relieved, when he noticed that Chill's harsh demeanor had seemed to soften up a bit. "I'm worried about you, loved one. That's all," he continued.

"Worried about me, for what, motherfucka'? Chill shouted. "What in the hell are you worried about me for? I ain't done a goddamn thing for you to be worrying about me! And you know that, Dub! " he blasted.

"Chill baby," C-Dub grinned. "I'm concerned about you, because your name happened to be mentioned practically all throughout my court proceedings. I'm talking about the whole time that I was locked up."

"What?" Chill shouted, and then he looked at his saddened and frustrated wife. Jen shook her head and stared at the black carpeting beneath her gold leather sandals.

"What in the fuck is my name doing all mixed up in your courtroom shit?" he yelled and punched his car seat.

"Look, Chill," C-Dub continued restlessly. He tried hard to keep himself calm. "I'm sorry, dawg, but I've got some really bad news for you."

"What kind of news, nigga'?" Chill barked.

C-Dub sighed. "It's about that punk, snitching-ass, Armand Agassi. That bitch ratted on us all!"

"Ain't that about a bitch?" Chill blurted, while he was staring out of his side window.

"Yeah man. That rag-head son-of-a-bitch gave up the complete blueprint, baby. I mean the whole lick, man. Everything! He told the pigs everything they wanted to know. I'm talking about everything that we did that day! And I do mean everything, young blood."

"Damn," Jen whispered. She sighed deeply and shook her head. Chill watched her as she fell into what seemed to be deeper frustration and despair.

Following a dreadful moment of silence, Chill slammed his fist into the seat again. "Damn, blood!" he shouted, peering into C-Dub's eyes. "You know that I ain't done shit!" he lied. "This is some bullshit, man!"

C-Dub sighed heavily. "Look here, Chill, that's neither here nor there, man. Because, between you and me, you know the real-deal. We both know what really went down that morning in them folk's house. But the fact remains, man, that Armand's good snitching-ass finked us all out to the cops."

Chill stared at his wife before glaring out of his driver's side window. "Fuck!" he yelled and punched his seat again.

He noticed C-Dub flinch at his sudden anger outburst. He also noticed his nervousness and the tense look on his face as his lips quivered.

"Man, Chill, Armand told the pigs the exact role that you played in the kidnapping, the role that I played. That stool-pigeon spared them no details, man. They know everything, now! I mean all of it!"

"Damn!" Chill blurted, and socked the seat again.

He took some deep breaths in an attempt to calm himself. "Well, man," he finally said. "Those cops can't prove shit. They ain't got a damn thing on me! That's your folks, C-Dub. Not mine!"

"I know, man. But, he knew that your nickname is Chill. That's all that he needed to know. Those damn detectives put the rest of the pieces of the puzzle together."

The car went silent

Chill twisted back around in his seat and faced the windshield again.

After a moment of ponder, he slammed the side of his clenched fist up against the steering wheel.

"Shit!" he yelled. "The cold thing about it was I was never even down with no kidnapping bullshit in the first place! That was your stupid-ass move, 'dub! Something told me not to mess with you, man! Now look what happen! Fuck!"

"Well, Chill," C-Dub uttered casually. He now seemed to be in control of himself. "I beat all of my charges on this bullshit. So, I don't know what to tell you, dawg'."

For a long moment, Chill glared at him in the rearview mirror. "I know you don't, motherfucker!"

He observed C-Dub staring fearfully out of his side window. He seemed to do everything that he could to avoid eye contact with Chill's powerful gaze. He knew that Chill was obviously livid.

Chill observed that C-Dub seemed to be overly fidgety as well. He scoffed and quickly entertained the thought of grabbing his Glock 9mm from the leather pocket in his door panel, and shooting a hole in the middle of C-Dub's forehead, but instead, he thought about his wife.

C-Dub was a lucky man, he mused.

305

"You know, C-Dub," he finally mentioned in the rearview mirror. "There's something that ain't right about you, homeboy!"

C-Dub was too afraid to respond.

After hearing the terrible news that he could possibly spend the rest of his natural life in prison, especially for a horrible crime that he actually got away with, Chill drove back to C-Dub's residence in silence.

He continued to ponder the idea of killing C-Dub right there in the truck, but once again, he thought about his wife. He shook his head in frustration, as he parked the Cadillac against the curb in front of the house, which was covered with debris.

Chill sat there for a long moment. He could not believe what he had gotten himself into, as he scowled through the front windshield at a lime-green 1978 A.M.C. Gremlin. He noticed that it had a cracked rear window. Apparently abandoned, he mused.

He glared at C-Dub in the rear-view mirror and yelled, "Get the fuck out my car, nigga'!"

"Willie," C-Dub pleaded, while he stared at the side of Chill's face. "Look, Homie, you obviously don't realize how sorry that I am about all of this bullshit. But how was I supposed to know that Armand was going to snitch on us all like he did? I'm really sorry, dawg. I really am!"

Chill continued to glare at the Gremlin and appeared completely unmoved by C-Dub's entreaty.

He scoffed, and then blurted, "Yeah, motherfucka'! Whatever, man! And you can miss me with all that 'dawg' shit, too! 'Cause I ain't your dawg, blood! And I put that on Six-Deuce Brims, nigga'!" He turned his head and locked eyes with C-Dub. C-Dub snickered. "You put that on your neighborhood, huh?"

Jen observed Chill's jawbone clinch, as he slid his left hand down inside of the door pocket and nonchalantly clutched his pistol.

"Babe," she begged, while she stared at the side of his face, and hoped like hell that he wouldn't commit a murder in the car, and, in front of her, no less.

Chill seemed to disregard her feelings, as he turned his head and glared directly into C-Dub's eyes, and then hollered, "You goddamn right I put that on my 'hood, nigga'! Now what, Blood?"

"Come on, Willie," Jen said, as she placed her hand on his shoulder, attempting to calm him down.

During the 1970's and 1980's, Chill had grown up in the mean inner-city neighborhoods of South Central Los Angeles.

In 1973, at the young age of 12 years old, he was violently initiated into a notorious "Blood" street-gang, which was known as the Six-Deuce Brims.

Never once forgetting his roots, he had always maintained a steadfast loyalty to his "loved ones," *his homeboys*. Not only to the loved ones who were still dwelling within his neighborhood but also to the ones who had moved out of their childhood homes and were now scattered across America, whom he continued to stay in contact with.

He firmly believed that, "You could take the nigga' out of the 'hood, but you could never take the 'hood out of the nigga'." Although, he had shared enough time amongst other folks to be considered more or less domesticated. However, there were often times in his life, when he would revert back to the behavioral profile, the one that he was accustomed to from his violent, gangster upbringing, usually, in times of extreme anger. That's when he would use the word, 'blood.' It was rather uncommon to hear him use that word, but when he did, he would undoubtedly be in a very dangerous state of mind.

C-Dub knew him well.

"Yeah, blood!" Chill continued. "Now, get the fuck out of my car!"

After a short period of silence and harsh stares between the two of them, C-Dub grinned, as he nervously gripped the door handle. "Okay, Chill. If that's how you feel," he said apprehensively.

"Yeah, blood! That's exactly how the fuck I feel, buster!" he blurted, becoming angrier by the second.

C-Dub appeared mildly shocked. "Now I'm a buster, huh?" He grinned.

"You heard what the fuck I said! You old buster-ass nigga'! Now what?" Chill yelled, and was hoping that C-Dub would respond. His tone was gravely serious, and if C-Dub continued, he had made it up in his mind that he was going to kill him right there in the car, no matter how his wife felt about the situation.

"All right then, Chill." C-Dub resumed nervously. "If that's how you feel, and that's how we're getting down now, I'll get up out of your ride."

Jen continued to stare at Chill and finally said, "You know babe, I really don't trust this dude. I never have. For all we know, he could be trying to set you up at this very moment, you know what I'm saying?"

Chill continued to glare at C-Dub, and chuckled bitterly. "No shit, baby. You might be right about that."

C-Dub all of a sudden, seemed overwhelmed with anxiety, and placed his hands up above his shoulders as if he were getting robbed at gunpoint. "I ain't trying to set nobody up! I swear to you guys!" he pleaded.

"Check this out, 'Dub! It's something about your swagger that ain't cool to me no more, man! So why don't you go on and lift up that hot-ass sweater that you're wearing right quick, so I can see what the fuck you're working with!" he demanded, as he spun around in his seat and pointed the gun towards C-Dub, who panicked. "Man, fuck this shit! You guys are trippin'!" C-Dub declared, and then he threw open the door.

"Come on, babe," Chill mentioned, as they watched C-Dub run inside of his girlfriend's house. "Let's get the fuck out of here." He placed the car in gear and drove casually away from the house.

"Damn, baby. I told you a long time ago not to trust him. Now look what happened. Man," she sighed heavily, as tears began to pool in the bottom of her eyes.

She felt so powerless and unable to help her husband. She finally hung her head and let the tears flow freely onto her denim jeans.

Chill clenched his jaw and shook his head. "I know baby. I know. Damn!" he whispered, as they made their way out of the neighborhood and onto the Northbound Interstate 110 freeway.

Chapter 31

C-Dub was instantly met inside of his girlfriend's living room by Los Angeles Police detective, Sergeant Cole. Also in the room was his 50-year-old, Caucasian partner, detective, Larry Woods.

Sergeant Cole smiled at C-Dub. "You've done a splendid job here, Charlie," he said, as he helped C-Dub to remove his heavy black sweater.

Underneath the sweater was a bulletproof vest with a digital audio recorder and a microphone, which detective Woods assisted in removing.

Sergeant Cole slapped C-Dub hard on his back and startled him. "Ease up a little, Charlie!" he chuckled. "Thanks to you, buddy, our case against Bruce for kidnapping for ransom is virtually airtight. I especially enjoyed the way that you painted Armand Agassi as being the snitch in this case. Because if Willie Bruce would have known that it was you who actually snitched on him, he would have shot you dead in the head right there in that gas station! But when you get out of jail, you'll be living large with the snitch fee that you'll be paid. Just think about all of the crack cocaine you'll be able to smoke, Charlie!"

The officers shared a laugh, as Sergeant Cole detached the recorder.

C-Dub seemed nervous as he asked, "Yeah, Sarg', but are you sure that Chill is finished? I mean, I know him like the back of my hand. If he ever finds out that I was the one who set him up," he shuddered violently before continuing, "He'll blow my goddamn brains out! That's for sure! Or, he'll have one of his crazy-ass homeboys do it. That fool is already suspicious!"

"Fuck Willie Bruce!" Sergeant Cole shouted. "Because he's through, you hear me? Curtains! Don't you worry about him! Besides, once you're finished testifying against him, that low-life son-of-a-bitch will never see the streets again!"

Detective Woods chuckled. "Shit, Sarg', he won't in this lifetime."

"You're right about that, Larry," he said, and then looked at C-Dub.

"Don't give it a second thought, Charlie, because if old Willie boy is ever fortunate enough to be paroled one day, he'll probably be able to vacation on Mars!" He chuckled.

Detective Woods laughed. "I heard that, Sarg'! And, he'll most likely be able to fly there in his own goddamn spaceship."

Everyone but C-Dub nearly doubled over from laughter.

Sergeant Cole recovered and uttered, "Charlie, you don't get it, do you? We've got all of the necessary evidence that we need against Willie Bruce. It's right here in this room." He pointed at C-Dub and then to the recorder on the table, and then yelled, "In any event, asshole! I'm the threat you need to be worried about! Don't forget that you are facing life imprisonment as well. It's only through my magnificent influence, that you have the opportunity to snitch on your buddy, Mr. Bruce. I mean, don't you agree that you spending the rest of your worthless, chicken-shit-ass life in prison is much worse than telling on your very best friend?"

The detectives watched as C-Dub contemplated while nodding his head.

Woods placed a comforting hand on C-Dub's back. "That's my man, Charlie. Don't you worry about a thing, especially Mr. Bruce? I'm serious, man." He pointed to the recorder. "Listen, you see that little audio recorder right there? Well, it's got enough incriminating evidence on it to put Bruce away for at least 80 years. He'll be too old to do anything to you by then," he snickered. "You'll be dead and gone anyway, by the time that day comes around. That conversation that you had with Bruce in his Cadillac... that is a prosecutor's dream! Trust me, it was. I was listening from the van and I heard it all. It was flawless, I tell you! It was like an expensive diamond. There will not be any deals offered to Mr. Bruce, none whatsoever."

"Shit, I hope not!" C-Dub blurted.

"Charlie, there's not one jury panel from Beverly Hills, or anywhere else in the world, for that matter, who wouldn't convict his sorry ass. He's a done deal!" Woods added, and patted C-Dub on his back.

Sergeant Cole smiled and nodded his head to his partner. "Well, Chucky, you've heard all the good news. Now it's time for me to tell you the bad news. As it turns out, we don't trust you very much." He stared C-Dub straight in the eyes. "So, to avoid us having to hunt your black, good-for-nothing ass down, when the time comes for you to stab your buddy in the back, and testify against him, you'll be returned to the county jail, pending his trial. You'll be in protective custody, of course," he chuckled. "It's got to be a hell of a lot better than spending the rest of your worthless-ass life in the big house, with the big boys, isn't it?"

C-Dub sighed. "Yeah, Sarg', I guess it is," he muttered, sulking.

Wednesday morning, September 7th, two days later, Chill was lounging on the couch in the den in his black silk pajamas. He had his daughter, Jolina, resting in his lap.

She was fully engaged in a cartoon, playing on the 42" plasma television screen which was mounted on the wall.

He seemed to be in a pleasant mood while he spoke to Chris Darrington in Dallas, Texas on his cellular phone.

"Look here, dawg," he chuckled. "You keep messing around with us, and you're going to end up rich. I'm warning you, Chris."

Chris was also using his cell phone, relaxing in a local park with Candy, his 26 year-old African-American fiancée. "Thanks for the warning, Chill," he replied. "I have never made this much cheddar in my life, and that's on the real, my brotha."

"It's sad to hear that, kinfolk," Chill chortled. "It's probably because you've obviously never dealt with any real brotha's before, like Jo-Jo and I. Anyway Chris, you'll have those forty-eight reports finished by the middle of the month, right? Isn't that what you told me?"

"Yeah, boss. That's not a problem, buddy. All I need is eight more days. I guarantee you that they will all be ready by then."

"Thank you, Chris." He was suddenly distracted by the entrance of his teary-eyed wife, who was visibly distraught. "Say Chris, I'll holler back," he said as he closed his cell phone.

"Damn, Willie!" Jen sighed.

"What's wrong, Momma'?" he asked worriedly, as he placed Jolina beside him on the couch. "What's up? Why you crying, baby?"

She hurried over to the couch and picked up Jolina and held her in her arms. "Because, Willie. There's a bunch of fucking cops

311

standing in our living room right now! They want to speak with you."

Her tears flowed freely onto her confused and scared daughter.

Chill suddenly felt sick to his stomach. "Damn!" he sighed. "I knew it!" he whispered, and then stood up and walked down the hallway to the living room.

He was sure that he was about to spend the rest of his life in prison as he instantly was met by Sergeant Cole and two of his Caucasian junior detectives. Each of the men had their guns drawn but were kept pointed toward the floor.

"Willie Bruce?" Sergeant Cole asked.

"That's my name. What's this shit all about, man?" Chill asked, while Jen, their children and Jen's mother all stood behind him.

"Mr. Bruce, you're under arrest," Sergeant Cole resumed, "Now, I don't want to cause a scene in front of these kids, but I will if you force me to. So, let's try to keep this civil, shall we?"

Chill reluctantly nodded his head.

Sergeant Cole grinned. "Very well, then, Mr. Bruce. I need for you to turn around, place your hands behind your head, and spread your legs apart."

Chill complied and was given a full pat-down by one of the junior detectives. He was then handcuffed and the four of them began to move toward the front door of his home.

"Jen, call my attorney and tell him what has happened! I'll call you soon. I love you, Baby!" he said over his shoulder.

"Don't worry, dear!" She cried out. "I'll call him right now. I love you, too!"

His eyes began to water after they passed the threshold and the local activity on the street stopped as he was slowly walked toward the curb by his three escorts.

His wide-eyed, slack jawed mother-in-law was rendered speechless. She couldn't believe what she was witnessing, as she observed her precious son-in-law being deposited into the back seat of a black-and-white patrol car.

"Isn't that cute," Sergeant Cole whispered to his detectives.

Jen continued to cry as she stared at her devastated husband, who sat despondent and handcuffed in the back seat of the police car. From her position on the walkway in front of the house, she could have sworn that he had tears in his eyes as he peered downward at the floorboard.

The youngest detective, who was standing outside of the car near the driver's door, said to Sergeant Cole, "I wonder how long that this lovey-dovey shit's going to last, once he hits a prison yard with a life sentence?"

"Well, you know what they say- out of sight, out of mind," the other junior detective mentioned, as he walked around to the back of the patrol car and entered the rear door, then sat next to Chill, who was sobbing.

"He's not lying about that, Sarg'," the younger cop continued. Sergeant Cole sighed. "Well, youngsters, that's not necessarily true. Because, as they also say, *different strokes for different folks*." He then proceeded to his own detective's car which was parked on the street, blocking the driveway.

He stopped and turned to face the detective. "Listen Kirk, don't forget to read Mr. Bruce his rights. Because it will be all of our asses if we lose this case on a fucking technicality. It's all right to inform him of the charges that he's facing, but try and keep the chit-chat down to a minimum. Any other questions will be answered by me when we get him downtown for booking and processing. Got it?"

"Roger that, Sarg'," he replied, as he and the Sergeant got in behind the wheel of their respective vehicles.

At 9:31 that evening, Jo-Jo appeared visibly distraught. He was thinking about his brother-in-law as he stared blankly across the bedroom at his big-screen television.

He had his Glock 9mm handgun resting nearby on his nightstand. He glanced at it, while he sat up in bed in his white silk pajamas.

His rock cocaine pipe was hot to the touch as he placed it to his lips and whispered, "I can't believe that they done gaffled-up Chill."

He re-lit the end of the pipe and smoked the remainder of the cocaine within its glass bowl.

Meanwhile, Lena was heavily intoxicated downstairs in the kitchen. She was making a pathetic attempt at preparing some fried bologna and cheese sandwiches.

She had fried an entire pack of bologna all at once, before transferring the thick mass of sliced meat into the side shelf on the freezer door, which remained open.

Lena stood there with her hands on her hips, and was staring uncomprehendingly at the kitchen sink, when suddenly, the doorbell rang.

313

"Oh, shit!" she yelled, and jumped like a frightened cat. "Who in the hell could that be?" She wondered, as she made sure that her black terrycloth robe was secured before she walked to the front door and looked through the peephole. "What the hell do these guys want?" She whispered, as she noticed a small group of official-looking Caucasian men standing on the other side of the door. "What the fuck are these guys doing here?" she said out loud, behind being irritated by the intrusion.

She sighed and then opened the front door. "Yes?" she snapped.

Her mood quickly shifted from irritation to panic, as she took stock of the four middle-aged men, who were all wearing black flight jackets, faded denim pants and black leather work boots.

She also noticed that all four of the men sported visible bulletproof vests, dangerous-looking sidearms and badges.

Lena attempted to suppress her fear, instead, she conveyed annoyance when she asked, "May I help you guys?"

Agent D.W. Dobbs stepped to the front of the group and tipped his signature Stetson cowboy hat to the lady. "Good evening to you, Ma'am. "I'm supervising special agent, D.W. Dobbs. I'm with the United States Secret Service," he declared, while he reached into his coat pocket and pulled out a crisp, neatly folded document. "We have a Federal warrant for the arrest of your husband, Mr. Joseph Milton. Is he here on the premises, Ma'am?"

He handed Lena the document. "Let me see this shit!" she blurted, before she dropped the paper, due to the fact that her hands were shaking so badly. The warrant fell squarely in between them. Being the gentleman that Dobbs considered himself to be, he mentioned softly, "Please, allow me, Ma'am," before he reached down to retrieve the warrant. He shook off any dust that may have accumulated on the paper, and handed it back to Lena, who wept openly as she accepted it.

"Fuck," she sighed. "He's upstairs. I'll go and get him," she uttered sadly, when suddenly, the distinctive report of a pistol shot rang out from the upper level of the house.

Lena screamed, "Oh, my god!"

"Excuse me, ma'am!" Dobbs exclaimed, as he quickly shoved her out of the house while he and the other federal agents un-holstered their weapons and made their way into the home and up the stairs where they cautiously entered the master bedroom.

314

"Holy shit!" Agent Dobbs blurted, as he observed Jo-Jo's lifeless body slumped over on the carpet near the foot of the bed. He noticed a small hole near his right temple, and on the opposing side, was a gaping chasm the size of a grapefruit.

Dobbs grimaced, when he saw that the majority of his skull had been evacuated, and that bits of his brains, along with spatters of blood were distributed over a large area around the room.

Jo-Jo's handgun was still gripped tightly in his right hand. Agent Dobbs cautiously kicked it away before turning to one of his junior agents. "Keep the wife out of here, and notify the local police. Damn," he sighed. "I wanted to keep them out of this shit," he sighed. He crouched down near Jo-Jo's body and whispered, "I don't blame you one bit, Joseph."

He shook his head as he grabbed the silk sheet off of the bed and covered Jo-Jo's body. "Jesus, Milton." he uttered softly, and then stood to his feet and took a position at the bedroom door, where he stood guard until the local police arrived.

Lena was across the street when she released a wail that was so loud and pure that it chilled agent Dobbs to his core.

An hour and twenty minutes later, Jo-Jo and Chill's despondent wives were comforting each other in the driveway of the Milton home. There two of them carelessly cried and wailed freely, which Dobbs and his men deemed understandable.

Jo-Jo's body was sealed inside of a black body bag which was resting on a gurney that two male Caucasian employees of the coroner's office were pushing into the rear doors of a waiting black coroner's van.

The grief-stricken women watched as the two men eased the rear doors shut before they entered the vehicle and proceeded to drive slowly off of the property.

"Come on, sis," Jen commanded, as she gently escorted Lena down the sidewalk towards her and Chill's own home at the end of the block.

Chapter 32

At 10:21 the following morning, two Caucasian male Secret Service agents entered the Credit Company of America building. They were there to arrest Chris Darrington in his work cubical, at gunpoint, if necessary.

Chris however, chose to make things much more difficult than they needed to be. As it turns out, he resisted valiantly, by swinging his right clenched fist at one of the agents, who quickly subdued him with a Taser-gun. He was then dragged half-conscious and drooling through the busy lobby area, where his friends, other co-workers, and the receptionist observed in total shock.

As the professionally dressed agents continued onward with their handcuffed prisoner carried in between them, Chris' head accidently made a sharp impact with the lobby doors, as the three of them pushed through it to the outside.

While the trio approached a late-model black Lincoln Navigator in the parking lot, Chris Darrington, in his electrically induced stupor, glanced at the very spot near the bench in front of the building where his misfortune first began. All that he could do was moan loudly and buck against his captors, one of whom slugged him brutally in the abdomen.

"Shut the fuck up! You piece of shit!" the man screamed.

Chris hissed before the two agents shoved him violently into the right-rear passenger seat. One of the agents seated himself in the back with Chris, while the other entered the car behind the steering wheel and quickly drove out of the area.

"If you keep fucking around back there, we'll scramble your stupid-ass brains with the goddamn electricity again!" the driver shouted over his shoulder.

The agent in the rear seat watched mercilessly, as his prisoner urinated on himself before he eventually lost consciousness.

Later that morning, Al was perusing some sales reports at his desk in the modular office of his car dealership, Universal Sales Automotive. He was chewing on a large bite from a chocolate candy bar when suddenly he heard a man's voice shout, "Federal agents! We have a search warrant!" Immediately following this announcement, the trailer door exploded inward, and two Caucasian men in dark business suits were standing several feet in front of him. Their guns were drawn and aimed directly at him.

"We're with the Secret Service, Mr. Al Hakeeshe, and you are under arrest! Now, let me see your hands, very, very slowly!" the older agent yelled.

Al closed his eyes and prayed for a moment. He then grabbed a hold of his Colt Python .357 revolver that he always kept hidden in the alcove under his desk.

"Show us your hands, now!" the younger agent shouted.

Al winked at the men and shouted, "Kiss my fat ass!" and drew his revolver and blasted one missing shot, which caused the agents to fire repeated shots into his body, until they were completely out of ammunition. Al's head came to rest on the desk.

"My goodness!" the older agent blurted.

"Fuck yeah!" his partner shouted, as they both witnessed a copious amount of blood from Al's wounds, which flowed freely onto the remainder of the uneaten chocolate bar. The wall behind Al was blood-splattered.

"Damn! What a rush! The younger agent continued. "I feel like I've got so much fucking energy, man! Goddamn!"

The seasoned, older agent smirked. "That's just great, you sick-ass son-of-a-bitch! Now, since you've got so much fucking energy, you can stay here and wait for the police to arrive. You can help them with their paperwork, you idiot!" and ducked out of the office before his partner could respond.

A short while later at the Landmark Investment Group, the round-up continued. Michael Leon was completely irate, as he stood near his office desk. Beside him was an African-American female agent from the United States Secret Service Agency who was placing him in handcuffs. Her middle-aged Caucasian counterpart was standing nearby and was reading Michael his Constitutional Rights.

"So, Mr. Leon, you do you understand these rights as I have explained them to you?" the agent asked.

Michael grinned. "Yes, I understand." "Okay, then. Having fully understood your Constitutional Rights, do you wish to speak with us?"

"Absolutely," he smiled and nodded his head. "You bitches can go choke yourselves with a bloody tampon, you fucking cunts!" he shouted.

The African-American agent scowled at her partner. "Let's get this nasty-ass mother-fucker up out of here, girl!" The two of them roughly escorted him out of the building.

As the morning gave way to the afternoon, Nick Crane at the Montoya Realty Group, Fred Macklin at Macklin's Income Tax Service, Stuart Magnum at Erotic Motoring Auto Sales, and Tony Kin, who was at his Mid-Wilshire office within the Capital Mortgage Corporation building, were all arrested and booked without incident in the downtown Metropolitan Holding Center.

Tony Kin, however, attempted to flee on foot before he was shot once in the buttocks.

The 40-year-old Caucasian male Secret Service agent who shot him stated, "He shouldn't have tried to run, damn bastard!" as he holstered his weapon.

"Should we read him his rights?" asked his Caucasian male partner.

"Hell, I thought that we already did!" the agent involved in the shooting quipped, before they both doubled over in laughter. Meanwhile, Tony was lying on the ground, crying and moaning in agony.

At 5:19 p.m., Chill was visited by Jen inside of the dreadful institution-gray visiting room of the Los Angeles County Men's Central Jail.

He wore a dark-blue two-piece uniform and was weeping while he sat on a metal stool in front of a thick bulletproof glass. On the opposite side of the glass was Jen who was also emotionally distraught, although she managed much more restraint in fighting back her tears than her husband did, who seemed resigned to his situation.

She wiped her teary bloodshot eyes before noisily blowing her nose into a tissue while they spoke to one another through telephone handsets.

Chill shook his head in frustration. "Damn, baby. Jo-Jo wasn't bullshitting when he said that he would rather die than go back to prison. That's fucking crazy!"

"I know, dear." She used some more tissue to dab away the tears from her eyes when she felt that they were spilling onto her light-blue wool sweater. "Lena's a total wreck right now."

"Jesus. I can't even imagine. I mean, I told you how she was acting during those times that I went to their house to drop off some money. Damn, momma, she was ready for the mental hospital before Joseph did this. I feel for that poor girl." He sighed. "I can imagine how she's doing right now."

He glanced up and down his side of the glass at a dozen or so similarly dressed inmates, all of whom were engaged in conversations with their family members and friends. "But she's not the only one," he resumed, looking into Jen's eyes.

"What do you mean by that, Willie?" she asked, as she tried to combat her tears.

"Well, I'm going through it, too. I mean, my bail amount is over five million dollars. I'll never be able to pay that. On top of it all is what my attorney, Larry Pearlstein, told me."

"What was that?" she asked curiously, looking him straight in the eyes.

"He said that the Secret Service is building up a case against me, but they are waiting on the outcome of my criminal kidnapping case with the State of California. They're betting that I'll get life in prison for the kidnapping charges alone. If I do, they'll be satisfied and drop their charges against me," he explained, as Jen became visibly choked up and cried heavily. "So tell me, Momma." He stared deeply into her eyes.

She met his intense gaze. "Tell you what, dear?"

"I want to know what you think about all of this shit."

She wanted to lash out and say, "I saw it coming from a mile away! I kept warning you, but you never listened!"

Instead, allowing her love for Chill to guide her thoughts and words, she said calmly, "It really doesn't matter what I think. What's done is done. When I married you, it was for better or for worse. Whatever God chooses for you, whether it's for you to spend the rest of your life in prison, or for you to live free with me and our children out here in society, it's really all the same. No matter what, my love, your family will never leave your side. We love you. Also, you and I have made a promise to love one another for 80 plus, remember?"

"I love you and the family too, baby. And of course I remember. It's eighty plus, baby. Eighty plus," he repeated softly, as he placed his right palm flat up against the thick visiting window.

"Eighty plus it is, Willie. You've got that right, my love," she replied, placing her palm flat up against the visiting window over his palm. "So don't you ever worry about us going anywhere. Because with me, it's until death do us part."

"It's the same with me, Momma."

The two of them began to cry together until a humongous, middle-aged African-American male Sheriff's Deputy abruptly ended the visit.

Monday morning, four days later, Jo-Jo was laid to rest in the Holy Acres Cemetery located in West Los Angeles. It was a beautiful ceremony as a large group of family members and friends assembled to pay their final respects.

Lena was weeping unabashedly as she stood under the crisp, clear sky, and observed. African-American Reverend, Mr. J. D. Haynes Jr., conveyed a moving eulogy.

Chapter 32

It was eight months later, Monday, May 8th, 2006, and the afternoon criminal court trial of Willie "Chill" Bruce was well underway.

The space inside of the superior courtroom belonging to the Honorable African-American Judge, Mr. Harry Jefferson Maxwell, was filled to capacity on the 9th floor of the downtown Los Angeles Criminal Courts building.

Chill, who was dressed very nicely in a black business suit, appeared to be rather upset as he forced himself to sit quietly next to his domineering attorney, Mr. Larry Pearlstein, Esquire.

The two of them observed Chill's longtime friend, Charles "C-Dub" Hicks, who sat smugly on the witness stand next to the elderly, obese, and aggressive Judge.

Suddenly, the Deputy District Attorney, Ms. Linda Chan, a 36-year-old Chinese-American, who wore a gray business suit, shot up from her chair and sauntered up to the witness stand. She smiled at practically everyone in the room, as she arrogantly rested her arm on the polished-wood railing near C-Dub, who enjoyed the scent of her Victoria Secret perfume.

"Mr. Hicks," she began with authority, glancing at the predominantly white male jury, who hung onto her every word. "On December 6th, 2004, at, or around 7:15 a.m., were you willfully engaged in the home invasion robbery, and kidnapping for ransom plot, against Beverly Hills residents, Mr. and Misses, Carlos and Joanna Diaz?"

C-Dub glanced at the members of the Jury panel, and then he looked Ms. Chan straight in the eyes, "I'm not proud of what I've done, Ms. Chan, but yes, yes I was, ma'am."

Attorney Chan nodded her head as she briefly looked at the jury panel. She patted her hand softly on the railing and looked back at C-Dub, whom she was absolutely sure was experiencing some erotic fantasies of having raunchy sex with her in his jail cell.

She smiled as she remembered what her father had told her when she was a young child. "You're a mind reader, sweetheart."

It appeared as though every one of her 32 teeth sparkled as she looked him in his eyes and said, "Okay, very well then, Mr. Hicks. Now, could you please tell me if you notice anyone here in this courtroom, today who was with you on that particular morning? Someone who, perhaps, helped you commit this horrible crime," she continued, gazing at her fingernails.

Larry Pearlstein's voice ranged out shrilly. "Objection, your Honor! Counsel is leading the witness, for Christ sake!"

Judge Maxwell's response was swift and decisive. "Your objection is over-ruled, Mr. Pearlstein."

He turned to C-Dub and pointed. "Answer the question, Mr. Hicks, please."

"Yes sir," C-Dub mentioned, and then looked at attorney Chan. "Um, yes Ma'am. Yes, I do see someone," he responded hesitantly.

"Very well, sir. Could you please do me a favor and point to him, or her, Mr. Hicks?"

C-Dub complied and jabbed his right index finger towards Chill, who stood up and yelled, "You punk, rat-ass son-of-a-bitch!"

He was immediately forced back down in his chair by two court deputies, who remained standing nearby during Judge Maxwell's admonition.

He pointed directly towards Chill's face and uttered, "Mr. Bruce, sir, I am a fair and patient Judge. However, I will not tolerate disorder of any sort in my courtroom! Do you understand?"

Chill scoffed and rolled his eyes.

The Judge grinned as he continued, "One more outburst from you, and I will find you in contempt of court!" He tapped his gavel angrily.

Attorney Chan turned to the court reporter, who was seated in front and to the left side of the witness stand.

"Your Honor, could you please let the record reflect, that the witness, Mr. Charles Hicks, has indicated the defendant, Mr. Willie Bruce."

"Yes, Ms. Chan."

As Chill glared menacingly into C-Dub's cowering eyes, he leaned over toward his attorney and whispered, "Hick's a fucking snitch!"

Larry Pearlstein nodded.

Later that afternoon, Chill and his attorney were sitting quietly at the defendant's table, while on the witness stand, Mrs. Joanna Diaz was pointing her finger at Chill.

"And how would you describe Mr. Bruce's behavior toward you on the morning in question, Mrs. Diaz?" Larry Pearlstine asked.

He knew that for a defense attorney to ask such an incriminating question to the victim would mean an unquestionable conviction for his client. However, he also knew that with C-Dub's testimony against Chill, there wasn't any doubt in his mind that Chill would be convicted for the crime of kidnap for ransom and would spend the rest of his natural life behind bars.

His intentions were simply to soften the harsh prison sentence that he was certain his client would receive based on the previous damaging testimonies.

Prosecutor Chan stood to her feet and yelled, "Objection, your honor! This is a question of relevance, sir. This trial is to determine whether or not Willie Bruce was an accomplice in the home-invasion robbery and the kidnap for ransom plot. It is not designed to characterize Mr. Bruce's behavior during the act itself!" she continued, wild-eyed.

Judge Maxwell sighed, "Yes, Ms. Chan, it is an unusual question for a defense attorney to ask, seeing as Mr. Bruce hasn't been convicted, as of yet, I will allow the question to be entered into the transcripts."

"Yes, your Honor," she sighed and smirked, as she sat down in her chair. Judge Maxwell used a white handkerchief to clean his gold-framed reading glasses and pointed to Larry Pearlstein. "Get to the point, counselor," he instructed.

When Mrs. Diaz seemed unsure as to how to continue, Judge Maxwell said, "It's okay, ma'am. You may proceed with answering the question." He smiled.

Mrs. Diaz nodded her head and drew in a deep breath. "It was almost as if he didn't belong there at all. Like he did not seem to share the evilness of the others, in fact, I distinctly remember Mr. Bruce bringing me a glass of water. I thought that was nice of him. I mean, considering the dreadful circumstances."

"Thank you very much, Mrs. Diaz," Mr. Pearlstein resumed.

He turned to the judge. "No further questions, your honor," he said, as he returned to his seat and patted Chill on the back.

After the prosecution and the defense team rested their cases, Chill was ordered back into the courtroom of Judge Harry J. Maxwell.

The Jury panel, which had been deliberating for an almost unprecedented three days, filed back into the courtroom and took their respective seats.

Chill was desperately seeking eye contact with any one of the eleven men and one woman for some clue as to his fate. They all avoided looking in his direction.

The bailiff announced dispassionately, "All rise for the Honorable Judge, Harry Jefferson Maxwell." He did so, as soon as the perturbed judge appeared from behind the door to his chambers, and then assumed his seat on the bench.

"This court is back in session. You may be seated," he instructed.

Chill was so nervous that he had to stop his teeth from chattering on more than a few occasions.

Larry Pearlstein looked at him pityingly and placed his hand on his shoulders.

Judge Maxwell addressed the Jury. "Distinguished members of the Jury, it is to my understanding that you have reached a verdict, is this correct?"

The sole female, who was also the fore person speaking on behalf of the others, stood up. "Yes it is, your Honor."

Judge Maxwell looked at Chill and his attorney. "The defendant will rise."

Chill and Attorney Pearlstein stood to their feet. The defendant had to struggle to remain standing.

"Madame Foreperson, please read your verdict."

"Yes, your honor," she replied.

She placed on her silver designer reading glasses and then began to read from an ordinary sheet of office copy paper. "On this, the 22nd day of May, 2006, regarding the matter of the people of the State of California, versus Willie Bruce, case number- LACBX-102-132, We, the jury in the above-entitled action, do hereby find the defendant, Willie Bruce, guilty of the crime of Home-Invasion Robbery, a violation of the California Penal Code section- 211 (a)."

She glanced briefly at the Judge, and then resumed, "We the Jury, on the above-entitled action, do hereby also find the defendant, Willie Bruce, guilty of the crimes of kidnapping for ransom, a violation of the California Penal Code, section- 209 (a)."

Silent tears began to stream down Chill's face, as he looked at Jen, who was crying so loudly, that Judge Maxwell made a demand for there to be order in the courtroom.

The two deputy sheriffs, who had been standing no more than a foot away while the verdict was being read, restrained and handcuffed Chill as soon as the word, 'Guilty' was announced.

The judge said to the jury, "Gentlemen." He respectfully nodded to the foreperson. "Ma'am, I need to know. Was this a unanimous verdict?"

"Yes it was, your Honor," she replied, glancing at Chill.

"Are there any amongst you who disagree with this verdict?" his honor asked, as he studied each member of the jury. No one responded.

"Very well," he resumed. "On behalf of myself and the good People of the State of California, I thank you. Have a good day," he hastily retreated to his chambers as the courtroom began to clear out.

Chill was taken to a holding area where his handcuffs were removed.

Later that evening, he was driven via jail bus back to his housing unit, known as, "The million dollar row." It was a heavily secured section within the downtown Men's Central jail, where the inmates' bail amount was in excess of one million dollars. It housed 199 prisoners in all. Chill's place in line was inmate number 182.

Once he returned to his cell, he confided in his cellmate, Ricardo Vega, a 36-year-old Puerto-Rican, and a man of means.

Rico, as he preferred to be called, had a great attorney. His name was Victor Lealman. Rico's older brother, Butch, had paid him handsomely to represent his brother. In return, Victor was able to get Rico a nine-month stint in the county jail, primarily, for being in possession of 11 pounds of methamphetamine. However, the Hispanic female judge had ordered Rico to spend his jail time on, "The Million Dollar Row."

Had Rico's family not been able to afford Mr. Lealman's expertise, he would have undoubtedly received a life sentence in prison, being that he already had two prior felony convictions for drugs and weapons related crimes.

Teardrops were building up in the corners of Chill's eye, as he sat on the edge of his bunk in his white boxer shorts. He was staring intently at the concrete floor and contemplating some dreadful possibilities. One, in particular, was suicide. He stood up and moved to the front of the cell, where he leaned against the security bars in deep frustration.

Rico was sitting with his legs folded on his upper bunk, silently playing Solitaire with a deck of cards when he observed that Chill seemed depressed and obviously had a lot on his mind.

He studied him for a long moment, but remained silent. He knew that Chill was a condemned man, but what could he do about it? What could he say to a man who was about to be sentenced to prison for the rest of his life?

He himself was due to be released from jail in six days, and Chill knew it. He watched Chill ponder and shake his head. He felt his pain, as he compulsively shuffled the cards and said, "Try to keep your head up, Chill. I'm sure that you're going to be all right. You're a soldier, man. You're about as solid as they come."

Chill sighed heavily and looked him in the eyes. "I don't know, Rico. This shit is way too much for me to handle, you know? I'm telling you, man. This shit is crazy! I mean, I've got the wife and kids at home. I just hope that they can handle this shit."

"They will dawg'. You've got a good woman who believes in you. She ain't going anywhere."

Chill let out a deep sigh. "I pray every day that she won't."

"Trust me, Chill. She's in your corner one hundred percent, man.

"Yeah," Chill managed to grin, as he continued. "On top of that, Rico, I've got the one nigga' that I trusted in this whole wide world, snitchin' on me! Man," he sighed and shrugged his shoulders. "What's next, you know?"

"I know what you mean, man. But you'll be all right, Chill. You've still got that appeal thing that you were telling me about. So, try not to give up, man. And don't be a quitter, you know? You're stronger than that. I know you are! Like I said, you're a soldier."

"Yeah, man. But, I feel like I'm going to lose it, though. I'm looking at a whole shit-load of prison time, Rico," he admitted, as the tears finally flowed down his face and onto his bare chest.

Rico felt like crying himself, but he fought back his tears. Instead, he focused on compulsively shuffling the deck. He finally said, "Well my brother, like my mother used to tell me before she passed away in 1996, "There be consequences to each and every one of our actions."

"She used to mention that to me all the time, Chill."

"She was right, you know? That's some true wisdom she was lacing you with. She definitely sounds like she was a smart woman."

"She was smart." Rico smiled. "She was beautiful, too," he replied, sorrowfully.

"I can feel what you're saying, man," Chill said, as he returned to his bed, faced the wall and began weeping.

Two weeks later, Chill was wearing his dark-blue county jail uniform inside of Judge Maxwell's courtroom, for what would most likely be the last time. There were two middle-aged Caucasian male deputies who flanked him from behind as he sat heartbroken at the defendant's table next to Larry Pearlstein, who tried his best to keep him calm.

Deputy District Attorney, Linda Chan, looked bored, as she sat at the prosecutor's table examining her French-manicured fingernails.

Lena's face was bandaged and her demeanor seemed admittedly more sober and lucid than Chill had seen since his return from Dallas, Texas, nine months earlier.

She sat huddled with Jen, who couldn't seem to bring herself to look at her husband. Not out of shame but because of the profound sense of loss that she felt when she first saw him being escorted in, shackled at the waist and legs, to where he now sat.

He glanced up at the armed deputies who glared him straight in the eyes. One of them even moved his hand to his Glock .40-caliber handgun which he had resting in a black quick-release holster on his side.

Chill wished that this whole circus would end, as Judge Maxwell finally entered the courtroom and banged his gavel three times, before his body came to rest in his black leather executive chair.

"We're back in session, you may be seated," he announced. "Now, we're here on the matter of the People versus Bruce, who is present in my courtroom, and is in custody."

He moved his attention to Chill, who was sweating profusely and looked away from his penetrating stare. "Mr. Bruce, you have been found guilty of the crime of kidnapping for the purpose of ransom, as well as the crime of home-invasion robbery, both of which, are violations of the applicable Penal Code sections. The verdict was handed down by a jury of your peers."

"That's some straight bullshit!" he said. "Jury of my peers, my ass!" Chill muttered to Larry Pearlstein, which was immediately noticed by the judge.

"Anyway," Judge Maxwell sneered. "Do you understand everything that I've explained to you today, Mr. Bruce?"

"Yeah, Judge. Whatever, man," Chill replied flippantly.

"Very well then, sir," His Honor continued. "I am now going to pronounce a sentence upon you, since you understand. You do comprehend what is about to happen, don't you?"

Chill scoffed. "Yeah, Judge. I think so. Just do what you got to do!"

Judge Maxwell grinned as he mused momentarily and then glared at Chill. "You know Mr. Bruce, you've got a bit of an attitude there, young man."

"Really?" Chill scowled. "You think?" he blurted sarcastically.

His Honor grinned. "Well, considering the circumstances, it is understandable that you would feel this way." He sighed. "Well, anyway, let's get on with it, shall we?"

"Yeah, man. Let's get this shit over with," Chill whispered to his attorney, but was clearly overheard by everyone in the room.

Judge Maxwell smirked. "Okay, Mr. Bruce. I'll do exactly as you wish. I'll get this "shit" over with. But, before I do, I must first inform you that I have a very wide discretion here. I have the total authority to sentence you up to the maximum penalty, or the minimum, should I decide to do so. You do understand this, don't you, Mr. Bruce?"

"Yeah, man, I hear you, loud and clear!" Chill smirked.

Judge Maxwell shook his head and chuckled, "You know Mr. Bruce? From what I've read of your probation report, as well as the police report itself, you appear to me to be a pretty sharp young man." He paused. "Yes, you appear to be very sharp, indeed. However, from what I'm seeing of you at this very minute, you seem to be about as sharp as a bowling ball." Laughter suddenly erupted in the courtroom. "And, from what I'm seeing of you from up here, I truly believe that the only way that you would know that this concrete building is falling down is after it has already crushed you," he continued, and received a hilarious response from the majority of the courtroom occupants, except for Chill's loved ones, who were seated directly behind him in the spectator seats.

He scowled at the Judge and whispered to Larry Pearlstein, "Fuck this hog-maw-eating mother-fucker!"

Pearlstein laughed and then whispered, "Yeah, be cool, Willie. Please, before we mess around and get another charge."

"At any rate, sir" Judge Maxwell continued. "As the presiding judge in the case involving the complaint filed by the District Attorney, on behalf of Mr. and Misses, Carlos Hector Diaz, and his wife, Joanna Maria Diaz, of Beverly Hills, I now pronounce sentence upon you, Willie Bruce. By the power granted to me by the great State of California, for the crimes of kidnapping for the purpose of ransom, I hereby remand you to the custody of the California Department of Corrections, for the remainder of your natural life. This is carried out without the possibility of parole."

He glanced up momentarily, as the sounds of shock and sadness filled the room.

Jen ran crying out of the courtroom.

At that very moment, Chill experienced an odd sense of detachment, and suddenly, he felt that his situation wasn't so bad, as he simply decided to stop caring.

The judge continued, "And for the crimes of first-degree armed robbery, I remand you to the California Department of Corrections for the remainder of your natural life. These sentences are to be imposed consecutively, I might add," he said, as he removed his reading glasses and looked up at Chill, who was grinning and shaking his head. "Mr. Bruce, have you anything that you would like to express, in regards to this matter?"

Chill jabbed Larry Pearlstein in his ribcage with a sharp elbow.

"Willie, I really think that we can beat this rap on appeal, trust me," Pearlstein whispered, truthfully.

"You're a dump-truck-ass lawyer, you know that?" Chill whispered

He glared at Judge Maxwell and cleared his throat. "Why yes, Mr. Maxwell. Matter-of-fact, there is something that I would like to express to the court this morning."

His Honor smiled. "Well then, Mr. Bruce, you have my undivided attention, sir. You go right ahead and express yourself however you see fit this morning." He looked at the deputies. "This should be very interesting, guys."

He then focused his attention back to Chill and nodded. "You may proceed, Mr. Bruce. The court is listening. "

Judge Maxwell smiled and placed a frame tip from his reading glasses in between his teeth, and leaned back in his chair and eagerly awaited Chill's response.

Chill gazed around the courtroom. He scoffed and then smirked at the presumably shocked and penetrating stares which were being cast upon him by some strangers. He suddenly grinned. "Look at all you punk mother-fuckers!" he muttered, and then scoffed again.

He turned and locked eyes with the Judge. "Man, you must be out of your goddamn mind this morning!" he exclaimed.

Laughter came from the judge and the prosecutor, while the rest of the courtroom occupants looked on in shock with their mouths wide open.

Judge Maxwell tapped his gavel once. "Order in the court!" he demanded, peering around the room. Silence occurred instantly, as he continued, "Now Mr. Bruce, to respond to your comment, if I may?"

Chill smirked. "Whatever, man! Just get on with it, shit!"

Judge Maxwell chuckled. "I'm sorry that you feel this way, young man. But I assure you Mr. Bruce, I am a rational individual. Ask anyone who knows me," he chortled.

"That's some bullshit, man! You can't be rational! Because this shit don't make any goddamn sense! There ain't no way in hell that I'm going to serve two consecutive life sentences in prison without parole! That's crazy, man! It's fucking impossible!"

Judge Maxwell casually placed his glasses on the bench. "Man," he sighed. "You've got quite a foul mouth on you there, Mr. Bruce," he said, as he crossed his arms and leaned back in his chair. "Well, son, to answer your question," he uttered slowly, obviously in deep ponder. "Just do what you can, that's all." He nodded his head. "Don't worry about the rest. The future will take care of itself. I promise you that, Mr. Bruce," he continued.

He looked at the deputies, who found his comment humorous. "Now officers, get this convict out of my courtroom, and deliver him to his fate."

"Fuck you, nigga'!" Chill shouted.

"Ditto, young man," Judge Maxwell smiled, and then motioned to the deputies to remove Chill from the room.

"Yes, sir," the deputy in charge mentioned, as he and his partner wrenched a mildly resisting Chill toward the rear door, which led to the holding cells behind the courtroom.

Jen, who had returned to the courtroom moments earlier, yelled out, "Don't worry Willie!" Her mascara was smeared from her incessant tears, as she resumed, "Besides, we still have an appeal! And it's still, 80 plus between you and I! And that's forever, baby!"

Chill yelled back, "Yeah momma'! 80 plus! I love you, Jen!"

"I love you too, dear!" she blurted, as she watched him being forced through the rear door behind the Judge's bench.

Chapter 34

At 1:03 the next morning, C-Dub was released from the custody of the county jail in exchange for his damaging testimony against Chill.

After stepping through the doors leading to the sidewalk, and to his freedom, he stopped for a moment and smiled.

"Yes!" he exclaimed and closed his eyes, reaping the benefits of his new found liberty. "Freedom!" he blurted, and filled his lungs with his first breath of fresh air since his arrest, nineteen months earlier.

He never thought that he would walk again as a free man in Los Angeles, or in any other city for that matter. Had he not betrayed his one-and-only true friend, the only walking that he would have been doing would have been on concrete pavement inside of a California State prison.

Charles "C-Dub" Hicks, was never one to agonize over tough moral decisions, however, being a sociopath had its privileges. One of those privileges was his uncanny ability to forget completely the unpleasant episodes of the robbery/kidnapping, and the betrayal of his loyal friend. He carried this out without even batting an eyelid.

After opening his eyes, it took him some time before he was acclimated back to the outside world. He had recently spent the better part of the last two years locked up within a small concrete cell with Mark, his middle-aged African-American protective custody cellmate. The two of them were placed under the constant watchful eye of the jail's deputies who hated snitches!

Often, their food would be spat in and their beverages, well… urine was the odd taste that they were experiencing, compliments of the staff, who found the act itself humorous.

He had to tolerate clinically psychotic inmates on the tier, who were constantly yelling awful profanities and the sound of a cold metal toilet in the cells that, when flushed, sounded like a lion roaring! It was therefore, psychologically understandable that a period of re-adjustment was necessary and natural.

After having enough of his bearings to confidently proceed onto step number 2, that being obtaining some money until he could receive the "snitch fee" that was promised to him by the police department, along with some new clothes to replace the dingy, wrinkled suit that he was arrested in, he began walking toward the street. He carried only a brown cardboard folder in his hand containing what little personal effects he had. To his surprise, he heard the gentle tap of a car horn and quickly spun around, in a state of panic. "Who the fuck is that?" he blurted with his eyes wide open, obviously scared to death. He sort of resembled a wild deer who was caught in headlights, as he stood there hunched over, frozen in place, and peering at a brand new black 2006 Dodge Ram truck. It was parked at the curb near the sidewalk.

The headlights flashed twice, beckoning him.

"Who in the hell is that?" he whispered. He knew that he was a man who was now marked for death because of his willingness to help to prosecute his friend.

The headlights flashed again, but more insistent this time. They were followed by another soft tap of the car horn.

C-Dub seemed frightened out of his wits as he began to move slowly toward the vehicle but was ready and willing to dive for cover if necessary.

Suddenly, the front passenger window lowered, revealing Sergeant Cole sitting behind the steering wheel, and wearing a big, toothy grin. "Howdy, Charlie!" he blurted, as he unlocked the passenger door while C-Dub approached the vehicle.

"What's up Sarg'?" C-Dub said, instantly appearing disburdened.

"Not too much, Chucky. I'm just doing my thing, you know? Why don't you climb on in? I'll give you a lift to wherever it is that you're going this morning. How's that sound, buddy?"

"That sounds cool, Sarg'. I wasn't very thrilled at having to take the bus, you dig?"

Sergeant Cole chuckled, "I heard that!"

"But anyway, Sarg', I'd like to go back to that bitch of mine's house on 109th Street. That's the same house that Chill had picked me up in front of that day. I mean, if you don't mind? You remember the house, don't you?"

"Of course I do, Charlie," he chortled, as C-Dub opened the door and entered the vehicle.

The two of them shook hands. "How could I forget?" he continued, while he pressed a button on his door panel and raised C-Dub's window, and then locked the doors. "And how could I mind, Charlie? You've been locked up for 19 months now. All throughout that time, you've willingly provided the prosecution team with any and everything that they needed to put Bruce's unlawful-ass away forever. So, I figured that giving you a ride home was the least that I can do for you."

He rolled down his driver's window a few inches, lit-up a non-filter cigarette, and took a deep drag.

"Well thanks, Sarg'. I really appreciate this."

"I know you do, Chucky." He exhaled a cloud of smoke out of his window, and then placed the vehicle in gear and accelerated away from the curb. "Care for a smoke?" He shook the pack, causing a single cigarette to protrude a couple of inches.

"No thanks, Sarg'. I'm trying to eliminate my bad habits. Cut my loses. You know what I'm saying?"

Sergeant Cole began coughing, which gradually converted to laughter. "Yeah Charlie, I know exactly what you're talking about. Anyway, suit yourself," he said, as he tossed the pack back onto the center console.

"So Sarg', I know that it's really none of my business, but I'm just curious, man," he mentioned, while he placed his folder filled with court documents on the floor.

"You're curious about what?"

"Well, it's late as a motherfucker! So, what in the hell are you doing all out and about, down here at 1 something in the morning?"

Sergeant Cole grinned, as he seemed to reflect upon a pleasant memory. "Well, I had to drop off a little lady-friend of mine. She works at the jail, 1st watch. Well, I made her a little late, if you know what I mean?" he chuckled.

C-Dub laughed as Sergeant Cole brought the truck to an easy stop at a red traffic light at the corner. "Yeah Sarg', I know exactly what you mean! You must've been fucking the shit out of her, huh?"

"Ah, yes indeed," he smiled. "You would've been proud of my performance tonight. Especially after swallowing three-quarters of a V-baby and chasing it down with a cold brew," he explained, as he activated his left signal indicator.

The signal light turned green and Sergeant Cole turned left onto First Street, and then headed eastbound toward the northbound onramp to the 101 freeway, a half-mile up the street.

"What in the fuck is a V-baby, Sarg'?"

"That's my little pet name for Viagra."

"Viagra?" C-Dub scowled. "Sarg', you actually need that stuff?"

"Hell no, Charlie!" he blurted defensively. "Shit no!" he continued, as he pulled over to the curbside and parked the truck in front of a 24-hour liquor store. "My ding-a-ling functions perfectly well, all by itself, thank you very much!"

"Then why do you use it then?" C-Dub grinned.

"Because, it makes my penis perform like a champion! It feels like it's hard as steel, you know what I mean? It's almost as if it's been lifting weights or something. It's amazing, I tell you! You should see the thing! I'll show you, if you like?" he said, as he reached down toward his pants zipper. C-Dub chuckled and placed his hands up. "Hell nah!" He scowled. "You're a fool, Sarg'! I'll take your word for it," he chuckled.

"You better go and get yourself some. I'm telling you, Charlie- it ain't no joke at all!"

"I'll check it out, Sarg'," C-Dub laughed, as Sergeant Cole pulled out a black leather wallet from the back pocket of his stone-washed jeans.

"It could be the best decision you'll ever make, Chucky."

"I got it, Sarg'," he chortled. "So tell me, is that lady-friend of yours at the jail anyone that I may be acquainted with?"

Sergeant Cole sighed. "Now Chucky, you know damn well that I can't divulge that kind of information to you. Although, I can tell you that she's about the best blond fuck that I've encountered in my entire life!"

"It must be nice, Sarg'." He smiled, as he briefly day-dreamed about his upcoming sexual escapade. "You know, it's been a long time since I had some good, hot-ass pussy. So, I'm definitely going to get my rod wet this morning. I'm talking about as soon as I get my black ass back to that bitch of mines house over on the eastside," he mentioned, as he glanced at the door to the liquor store.

"Well, Mr. Hicks," Sergeant Cole chuckled. "Try not to hurt the poor woman, okay?"

"Hurt her?" C-Dub scowled. "Sarg', I'm going to beat it up when I climb up in it!"

He placed the vehicle in park. "Beat what up, Charlie?"

C-Dub sighed in exasperation. "Man Sarg', y'all police cats some square-ass motherfuckers!" He laughed. "I'm talking about the pussy, Sarg'! I'm going to tear it up!"

"Ah-ha, I get it," he laughed softly. "That's real funny, Chucky boy. Beat up the pussy! I like that. I might have to steal that phrase from you, if you don't mind? Tell it to the boys, you know?"

"Yeah, man. Go ahead, Sarg'. Get hip, dawg'!"

"I'm trying, Chucky. But I'm really just an old, square-ass country boy, you know?" He opened his wallet and pulled out a $100 bill. "Anyway, you feel like an ice-cold brew or something? I'm sure that it beats the hell out of that bullshit homemade jailhouse crap, which you convicts are always sipping on in there. What do they call that stuff? Ah, yes- 'Pruno'. It sure doesn't sound very attractive."

"It's not. But yeah, Sarg', a cold-one would be real nice about right now. Because I've been drinking that Pruno shit for 19 months! I've been craving the real deal the whole time, too!"

"Yeah man, I know. Here," he said, as he handed C-Dub the bill. "Get whatever you want. Just pick me up an ice-cold, longneck brew, okay? You keep the change for yourself."

"Thanks a lot, Sarg'. That's good looking out, man!"

"You're very welcome, Charlie."

"A cold brew, now that's what I'm talking about!" he said, as he climbed out of the truck and entered the liquor store.

He suddenly noticed that the African-Nationalist cashier, a tall man whose back was facing him, was busily using a pink feather duster on an array of liquor bottles, which were prominently displayed within some metal shelving against the wall.

Without so much as a word to the man, C-Dub made a bee-line for the back of the store and picked out two bottles of beer from the refrigerator.

Backtracking a few steps, he then grabbed a family-sized bag of flaming hot barbecue pork skins, and made his way back to the front of the store and deposited the items on the counter.

He marveled at the proprietor who was still absorbed in his dusting. He stared at the back of the man's head for a short time, and then becoming somewhat impatient with the lack of attention, he cleared his throat, loudly.

Suddenly, four very large African men entered the store jabbering to one another in their native language.

As C-Dub glanced over his shoulder at them, the men all at once stopped speaking and gave him a look that suddenly made him want to hurry up and leave the store.

"Ah, pardon me, brother," C-Dub directed towards the back of the clerk's head.

"Yes, what can I do for you, Charlie?" Agonda asked, as he spun around with the pink feather duster in his hand. He smiled and winked at C-Dub, who was suddenly petrified.

"Agonda?" he squeaked.

As C-Dub began to panic, the four African henchmen, who were now holding guns, seized his arms and held him immobile, even as he struggled mightily against their powerful grasp.

"Yes, Charlie, it's me," Agonda uttered evenly. "I heard that you were looking for me. Well Charlie, here I am. Boo!!!" He screamed directly in C-Dub's face, and then laughed, as he watched him shudder in fear.

"You fucking coward!" Agonda exclaimed, and then he playfully tickled C-Dub's face with the feather duster. He seemed to be thoroughly enjoying the misery that he was inflicting upon him.

"I don't have a problem with you, Agonda! I swear I don't!" C-Dub blurted, as his eyes became filled with tears, which quickly spilled down his cheeks. "I ain't tripping on nothing man! So fuck the fifty-thousand dollars that you took from me in the Sky Tower Hotel!"

Agonda laughed. "No, Charlie. Don't you mean fuck the five thousand dollars that I took from you in the Sky Tower hotel?

337

Because you and I both know that the rest of that money in your briefcase was bullshit. It was phony!"

C-Dub began to hyperventilate. "Phony? What do you mean, Agonda?" he yelled helplessly, as the henchmen continued to hold him against his will.

Agonda laughed scornfully. "Yes, it was phony, you stupid-ass son-of-a-bitch! Do you take me for a fool, Charlie? I make that counterfeit shit, remember? I could see from a mile away that it was some counterfeit money in your briefcase. But you lied to me." He smiled and tickled C-Dub some more with the duster. "Charlie, you're a naughty, naughty boy. You led me to believe that you were a man of your word, which I soon found out, you weren't. Well," he said, as he twirled the duster and rolled his eyes. "Everyone knows that your word ain't shit! Besides, that wasn't the first time that you burned me- or my family," Agonda added, and gave C-Dub a punishing backhand slap, which sent his head twisting.

When C-Dub recovered, a thin trickle of blood was running down the right corner of his mouth. His facial expression changed from abject terror, to one of intense curiosity.

"What do you mean, it wasn't the first time?'"

"Well, ass-hole, you happen to rob my younger brother, Mustafa," he hissed, and peered at a dumbfounded C-Dub through his narrowed eyelids.

"What in the hell are you talking about, man? I have never heard of any goddamn, Mustafa! I'm telling you, you've got the wrong guy!" He pleaded.

Agonda buried the feather duster in C-Dub's face, twisting it wildly and cackling as he did so.

The four henchmen glanced at each other with extreme concern.

"Oh Chucky, you silly, silly boy," Agonda chuckled and shrugged his shoulders. "Well," he sighed. "How about we take a nice little trip back down memory lane, shall we?"

He walked around from behind the counter and stood face-to-face with C-Dub. "Mm," he moaned and closed his eyes while he inhaled slowly. He seemed to be relishing the very real and pungent scent of fear that was radiating from C-Dub's body.

C-Dub attempted to bolt, but his captor's hold was steadfast and true. Finding it useless, he began to cry and sniffle.

338

Agonda smiled. "Chucky, dear, don't you remember what happened exactly three years ago, at the house on the corner of Crenshaw and 83rd place?"

"Oh my God!" C-Dub cried out, as the memory of that crazy night came flooding back to him.

It was three years earlier, on January 17th, 2003. The time was 8:29 p.m., and C-Dub was speeding up Crenshaw Boulevard near Manchester Avenue in the city of Inglewood.

He was on his way to the house of a well-known and trusted cocaine connection, someone called, "Mustafa." He was an African immigrant from the small war-torn nation of Nigeria.

Mustafa was a large and powerful man, but for some people, he had a soft spot.

C-Dub, however, was definitely not someone for whom Mustafa felt anything at all. But he always figured that there was something not quite right about C-Dub, nevertheless, he wasn't about to blow a $160,000 cocaine sale, simply because he wouldn't invite him to his home for Christmas.

C-Dub pulled his gray 2001 Chevrolet Impala over to the curb and parked it in front of a neatly kept single-story home. He noticed that the home looked much like every other home in this particular neighborhood.

He shut the engine down and verified that his Glock 26, 9mm, semi-automatic pistol was locked, loaded, and hidden from view inside of his black leather-coat pocket. He grabbed his black attaché case from the passenger seat, which contained what would appear to be $160,000 in cash, but in reality, was filled with sixteen stacks of paper, on top of which, was a single counterfeit U.S. $100 bill.

He grinned and thought, this would turn out to be my biggest lick, as he walked up the concrete path which was flanked by beautiful red-rose bushes.

He saw that the porch light was off. "Ready Daddy-O?" he whispered to himself, as he took the three steps up to the porch in a single bound. He then reached out his finger and pressed the doorbell three times in a rapid succession.

He casually checked over his shoulder as he stood there gripping his attaché case in his left hand and his pistol, concealed within his coat pocket, in his other hand.

The front door opened and C-Dub was suddenly staring at the shaved chest of an extremely tall man who was obviously a homosexual African-American who immediately introduced himself.

"Well, now," he smiled. "Look what the cat done dragged in!" he blurted over his shoulder to Mustafa who was sitting on the couch.

He winked at C-Dub. "Hi, baby. You must be C-Dub, right?"

"Yeah, man," he replied, dryly.

"Well, I'm Mrs. Humboldt, honey. Come on in! Mustafa and I have been expecting you!" he said in his best feminine voice, as he held out his hand, palm-down.

C-Dub released his hold on his sidearm and pulled his hand out of his pocket and slowly extended it to him.

Mrs. Humboldt snatched C-Dub's hand and shook it roughly, and flashed a maniacal smile as he pulled him into the house and invited him to sit on a black leather loveseat, as he himself, sat down easily next to his husband, Mustafa.

C-Dub was slack jawed as he brought his gaze up to the 19" color television, which was nestled within the chrome entertainment center. It appeared to be a normal, straight pornographic movie, but upon his double-take, he saw to his surprise, a rather large black penis that was attached to what he thought a moment before, was a woman.

What a couple of freaks that these two were. His disgust suddenly strengthened his resolve to take them for everything that they had.

"I certainly hope that what you have seen here in this room this evening will not leave this house, yes, C-Dub?" Mustafa smiled and winked at C-Dub, which made him nauseous.

"Yeah, whatever, Mustafa," he replied, avoiding the lascivious stare of the homosexual, who licked his lips obscenely. "Excellent. Now, if you don't mind- let's get down to business, okay?"

"Please, let's do this shit, so that I can get the fuck on, Mustafa," C-Dub mentioned, while he placed his attaché case on the chrome coffee table and opened it, displaying the neatly placed stacks of fake money.

"Damn!" exclaimed Mrs. Humboldt, as he eagerly turned toward Mustafa. "I've never seen this much money before, honey bunny!"

Mustafa smirked. "I've seen more, Sweety. This ain't shit! I've dealt with a hell-of-a-lot more cash than this." He picked up a stack from the case and noticed that there was only one bill- the rest were only sheets of plain white copy paper.

Before he could draw his next breath to protest, C-Dub's Glock was pointed directly in his face.

"Where's the motherfucking keys at, Nigga'?" C-Dub shouted through clenched teeth.

"What the fuck?" Mrs. Humboldt blurted, as he jammed his hand underneath the couch cushion and began screaming like a mad woman.

In one fluid movement, C-Dub shot him in his right hip. As he collapsed on the floor and moaned in agony, C-Dub forced Mustafa to the ground and removed the man's belt. "You're going to die tonight, man!" he whispered, as he used the belt to secure his hands behind his back. He then went over to Mrs. Humboldt whose screams had the very real potential to bring in unwanted attention to his little covert operation.

He noticed his bleeding bullet wound. The entrance was slightly above his left hip and the somewhat larger exit wound appeared to have obliterated a sizeable portion of his left buttock.

"I can't move my leg! Oh my God! You fucking bastard!" Mrs. Humboldt screamed.

C-Dub grinned and then kicked him in the side of his face. "If you don't shut the fuck up, I'll make your little leg problems go away! Quick!" he mentioned, as he jammed the pistol against the side of Mrs. Humboldt's face, who whimpered like a wounded dog.

He turned toward Mustafa who was lying face-down on the floor. "Now man, where's the goddamn dope?"

"Fuck you, nigga'!" Mustafa shouted defiantly.

"Fuck me, huh?" C-Dub chuckled, as he raised his gun above his head and brought the butt of the pistol grip crashing down against the side of Mustafa's mouth.

"Oh, damn!" Mrs. Humboldt muttered instantly, as the sickening unmistakable sound of shattered teeth was heard upon impact.

Mustafa buried his face in the carpet, as he cried out in agony and began to spit up blood and bits of his teeth. "You like that rough shit, don't you, boy?" C-Dub laughed, before he kicked Mustafa in the ribs. "Yeah, motherfucker, you like it," he continued, and then turned his attention to Mrs. Humboldt, who was half-conscious from the pain.

C-Dub's eyes widened as he approached him, noticing that he was bleeding on the carpet. He knelt down on one knee and used the homosexual's silver-sequin belt to secure his hands behind his back, much like he did to Mustafa.

"So tell me, how are you doing now, Mrs. Humboldt?" He smiled. "How are you feeling, Sweetie?" he asked softly, as he crouched over him and slapped him across the back of his head. "Stay with me now, bitch!" he whispered, and then grabbed a pen from the coffee table, uncapped it, and used it to violently probe the bullet wound.

Mrs. Humboldt screamed, "Oh God!"

C-Dub grinned. "You like that, don't you, bitch? Yeah, you like it. You sick, fucking punk! Does that feel good to you, Mrs. Humboldt?" He smiled, as his victim began to writhe in silent agony on the carpet. "You're nice and awake now, aren't you? That's good." He smiled again. "Now bitch, tell me where the dope is?" he insisted.

"Fuck yourself!" Mrs. Humboldt whispered, before his eyes rolled back in his head.

C-Dub nodded his head thoughtfully. "I see that you are not hearing me and what I have to say. Well, that's just too bad, bitch!"

He kicked him in the ribs, and then walked off in search of the bathroom, which he quickly found.

Once inside, he opened the drawers and then the cabinets, until he found what he was looking for. "Yeah, that's it," he smiled, as he grabbed hold of a large plug-in type hair curling iron and a large family-size tub of petroleum jelly.

He took the items in his left hand and barged back into the living room and stood above Mrs. Humboldt.

"Wake up, mother-fucker," he whispered, as he rudely dropped the petroleum jelly container and the curling iron on top of his head, which temporarily jolted the dying man back to full awareness.

"Good morning, sunshine!" C-Dub grinned, as he knelt down beside him and pulled down the loose-fitting denim jeans that Mrs. Humboldt wore.

He then stood up and sought out an electrical outlet, but the nearest one was clear across the living room.

C-Dub grunted and flung the coffee table out of his way, and grabbed the enormous homosexual by his right foot and dragged him screaming across the carpet near the entertainment center.

"Shut up, bitch!" he yelled, as he proceeded back to where he had dropped the petroleum jelly and the curling iron.

He appeared to enjoy himself, as he kicked the items across the room next to Mrs. Humboldt, who quickly began to understand what his intentions were.

C-Dub plugged in the curling iron and made the wounded homosexual lie still on the floor, which exposed the bullet wound.

"You've got this one last chance to talk to me, you monkey-ass motherfucker! Now, where's the fucking cocaine at, you faggot?" he hollered. Mrs. Humboldt stuttered, "I... I don't know where it's at! I swear to you, man! Please don't kill me! I don't know shit!" he yelled in a state of panic.

C-Dub looked at Mustafa, who appeared to be terror-stricken, as he closed his eyes and began praying.

C-Dub grinned. "Old bitch-ass nigga'," he mumbled, as he opened the tub of petroleum jelly and stuffed the hot curling iron down into it.

He laughed as it sizzled and gurgled almost immediately.

For a brief moment, C-Dub entertained the thought of ramming the scorching mechanism up the rectum of his horrified victim, Mrs. Humboldt, but instead, he chuckled, "It looks like you're not so tough now, are you, Mrs. bitch? Where's the tough talk now, Mrs. Humboldt?"

"Please don't do that, man!" Mrs. Humboldt begged.

"Shut up, punk!" he shouted, and then he plunged the lubricated curling iron all the way down inside of Mrs. Humboldt's bullet wound. "How you like that, bitch?" he blurted, and then smashed the homosexual's face into the carpet, as soon as he heard the ear-piercing cry that filled the house.

"Yeah Charlie, messing around with you," Agonda said to C-Dub, as they stood inside of his liquor store. "My baby brother, Mustafa, had to get some very expensive dental implants behind what you did to him. Yep." He grinned. "Yeah Charlie, that's right. And I'm sure that you remember that poor, Reginald Hawthorne? He calls himself, Mrs. Humboldt. He's the man that you maimed for the rest of his life. You know that he had to end up getting a colostomy bag? He sure did." He nodded. "You know what that is, don't you? It's when you can't take a shit anymore. The doctors have to cut a hole in your side, and then they have to shove a tube up in there that hooks up with your guts. The other end of the tube empties into a goddamn bag, you worthless piece of shit!" he shouted, and paused, as he shoved the tip of the feather duster into C-Dub's face.

He laughed as C-Dub cried like a baby.

"How in the hell could you be so cruel and do that to someone?" he whispered.

"I'm sorry about Mustafa! I really am, man!" C-Dub pleaded.

Agonda backhand slapped him in the face again. "Sorry didn't do it, Charlie. You did. But, it turns out that this wasn't the first time that you've hurt someone. Because I hear that you've been doing some dirty shit your whole life."

"What do you mean?" C-Dub wept.

"This will be explained to you shortly," Agonda mentioned, and then he used his fingers to whistle towards the warehouse in the rear of the store.

A moment later, to C-Dub's surprise, Armand Agassi walked in from the back room and approached the group of men standing near the cash register.

He smiled at C-Dub. "I'll bet you weren't expecting to see me ever again, huh Charlie?"

C-Dub stuttered, "A... Armand! My God, it's you, buddy! But how?"

Armand laughed at C-Dub. "You never were very bright, Charlie. You see, when I had my lawyer to get my criminal court case separated away from your case, I ended up beating my charges the honorable way- without snitching on my best friend. I was acquitted of all charges last week."

C-Dub lowered his head shamefully.

"Now Charlie," Armand continued. "It is to my understanding, that you lead your friend, Chill, to believe at one point, that it was I who snitched him out to the cops. When in all actuality, it was you who were the real stool pigeon."

"Man, Armand, I ain't never snitched on nobody!" C-Dub frightfully shouted.

Everyone in the store pointed at him and laughed.

"Bah! That's some bullshit, Charlie!" Armand spat, waving his hand dismissively. "That's some hog-wash! But, it's your lie. Therefore, I'll let you tell it. Oh yeah, by the way; I figured that you should know something. It was I who actually set you up to get robbed on the evening that you were in my hotel suite. If my memory hasn't deceived me, you were robbed by that gentleman right there." He nodded toward Agonda, who smiled. "Yes, the one holding the feather duster." Agonda giggled and leaned in and kissed C-Dub on his cheek.

Armand thought that Agonda was sort of a strange fellow, as he continued, "You were supposed to be the fall guy for the whole Diaz robbery operation. Ken and Mike, who were also acquitted with me last week, they were supposed to kill you that same morning at your little piss-ant detail shop. This was supposed to happen when you were talking about killing the kid, Chill. And by the way, we weren't about to let that happen! But, as it turned out, you got stupid, and eventually the cops got involved. So my dear friend, Agonda here, he had to wait just a little while longer to seek his revenge. And here we are now, the finale." He smiled.

C-Dub started panicking. He tried his best to buck against the strong grip of his captors, who didn't budge one bit.

"Yes, Armand," Agonda cut in.

He glared at C-Dub. "You did some terrible things to my little brother, and also to his beloved husband, Mrs. Humboldt. And you did that over ten lousy kilos of cocaine, at that! Therefore, you must pay for it, Charlie. Matter of fact, now is the time for you to pay for all of your wrong doings."

"Now look here, you guys!" C-Dub exclaimed arrogantly through a toothless grin. "I was released from the county jail less than ten minutes ago. There's a cop outside right now, he's waiting for me in a black truck at the curb. I'm sure that he's going to get suspicious and come in here at any minute to investigate, if I'm not out there pretty soon with his beer. So, you guys go on and let me go, and I'll forget all about this little bullshit. What do you say, fella's?" he said nervously, before Agonda suddenly kneed him in his groin.

All of a sudden, the door chime sounded and in walked Detective Sergeant Cole. He was rubbing his hands together as if he were freezing.

"Boy, its cold outside!" he blurted, as he walked up to C-Dub, who was still moaning from his groin impact. He smiled at the group and exclaimed, "Howdy, fella's! What seems to be the problem here?"

C-Dub screamed, "Sergeant Cole! Help me, man! These guys want to kill me!"

Sergeant Cole backed up a few steps and quickly drew his Glock 9mm handgun. "Is that right?" he asked, and then he pointed it directly at C-Dub's head.

He looked at Agonda. "Come on, Agonda! Let me do it, okay? Please!"

"No Sarg', not right now." Agonda waved him off.

"Why you always get to have all the fun?" Sergeant Cole uttered, jokingly.

C-Dub knew at that very moment that his good-for-nothing life was over.

He looked at Agonda, who appeared to be the man in charge. "Please Agonda, don't kill me, man! I'm begging you! I'll do whatever you want!"

Sergeant Cole whispered something into Agonda's ear.

He smiled suddenly. "That sounds fair enough, Sarg'."

"Okay then," Sergeant Cole continued, as he holstered his sidearm and placed a comforting hand on C-Dub's shoulder, and said, "We're not devils, Chucky. In fact, we are some very fair people. So, with that being said, we've decided to put this issue to a vote, my friend."

"Ah... how American," Armand mentioned sourly.

"Now, now, Armand, sweetheart," Agonda began, "Don't be so cross about this. I promise you that justice will be served in here. Trust me on that," he mentioned, as he tickled Armand's nose with the feather duster.

Armand sighed. "Come on, Agonda! Let's get on with it!"

"Very well, gentlemen," Agonda resumed. "Now, by a show of hands, how many of you think that Chucky-boy here should die?"

Agonda, Armand and Sergeant Cole all raised their hands. C-Dub looked terror-stricken from side-to-side at the four henchmen and grinned. "So you guys don't want me to die?" he exclaimed, appearing extremely excited.

"Dammit!" Agonda blurted, before he fired off a short salvo of Nigerian prose to his henchmen, who laughed and slowly raised their hands.

C-Dub's eyes grew wide in terror, as he shouted, "Please don't kill me!"

He lost control of his bladder and his bowels at that very moment.

"Good God, man!" Sergeant Cole mentioned, and then pinched his nose. "At least have a little dignity in the face of death! Pee-yoo!" Agonda told the henchmen- in their native tongue, "Take this poor excuse for a rotten piece of cow-shit to the back room, and remove his fucking head from his neck on the first whack." He paused. "No, second thought, do it in about three of four whacks, okay? I want him to suffer a bit, for the shit that he did to my loved ones."

The henchmen nodded their heads enthusiastically and dragged C-Dub, kicking and screaming, into the back storage room.

"Make sure that you get that $100 bill that I gave him. He's got it stuffed inside of his pockets somewhere. It's got my fingerprints on it," Sergeant Cole requested.

"No problem, Sarg'. Don't trip. I got you," Agonda replied, as they suddenly heard the distinctive sound of a decapitation replace C-Dub's futile cries for help. He scowled towards the warehouse door and shouted, "Dammit! I told those fools to take their time! I wanted him to suffer a little! Man, those fucking idiots!" He sighed and shook his head, as a bright red pool of blood began to flow underneath the door and into the store.

"Armand noticed it and quipped, "Clean up, on aisle four!" Everyone laughed.

"Well fellows," Sergeant Cole began. "That's my cue to go," he pointed to the blood pool on the ground. "I'd love to stay around and chat for a while with you gentlemen, but... duty calls. You guys have a good evening."

He pointed to Agonda. "And Big fella', do give my regards to the four young lads who worked so hard for us tonight, will you?"

"Will do Sarg'," Agonda replied.

"I'm out of here, too, Agonda. I'll call you later," Armand mentioned.

"Sure, Armand," he answered, as Armand and Sergeant Cole walked through the front door.

347

Chapter 35

The following week, Chill was asleep in his cell in his white boxer shorts. The tears from his silent cries had stained his face and it was obvious that he was in a very depressed mood. All that he could think about was his ominous future as he awaited transfer into the prison custody of the California Department of Corrections.

Staying unconscious was the best way that he had found to kill the monotony of cell-living in a county jail, with no yard, phone, radio, or television to occupy his time.

Rico, his former cell-mate had been released from custody two days prior, therefore, he became quite lonely. All that he basically had was the weekly visits and the encouragement letters from his wife to keep him from going over the edge. Thus, the long periods of slumber were something that he felt to be a necessity.

Suddenly, he was jolted awake by the loud, un-locking mechanism, which was disengaging on his cell door. He quickly placed his bare feet on the floor and watched it as it slowly rolled open.

To his surprise, the Caucasian facility Captain and two of his Caucasian male deputies entered the cell.

"What's up, Captain?" he asked, as he stood to his feet.

"What's up, is you, Bruce. It looks like God loves you after all."

"What do you mean, man?" he said, as he rubbed the corners of his bloodshot eyes.

The Captain smiled. "What I mean is... you need to hurry up and roll up your shit. You're going home, boy."

Chill smirked. "Is this some kind of a sick-ass joke, Captain? If it is, your little humor ain't shit!"

"I was just about to ask you the same thing, Bruce. I mean, you can't leave up out of here in your underwear! So, get your uniform on!" He chuckled, as his deputies guffawed heartily.

After making his way through the final release processing, Chill found himself standing in the exact same spot outside of the county jail which C-Dub had stood a week earlier. He was absolutely shell-shocked, and he still half-expected for this release of his to turn out to be the ultimate practical joke ever created. But free he was, and free he stood on the sidewalk holding a brown cardboard folder, which contained his court documents and his wife and kids' letters. He had to steady himself on more than a few occasions, as the sheer enormity of what had taken place began to hit him like a ton of bricks. He suddenly became physically dizzy and disoriented.

From his left side, he heard a car horn blowing, rather insistently. He turned his head and saw a pristine snow-white 1974 Lincoln Mark IV. Music was blaring from the open windows as it screeched to a stop directly in front of him.

His eccentric attorney, Larry Pearlstein, waved through the passenger-side window. "Hey, Willie, get in bud'!" he yelled from behind the steering wheel of his beautiful behemoth.

Chill admired the car for a moment before getting in. He was struck by how new that the Lincoln appeared. It looked almost as if it had recently rolled off the factory floor, he thought, as Pearlstein accelerated smoothly away from the jail.

"I'm sure that you've got a bunch of questions for me, Son," the lawyer began. "But first of all, I want for you to thank me. Go on, don't be shy. Thank me!" He grinned.

Chill smiled. "Thank you, Larry. My God, man! How did you...?"

Larry winked. "I know. She's an absolute beauty, isn't she? She was built from the bottom up, nearly two weeks ago. They used original equipment, no less. It's straight from the factory floor. Original specs even. It's hard to believe, isn't it? Yes, it is, Willie. It's about as hard to believe as me persuading my long-time buddy,

Justin Francis, who happens to be an Appellate Court Judge. He's the one who granted your appeal. Can you imagine that? God is good, huh?"

"He sure is!" Chill sighed, as he shook Pearlstein's hand.

"And also, your federal charges were dropped. They really wanted Joseph Milton all along, who as you know, shot himself."

Chill nodded, "Yeah."

"Anyway, Willie, isn't life grand?" He sighed dreamily and turned up the stereo.

He picked up an 8-track tape and fed it into the player. "You know, these 8-tracks have better sound quality than the chintzy, smaller cassette tapes which superseded them," Larry grinned, as the legendary "Led-Zeppelin's" song, "*Stairway to Heaven*" played clearly from the speakers. "Larry, I can't believe that you did that for me," Chill mentioned, as his eyes grew watery.

"Hell Son! You were railroaded from the very beginning by your own crime partners. I did this for you in the interest of justice," he explained, while he brought the Mark IV to an easy stop at the red light. "I'll bet you wish that you'd never called me, "a dump-truck-ass lawyer", huh?" He smiled.

Chill looked embarrassed. "Well Larry, you know that I can never repay you enough for what you've done for me. Please forgive me for my harsh words towards you. But, you've got to understand, man. I was up under a lot of stress."

"I know you were, Son. And I do forgive you. But oh, you can repay me! I want for you to re-establish yourself in the credit-cleaning game. I think that if you can run a couple of reports a month for me on a pro-bono basis, for the rest of your life; that would be just fine." He smiled and patted Chill on the back. "In an instant, Willie, life can change so quickly... and so completely," he mentioned, philosophically.

Chill nodded his agreement. "I see."

Pearlstein chuckled. "I know. And, oh yeah... pretty soon, you'll be contacted by a mutual friend of ours. So keep your phones on."

"Contacted by whom?" Chill asked curiously.

Larry smiled. "You'll be contacted by someone who is very special to the both of us. You'll be happy! Trust me. Just give him a chance, hear him out. And by the way, your apology is accepted."

"I'm forever in your debt, man. I could kiss you, Larry!"

"Ah!" he chuckled. "And if you do, I'll tell your lovely wife! I'm taking you to your house right now," he laughed. "Your family's waiting on you."

Chill was so happy that he could not do anything but weep.

When Larry Pearlstein pulled into Chill's Tarzana Hills driveway at 5:33 that evening, his children, Jen, his mother-in-law and Lena all ran up to the Lincoln and all but dragged Chill out of the car. Jen planted kisses all over his face and hugged him fiercely. "Welcome home, babe," she whispered in his ear, while Larry Pearlstein stood outside of the car with his arms folded across his chest, like a proud father.

Jen broke away from Chill, leaving him with Mai, Lena and the kids, and approached Larry and gave him a big hug, "Thank you so much, Larry. You've done such a wonderful thing for us all. If you ever need anything, you let us know, okay?"

"My good woman, the only reward that I seek, is the satisfaction of having followed my conscience. Doing what's right, that's a reward in and of its self." He smiled.

Jen nodded her head and called out to Chill, "Come on baby. Your dinner's almost ready. I made your favorite, some gumbo, spicy fried chicken, and a pot full of dirty rice," she winked her eye suggestively at him.

He smiled gloriously. "I think that I've done died and gone to heaven," he said to himself, as he herded his family towards the front door of their house.

He looked over his shoulder at Larry Pearlstein. "Come on in, Larry! Let's eat, man!" he yelled, filled with excitement.

"No thanks, Willie," he smiled, enjoying the moment. "I'm taking the wife out to dinner tonight. I got to save some room, you know?" He rubbed his stomach for emphasis.

"Yeah, I dig what you're saying, man." Chill smiled.

"But don't you worry, Willie. I'll definitely be in touch. You guys go on and enjoy your meal. You deserve it, son," he told him, and then entered his car and slowly backed out of the driveway.

The "Led-Zeppelin's" song, "*Since I been Lovin' You*", was blasting from the vehicle as he proceeded down the street.

Chapter 36

Chill and Jen were relaxing in bed after a long session of passionate lovemaking. He lay on his back while she nestled into his side. "I love you, baby," he uttered, as he lovingly stroked her face and hair.

"I love you too, dear," she whispered, and kissed him softly on the lips. "You know, it's so hard to believe that you're finally home, Willie. I was convinced that I had lost you to the prison system forever." She hugged him tightly.

He sighed. "Yeah, momma', you're telling me! It's almost like I'm dreaming or something." He kissed her on the top of her head.

"Now, I know that you are going to stay away from people like C-Dub in the future, right? Please!"

"Don't trip on that, baby. Everything's going to be all right." He sighed again.

Jen patted his stomach gently. "Did you notice how rested that Lena looked in the driveway yesterday when you came home?"

He smiled. "How could I not notice her? She looks a lot better than she did the last time I saw her. She must be staying off that cocaine, huh?"

Jen propped herself up on her elbow and gave him a sharp look. "Of course she is! She's been drug-free for six months now. She recently graduated from the Woodland Rehabilitation House. She lived on the campus there practically the whole time you were in jail. I'm so proud of her! I really am."

"Wow, that's great baby. I'm very happy to hear that! She doesn't need that type of bullshit in her life, anyway. It's nothing but trouble."

"Yeah," she said, and then lay back down and stroked his chest. "She's come a long way baby."

Chill nodded, when suddenly his attention was captured by an image on the television on the wall. "What's this, babe?" he mentioned, as he and Jen caught sight of a square graphic image. It depicted a chalked-outline of a body that was lying on the ground. Below it, the word, "Murder", was emblazoned in large red letters.

He grabbed the remote control from the nightstand and increased the volume, just as the voice of a Caucasian man announced, "...Police investigators are unable to comment further on the grisly discovery of this decapitated body, belonging to a Charles Hicks of South Los Angeles. The scene was happened upon by a man jogging on a well-traveled trail right here in the Santa Monica Mountains. The victim's head was lying next to his body. The lack of blood at the scene has led the investigators to believe that, although this was obviously an execution, it was not gang-related. For the channel 8, All-Inclusive News, I'm Bret Mitchell, reporting."

Chill lowered the volume and sighed. "No wonder why I haven't heard anything about that punk-ass nigga! Well, if it is that fool up under that sheet, that's what C-Dub gets, that fucking bastard!"

Jen finally took her hand away from her mouth. "You see what happens to people like that? I lost you once, I'm not trying to lose you again!" She began crying and heaving her chest up against his while she gripped him tightly.

He hugged her and firmly. "Baby, I am not going anywhere. I've learned my lesson, trust and believe that!"

Two weeks had passed and Chill was driving northbound on the Interstate 405 freeway in his Mercedes-Benz. He was about a mile south of the Interstate 10 freeway interchange and was traveling at 72 miles per hour in the light late-morning traffic.

He was wondering what his next move should be when his cell phone on the center console began to ring. He pressed the call button. "Hello?" he said into his Bluetooth earpiece.

To his surprise, an automated female voice announced that an inmate in a Federal Correctional facility was calling him collect. "Boss-Hogg", was the name identified as being the caller. Chill's eyes flew wide open. "Boss-Hogg's ass," he mentioned, as he pressed the number "5" button on the phone and accepted the call. "Boss-Hogg is that you, man?" he asked, surprised.

"Yeah, son, it is. I'm alive and kicking, no doubt. Which is much to the dismay of my detractors. Now, listen, Willie. I can't talk to you on this line other than to tell you that Jo-Jo was responsible for my present incarceration. My God, man, he was like a Son to me. But when he got drunk, he ran his mouth too much! He attracted too much attention to himself. In doing so, this shifted the feds to focus their attention onto me. That's a bad thing, Son."

"Yeah, I can understand that, Boss."

"I'm sure that you can." He sighed. "Man, Willie, these feds had me pinned-up in a tight-ass corner, I'm telling you. Do you know that they actually had threatened to turn me into a fucking terrorist, and ship my ass on over to Guantanamo Bay! Can you believe that shit?"

"Damn! That is unreal, Boss-Hogg! But I do know that Jo-Jo was way-out at times. Anyway, how can I help you, sir?"

"That's what I admire about you, man. It's your loyalty. Even though you and I have never officially met one another, except through telephone conversations by way of Jo-Jo, God rest his soul."

"Yeah, may his soul rest in peace, Sir." Chill wished, and then paused for a moment before he continued, "And I'd like to thank you for the compliment."

"You're welcome, Son. Now, if you will, what I need for you to do is call my wife, Vicky. She's at my mother's house in Whittier, California. She'll give you the whole rundown on everything that I need for you to know, okay?"

"Man, okay, okay, Boss-Hogg. Just give me a minute to get my head together. It's spinning so fast right now. I'm on the freeway and I really don't feel like crashing my ride, you know?" he explained, as he eased his car through the leftward curve which deposited him onto the westbound Interstate 10 freeway.

Boss-Hogg chuckled, "Good heavens, Son! Don't crash! We need for you to stay alive and in one piece, please!"

Chill laughed as he drove into the freeway off-ramp to Bundy Avenue. He then made a sharp right turn and steered the car into a gasoline station parking lot.

"Okay, Boss-Hogg, I'm here. I pulled in a gas station over here on Bundy in Brentwood. But yeah, you aren't the only one who needs me alive and in one piece!" he resumed, as he parked the vehicle near a pay phone booth in the rear of the lot.

"I know that's true, son."

"That's without a doubt, sir. Man, Boss-Hogg, they must've broken you off a lot of time in the federal prisons system, huh? When are you getting out of there?"

Boss-Hogg sighed. "Initially, I was looking at life in prison, son. A lot of time, just like you. Mainly because of the weapons and some other shit they 'say' that they found on my property, which was a bunch of bullshit. But thanks to our good old folks, Larry Pearlstein, he was able to get me a sentence reduction through some people he knows. Thank God! Because of which, I'm able to be released from here in about 18 months from now."

Chill whistled. "That's great, man! Good old Larry P., he saved my life. I've got nothing but love for him, Boss-Hogg."

"I do too, Willie. Besides, who do you think sent him to you?"

"I thought that Lena did. That's what she told me."

"Initially, she did. But she didn't have the two-hundred and twenty grand that he was charging. I did. So, he dealt with me. We're old friends, anyway," he laughed. "I heard that you called him, '*a dump-truck-ass lawyer.*' Is that true?" He chuckled.

"Yeah, it's true, Boss'," Chill admitted, sheepishly. "But, I was really upset, man. Hell, I was getting a life sentence, you know?"

"No shit, son. I don't blame you at all. Because life in prison will make you kind of bitter. I understand."

"Tell me about it!" Chill sighed. "Well sir, I'd like to thank you, man. How can I ever repay you?"

"Well, Willie, we'll discuss that a little bit later. But yeah, I'm out of this place pretty soon. Thank God."

"That's great, Boss-Hogg!" Boss-Hogg chortled. "Yeah, son, it is. But yeah, a year and a half is a hell of a lot better than never getting out of here. Anyway, Vicky will explain the Joseph situation to you in detail when you speak with her. I'm sure that you'll see my point of view. But it's imperative that you call my wife. My mom's name is Pearl. She's awaiting your call as we speak."

Boss-Hogg gave Chill his mother's telephone number and promised him that he would contact him weekly.

Chill was happy to hear that he was alive and well. He knew how good that Boss-Hogg had been to Jo-Jo. Almost like a father figure, according to Jo-Jo himself. He also knew that whatever had happened in the past with Boss-Hogg and the Secret Service, well, that was the past. It's forgiven.

They talked for another thirteen minutes, and then Boss-Hogg's telephone time was up.

Chill quickly dialed Boss-Hogg's mother's number and pressed the call button on his cell phone.

Her phone rang twice. "Good morning, Pearl speaking," she answered in an elderly and friendly Southern voice.

"Yes, good morning, ma'am," he responded respectfully into his Bluetooth. "My name is Willie Bruce. I was informed by Jesse Braxton that I could reach his wife, Vicky, at this number."

The woman exclaimed. "God Bless you, son! You're such a good boy! My son and my daughter-in-law told me all about you! But don't let this old gal keep you from important matters. I'll go and get Vicky for you," she told him, and set the phone down before Chill could reply.

A few moments later, a younger sounding woman picked up the telephone. "Willie? Is that you, honey?"

"Yes ma'am, it is. I take it that you're Mr. Braxton's wife, Vicky, correct?"

"You've got it! Thanks for calling, Willie. Good grief!" She sighed. "It's amazing how crazy that stuff has been in the past several months."

"Yes, it is, ma'am. I know exactly what you mean."

"I'm sure that you do," she chuckled. "Well anyway, look, Willie' Jesse trusts you very much. He knows that your tenacity and work ethics are damn near unequalled. He wants for you to pick up the torch that poor unfortunate Joseph Milton dropped. He then wants for you to carry on with the family business. It'll bring fortune to all of us," she mentioned, and took a deep breath before proceeding, "My husband and I have nearly twelve hundred clients, sweetie."

Chill gasped. "My God, Mrs. Braxton! You guys have got twelve hundred clients? Are you serious?"

Vicky chuckled. "Yes dear, twelve hundred. Well, somewhere thereabouts, I guess. Give or take a dozen, or so. And trust me, Willie, these clients are clamoring to get their credit reports cleaned. However, we need to find a new contact within the Credit Company of America. It needs to be someone whom we can totally trust. But before we go on with business talk, I want to share a little something with you, if I may?"

"Sure Mrs. Braxton. By all means, you go right ahead."

He leaned back in his seat and watched the traffic pass him by on Bundy Avenue.

"Well, I know my husband, Son. We've been married forever, it seems. He's a good and caring man. He's also from the same type of places where you grew up. He knows the codes of the game. You know, the no-snitching clauses. The codes of silence, so to speak. I don't know if you know this or not, but Jesse was basically told on by Joseph and his loose tongue by him running his drunk mouth to some white woman in a nightclub one evening. But the things that he mentioned to that woman, who happened to be a Secret Service agent, were things that only he, my husband and I knew about. Those things he mentioned to that woman is what ultimately led to Jesse's arrest. So Jesse did what he had to do to save his own life. Anyway Willie, what I'm saying is this, it was Joseph's wrongdoings that placed my husband where he is located today, instead of being at home with me. But God rest Joseph's soul. I hope that you understand?" she concluded honestly."

"Yes ma'am, I totally understand. Jo-Jo was out of control sometimes. I knew him well, very well, in fact. So, I do understand."

"I'm happy that you do, Willie."

"Please, do me a favor and inform Jesse that it's all good. And that I am not Joseph Milton. So, let's get this money, shall we?"

She was relieved to hear Chill say those words. "Oh thank you, dear! Thank you very much! I'm glad that you have no grudge against us," she said nervously, as she took a seat at the kitchen table.

"I don't hold a grudge, Mrs. Braxton! There isn't anything to have a grudge about. You guys are some really good people. I've got your back, I want you to remember that. I also want for you all to consider myself and my family as being a part of your family. And maybe when Jesse comes home, you guys will invite me and my family to some of those Sunday get-togethers that Joseph use to tell me about," he chuckled.

Vicky laughed. "That's mandatory, son! We'd love to play host to you and your family. It would be an honor!"

"Thank you, Mrs. Braxton."

"Please, Willie, call me, Vicky."

"Okay, Vicky. Thank you very much. And please tell Jesse that I can't wait to meet him and be a part of his new family."

"I will, Willie. I'll do that just as soon as I speak with him. Now, my husband requires that you fly immediately to Dallas, Texas. Using your considerable charm and wit, he needs for you to acquire for the family, a new inside person, preferably a man. We need to find someone with a little more finesse than that hopeless, Chris Darrington guy that you and Jo-Jo hired." She smiled.

"Chill looked shocked. "You knew about him?"

"Of course we did!" She laughed. "Jesse found that out from the Secret Service guy. His name is, D.W. Dobbs."

"Wow, those cats aren't playing!" Chill said, as he enjoyed the promise of wealth that this particular phone call would bring him. "*I'm back in business, baby*," he thought, as he continued to gaze at the boulevard traffic.

"Yeah, those federal guys ain't no joke," Vicky continued. "The Secret Service can make you vanish if they want to."

"Yeah," he chuckled. "Vanish straight to Cuba, huh?"

Vicky laughed. "Yeah, Willie, Jesse told me about that. He said that guy, Dobbs, had threatened to send him to Guantanamo Bay."

"He probably wasn't playing, either!"

"I know. But anyway, you'll be compensated for your expenses, of course. Will you be able to handle this task, honey?"

"Absolutely, ma'am. Matter of fact, I'll fly out first thing tomorrow morning," he told her, as he increased the air-conditioning in the car.

"That's fantastic! We're so glad to have you on board. When you find what you're looking for in Dallas, please give me a call, okay?"

"I will, Vicky, and thank you, ma'am. You and your husband are some really wonderful people. I can't wait to get back to work."

She laughed. "You're welcome, son. I want to thank you, too!"

"You're welcome, Vicky. Okay then, I'll get ready for my flight tomorrow."

"Well, don't let me keep you from handling your business. Be safe and good luck, honey. Bye now."

"Take it easy." Chill smiled as he closed his cell phone.

He laughed briefly, and then shook his head and screamed through clenched teeth, "Fuck yeah! Now, that's what I'm talking about!"

The next day at 10:21a.m., Chill's South-Eastern flight out of L.A.X., touched down safely on the tarmac at the Dallas-Fort Worth International Airport.

Upon disembarking the 747, he was directed by an employee to the On-time Rent-A-Car agency nearby.

He used one of his credit cards that Jo-Jo had helped him to attain, to lease a respectable silver late-model Cadillac Escalade. After loading his luggage into the rear seat, he drove the vehicle out to the Credit Company of America building. He knew exactly where it was located. The noontime weather was scorching when he pulled the shiny vehicle into the parking lot.

"Nice car!" he uttered, as his eyes fell upon a convertible 1964, Chevrolet Super-Sport low-rider. It was painted a really good-looking Candy-apple red, and its owner had it parked near the building's entrance with its tan leather top lowered.

Chill pulled into an empty stall and parked the S.U.V., when suddenly, he noticed a young Hispanic man. He was sitting by himself on the bench in front of the building near the entrance doors. He seemed to be keeping a close eye on the low-rider.

Chill exited the Escalade and walked toward him. "That's got to be his shit," he mentioned, while he observed that the man seemed to be out of place in the vicinity; being that everyone else in the area wore some smart business attire. However, this young man of 24-years wore a plain, white neatly starched T-shirt that barely concealed the array of tattoos that he had covering his arms and neck.

He also wore some nondescript, yet clearly creased beige khaki pants with a pair of black leather tennis shoes.

He leered suspiciously at Chill as he approached him.

"That's a nice-ass ride you got there, homie," Chill said, approvingly.

"Thanks, man. I put a lot of money into her. She's my pride and joy," he replied, before eyeing Chill's Rolex. He also noticed his brown tailor-made suit and brown Crocodile shoes, which were compliments of Jo-Jo. "Are you a manager in here or something?"

Chill chuckled politely. "Hell nah', man. I'm just waiting for somebody, that's all."

"Well, so am I. I'm waiting on my older brother. His name is, Oscar. He works here." He tilted his head towards the building.

"His name is, Oscar, huh?"

"Yeah."

"Well, by the way. My name is, Willie. But my friends call me, Chill."

"It's nice to meet you, Chill. My name is, Tino."

"It's a real pleasure to meet you, Tino."

"Yeah, man," he replied, as he rose to his feet and shook Chill's hand.

Chill used his right thumb to point over his shoulder towards the entrance doors to the Credit Company. "You said that your brother, Oscar works here, huh?"

"Yeah, he works around computers an' shit."

"Is that right?"

"Yeah, Chill."

"Well, what does he do? I mean, if you don't mind me asking?"

Tino smiled. "I don't mind at all, man. He says that he's some kind of a computer programmer in there." He pointed toward the entrance doors. "He started working here some-time ago. It was right after some federal agents dragged this Black brother through those doors. The word is, he was kicking and screaming, too."

"Is that right?" Chill said, playing the unknowing role.

"Yeah. Here comes Oscar right now."

Chill turned his head and observed a 30-year-old Hispanic man walking out of the building. He waved to Tino as he approached him.

Chill took note of the guy's dark gray polyester suit and his scruffy black leather shoes. *He definitely needs my assistance*, he thought.

Tino made the introductions. "Oscar, this is Chill. He has an interest in your work," he mentioned, and tilted his head towards Chill's sparkling Rolex wristwatch, which Oscar immediately noticed.

Oscar shook Chill's hand with hesitation. "And why are you so interested in me and my work, sir?"

Chill smiled. "Because, Oscar, I want to make you rich, if you let me."

The brothers laughed.

"No fella's, really, I'm very serious you guys," Chill continued. "I represent some very successful business people all over Southern California, as well as people in other sections of the country. My clients have some, well, agency-specific needs. To make a long story short, I need you, Oscar." He pointed. "I'd like to increase your weekly income by five-thousand dollars, maybe even more, depending on your performance. It's up to you. Does that sound appealing to you?"

"Hell yeah, shit!" Tino blurted, gazing at Oscar, who seemed interested, yet still suspicious.

Observing this, Chill said, "Look, fella's- it's lunchtime now. I don't know about y'all, but I'm hungry! No, matter-of-fact, I'm starving! Let me take the two of you out to lunch. Anything you want- it's my treat. I'll tell you what? What do you gentlemen think about this French's Tenderloin establishment over there?" He tilted his head toward the World-Class Gourmet Cajun restaurant across the street.

Oscar laughed. "You mean, French's? Man, that's got to be one of the most exclusive and expensive restaurant's in all of Dallas, Texas!"

Tino nodded and pointed to his clothing. "Yeah, Chill- they wouldn't let me through the front door! Not dressed like this anyway."

Chill chuckled. "It's cash over clothing, Tino. Money talks, and bullshit walks. Now gentlemen, lay your fears aside and take a leap of faith if you will. You guys follow me into that restaurant and I'll share with you the secrets to my success. Hey, at the very least, you'll enjoy an unforgettable meal. So gentlemen, what do you have to lose?"

The brothers exchanged looks and shrugged their shoulders.

"Lead the way, Chill," Oscar mentioned.

"Very well gentlemen." Chill smiled, as the brother's began to walk with him towards the restaurant.

Oscar appeared to have trouble suppressing his excitement. "Damn, Chill, can a man really make some big bucks working with you?"

"Oscar my friend, you'd be surprised. By the way, did I tell you guys that I am a part of a Royal family? I'm one of the kings." Chill smiled.

"The kings of what, Chill?" Tino asked curiously.

Chill winked at him. "The Kings of Credit, my brother!"

The brothers laughed as they followed Chill towards the restaurant.

THE END.

Excerpt from The Roux In The Gumbo

Gizelle

Gizelle welcomed the feel of the cool sheets against her skin. She crawled exhausted into her bed, naked as always during the humid summer. As Gizelle slept, her subconscious took her back to a night twenty years ago in 1850. She was twelve years old and alone in the middle of the night. Scared, tired, hungry, and sick, she sat crying and shivering under a huge magnolia tree in driving rain, deep in the bayou near Lake Charles, Louisiana.

Gizelle decided to sit and wait. Surely, one of the water moccasins or some deadly spider would put her out of her misery. No matter what, she was not going back to the plantation.

Before Gizelle was old enough to be weaned, she had been wrenched from her mother's breast and sold to the Sunrise Plantation. They should have called it the Graveyard because so many slaves were buried there. They worked clearing the bayous so the boats could navigate through the waters to bring in materials to build plantation homes and slave quarters. They also brought in seed and supplies to cultivate the fields of cotton, rice, and sugar cane; anything that was agriculturally profitable.

The overseers did not allow slaves who labored in the fetid water to get out as they watched others pulled under by the alligators. If the poisonous snakes and spiders did not kill them, the elements would. They worked regardless of rain or snow. Those who fell ill were left on the bank to die. The owners could always buy more slaves.

During the epidemics, cholera and yellow fever laid claim to many. Hundreds expired from colds, croup, or the many diseases that thrived in the swampy water. The soles of their feet split open from the fungus brought on by standing in dirty water for too long. They bound their feet with bandages but without proper treatment, the cuts developed gangrene. The limbs were amputated. Cripples sat in pirogues to transfer the debris from the water to the bank. A slave was lucky to make it through a year working at Sunrise.

Gizelle's dark skin dictated that by the age of four she was sent to the fields to pick cotton. When she was nine years old, the overseer gave her a gift. He raped her. He had been doing so for three years now. He had very strange and unnatural desires, and she could not take it anymore. She would prefer death to the tortured existence she was living.

Each time lightning brightened the sky, Gizelle prayed for God to end her life. Finally, the storm passed. She gathered Spanish moss from the trees and made a pallet. She closed her eyes, hoping they would never again open.

"Cher, Cher, Wake up chile! What are you doing here? Get up *Cher* you are soaking wet. Come with me. Open your eyes," the voice said.

Gizelle heard the words but did not want to open her eyes. She did not want to be alive. Maybe God was a woman, or maybe he was busy and had sent an angel for her. She peeked out with one eye. Nope it was not God; God did not have long white hair that hung down to his waist. She opened the other eye and looked into eyes that looked like a cat, colored a greenish-gray. Her face was soft with what seemed to be concern. No one had ever looked at Gizelle with such kindness.

"Can you stand, *Cher?* Are you hurt?" The woman touched Gizelle's forehead and found it burning with fever. "You poor chile, you come with Tallulah; I will make you better," she said.

Gizelle rose shakily to her feet and leaned against the strange woman. Tallulah was the tallest woman she had ever seen. When Gizelle got dizzy and could not walk, Tallulah carried her.

Tallulah took her to a cabin built three feet above the ground alongside a creek, allowing the water to flow under rather than through the house when the water was high. It was a cozy habitat.

Three large rooms were more than adequate for Tallulah. One, a large inviting kitchen kept warm by the stove where she prepared her food. Another was the bedroom, which boasted a four-poster bed with night tables and an armoire that covered an entire wall. The custom furniture would have done any mansion proud. The last room had a massive desk on one wall. The other three walls were bookshelves, overflowing with books and mementos of her life. The collection of Indian and French artifacts spoke volumes about Tallulah's heritage.

Gizelle dreamt that someone removed her wet clothes and placed her in a large metal basin filled with lavender scented water that had been warmed in a teakettle that sat on the top of a big pot-bellied stove. Her hair was gently washed and braided. She was spooned hot soup; the tastiest she had ever eaten, nothing like the slop at Sunrise. The woman held a cup for her so she could sip delicious honey-sweetened herb tea. It soothed and warmed her from the inside out.

When she was out of the tub, Gizelle's body was rubbed down with oils that made her skin feel smooth and soft like a baby. The towel was soft, like freshly ginned and cleaned cotton. She wondered if she

was dreaming, or maybe this was heaven. Wherever she was, this was where she wanted to be.

Gizelle awoke in the comfort of a soft feather mattress. *This must be how the people in the big house slept,* she thought. She was afraid that if she moved, her surroundings would disappear and she would find herself back on the floor of her cabin. Tallulah warmed the sheets by filling a bottle with hot water and rolling it between them. The quilt smelled as if it were filled with fragrant flowers. She drifted back to sleep.

Excerpt from Street Life to Housewife

1982

Bad Girls
Donna Summer

Francois let out a loud moan, his body shuddered, and it was over. The first time I had seen him it took ten minutes of conversation to put this trick "to sleep," which meant putting him at ease so that he could relax enough in my company to attain a happy ending.

Every black girl had to be adept at this in order to assuage the fears that lurked in client's minds planted by experiences, rumors and assumptions that all black girls wanted to rob them. Funny thing, it didn't stop them from taking the chance.

As a hooker, prostitute, call girl, I did not mind the talking part, it's when the client wants to touch me that I disassociated my mind from my body and hover around on the ceiling. I go into automatic pilot, robot mode, so it isn't me that they are huffing and puffing over.

I learned a lot of tricks of the trade listening to my Uncle's women while growing up. A good working girl never got off with a trick. If you did then you were the trick. Having been beaten and tortured by a few psychopaths I had a level of disdain for men who paid for my time and body. Within the first few months of my career, I mastered techniques that helped me avoid sex, while at the same time satisfying the needs of the client so they got their moneys worth.

With this particular client, work could not be avoided. Now I had to remember the other advice I had received, "Do what you got to do to get paid, stay down for your crown, and don't turn down nuthin' but yo' collar."

The $400.00 Francois paid me for two hours of my time made it worthwhile. The first hour we talked about his work and problems. Reading the paper every morning certainly paid off. I wasted a lot of

homes where I wasn't treated too nicely. I ran away from the last one when I was fifteen. I figured the streets couldn't be any worse than that house."

"What happened there?" Francois got a tissue from the bedside and wiped the tears from my face.

"The Father and teenage son were raping me. Almost every night they came into my room. The mother beat me because she knew."

"She beat you because her husband was raping you? She knew about it and did nothing to stop it?"

"Oh, she knew alright, sometimes she joined in."

"I don't believe such despicable people walk this world. Why didn't you tell someone?"

"Girls who told ended up in worse places. No one believed them and they were labeled troublemakers."

"Someone should have helped you."

"I looked at Francois and through my tears said, "I helped me."

"One night when my foster parents were out, the son brought home his football teammates. I heard them talking through the vent in the basement where my room was. They were pulling straws to see who would rape me first.

"My God, he planned to pass you around?"

"I threw some clothes and my piggy bank into a pillow case. I had saved my lunch money and allowance for over two years. My jar held $200.00. I climbed out the window and never looked back."

"How did you survive?"

"I hitchhiked to Venice beach. The beach held so many good memories from my childhood. My parents took me camping there every summer. My Father and I fished during school vacations. It was a place where I felt like they were still with me. I even saw them sometime."

"You mean you saw their ghost?"

"I think it was there spirit. They kept me safe. One day I was bedding down in the beach bathroom, when a man followed me in. Suddenly I saw my parents, and felt the man being lifted off of me. He went running down the beach naked, screaming at the top of his lungs. I slept in that bathroom every night for two months and nothing bad ever happened. I stashed my sleeping bag and pillowcase in a locker at the bus station during the day, and went to my under the table job at the skate store. The woman who owned the place paid me to clean up the skates and eventually I started

369

working the rental counter. I never told her that I was homeless but she figured it out and presented me with a key and bought a bed and a radio so I could sleep in the back room."

"You poor child, my heart bleeds for you," he hugged me.

"I met some girls who were a couple of years older than me. It seemed like we had all been through hard times and opted to be on our own for one reason or another. They invited me to be their roommate. I jumped at the chance to have a roof over my head."

"How did they live? Where did they get food, shelter, and clothes?"

"There was an old guy, Mr. Charlie who rented an apartment and paid the utilities in exchange for one night with each of us every month. We did whatever it took to feed ourselves. Mr. Charlie forged birth certificates and enrolled us in school as his foster children."

"Wasn't he a nice pedophile?" Francois' voice dripped with sarcasm.

"We are all in college now and I'm proud to say getting very close to   accomplishing our goals."

When I looked at Francois, there were tears in his eyes. I knew he was thinking about his spoiled daughters. He spent a fortune putting them through college and they did nothing with their sheepskins but get pregnant and marry bums that he was forced to hire at his construction company so they could keep a roof over his girls and grandchildren's heads.

"You know my daughters are grown women in their thirties and forties and if they had to take care of themselves they would starve to death. Here you are twenty-two years old and you've been taking care of yourself for seven years now. Look at you, furthering your education so you can do something with your life, something that will make a difference in spite of everything you had to survive."

"Hey, what else do I have to do? Without an education I won't ever be anything that I can feel good about."

"You deserve a break and I am going to give you one. How much money do you need to finish school?"

"Well, I have about three more years to go. I just finished community college and got into a state college this year. I don't know twenty-five grand for this semester alone. I'm taking a heavy load trying to finish quickly, books are expensive as hell."

"I don't want you to worry about any of that, hand me my jacket."

Francois wrote me a check for $30,000.00 and placed it in my hand kissing my wrist, "If you have any problems here's my card. This should allow you to concentrate on what's important. I'll give you more for next semester and if you need anything, anything at all you promise to call me."

Hook, line and sinker. I looked at the check and squeezed out a few tears, "I can't take this Francois," knowing full well there was no way I would give it back.

"Yes you can. Sparkle I throw away more than this every month on alimony and it doesn't make me feel good. Doing this for you makes me feel like my money is doing some good and I can write it off on taxes."

"The Francois College fund huh?" I laughed and hugged him.

"Maybe I'll start a foundation."

"Thank you Francois, you don't know how much this means to me, no one has ever given me this kind of help without wanting me to do something crazy." I sniffed.

"There are no strings attached. If I never see you again, which I know I will, you don't owe me a thing."

"I think you are my guardian angel." I kissed him on the forehead before raising my 5' 9" 130 pound, long-legged frame from the bed. I stepped into my five inch stilettos. "I need to freshen up and get out of here, got to pick my baby up from the sitter."

"You have a child?"

"Yeah, I didn't tell you?" I reached in my wallet and pulled out a picture of a little girl. She was about three years old, her caramel skin was close to my own complexion, and she had a head full of wavy hair. "This is my baby girl Keisa."

I picked up my leather dress, jacket, and panties and walked into the bathroom to wash up. I touched up my eyeliner, mascara, and lipstick. I didn't need foundation or powder. I took the $400.00 cash that Frank had given me upon arrival and wrapped it around the check and placed it in the hidden pocket in my jacket lining.

I smiled at the dark eyed, full mouthed, pretty girl reflected in the mirror, *Damn girl; you are good at what you do. $30,400.00 for two hours of my time was a personal best.*

I took the silver-plated two-shooter from my purse, checked that the safety was on before placing it in the pocket sewn into the nape of my neck where a 22 inch, curly wavy, human hair weave covered it. *Time to go.*

Francois was dressed. He handed me back the child's photograph along with a roll of money. He held my hand with both of his, "Do something nice for your daughter. She's very beautiful. I can tell you take good care of her. Maybe one day I can take you and Keisa on a trip to Disneyland or Knott's Berry farm?"

"Maybe, you never know what can happen in the future. I've never taken any men around her. I've never told any clients about her, so please keep this confidential. The agency doesn't know about her. I don't know why I told you."

"Don't worry Sparkle; your secret is safe with me. It is understandable that you would be protective of her in light of all you have been through."

I leaned in to kiss him on the cheek and he turned his head and tried to kiss me on the mouth. "You know better than that."

"You still won't let me kiss you?"

"Don't take it personal Francois. I usually don't even kiss on the cheek. I feel that I have to save something for later in life. One day I'm going to meet a man and he isn't going to know anything about this life, or care when I tell him. He will love me unconditionally and take me away from all of this. We'll date like normal people, and he will ask me to marry him. That is the person I want to kiss. You see I give everything else, I have away for money. You understand don't you?"

"I understand. You know the more I get to know you, the more I like you. Who knows maybe I can be that guy for you. You keep working on your dreams; I'll do anything I can to help. No strings attached. I promise I'll be there for you," He hugged me tightly, too tightly.

When he let go I turned and headed for the door. I took one last look in the mirror on my way out the door to make sure everything was in place. Three pair of lions-head earrings, three gold chains, one with a Lions-head sporting a two carat diamond in its mouth. I loved lions, didn't hurt that I was a Leo.

I was heading for the elevator when Francois peeked out, "Hey Sparkle, I'm going to call for you next week?"

I walked back and gave him a card with my pager number, "Call me direct, you do know to keep this between you and me, right?"

He took this as a sign that I was getting closer to having a relationship with him. What I was really doing was cutting out the agency out of its forty percent. They had made enough money from me off of this client. If he was going to start calling every week that was 40 dollars an hour that I would be putting in my own pocket.

I got off the elevator and made my way through the parking lot to my little blue Nissan. I loved my little stick shift car. I realized I was still holding the money and the picture in my hand. I counted it. Oh how sweet, Francois had given me $200 to spend on precious Keisa. I kissed the picture and returned it to my wallet where it was when I purchased it.

I didn't have any children, unlike most of my friends who had kids before we graduated high school in 1977. Why had I used Keisa's name? Maybe it was because my little cousin was on my mind. I had told my aunt that I would babysit this Saturday night. I planned to take Keisa and her brother Jay to the movies Saturday.

I turned off my radio and pushed the last button then used the key to open the hidden compartment that was welded into the center panel. If I got stopped, the police would not find anything. I retrieved an envelope folded from a hundred dollar bill and used a gold plated, one inch fingernail to powder my nose with cocaine that would clear my head of the date I had just turned.

It was five p.m. on Friday and traffic was going to be a bear. I anticipated being on 101 for at least an hour to get from Hollywood to Compton, so that I could take my parents to dinner.

My parents were still very much alive, married, and living in the house that they bought when I was five years old. Every year the week after New Years, I used my Christmas money to treat us to dinner at our favorite restaurant, Tracton's on La Cienega Boulevard and Rodeo Road. It was a very colorful place that was owned by a boxer.

I laid my head back against the headrest and let the cocaine and the Gap Band's "Burn rubber on me," relax me. Soon I was snapping my fingers and back to the real world. On the way to the freeway, I went to the bank drive through window on Wilshire Blvd to deposit the check into my account.

I went back into my stash and removed one of three identifications. I had four bank accounts one in my real name. I never let the balance get over ten thousand for tax purposes so I would have to move some money around as soon as the check cleared. I knew better than to play with the IRS.

I was feeling the beat of The Dazz Bands "Let it Whip," as I waited in the long bank line. A man in a white Mercedes was flirting with me through his rear view mirror. When I drove out of the bank, he was parked on the street standing next to his car waving at me. I parked and he came to my window.

"Hey pretty lady."

"Hey yourself," I smiled at the guy and assessed his expensive clothes and Rolex; I did not miss the fact that he was wearing a wedding band.

"So how long have you been married?"

"You saw that huh?"

"Yeah, what's your name?"

"Martell Sham," he said handing me his business card. And yours?"

"Sparkle." When I took the card he captured my hand and kissed the back of it."

"Aren't you a charmer? So what's really going on Martell?"

"I'm attracted to a pretty lady."

"Really now?"

"What's wrong with that?"

"What's wrong with that is you have a wife sitting at home, with all the luxuries that come with station. That means that the number one position has already been filled, where does that leave me?"

"I would not leave you anywhere, besides you don't look like a lady who would go for it anyway."

"Right, right."

"I like that. Why don't we work out the details over dinner?"

"I have a prior engagement."

"Oh, you got a man huh?"

"Nope, my engagement is with my parents. I'm taking them to dinner."

"That's so sweet. So when can we get together?"

"Sunday night good for you?"

"How about Monday?"

"That'll work. I'll call you in the afternoon."

"Don't I get your number?"

"Yeah, after we work out the details."

When I looked in my rear view mirror, Martell was watching me drive off. I wrote down his license number. So I could find out who he was.

The sky was a beautiful mixture of orange and pink as the sun went down on the smoggy, palm tree lined freeway. I loved this time of day. A few years ago I worked downtown Los Angeles in a bank and had to take this ride every day. I always worked until the sun started to set so that I could enjoy it. Sometimes I just sat outside and watched the sun go down.

Rick James and Tina Marie kept me company. I was pleased to find traffic moving at a brisk clip, which was unusual for after work traffic hour. I pulled into my parent's driveway in 40 minutes instead of the anticipated hour. I opened the gate and parked in the back yard and used my door key. Once inside, I got myself a glass of water, "Hello I'm here," I announced.

"You know your mother can never be ready on time," My Father said from the living room. I hugged him and kissed him on the cheek. He was wearing Russian Leather, I loved that fragrance.

"You better go help her Daddy. If we ain't on time for our reservation we will be waiting all night to get in, and I'm hungry."

"Your hungry, I could eat a bear. I didn't eat lunch so that I would have extra room." He went into the bedroom, "Come on woman we got to go."

I phoned the agency to let them know that I would not be on call until Sunday night. I had made enough money to take a couple of nights off.

I called a friend who worked at the Beverly Hills police precinct and gave him the license number for Martell Sham so that he could run it. My pager had gone off several times while I was on the freeway. I checked the numbers and returned my friend Laisyv's call. We made arrangements to meet at "The Speakeasy" later that night for a bachelorette party.

"I'll have my parents drop me off after dinner and roll with you if you can bring me to get my car tomorrow?"

That settled I went into the living room and sat on the brown leather couch. I picked up a photo album that my Father had been working on. That man had a camera glued to his face every since I could remember. He had a photographic diary of our lives. As I looked at the pictures, I drifted back down memory lane.

Kim's
PUBLISHING

1901 Los Rios Boulevard   Plano Texas 75074

Name:

_____

For Inmate ID#:

_____

Address: _____

City/State:

_____

Qty	Title of Book	Price each	Total
	Kings of Credit	15.00	
	The Roux in the Gumbo	15.00	
	Street Life to Housewife	15.00	

Total Books ordered _____   Subtotal _____

                                    Shipping   4.00

                                    Total _____

Bulk orders will receive special discount pricing. Please contact Kim's Publishing at kim@kim-robinson.com

Forms of accepted payments: Money order, certified or Government Issue checks and paypal Kim@kim-robinson.com. All mail orders will take 7-10 business days for delivery. Books can be published on websites www.Kim-Robinson.com or Amazon.com or your local retail store. Incarcerated readers receive discount and pay 11.00 per book and apply same shipping terms as stated above.

Willie Bruce was born and raised in south Los Angeles. He now lives in Van Nuys California with his loving family. He is devoted to his writing and promises to keep his fans entertained with more of his chilling stories to come.

Kim Robinson was born and raised in Compton California. She now resides in a Dallas suburb with her three children and husband. She is the author of a family history entitled The Roux In the Gumbo, and it's sequels Street Life to Housewife parts 1 and 2. She also has two virtual cookbooks that feature over two hundred authors, their recipes, book covers, excerpts and photos. Several more series are on the horizon for her and family members. Stay in touch at www.kim-robinson.com and feel free to write to her at Kim@kim-robinson.com

Two cookbooks featuring authors and their books are on Kindle and my website
http://groups.yahoo.com/group/kimsCrew
Join us on Kim's Crew a writer, reader, publisher and reviewer group
kim@kim-robinson.com   www.kim-robinson.com
http://groups.yahoo.com/group/sewingsouls